BLUEMANTLE

BLUEMANTLE

KAREN LANGSTON

The Book Guild Ltd

First published in Great Britain in 2021 by
The Book Guild Ltd
9 Priory Business Park
Wistow Road, Kibworth
Leicestershire, LE8 0RX
Freephone: 0800 999 2982
www.bookguild.co.uk
Email: info@bookguild.co.uk
Twitter: @bookguild

Copyright © 2021 Karen Langston

The right of Karen Langston to be identified as the author of this
work has been asserted by her in accordance with the
Copyright, Design and Patents Act 1988.

All rights reserved. No part of this publication may be
reproduced, transmitted, or stored in a retrieval system, in any form or by any means,
without permission in writing from the publisher, nor be otherwise circulated in
any form of binding or cover other than that in which it is published and without
a similar condition being imposed on the subsequent purchaser.

This work is entirely fictitious and bears no resemblance to any persons living or dead.

Typeset in 12pt Adobe Jenson Pro

Printed on FSC accredited paper
Printed and bound in Great Britain by 4edge Limited

ISBN 978 1913551 599

British Library Cataloguing in Publication Data.
A catalogue record for this book is available from the British Library.

To Mark, for opening the door and
encouraging me to follow a brighter path.

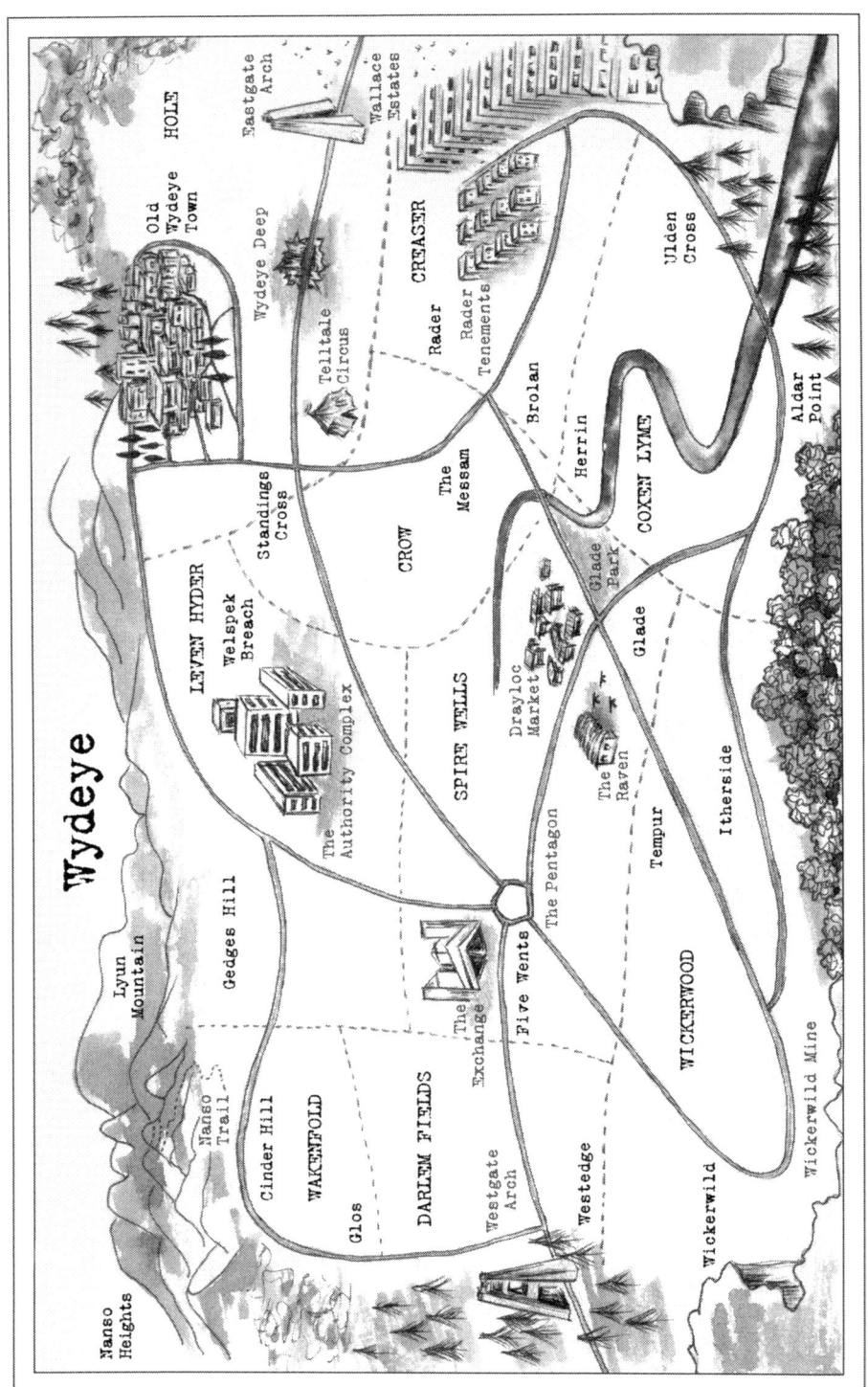

PROLOGUE

The woman sat up in bed, her naked skin prickling as her breath quickened.

"What is it?" said the man lying beside her.

"I heard a noise."

Her ears strained to decipher the silence. Wide-eyed, she stared ahead, blinded by the darkness that shrouded their bedroom.

"I don't hear anything," said the man. He grunted and turned over, submitting to sleep.

The woman remained sitting up, her body tense. She reached over and turned on her bedside light. As her eyes adjusted, she noticed the glass of water beside the lamp. Tiny rings rippled across its surface.

Creaks and groans of a building in agony broke the silence.

The man bolted upright. "What the…?"

The woman screamed.

Their room tipped violently, spilling the couple from their bed. They slid across the floor, slamming into a wall. The woman's head smashed against the concrete blockwork, cracking her skull. She could feel warm blood seeping into her hair, snaking down the side of her face, pooling beside her mouth.

A few feet away, the man called to her, but his voice was drowned by a grinding roar. Then the concrete floor beneath the woman cracked and collapsed. Instinct compelled her to reach out, to grab and cling on. Her trembling hands gripped a loop of exposed rebar, suspending her body over a pitch-black abyss.

The man screamed from his precarious platform, the slither of floor beneath him having remained intact. Leaning over the edge and reaching out to the woman, he cried out, "Here. Take hold of my hand."

Just as their hands clasped one another and the man began to pull, there came another roar and a rush of warm air. A huge slab of concrete plummeted from above, crashing down, wrenching the woman from his grip.

Alone on the ledge, his empty hand still reaching down, the man howled in horror at the fathomless maw below.

–

The hole had yawned in the night, devouring concrete and steel, skin and bone. By the yellow haze of dawn, the full horror of the devastation had become apparent. A gaping blackness loomed beneath vertiginous walls of rock. Barely visible in the gloom, the dust-covered roof of an apartment block lay three hundred metres below its own foundations.

The swallow hole was as wide as it was deep. It had sucked down three buildings and a tooth-gap chunk of the Westway Road.

Part of the third building remained standing. Five storeys of rooms stood exposed to the elements: a model dolls' house with the front removed. A woman crouched in a pigeonhole room on the fifth floor, wailing at the drop below her. A dog barked on the fourth floor, its owner quivering in the shadows behind. On the third floor, a man lay on a narrow ledge, a trembling hand reaching down towards nothing.

The sirens had screamed on arrival, adding to a soundtrack of terror. Searchlights of the Emergency Division sought out the stranded in the pre-dawn gloom, illuminating white masks of horror praying this was a nightmare.

By daybreak, the clamour had fallen to an eerie quiet. Emergency officers knelt as close to the edge of the hole as they dared, leaning forward, straining to hear. The rescued residents of the severed building lingered behind them, listening for traces of loved ones. Stillness filled the void, tangible and laden with loss.

The rescue operation was an exercise in protocol, with little hope of success. Emergency officers were winched down, their lines running out before they even came close to twisted steel and concrete. A unit of Allears was deployed: an elite division of the Authority's Special Forces, armed with the physiological capacity to detect sound beyond the range of human hearing. No sign of life was found.

After thirty-six hours of delicate operation, labouring in fear of further collapse, the Authority called off the search. A cordon was erected around the swallow hole and military personnel were placed on guard until the area could be made safe.

No bodies were ever recovered.

Following an assessment of registered residency and reports of missing persons, the Authority declared that the death toll was thirty-two adults and fifteen children.

This did not include Saltire and her players.

PART ONE
ABOVE AND BELOW

CHAPTER ONE

"Naylor, it's Chase. Wella's missing." It was two days after the swallow hole had left a bite out of the city of Wydeye. "She was supposed to meet me this morning, but she didn't show."

"Now, don't panic, Chase. Where are you calling from?"

"A kiosk on Second Went. Can you meet me?"

"I'm on shift. I shouldn't even be taking this call."

"When you finish, then. What time is that?"

"Four. I can be at the market by half past."

"I'll meet you at the north gate."

Chase Newell should have been at work too, but he couldn't face a twelve-hour shift at the quarry. His sister had contacted him the previous week, asking for money. This was unheard of. He knew Wella was fiercely independent; she hated asking him for the time, let alone a bail-out. They were far from close; Chase struggled to remember the last time he had seen her. Yet, out of the blue, she had contacted him and asked for two thousand ketrels. Not a vast amount, but enough for it to be meaningful. *Maybe to cover the rent in her shithole of a room in Rader Tenements*, he had thought.

They had arranged to meet that morning so he could hand her the money. He felt sure she wouldn't have missed their appointment unless something had happened. Something unexpected.

Chase honed in on the swallow hole.

He had heard the reports on the radio. State journalists had been at the scene from early dawn, interviewing Emergency officers, local residents, the weeping separated. It had dominated mandatory broadcasts for over forty-eight hours.

Now, with a potential connection to the disaster, he couldn't rid his mind of the pictures the radio had painted. He imagined the scene, the vast scale of the hole. The unfathomable depth. He tried to visualise three hundred metres, gauging it against a familiar frame of reference: the high-rise blocks in the Wallace Estates where Naylor lived. They were eighty storeys and towered 250 metres from the ground. Chase's stomach turned.

He remained preoccupied by the horrors of the hole until he wandered into Drayloc Market, a sprawling maze of stalls and shacks, bordered by low-rise buildings. These were built in the old style: hand-carved limestone, with shuttered apertures in weathered oak. Faded posters peeled from the walls – blocks of washed-out colour amid the yellow ochre and raw sienna of the limestone buildings and sun-baked ground.

The market stalls were ramshackle, covered by hide awnings that created much-needed shade. Vendors called out their wares to passing trade, pushing cloth, ironware, pottery, bric-a-brac. Food shacks filled the air with toasted spice and sugar syrup, cooking street food such as kobbos, roll-tops and balkra over roasting braziers. The narrow passageways between the stalls were filled with citizens, moving with purpose without haste. Most wore tunics in shades of grey, or strap shirts and lose slacks – practicality, the only design principle.

Chase sought shade from the sun but could not escape the sultry air. His strap shirt clung to his broad chest; the tattoos along his bare arms glistened with sweat. Pushing back his dark hair, he tried to imagine a stroking breeze cooling his neck. He glanced up at the clock in the centre of the market. It was time.

Naylor was already waiting at the gate. "So, fill me in," he said. He was approaching sixty, more than a decade older than Chase. Tall with a wiry frame, he hid beneath salt and pepper hair that was curly and unkempt.

"Not here. Let's find some shade." Chase led the way, weaving through the crowded market to a tea bar. Long wooden benches ran either side of narrow trestle tables. The two men sat down opposite each other. A boy came over with glasses of cold green tea. "Thanks for meeting me," said Chase.

"That's what friends are for. Now, tell me what you know."

"Wella was supposed to meet me this morning. It was something important, but she didn't show. I went over to Rader, but she wasn't home."

"Work?"

"I phoned in. They couldn't connect me. She wasn't at her station."

"Maybe something came up?"

"It's the furnaces, Naylor. You don't just not go because something comes up."

Naylor studied Chase's face. "What is it?"

"I keep thinking about that hole."

"But that's over in Glos – opposite side of the city. Why would she be there in the middle of the night?"

"She could've been with Tinashe, or Weldon."

"But they live in Darlem Fields. And they'd have no reason to go up to Glos, or anywhere else in A territory for that matter. I'm sure she wouldn't have been anywhere near the hole."

"Bit of a coincidence, though, don't you think?"

"Yes, I do. Coincidence is exactly what I think. And anyway, you must've heard the radio. The Authority says they've assessed their records and named all the dead."

"They would say that."

"Yeah, but—"

"No bodies, Naylor. No proof there weren't more victims. Just the usual 'job done', 'case closed', 'we know what we know'."

Naylor glanced around them, then leant forward, dropping his voice. "Careful with that talk, Chase. We're not in The Raven here. You know what goes on in the Exchange." He sat back, eyes wide.

"Relax. I'm not criticising the A; I'm simply stating facts. They like things neat and tidy." He shook his head. "All I'm saying is this isn't like Wella. She never calls, let alone asks for help. She wouldn't have done it lightly. That's why I'm convinced, if something had come up, she would've put a call out to me."

"So, we'll look for her. Think who her friends are, where she hangs out."

"I've no idea."

"Well, there must be places near here, in Five Wents. Then I suggest we go back to her quarters, see if we can find anything that might give us a lead." Naylor stood up and dropped a ten-ketrel coin in each of the glasses. "Let's go find your sister."

—

They walked the length of Second Went, clinging to the shade beneath the iron ribcage of the elevated tramway. Steam railmotors rattled overhead, their wheels clack-clacking over neglected joints. The supporting girders strained under the weight of crawling engines and their coupled trailers loaded with weary passengers. The Elevated wove through the city: a rusted chain binding the Hundreds of Wydeye and their constituent districts.

Beneath the straddled legs of the Elevated ran a concrete underpass. Pedestrians competed with Authority vehicles, bicycles and an assortment of carts, mostly goat-drawn. Chase jumped to one side, narrowly escaping a knock from an oncoming carter, his goats oblivious.

Flustered as much from the long walk in the sultry heat as from the near miss, Chase grabbed Naylor's arm. "Let's ask in here."

He led them into Riat's, a noodle bar of sorts. Inside was dark, the only light coming from the open double doors that constituted the bar's frontage. The building was vintage Wydeye: thick limestone walls, low timber ceiling, ceramic tiled floor. Along the far end of the long room ran the food counter, selling bowls of highly spiced noodles served with a choice of undefined meat or vegetables. Customers invariably washed this down with a pint of Kitson or a gill of Pyncher schnapps, both brewed at the local Tramways Brewery in the Hundred of Creaser.

Furniture in Riat's was hotchpotch and sparse: an uncoordinated assortment of stools and makeshift tables, mostly occupied by small groups of lean and muscular men and women – the contours of manual labour.

Chase and Naylor weaved through the room, navigating a course to the counter. Chase glanced at the huddled groups. He doubted he would even recognise any of Wella's friends.

Behind the counter, a radio played. There was no music, just the monotonous voice of a woman, her expression sales-pitch and scripted. "*Citizens of Wydeye, fear not the events in Glos. The situation is under control. A distracted mind is a suboptimal mind. Those targets won't reach themselves. Workers of Wydeye, remain focused on your job, just as the Authority is. We are protecting you. You've nothing to fear. Good citizens…*"

"Meat or veg?" said a short man behind the counter, his voiced raised to compete with the mandatory broadcast. The man looked at Chase, ladle poised, expectant.

"Neither. Sorry," said Chase.

"What you want then?"

"I'm looking for my sister. Wella Newell. I think she comes here. Do you know her?"

"Lots of people come here. What she look like?"

"Taller than you. Short fair hair. Wears a black tunic with a purple patch on the back."

"Ah yes, I've seen her. Pretty. Comes in here couple of times a week, maybe."

"When did you last see her?"

"Few days ago, I guess."

It was Friday. The swallow hole had appeared on Wednesday night. Chase leant forward, his voice strained. "You sure you didn't see her yesterday?"

The man rubbed his chin with the tip of the ladle's handle. "No. Definitely Wednesday. I remember now because something got me stirred."

"What?"

"Well, one of the people she was with got out a street map for Wakenfold. Got me thinking they might be from the A. I don't trust them bastards." The man dropped the ladle and stared at Chase. "You don't…? I, er…"

"No. We're not from the Authority. Neither is Wella. So, drop your guard and tell us what you know."

"Merciful Deep. Thought I'd tipped the crow there." A line of customers had formed behind Chase and Naylor. "But that's all. Can't tell you nothing else. Now, if you don't mind, I've got to serve." He looked over their shoulders to a woman behind. "Meat or veg?"

"Listen, if she comes in here, tell her to contact me straight away. Tell her I'm worried."

The man nodded as he spooned a pile of grey meat onto a bowl of noodles and passed it over Chase's shoulder.

"Come on, let's go," said Naylor. He pulled Chase by the arm and led him back through the crowded room, into the glare of the sun. Blinded for a moment, they both stood still, wary of stumbling into the path of another carter.

With his vision restored, Chase remained motionless, eyes horror-wide. "The street map. It covers Glos. She could've been near the swallow hole after all…"

"He said someone else had the map."

"Yeah, but they were all together. He said they were all talking. Maybe they were planning to go somewhere that evening. She could've been there."

"There's nothing in Glos. Wakenfold is off limits. And it's a curfew zone. She'd have no reason to be there."

"But the map…"

—

"I can't believe the state gets away with charging rent for these shitholes. It's criminal," said Naylor, glaring grim-faced at the tenement block where Wella lived.

They had checked out a couple of other places in Five Wents, blindly second-guessing where Wella might have frequented. Whilst a few barmen and stall holders recognised her description, no one had seen her since Wednesday.

Weary from the draining heat, Chase had sought shelter in a phone kiosk: a steel cubicle the shape of a giant bullet, one of millions positioned around the city. He had put in calls to the furnaces, the Bayley Road sports centre, random bars and restaurants. He had even chanced a call to the kiosk outside Wella's tenement block in Rader.

He had let it ring for over five minutes. No one picked up.

"You know what it's like this time of day," Naylor had said. "People returning from work. They just want to get home, clean up and cool down. Too hot and tired to do favours for strangers."

"Bastard A. They have to control everything. The system's fucked."

"Forget it, Chase. We'll take the Elevated over to Rader and look for ourselves. Worth a try."

They had travelled the tramway in silence, squeezed inside a packed trailer on the upper deck. The air at this height was still humid but less suffocating than at ground level. And whilst the steam locomotives emitted their own distinct smell, the air was free of the potent cocktail of odours that lingered in the streets: a blend of spice, rotting garbage, sewers and goats' piss.

Chase had stared out of the window, his bulky frame wedged into one of the trailer's narrow seats. Despite the discomfort, he liked to ride the Elevated. The view afforded a striking perspective: the dividing line between a city of two landscapes, above and below.

As the railmotor left the bustle of Five Wents, arcing north-east through Spire Wells, Chase gazed at these parallel planes. Below, the snaking underpass, lined with the stalls of street traders, smoke rising from coal braziers, citizens hugging the shade, homeless Wethers scavenging for scraps.

Above, a vista of imposing concrete structures, commanding and severe.

The architecture was brutal – an uncompromising statement of intent. Most of it was built during a period of rapid expansion, under the ambitious rule of Governor Wallace. Introducing a programme of controlled migration to boost the city's workforce and productivity, Wallace had ordered the construction of tens of thousands of low-cost housing units to accommodate the bloated population. The Hundred of Creaser was created, incorporating the Rader Tenements and the twenty-four tower blocks that constituted the vast Wallace Estates.

Aside from addressing residential demands of a burgeoning population, Wallace had commissioned sprawling public buildings such as the Exchange, New City Bank and City Hall. The Messam, the business district and mercantile heart of Wydeye, was dominated by monolithic structures, bearing hard angles and jutting promontories, with blind façades or inside-out apertures revealing slices of glass.

As the railmotor looped through The Messam, Chase witnessed the full force of Wallace's intent. The city seen from above the line was an imposing demonstration of industrial might: huge edifices made from steel and concrete – vast, muscular and aesthetically aggressive.

On reaching part of Wallace's legacy, Chase and Naylor descended the Elevated and stood before the tenement blocks of Rader. As they entered the intimidating maze, they found themselves surrounded by row upon row of six-storey terraced dwellings, cowering beneath the shadow of the neighbouring high-rise.

In common with their attendant giants, the terraces were identical and constructed from concrete – unrendered blockwork, rather than precast. Small letterbox apertures barely broke the grey – the only feature on the façade, aside from six-foot-high iron grills at intervals on the ground floor, providing the means of entry and escape. Street after street, the tenements of Rader led the eye down long channels of soulless repetition and anonymous isolation.

Street twelve, block H. Passing the bullet kiosk no one had answered, they approached the building, pushed open the grill and stepped inside. They climbed a dark, concrete stairwell until they reached the fifth floor. Four doors led off a narrow corridor. Chase approached the furthest door, marked 'H20', and knocked. No answer. He pulled a bunch of keys from his pocket and used one to open the door.

Wella's quarters consisted of two small rooms and a broom-cupboard bathroom. The space was dark and undecorated, the walls the same blockwork as the exterior. Two narrow apertures let in negligible natural light. Naylor flicked a switch by the front door, turning on a bulb that hung limp from the low ceiling.

Chase stood in the centre of the first room, head down and fists clenched.

"How long since you've been here?" said Naylor.

"Six years. I helped her move in. She's not invited me back."

"I didn't realise they were so small."

"She's so damned independent. Refused to share, even though she could've ended up somewhere nicer. And living with our folks was out of the question, apparently. This is all she could afford." He shook his head.

Naylor clapped his hands together. "Okay, then. Let's get looking. I'm guessing that's her bedroom next door, so you look in there. I'll search in here."

"Remind me what we're looking for."

"Anything that might be something. Names, phone numbers. A diary would be good. Signs that she might have packed up and gone somewhere. Clues."

"Clues…" said Chase, his voice flat. He walked into the adjoining room, struggling to imagine what such a thing might look like. He knew he wouldn't recognise if anything appeared different or out of the ordinary.

They searched in silence, scanning pieces of paper, peering into cupboards, looking behind cushions, mindful of the reluctant transgression of privacy. Eventually Naylor called out, "Chase, take a look at this."

Chase hurried over to Naylor, who handed him a pamphlet of sorts. It was folded concertina-style, creating ten pages, front and back, around ten inches by six. The paper was covered in blocks of text in various fonts, arranged between sketched illustrations and stylised border art. The sections of text were at odd angles – a manual cut-and-paste job – with the pamphlet representing a grainy copy of a master. "What do you think it is?" said Naylor.

Chase scanned the text. It referred to music, bands, snippets of news relating to them. "I'm not sure, but I don't like the look of it." His eyes darkened.

"Looks odd. Maybe it's nothing," said Naylor, sensing the change in Chase's mood.

"Oh, it's definitely something alright." He opened it up, scanning front and back. "Where did you find it?"

"Inside one of the books on the shelf over there. Saw it poking out the top."

Chase approached the shelf and picked up books at random, flicking through the pages. Another pamphlet dropped to the floor. Then another from a different book. "Hidden."

"Why would she hide them?"

"Music, Naylor. Why do you think?"

"But there's nothing wrong with music, only—"

"Tell that to Brann."

Naylor turned away, knowing the reference to Chase's younger brother was a clear end-of-subject jab. He reached down. "Look at this," he said, picking up one of the pamphlets that had fallen to the floor. He pointed to handwriting, obscured amid the greyscale blur of one of the illustrations, and read, "Ursel – Telltale Circus." He looked up at Chase. "This is it. This is our clue."

CHAPTER TWO

Governor Blix stood in her office, staring out of a tall window that overlooked the Authority Complex: huge concrete edifices that dominated the Hundred of Leven Hyder. She was in her mid-sixties, with silver hair scraped back from her pale, humourless face, into an immaculate bun. Her sharp grey suit blended well with the view.

A knock at the door pulled her attention back into the room: a sparse office swamped by a huge black desk and a high-backed swivel chair. "Enter."

A tall, heavyset man walked in. He had spiked black hair and wore a long, leather trench coat, despite the heat. A deep scar ran across his left cheek down to his upper lip, carving the impression of a permanent sneer. "You called for me, Governor."

"Ah, Commander Wulfwin. Sit down." Blix gestured to a low seat before her desk, while she slid into the swivel chair opposite. "The latest on the Glos investigation."

Wulfwin remained standing. "We've stabilised the area. Utilities have rerouted supply. Construction are on standby while we assess options around in-fill."

"Good. The citizens' reaction. Describe."

Wulfwin had worked under Blix for twenty years. He'd grown accustomed to her manner of communicating: staccato statements, never asking a question. He suspected she would regard the latter as a sign of weakness. He took the contrivance to be a symptom of the same. "They're afraid," he said.

"The broadcasts. The script makes it quite clear." Her eyes bore into Wulfwin, who met her gaze without faltering.

"It does. And they're listening. But there's also been talk of Wydeye Deep. They're beginning to recognise what it is. Word is spreading."

"Your point."

"They're realising it's happened before. Now they think it's going to happen again."

"That's ridiculous. We've investigated the cause. We've dealt with the problem. It's under control."

"With all due respect, Governor, you can't control nature."

The base of Blix's neck flushed; her face remained stone white. "Nature is not my concern. We have the situation in hand. Your job is to communicate that fact. And step up ground presence. Their unease cannot be allowed to escalate. Order must be maintained. I'm not prepared to let it slip for the sake of a hole in the ground."

"Yes, Governor."

Blix rose and returned to the window, her back to Wulfwin. She put her right hand to the glass, tracing shapes with her long fingers. "Instability is inherent in the masses," she said. "It's endemic of the crowd. The larger the crowd, the more fragile it is. Therein lies its cancer. Volatility." She turned slowly and walked towards Wulfwin. "I will not let this cancer grow."

Wulfwin stood firm, his dark eyes pinned to Blix. The permanent sneer caused by the scar made his expression difficult to read. He waited for more.

"Tell me what we've learnt from the Exchange," said Blix.

"Trade is down. Ears on the street say citizens are agitated. They think more needs to be done to make them safe."

"They are a swarm of hysterical ants, teaming around their disturbed nest." She walked to her desk and slipped into the chair. "I invite your counsel, Chief of Command."

Wulfwin's face twitched; his eyes hardened. "Toughen our response. The radio messages may be giving the impression we care. Meanwhile, the citizens have become a whining distraction. I've still got men at the scene – a wasted resource. We could be missing something."

Blix leant forward, her hands splayed on the desk. "Word of an event."

"No. But while we pander to the people, our guard is down. I say we step up operations. Visible manpower. The messages should reinforce the fancy we're there to protect and serve. Meanwhile, we'll be ready to strike the moment anyone takes advantage."

"You are right. We cannot afford to jeopardise our chances for early detection. Call the Deaf Squad to action. Have them patrol the streets. Target Spire Wells and Creaser. Intimidate the citizens into feeling safe while you focus on the prize."

"And the Allears?"

"Send Commander Lore to me."

—

Wulfwin had left by the time Allear Commander Dent Lore arrived. He stood in front of Blix's desk, his well-built physique partially the result of his daily run along the gruelling Nanso Trail. His dark, thick beard was in contrast to his closely shaved head.

Dent was a natural Allear, born with hypersensitive hearing that made him an asset to the Authority. This natural gift also meant that he did not have to endure the adjustment measures that the majority of recruits had to suffer: surgically induced anosmia and permanently sealing both eyelids at the knife of a plastic surgeon. By compromising an Allear's superfluous senses, their hearing intensified.

Following his recruitment and training, Dent rose through the ranks and became Unit Superior twelve years ago. He served with unwavering commitment to achieve the goals of the Authority, with unquestioning loyalty to the rule of its Governor. He stood before Blix, calm and eager to obey.

"I commend you and your unit for your contribution to operations following Wednesday's event in Glos," said Blix. "I know you did all you could to detect trace of survivors."

"It was an honour to serve the Authority, Governor."

"The presence of the Allears was a reassuring influence on the citizens of Wydeye. They are fully aware of your capability. If anyone could locate survivors of the tragedy, it was you and your team." She sat forward, her fingers drumming on the desk. "Which is why I wish you to continue to reassure our needy masses, whilst actually listening for the sounds for which you are trained."

"Is there word of an event?"

"Not yet. But while the city grows nervous of another swallow hole, there are those among the throng who will take advantage of the distraction. So, we shall do likewise." Blix was not known to smile. A slight twist to her mouth and a glint in her eye betrayed her satisfaction with her plan. "Put your Allears on full-rotation duty. I want all whisper dishes in operation, twenty-four seven. Visible presence. Let citizens see you in action. They will feel reassured, believing you are listening for signs of further collapse. The Authority's messages will corroborate that assumption. While, in actual fact, you will be listening for a far greater threat."

—

Commander Dent Lore stood on a rostrum in the Allear Training Centre, surveying the blind faces before him. Two hundred and sixty expressionless masks, pocked with a pair of shallow craters from where eyes had once seen. The adjusted Allears stood to unsighted attention, their heightened hearing obediently waiting for orders.

"We have an important mission," said Dent, his voice calm and deep. "Governor Blix personally commended your contribution to the Glos hole recovery operation. She now requires our skills in the service of the entire city and the protection of its citizens. Our orders are to be the pervasive ears of Wydeye, listening for every heartbeat, every whisper, every note. In action, we are the sum of our parts; we form a single apparatus, which we operate as one. Together we heed the echo, sense the vibration, trace the illusive source of sound. Together we fight that which seeks to destroy the harmony of our city. If one of you fails, we all fail. And the Allears are not built to fail. Are you with me?"

"Sir!" they roared, proud heads raised, battle-ready, skin sockets unblinking.

"Then let us descend upon the city, take up our stations and put our ears to the ground."

The Allears mobilised, leaving the Authority Complex in Leven Hyder and dispersing throughout the Hundreds of the city. They were transported to their posts by a fleet of Logistics Division Ops trucks, weaving in convoy beneath the arches of the Elevated. Some were stationed in pairs beside towering, cast concrete whisper dishes. Ten metres in diameter, the parabolic acoustic mirrors were sited throughout the city to capture and amplify even the faintest trace of live music. Huge hemispheres in bold relief, poised and listening – stethoscopes held firm against the city's chest.

Other Allears moved silently through the streets, navigating by mental maps, memorised as part of their training. They paused on street corners, listening for trace of contraband sound. Usually their presence on the streets made the citizens feel apprehensive. The Allears signified a potential Deaf Squad raid. Too many citizens had witnessed the consequences of positive detection. Those who hadn't, had heard enough stories to imagine the brutality of 'reasonable force'.

However, on this occasion the radio had explained everything: *"Citizens of Wydeye, our brave Forces are working tirelessly to protect you. They will prevent another Glos hole. Their presence is for security reasons. See for yourself. You are safe to focus on your targets. Repay our Forces' diligence with productivity."*

The Authority was there to serve and protect. Fears were allayed; nervous minds were reassured. Everyone could sleep soundly at night. The situation was under control.

Meanwhile, Dent Lore and his Allears listened. They pulled apart the layers of sound, delving ever deeper, searching for a whispered breath amid a howling storm – trace of the Music Makers.

CHAPTER THREE

"I cannot believe that Saltire is gone." Bend Sinister sat on a rock with his head in his hands, his long black hair falling across his face.

Chief paced the cave, her generous stride making short work of the distance. "She was definitely in her camp. I had left her not an hour before."

"And her players?"

"All with her. All gone."

Bend Sinister shook his head and looked up to the stone dome above them. "To think we moved down here to be safe." He had a small tattoo on his left cheek, a diagonal line, which he touched absentmindedly. "This loss is beyond words."

Chief stood beside him, observing how grief could reduce such a tall, broad frame to this huddle of pain. She flicked back her silver dreadlocks and folded her arms. "I cared for Saltire too. We all did. She was a true artist. And a fair leader."

Bend Sinister looked up into Chief's cobalt eyes, searching for something he anticipated but couldn't find. "Yes," he said. "A fair leader. And a strong woman. She held my respect and trust."

Chief nodded, adding to the weight of sentiment through her silence. Then she cleared her throat and said, "Where's Pale Dexter?"

"He's on his way."

Kicking the dirt beneath her boots, she said, "You know, this shouldn't affect the schedule. I'm due to play. I can't afford to postpone."

"Now is not the time."

"I'm not suggesting immediately. But soon. I can't delay for long."

"We must wait until Pale Dexter's here before we discuss anything."

Silence filled the cave, then ebbed away as a man entered. He was well built, with dark features beneath a closely shaved head. Along his arms ran strange tattoos – cryptic formulae that hinted at secrets. "Chief. Bend Sinister," said Pale Dexter. "My apologies for keeping you waiting."

Bend Sinister rose and the three Troubadours stood on ceremony, their heads bowed with eyes to the ground. A different type of silence now filled the cave, dense with latent energy. Gas lamps flickered on the limestone walls around them; stalactites and stalagmites cast dancing shadows in the yellow ochre glow. The sound of dripping water, amplified by the cave's acoustics, set a slow, steady rhythm.

There was no form, no precedent to prescribe what was to be done. They each applied a different measure to the gesture of respect.

It was Pale Dexter who moved the moment on. He raised his head and said, "It is with great sadness and reverence that we gather to mourn the passing of Saltire and her players. The loss to our community cannot be weighed in words. Her legacy is the spirit by which we survive. Our debt to her will outlive the end of days." He looked to Chief and nodded.

"Spirit of Saltire," said Chief, "take flight and, in peace, be free."

Both Chief and Pale Dexter looked to Bend Sinister, who felt the weight of expectation upon him. He cleared his throat and looked around, recalling the cave that had become the grave of his friend. "Two centuries," he said. "We've never known a lifetime until now. Your end has come too soon, dear friend." He could speak no more.

The three Troubadours stood in silence once again, before drifting away to occupy separate parts of the cave. Bend Sinister sought shadow, sitting on a rock between pools of amber light. Chief leant against the cave's curved wall, twisting her silver dreads while glancing at her counterparts. Pale Dexter remained close to the centre, tattooed arms folded across his chest. "This leaves us with a problem," he said.

Cobalt eyes flittered.

Bend Sinister sighed. "Not today," he said.

"Yes, today. We can't leave the position unfilled. Saltire would agree."

"Pale Dexter is right," said Chief. "We need a plan."

"She's barely cold and already you speak of succession?" said Bend Sinister, palms raised in appeal. "Can't we trust each other enough to cooperate in peace without a leader whilst we show due respect?"

"It is through due respect that I argue the contrary," said Pale Dexter, his deep voice hardening. "Saltire became lead Troubadour because we could no longer live in harmony without sovereignty. The hierarchy created balance. We risk instability without it."

Chief stepped forward and placed her hands on her hips. "We've also earnt this opportunity. We've cooperated under Saltire's lead for forty-five years. Time someone else had a turn at the top."

"We managed perfectly well before, in the early years," said Bend Sinister from the shadows.

"Life was different then and you know it," said Pale Dexter. "We need a plan. I see no point in delaying what is in the best interests of us all. Balance must be restored. We just need to decide how."

"But not today," said Bend Sinister.

Pale Dexter glared at him, his cryptic ink glistening beneath the gas lamps' glow. "We move on, then," he said, his tone clipped. He turned to Chief. "To the business of the hour. You called us together, Chief. You have our attention. Say your piece."

Chief stood before them and cleared her throat. "I had wanted to delay raising the issue out of respect for Saltire, but I cannot. My hand is forced."

"Explain."

"The schedule. I am due to play. In the absence of a leader, I am seeking your approval to prepare."

"Now is not the time," he snapped.

"It is my time. The schedule confirms this."

"It is a distraction from what must be our priority."

"I take it you don't mean a respectful mourning period for Saltire?" said Bend Sinister.

Pale Dexter spun around. "You know full well what I mean."

"The matter of leadership can wait," said Chief. "My turn cannot. I need to play."

Bend Sinister turned to Chief. "It's too dangerous. My followers have warned of heightened activity overground. The hole has left citizens afraid. The Authority is attempting to hear disaster before it happens. Whispers of prophecy."

"We can't risk detection," agreed Pale Dexter. "Their fear is reactionary. The precautions will be short-lived."

"I can't risk putting that assumption to the test." Chief held out her arms. "Look at me. Look at my colour. I grow weak. I'm overdue as it is. Consider yourself in my place. You know full well what this means."

Bend Sinister sighed. "She's right."

"No. It's too great a risk, as you said. And a distraction. We should focus on the leadership question first. Then return to the schedule."

"Please," said Chief.

Pale Dexter shook his head and crossed his arms.

Chief looked imploringly to Bend Sinister, who stepped forward and said, "Saltire was our leader for nigh on half a century. But prior to that, we enjoyed balance through democracy for over 150 years. It strikes me that, until such time as we determine Saltire's successor, we can return to that once-familiar state." He held up his right hand. "Let us put it to a vote."

Chief held her hand to her chest and nodded, a faint smile betraying her relief.

Pale Dexter set his jaw and said, "May the cost of this risk fall entirely in your hands. My players and followers must remain safe." He turned to Chief. "You bring detection upon yourself. I will have no part in this plan." He spun on his heels and stormed out of the cave.

"Two against one," said Bend Sinister. "You may play. Summon Bluemantle."

—

Overground, Cole crushed the nettle leaves in a mortar and pestle, scraping the pulp into a chipped enamel jug. He poured hot water into the jug, then stirred with a wooden spoon. Behind him, sat Evan.

They were in the kitchen of Cole's box flat in Tempur in the Hundred of Wickerwood. Cole was forty, with a slight frame, curly brown hair and an intense expression that made people feel anxious without knowing why. Anxious, that was, unless you knew him well. Evan was Cole's partner. He knew Cole better than anyone. Evan didn't feel anxious in response to Cole's expression; he felt helpless, and sometimes afraid.

Evan studied Cole's movements as he made tea – a pattern of actions that appeared more ritual than culinary. He observed how Cole lifted a jar of honey from the shelf in front of him, reaching up and grasping without looking. His left hand felt blindly to the side, pulled open a drawer and felt for a spoon. Evan studied the back of Cole's neck. A pulse at the nape pumped the sweating skin. He refused to look at the scar that streaked across his back. Even knowing it was there pained him.

Cole added honey, stirred again, then poured the liquid into two small glasses. Flecks of nettle floated in silent suspension. He hesitated a moment, his hands resting on the worktop. Evan watched. The pulse quickened.

It was the briefest of moments, almost over the instant it began. But it was long enough for Evan to read its portent. Before he had time to ask the question, however, Cole flicked the radio on. "*...stationed throughout the city. Highly trained personnel, best placed to detect sounds that indicate movement. An early warning system poised in protection of the city. You are safe. Think about it. It's all good. Citizens of Wydeye...*"

Cole grunted and switched off the radio. "Drives me fucking crazy," he said.

"I saw them earlier. Allears and Deaf Squad everywhere. Maybe they know something we don't, that there's going to be another hole."

Cole placed the glasses of tea on the table and sat down opposite Evan. "It's a farce. As if they could hear something in time to do anything about it."

"Still, better than nothing."

"Careful, now. You've been listening to the radio too much. Influence by stealth. Their bullshit works through osmosis." He held up his fists, boxer-style. "Guard up, remember."

"Just now, before you turned the radio on…"

"What?"

"There's something you need to tell me."

Cole picked up his glass, turned it slowly between ink-stained fingers, then placed it back on the table. "I've had word from underground. Chief wants to see me."

Evan's face dropped; his shoulders sagged. "Must you go?"

"Must we go through this every time?" Cole caught his partner's wince and the regret of his words stung. "I'm sorry."

"It's just that with Special Forces out on the street… They're not just listening. They're watching too."

"I know." He shook his head and sighed. "But you know the score. I have a duty. Responsibilities. I can't ignore the call, even if I wanted to. Which I don't."

"But—"

"I've been straight with you from the start. I explained what I do and why. Please, don't let's fight about something I won't stop doing."

Evan's gaze fell to the table. Helpless and afraid.

Cole was right, of course. Evan had known from the outset about Cole's creation – his singlehanded mission. *Bluemantle*.

Cole had produced the inaugural copy of the fanzine when he was just sixteen. He had attended his first event – an experience that changed his life forever. Although he had been far too young to witness the Rideout Rebellion, his outrage at what had happened fired his spirit beyond his own adolescent grasp. It was only when he saw Bend Sinister perform for the first time that he finally understood. *Bluemantle* was born from a faith that truth was there for the finding.

For that first edition, he worked through the night in his bedroom in his parent's house in the Old Town. Equipped with a typewriter, pens, scissors and glue, he constructed a magazine-style montage of music journalism.

When legislation outlawing live music was passed, the Authority was heavy-handed in enforcement. Citizens were afraid of blurred distinctions so steered clear of music altogether. For this reason, the fanzine's content was entirely fictitious: reviews, interviews and biographies of bands dreamt up in Cole's spirited imagination.

Yet, buried beneath the cut and paste text, between stylised sketches and graffiti-esque motifs, were traces of fact. Information hidden through advanced encryption, a skill he'd learnt from his father. An elusive treasure: date, time and place of the next event.

Cole was under no illusion. He knew that what he had created, and what he continued to create and disseminate each time an event was planned, was highly illegal and incredibly dangerous. He'd once been beaten, his flesh torn by the Deaf Squad. He knew about their raids on suspected sites, of the torture of those arrested, the indefinite incarceration without trial or parole. He knew people who had gone missing, their families too afraid to ask questions of the Authority. Sometimes their loved ones reappeared following an intel trade at the Exchange. More often they remained a greyscale headshot posted on a row of huge boards beside the building – the 'Wall of the Missing'. It was a haunting parade, created by citizens and maintained by the Authority as an effective aide-memoire.

Even so, Cole saw the danger pale in the light of purpose. He'd once described himself as a graffiti existentialist –

Bluemantle, an expression of his will. He knew the risks. He simply believed they were worth taking.

He reached out and held Evan's hand. "I must do this."

—

Despite the approaching dusk, the air remained hot and sultry. Cole left his flat, ascended the nearest iron stairwell to the Elevated and caught a railmotor into Spire Wells. The double-deck trailers were packed, hauling hundreds of stony-faced commuters home from work. No one spoke. The clatter of the wheels over rusted track created a rhythm that lulled the weary workforce. Few looked through the open windows at the concrete view. Most travelled with their eyes closed, straining to ignore the smell of sulphur that seeped from the locomotive.

Careful to shake any potential tail, Cole changed lines several times. His route looped through the concrete monoliths of the Messam, the street below flooded with office workers, hurrying to reach home before curfew. At the tramway's terminus just north of Drayloc Market, he switched to the Darlem line, taking him west into less frenetic suburbia. He got off at a stop on the tip of Westedge, a residential district on the outskirts of the city. From there he proceeded on foot, avoiding the main road through Westgate Arch that led out of Wydeye. Passage was unrestricted; however, WatcherCams were trained on the thoroughfare. Cole never took the risk.

Once clear of the city's limits, he faced a long trek north into the Nanso Heights – a mountain range that shouldered the north-west corner of the city. The climb was tough, the air thick with humidity. Cole was accustomed to its demands, but it wasn't that that lessened the strain. These periodical summonses instilled in him a fierce loyalty and a modest pride – rich fuel for the journey.

Despite his familiarity with the area, it always took him a while to find the narrow crevice, effectively obscured by the ridges in the escarpment in which it lay. He eased himself through the opening and felt the familiar relief of cool air as he moved along the limestone passage. It was dark; he had to feel his way. Tentative fingertips reading stone; feet shuffling in cautious half-steps. Eventually he reached an opening: a small cave dimly lit with a single gas lamp. The Reception.

Cole waited.

Before long, Chief entered, her silver dreadlocks framing her pale face like a frozen Medusa. "Thank you for coming," she said.

"It is my honour, Chief." He always felt the urge to bow, although he knew it wasn't necessary and he feared she would think him foolish. Instead he gave what he hoped was a courteous nod.

"You took the usual precautions?"

"Yes."

"That is good news. We appreciate the risk you have taken in coming here. And the risks inherent in what you are about to do for us."

"A small price to pay."

"In which case, here is what you need to know." She handed him a small slip of paper, folded in half. "We are aware of the heightened activity overground. The risks are greater than usual. However, it is a necessary step." She held her hand to her chest and paused, catching her breath. "I anticipate numbers will be low, but as long as people know."

"I will get the information to them. You have my word."

"Thank you, Bluemantle." She smiled faintly, stepped back, then turned and slipped away.

Cole stood motionless, waiting for the awe to subside and release his muscles. He followed Bend Sinister and would never switch allegiance. But meeting any of the Troubadours had this effect on him – still, after all these years. He looked at the space that Chief had filled and took a deep breath. Then he looked down at the piece of paper in his hands and carefully unfolded it.

Three sets of numbers.

Date, time and place.

CHAPTER FOUR

The Telltale Circus was not a circus at all, but a travelling theatre troupe who performed on a stage inside a big top. For generations, they had crossed continents, performing to audiences in countless countries. The founding families each originated from a different part of the world, bringing with them stories from their own cultures – folktales that held special meaning beyond mere character and plot. It was these folktales that they adapted and performed as plays, along with tales they had collected through their life on the road.

One day, they had set up their orange and green striped tent on Standings Cross on the edge of Old Wydeye Town, a short distance from the revered Wydeye Deep. The Old Town itself had been founded upon superstition and folklore, much of which revolved around the mysticism of Wydeye Deep – a vast crater with a sheer drop to its fathomless base.

The Circus had performed its plays for the standard run of twenty-one nights. Then a twenty-second night. Then a twenty-third. That was almost eighty years ago.

Elders of the Old Town attributed the extended residency to the influence of Wydeye Deep; it was safer for the Circus to remain under its protective eye, they said. Others maintained it was the city's own folktales that held the attraction, most notably *The Travelling Minstrels* and *The One-Legged Crow*. The theatre troupe themselves were not swayed by local superstition, despite building their livelihoods on similar such tales. However, they could not account for their mutual desire to settle.

Over time, the next generation of actors took to the stage – men and women born into the life of a travelling theatre, but who had never left the limits of Wydeye. One of those native successors was Ursel.

In her late thirties, Ursel had cropped hair, dyed black with a blue streak on one side and a tattoo of a question mark on her left upper arm. Born with a congenital amputation, she had no right arm. Her parents and grandparents had been accomplished actors. The stage was her home – performing, akin to breathing.

By the time Chase and Naylor arrived at the Circus from Wella's quarters in Rader, Ursel had just returned from her day job at the iron refinery in Coxen Lyme.

"Are you Ursel?" said Chase.

"Not quite, but that'll do. Who's asking?" she said. She faced them through tall iron gates, security having barred their entry.

"I'm Chase. And this is Naylor. We're looking for my sister, Wella. Your height. Fair hair. Forty. She's gone missing. Do you know her?"

"I might. If I do, she didn't mention an older brother."

"She's a private person."

"Sounds like I know your sister better than you do." She studied her visitors through narrowed eyes. "How do I know you're not from the A?"

"Do we look like we are?" said Chase, a hard edge to his voice. It had been a hot ride up from Creaser, an exhausting day of searching.

"Now you sound like you are." She turned and began to walk away.

"No, wait," said Naylor, elbowing Chase. "Please. We're sorry."

Ursel stopped but didn't turn around.

"We're just worried for Wella. Chase here's convinced there's something wrong and I'm of a mind to agree. We just want to find her, to know she's okay."

Ursel turned to face them and walked back to the gate. "If you're after Wella, why come looking for me?"

"We found this. In her quarters." Chase handed her the folded pamphlet through the bars of the gate.

"Are you mad?" she hissed, snatching the pamphlet and stuffing it into her tunic. She glanced around her, eyes wide and searching.

"Listen," said Chase, gripping the bars, "I don't know what it is, but I know what it's about. Which means I know enough to fear for her safety. There were others, too. But this one had your name on. So, if you know something, tell me." He could sense she was about to turn and leave. "Wait. Okay, so you probably do know her better than I do. But she's my sister. I just need to know she's alright."

Ursel hesitated. She looked at Chase's hands, his knuckles white from where he gripped the bars. She noticed his strap shirt, soaked from the heat and soiled from dust and clinker, and the open canteen hanging from his belt. She gave a brief nod to the security guard, then said to Chase, "It looks like you could do with some water. Follow me."

—

"I've known Wella for a couple of years. She's a good friend." Ursel had led Chase and Naylor around the side of the big top to an area of smaller tents, yurts and colourful wooden caravans. They were now sat on the floor inside a small yurt, no more than twelve feet in diameter, which Ursel introduced as her home. "If you don't see her, why do you think she's missing?"

"We were due to meet. This morning. It was important. When she didn't show, I knew something must be wrong." He looked to Naylor.

"He's worried about the swallow hole," said Naylor. "Do you know if she would have had a reason to be in Glos on Wednesday night?"

"Not as far as I know. She hates the A as much as I do. And they're the only people that live around there, right?"

"That's what I figured. But Chase here can't help but interpret coincidence as conclusion."

"When did you last see her?" asked Chase, his broad frame hunched over as he knelt awkwardly on the floor.

"Not since the hole, I'm afraid. But that doesn't mean anything. She works long shifts and I'm tied up here when I'm not at work. We normally only get to meet up on Sundays."

"When you last saw her, did she say anything to you? Did she sound like she was in trouble? Someone after her?"

"No. Nothing like that."

"Well, did she seem worried about anything? Was she upset?"

Ursel hesitated, her fingers pulling at a thread from the frayed hem of her tunic. She sighed and looked up at Chase. "I may be betraying a confidence here…"

"Go on," urged Chase.

"She's struggling to cope. She has been for some while. I'd told her to go to the medical centre, but she doesn't want anything on her record. She's worried they'll downgrade her job or confiscate her quarters."

"I knew she needed money – that's why we'd arranged to meet."

"It's more than just money. She's low, spirit-sick. The furnaces is a hard job; it's wearing her down." She studied Chase, as if trying to reach a decision based on what she read in his face. Eventually she said, "She's found a way to manage, though. In the last year or so, she's kept on top of things."

Chase sat up, his face flushed. "Meezel? You're telling me she's on drugs? Is that what the money was for? To get high?"

"No, it isn't Meezel."

"Then what?"

Ursel pulled something out from the folds of her tunic and let it fall to the floor between them. It was the pamphlet Chase had handed her. "Do you know what this is?"

Chase and Naylor looked at each other, then back at Ursel, expectant.

"It's *Bluemantle*," she said. "The fanzine for the Music Scene. I can't tell you anything more than that. And I've only told you that much as you have a copy."

"What in crow's fall is Wella doing with it?"

"She's a follower of the Scene."

"She's what?" Chase stood up, his eyes glaring. "No, she's not. She wouldn't do that. Not after what happened."

Naylor read confusion on Ursel's face. He leant towards her and dropped his voice. "Brann, their younger brother, was arrested by the A. Possession of an instrument. Imprisoned for five years without trial."

"I know about Brann," she said. "Wella told me."

"Then you know she wouldn't be so fucking irresponsible as to have anything to do with the Scene," said Chase. "She wouldn't run the risk. After what our family went through?

How Brann suffered just for carrying a guitar case, for fuck's sake? No one would be that stupid. Not if you saw him now. They broke him. He was just a kid and they fucking broke him."

Ursel's eyes were wide. She stood up and faced Chase. "I'm sorry about what happened to your brother. But Wella is not stupid. She's an intelligent woman. She knows what she's doing. She joined the Scene two years ago. That's where we met. I'm part of it too."

"This is insane. You realise they torture people over this? You don't even have to be caught at an event. If they so much as suspect you were there, you're treated the same. If they think you know someone who knows someone who went, you're arrested and beaten half to death. How the fuck did Wella get mixed up in that shit?"

Ursel sighed. "That's the wrong question."

"What?"

"Ask yourself why. Don't jump to the first prejudicial conclusion your narrow perspective can reach." She turned sideways and raised her left shoulder. "Always ask yourself why."

Chase stared at Ursel, his pulse racing. Ursel stood her ground, staring back, battling inside her mind. Naylor, who was still sat on the floor, slowly rose, struggling to think of a way to break the stalemate. In the final moment, he no longer needed to. Ursel blinked first.

"I believe Wella is okay. And I believe I can find her. You don't have to agree with me, but you will need to trust me. Can you do that?"

—

"I still don't believe you're right about this," muttered Chase, rattled and reluctant.

It was the following day. Chase was sat with Naylor and Ursel in The Raven, a traditional tavern on the fringe of Drayloc Market. The space inside was sparse and gloomy. Timber panelling and a flagstone floor absorbed the limited light that seeped through the shuttered apertures. Wooden tables and chairs were scattered with no sense of order. The bar was makeshift and utilitarian.

The previous evening, Ursel had had to prepare for her performance in the big top. She had said she would be in The Raven at noon if Chase wanted to talk some more.

They were sat huddled around half-empty pints of Kitson, surrounded by other close groups talking in hushed tones. Most taverns, bars and cafés tended not to play music in the background in an effort to avoid attracting the wrong sort of attention. As a consequence, everyone spoke in whispers, creating an atmosphere of secrecy and paranoia, even if there was no cause.

"This is why you need to trust me," said Ursel.

Chase shifted on his stool, appraising Ursel and those around them with suspicion.

"And try not to look so uptight," she said. "I know a lot of these people. We're safe to talk in here."

Chase glanced at Naylor, who shrugged. He turned back to Ursel. "So, what do you suggest?"

"Wella was struggling to cope. For the followers who attend, the Scene is a release from the shit they have to deal with in the real world. It's an escape. And an effective one." She leant forward. "I'm not saying she's definitely there. But, if you want to find your sister, that's the first place I'd look."

"I still don't believe she'd get involved. She hates the Authority, sure. But she's no rebel. She wouldn't risk torture and prison just to fuck with the system."

Ursel sat back, shaking her head. "Well, the A have worked their magic on you alright."

"What do you mean by that?"

"That's not what it's about. The Scene. The events. It's not some dissident vehicle constructed for the sake of rebellion, much as the A would like you to believe. It's not posturing for the sake of insurgency."

"Then why?" asked Naylor. "Why take the risk when you know what the A will do if you're caught? It doesn't make sense."

"Because it's not about breaking the law. It's not about defiance." She paused, rubbing her right shoulder, above her absent arm. "It's about the music."

"For fuck's sake," hissed Chase, banging the table with his fist. "You don't flirt with torture because you like a few songs."

"You don't understand. You're so full of the A's spoon-fed prejudice. You can't judge if you've never been to an event. This is the trust part, okay? I know what I'm talking about."

Naylor turned to Chase. "Hear her out. She's our only lead."

Chase downed the remainder of his Kitson, then sat back, jaws clenched.

Ursel watched him, noticed the flush in his face, the anger in his eyes. Finally she said, "Wella is my friend. With or without you, I'll find her, make sure she's alright. I'll attend the next event. If I'm right and she's there, I can't promise I can persuade her to come back. But at least you'll know she's alive and she's where she wants to be."

"Why do we have to wait? Why can't we go now? Where the crow is it anyway?"

"I can't tell you that."

"Why not?"

"Everyone involved is committed to its preservation. Secrecy is a necessity. Besides, it's transient to avoid detection. I honestly have no idea where it is right now."

"Ha! This is ridiculous. How are you going to find her then?"

"As I said, I'll attend the next event."

"Even though you don't know when or where it is?"

"No, I don't. But I know how to find out."

—

As Ursel rode the railmotor, she sensed a tension in the trailer – the contagious influence of intimidation. Passengers didn't look out at the vast concrete structures in uniform grey. Instead, they looked down at the streets below, catching glimpses of Allears. Then they searched for attendant Deaf Squad – the signal that a sound had been detected.

Before, that sound had meant a potential event, which, in turn, signalled a raid. The terror of past raids remained like a wound that would not heal. The brutality, whether suffered or witnessed, caused citizens to flinch and cower at the sight of a Deaf Squad trooper.

Now? The broadcasts had been clear on the reason for their presence. Terror levels intensified. Passengers pictured the hole in Glos. Their pallor blended with the buildings before them.

Immune to the contagion, Ursel stared ahead at the concrete office blocks of the Messam, imagining fresh air and the sweet scent of bava blossom in place of stale body odour and burning coke. She tried to close her ears to the in-trailer speakers, broadcasting Authority messages in a Mobius monologue: *"…confidence in your safety. Citizens of Wydeye, help us help you. You have ears too. For the sake of us all, share what you hear. Rent reductions, target adjustment, pharmaceutical relief; the Exchange has the price that's right for you. Good citizens, fear not…"*

Eventually the railmotor approached Standings Cross, skirting the green and orange spectacle of the big top. Ursel always found the sudden splash of colour striking, even though she had spent her whole life at the Telltale Circus. It wasn't just the notion of home, she thought. It was the absence of permanence, the relief of choice. The Circus hadn't ceased to be a travelling theatre just because the troupe had failed to move on for so long. Their sense of freedom lay in having the option.

Instead of alighting at her usual stop, she rode the tramway to the end of the line, Old Wydeye Town. Climbing out of the trailer, she descended the iron stairwell and sought shade in the narrow, cobbled streets.

Old Wydeye Town was in stark contrast to the rest of the city. The site of the original settlement, the buildings were made from hand-carved limestone, all single or two-storey with flat roofs. Much of the life of the Old Town occurred at roof level, on which were private residential terraces and goat pens, alongside public roofs filled with Ribatchi game tables, cushioned story corners and makeshift stalls selling food and drink, home crafts, books and fabrics. Precarious wooden platforms and rope ladders connected the buildings, making it possible to cross from one end of the Old Town to the other without touching the ground.

At street level, the narrow lanes were dark, cramped and oppressively humid. Ursel zigzagged through the lanes, occasionally glancing over her shoulder. Convinced that she had not been followed, she switched back and stopped before a squat building she had passed some time before. She knocked hard, three times, a pause, then twice more. The door creaked open and she stepped inside.

An elderly man, bent over a crooked cane, stood before her. "How may I help you?" he said.

"The crow flies low over Glade Park." She had spoken these words to the man so many times before; she knew he recognised her. Yet this was the form, and such caution was warranted. The person she had come to see risked his life for the cause. Security and secrecy were survival's armour.

"He's in the basement," said the old man, gesturing the way.

Ursel stepped forward towards a wooden cupboard built into a recess in the stone wall. She opened a door at its base and pulled out a hat box stuffed with balls of wool. Beneath where it had stood was a trap door, barely noticeable amid the ancient floorboards. Ursel ran her hand along one end, feeling for a slight lip, under which she wedged her fingers. Struggling slightly with her one hand, she pulled up the trap door, crawled into the cupboard and slipped through the opening. Her feet found the wooden ladder that led her down to the basement.

The space below was cramped and dark, dimly lit by a couple of gas lamps fixed to the damp stone walls. A man was sat at a desk, pecking a typewriter with his two index fingers. He looked up as Ursel climbed down the ladder, then promptly returned to his task.

Ursel stepped up to him, wary of the interruption. "Hello, Cole," she said. "I need your help."

—

Two hours later, Ursel was at the Circus, negotiating Chase and Naylor's entry past security. She led them to her yurt and gestured for them to sit on the floor. "I have the information," she said as she knelt down beside them.

"What? You know where Wella is?" said Chase, his earlier frustration tempered.

"No. But I know where to look."

"Well, let's go then."

"No, we can't. Not yet. I went to see the person who creates *Bluemantle*. He was finishing work on a new edition."

"What does that mean?"

"It means an event is planned. Each edition of *Bluemantle* contains the date, time and coordinates for the next show." She pulled out a copy of the fanzine from her tunic. "I know where it's going to take place. And I know when."

"When?"

Ursel hesitated, studying her guests' expressions, weighing up. Eventually she said, "Monday night."

"But that's forty-eight hours away. What if you're wrong? What if it was the hole? She could still be alive down there. Or what if the A have taken her? She had copies of that damn thing in her flat. They could've already been on to her. I can't wait two days for you to follow up on a hunch." Chase stood up. "Come on, Naylor. We're wasting time."

"Keep looking, by all means," said Ursel, getting up. "But you won't find her. I tell you, she's with the Scene. And she'll be safe there."

"You can't know that. Have you had the A take someone you love? Have you had family tortured and held for no reason?"

"No…" Ursel took a deep breath and looked down at the tattoo on her left shoulder. She closed her eyes and frowned. Then she opened them again and turned to Chase. "Why do you think she never told you? The Scene is the most important thing in her life right now. Why do you think she kept it from you?"

"Because she knows what I'd say. The risks are insane."

"Yet she's been taking them for two years. What does that tell you?"

"If she has, she's been caught up in something. She's not been thinking straight. Like Meezels. Once they start using regularly, they stop being themselves. And that's what the Authority says. The music's a drug; it influences you. Takes control. That's what's happened to Wella. You said she's your friend. You could've stopped her."

"Now, Chase," said Naylor, getting up and holding Chase by the arm. "Ursel's on our side. She's helping us."

"It's okay, Naylor," said Ursel. "And you're wrong, Chase. She never told you because she knew you wouldn't understand. So why not try to see it from her perspective? Come with me on Monday night. See for yourself."

—

Cole moved silently through the city. His deposits were always in the same place so that followers would know where to look. However, each time he had a drop to make, he would change the route, caution being his guiding principle.

It was Sunday morning, the only day off for most citizens, so the railmotor was less crammed than usual, making the long, looping detours less arduous. Tramway travel was fully subsidised by the state, so it didn't cost him a ketrel in fares. He could, and did, criss-cross the city all day, alighting at certain stops to hide bundles of *Bluemantle*.

By the time he'd made the final drop, it was early afternoon. Hot and weary from the sultry heat, he walked the final mile in the slim shade of the Elevated and arrived at The Raven. The tavern was already busy with people determined to make the most of their scant free time. He squinted across the room, his eyes adjusting to the dim light. He made out Evan waving from the far corner and smiled.

"Lifesaver," said Cole, sipping the chilled Kitson that Evan had just bought him. "It's felt a long day already."

"All done?"

"Yep. Not much notice this time, so it was tight. But yeah, all done. Feels good." He beamed at Evan, who strained to return the smile. "What's wrong?"

Evan dropped his already hushed voice to a faint whisper and leant in. "I'm worried about this one."

"It'll be alright."

"You say that because you want it to be. But you must've seen them today. Allears everywhere."

"Chief said they're aware of the situation overground. They'll take precautions." He held on to Evan's arm. "It's a good thing. Especially after Saltire. They need to play again. Momentum's important."

Evan shook his head.

"It is. Come on, you know this. Growing the audience is what it's all about."

"That's what it's about for you."

"That's not fair," said Cole, letting go of his arm. "I'm not doing this for me."

"Then don't go. You've done what you need to do for the Scene. You don't need to be there." He took Cole's hand. "Please. For me. It's not even Bend Sinister playing. I understand enough to know that'd be different. But it's Chief."

"It's still important."

"I know, I know it is. But the A, they might hear it this time. Then there will be raids. And…" Evan shook his head, struggling to keep his voice down. "If they arrest you, you'll be tortured. If they find out your role in the Scene, they'll kill you."

"But they won't find out. I won't tell them shit."

"You might not. But someone else they torture will. However loyal, followers are still human. There's only so much pain a person can take before they break."

Cole stared at his pint, his earlier joy destroyed. Evan watched him, close to tears. Neither spoke, each battling with the unreconcilable impasse.

Evan dropped his head into his hands. "If it wasn't for that damned festival," he sighed. "If it wasn't for Rideout, we wouldn't have to live like this."

CHAPTER FIVE

FORTY YEARS AGO

It was Governor Morgan Wallace who declared Rideout a rebellion.

It began as Rideout Festival, a live music event organised by a group of community volunteers. This was forty years ago, eight years into Wallace's term in office. His stringent measures to increase productivity and economic output had left the citizens of Wydeye weary and worn. Morale was at an all-time low.

Despite the state's curb on cultural activity, deeming it non-contributory to the growth agenda, a cluster of arts organisations had managed to survive. In an effort to boost morale, the volunteers approached the Authority with a proposal for a music festival. They sold it as a fundraiser, with the proceeds to be invested in the restoration of Glade Park. After months of lobbying, the Authority finally agreed, on the condition that it would manage the funds raised from the event.

Wallace also insisted that the state had control over security. A curfew of nine o'clock was imposed; people had to be fit for work the next day, after all. State police would be positioned around the perimeter of the venue, under the command of the newly appointed Chief of Police, Commissioner Estel Blix.

The festival was to be held in an open-air sports stadium near Glade Park, on the edge of Spire Wells. The once-thriving music scene had all but disappeared. However, a handful of bands had persevered, playing low-key shows in taverns and cafés. Headlining the event were two groups among the most popular in the scene. Their names were Saltire and Bend Sinister.

The day of the festival was particularly hot and humid. The open stadium afforded little shade for the tens of thousands gathered for the event. Some citizens loitered under the awnings of food stalls and Tramways Brewery tents that were dotted around the perimeter. Most, however, paid no attention to the heat. Life had been hard under Wallace. The promise of the festival had felt like a holiday. Spirits were high.

Families flocked into the stadium, waving streamers bought from street traders. Children darted between the crowds or sat on the shoulders of their parents. Smiling couples loitered, hand in hand. An eighteen-year-old Naylor Hammett laughed with a group of fellow apprentice miners, faces glowing, relishing the taste of freedom.

Fans of the two headline acts held aloft flags and banners, parading their allegiance to either Saltire or Bend Sinister. The flags bore bold emblems – symbols of proud patronage, unchanged in their design for over 150 years. These followers filtered through the crowd, pushing headlong towards the front of the stage.

The first few bands on the bill were met with cheers and applause. Those in the crowd who didn't know the music probably knew one of the band members – a friend, perhaps, or a work colleague. It was community cohesion at its most powerful; this was what it meant to belong. The hardships of the last eight years were forgotten. People fell in love with Wydeye once more. This was their city, their home.

By the time Saltire took to the stage, the stadium was full to capacity. Loyal fans surged to the front, leaving the rest of the audience staring in eager anticipation. From the opening riff on an electric guitar, the crowd fell silent. Gnarling bass reverberated around the stadium. Pounding drums thumped from the PA into the chests of everyone present. Saltire herself commanded centre stage – a Titaness appraising her faithful.

As Saltire played their unique blend of rock and metal, the crowd slipped into a warm enchantment. Those still sheltering under the shadow of an awning, stepped forward and joined the throng. Eyes were either transfixed on the stage or closed as bodies swayed. Some people cheered, others sang along. Most remained silent, absorbing the energy that emanated from the stage. Even the police officers succumbed to the lure. First one, then another, broke a cardinal rule of duty and removed their helmets. They stood enraptured, faces beaming, marvelling at the music.

The duty Superior regained control of his senses and roared to his unit to put their helmets back on. His voice drowned out by music, they remained staring at the stage, gaping at the sonic assault. Sensing the start of something he was at a loss to control, he shouted into his radio. Receiving or, more likely, hearing no reply, he barked orders at his oblivious unit and hurried away through one of the tunnels that led out of the stadium.

In his absence, Saltire disappeared from the stage and Bend Sinister emerged. The players were dressed in black, wielding their instruments like tridents. Bend Sinister raised his guitar over his head and roared into the microphone. The crowd responded in kind, arms in the air, hands reaching forward, chanting his name. With barely a break in the music, Bend Sinister filled the stadium with their sound: heavy, dense and complex. Utterly captivating. The crowd were ecstatic, swept up in an irresistible reverie.

By the time the duty Superior returned, the energy in the crowd was palpable. On his heels marched Commissioner Blix, surveying the unprecedented scene. Ignoring the stage, she scanned the perimeter, clocking the police officers standing dumbfounded, helmets hanging empty by their sides. The Chief of Police wasted no time; she spun around and stormed out of the tunnel, the Superior trotting clueless behind her.

Meanwhile, the atmosphere within the bowel of the stadium was reaching fever pitch. Bend Sinister's vocals mesmerised the crowd. The players' performance intensified. Nothing could break the spell.

No one heard the thud of combat boots or the thunder of hooves approach. No one noticed the troopers pour through the tunnels and take up position around the edge of the stadium, ear defenders straddling their Forces-issue helmets. No one turned to see the unit of horse-mounted soldiers arrive. Even when the power was cut and the PA fell silent, the crowd remained staring forward, shouting for more. They continued to cheer and applaud, staring at the empty stage.

Bend Sinister and his players had disappeared.

—

The first shot was fired into the air. No one reacted; they barely seemed to notice. The second shot was fired just over the heads of the crowd.

Then the horses charged.

People screamed. The stadium was packed; there was nowhere to run. The crowd surged in waves – a tidal swell of bodies. Some fell. Unable to get up, they were trampled over, their cries unheard. The heat and the terror intensified. Bodies crushed together, lungs unable to breathe. Many fainted, adding to the fallen underfoot. As further shots were fired, parents huddled over crying children. Everywhere, the chilling colour of carnage.

Citizens called out for the troopers to stop, yelled for lost loved ones, cried in horror. Those on the edge of the crowd tried to escape through the tunnels, but foot troopers, deaf to their screams, barred their exit. With nowhere to go, the crowd were trapped, helpless, terrified.

Then the horses moved in, crushing bodies like grapes beneath their iron-shod hooves.

Thirty-seven people lost their lives.

—

In his vitriolic assessment of the disaster, Governor Wallace denounced the behaviour of the citizens attending, declaring it 'a wilful act of rebellion'. As festival-goers struggled to regain their wits and regroup, Wallace asserted that they were 'resisting arrest'. The use of live ammunition was 'standard practice', he said; state troopers had 'no cause to expect, nor tolerate, such acts of defiance by the citizens they were trained to protect'. It was 'unfortunate', he conceded, 'that a number of bullets ricocheted within the stadium, causing unintended fatalities', including twelve children. The 'hysteria of citizens caused the horses to stampede', resulting in 'regrettable, yet inevitable loss of life'. In his scathing conclusion, Wallace blamed the deaths on the 'wantonly rebellious and defiant behaviour of the crowd', claiming they 'resisted proportionate measures of control'.

Meanwhile, Wallace locked his sights onto what he perceived as the true culpable cause. Besides, he had face to save; that meant parading scalps.

The Authority charged the last two bands to perform with inciting violence through a hypnotic influence exerted through their music. The influence could not be accounted for, yet the police officers who had removed their helmets and succumbed to the lure attested to its power. These accounts provided sound justification. Tagging them 'Music Makers', Wallace declared the accused 'enemies of the state' and ordered their immediate arrest, at any cost.

The Music Makers became the smoke screen for what the Authority couldn't understand and what its governor feared most: a challenge to control and order. Wallace believed in the scapegoat of his own making. He set his sights on their capture and vowed they would not evade due punishment.

Blinkered by determination, he misread the mood of the city, overlooking the rumbling unrest – the growing resentment that yielded the fruits of true rebellion.

—

Prior to Rideout, Wallace's agenda had focused exclusively on productivity and fiscal growth. A number of his early interventions proved popular, distracting attention from his less-than-transparent election into office. These included free travel on the expanding tramway system, capped rents in the purpose-built Rader Tenements and Wallace Estates, food stamps for families participating in the Three Child Initiative. Although never well liked, Governor Wallace was regarded as a progressive reformer with the interests of Wydeye at heart. Once they had adjusted to the changes, citizens recognised merit in his ambition and bought into his vision of prosperity.

Perspectives soon changed.

The first policy to provoke protest was the introduction of the Milk Tax to fund the construction of the self-aggrandising Authority Complex. Cows' milk became unaffordable for the majority. Families who had benefitted from the Three Child Initiative struggled, holding down multiple jobs just to afford milk for their babies. Enterprising minds spotted an opportunity and began breeding and selling goats for their milk. Ten months after the introduction of the Milk Tax, over thirty per cent of households owned or held shares in a goat. Two years and several heated protests later, the Milk Tax was abolished.

A further measure that proved unpopular was the demolition of popular arts and cultural venues across the city and the removal of creative subjects from the curriculum. Wallace maintained that arts and culture were an irrelevant distraction, without any measurable contribution to productivity.

Frustrated citizens took to the streets once again. However, their collective voice was an ineffectual murmur. The rights and will of the people were not part of Wallace's lexicon of leadership. Empty demands posed no threat.

Then came Rideout and subsequent demonstrations, prompting Governor Wallace to revise his opinion of the collective voice.

When the witch hunt against the 'Music Makers' was triggered, followers of the Scene organised a public protest. They gathered on the Pentagon, flags of allegiance unfurled. Then they marched up First Went and congregated outside City Hall and the Exchange. Impassioned chants demanded charges be dropped and the bands' freedom of the city be reinstated.

Citizens unassociated with the Scene also joined the protest. They empathised with the plight of the persecuted bands, drawing parallels with the struggles they endured at the hands of the Authority. They vented their anger at the cover-up over Rideout, which had exonerated the Chief of Police and trooper Commanders. They discovered a release for the pent-up pressure they had begun to take for granted, the strain of life under the weight of productivity targets.

The protests grew in scale and intensity. Citizens had had enough. They demanded change. With one voice, they challenged. With one fist, they fought back.

As did the Authority.

In swift retaliation, Wallace countered the escalation with a full-scale assault. Special Forces descended on the protestors in a storm cloud of terror. 'Any means necessary' was a free pass taken to the limit.

Troopers surrounded the protestors, weapons raised. The followers who had led the campaign stood their ground, faces defiant in their call for justice. They did not falter as their emblazoned flags were torn down and set alight. Behind them, citizens who had joined in noble solidarity, huddled like cornered prey. Some raised their hands in surrender. Others cried pleas for mercy.

Yet, orders were orders. The troopers had a job to do. They closed in, relishing the task.

Limbs were broken, blood was shed, lives were lost.

Within an hour, brute force lay waste to the protest – the collective voice silenced for good.

—

Wallace declared Rideout and the ensuing 'Rebellion' incidents of epidemic mass hysteria – a sociogenic illness that must be prevented from reoccurring at all costs.

To this end, live music was declared a first-degree drug on account of its perceived hypnotic influence and volatile effect on behaviour. Legislation was passed making it illegal to participate in, perform or associate with any activity related to live music. Enforcement would be ruthless, he warned, punishment severe.

The emblems that represented the four bands at the heart of the Scene were also outlawed. Wallace had long been looking for an excuse. He distrusted the musicians that commanded such loyalty, suspicious of the respect so freely given by those who followed. The relationship was incompatible with his version of what it meant to lead and what it meant to follow. He read a subtext of power that posed a threat to his own. The emblems had to go.

Flags were confiscated and destroyed; badges stitched to tunics and caps, torn off; tattoos surgically censored. Visible association with any one of the Music Makers became a criminal offence, carrying excessive penalties designed to deter.

In addition, any form of protest or public demonstration, peaceful or otherwise, was pronounced an act of treason against the state. Legislation on sentencing was toughened substantially.

To cater for the impact, Itherside Hold high-security penitentiary was built. It was an unequivocal demonstration of the Authority's intent – a message clearly stated in steel bars and concrete.

These interventions were punitive – an exercise in consequence for challenging the rule of the Authority. Meanwhile, Wallace and his Chief of Police, Commissioner Blix, remained focused on the only consequence that meant anything to them.

Blix had witnessed the mesmerised crowd, how the musicians' intangible power dwarfed her own. She concluded there was something in the Makers' music, a force words could not describe. She saw first-hand how this significantly undermined the control of the police officers present and, by default, the sovereignty of the Authority.

United in their ambition, Wallace and Blix both feared this new threat to achieving absolute control. Privately, they swore they would have their revenge upon the Music Makers – the source of the sociogenic disease.

Through a carefully crafted communication campaign, the Authority demonised the illness, claiming it a catastrophic threat to the peace and stability of Wydeye. The messages were tailored to sway public opinion on the cause and the cost. Citizens were to regard the festival and rebellion dead as culpable participants in mass hysteria, rather than innocent victims of an avoidable tragedy.

While the propaganda machine maintained its course, words were backed by action. The Authority's Special Forces diversified. The Deaf Squad were created first, mindful of the lessons on vulnerability learnt from Rideout. They operated with impunity and without restriction on the use of force. Unit Superiors were recruited from the state police and the military. The Squad's foot soldiers were made up of civilian volunteers and convicted violent criminals who opted for re-education and a full term of service in favour of indefinite incarceration in one of the state's unregulated detention centres.

Then came the Allears. Invasive experimentation was conducted on early recruits to establish viable methods of sensory manipulation to enhance aural capability. The resultant methods of adjustment proved effective.

Adding to ears on the ground, the first whisper dishes appeared around Coxen Lyme and Crow, Hundreds historically synonymous with the city's once-thriving music scene.

Despite the severity of risk and repercussion, the Scene continued, albeit at a far-reduced level and with elaborate precautions to preserve secrecy. Even so, events were raided, musicians lost to Itherside Hold, followers brutally beaten and imprisoned.

Soon, the only bands remaining were those the Authority had labelled the Music Makers: four groups of players who had dominated the Scene for decades.

Their capture became Governor Wallace and Commissioner Blix's all-consuming obsession.

And once, only once, they came very close indeed.

A raid was made on an old warehouse in Coxen Lyme, following positive detection by a unit of Allears. The warehouse was stormed in a dramatic display of excessive force and disproportionate aggression. A number of the audience were killed in the assault. Scores were arrested and subsequently tortured for information.

Of the band who was performing at the time, the drummer was captured and promptly transported to the most secure detention unit in the Authority Complex: the notorious C-Block. There, the drummer endured a protracted interrogation.

Rumours regarding his horrific torture became the subject of legend down in the streets and markets of Wydeye. Yet, as far as any citizen knew, the drummer did not betray his band, for they were never captured.

The band was Bend Sinister.

CHAPTER SIX

"Today, we prepare. Tomorrow, we play."

Deep underground, Chief looked to each of her players, who formed a circle around her. They all dressed the same: bespoke outfits constructed from pieces of grey cloth adorned with strips of leather, buckles and steel chain. Their faces were pale and ageless, their eyes intense.

"It will be a poignant occasion," she said. "Many followers may not know of Saltire's passing, but word will soon spread. Our music will not diminish their sorrow, but it can cradle it. This is our responsibility. Tonight, we play in memory of our lost leader and her players. Let us feel their presence and remember."

They were stood in a cavernous space, the cave's ceiling arching high above. The limestone walls were smooth and undulating. Soda straws hung from the ceiling like the pipes of an inverted church organ. As they stood, heads bowed, a steady trickle of water denied them silence.

After a period of reflection, Chief raised her head. "Any questions?"

"Will the others be there?" asked the drummer.

"Bend Sinister, possibly. I doubt very much that Pale Dexter will attend."

"Do you anticipate followers of Saltire will come?" said the bassist.

"Yes. Of those who know her fate, I imagine a number will. They must feel displaced. Despite their grief, they will need to find a new home."

The guitarist raised his eyebrows. "Is that why Pale Dexter opposed our request to perform?"

"Quite possibly." She flicked her silver dreads and crossed her arms. "Although, I am sure he will find a way to attract more than his fair share."

An echo of footfall crept into the cave. Then the source could be heard, becoming steadily louder. The players glanced at each other and turned towards the arched opening that formed the entrance to their camp. A shadow appeared first, bleeding across the floor like an oil slick, followed by a tall silhouette. "Chief. Forgive my intrusion. May I speak with you a while?"

"Bend Sinister. Please, enter," said Chief. "We were about to head to the location to prepare, but I can spare some time." She looked to her players. "You go on ahead. I will join you shortly."

The bassist, guitarist and drummer gave a courteous nod to Bend Sinister and filed out of the cave.

"I apologise for interrupting and for coming without prior arrangement," said Bend Sinister.

"That is quite alright. What is on your mind?"

"I've heard word from one of my followers. Activity on the streets is escalating far beyond what we would ordinarily expect." He stepped forward and spoke gravely. "I tell you this not to dissuade you from playing. I understand your motivation to perform."

"Then why?"

"To warn you of the danger, so that you may take whatever precautions are necessary. End as soon as you feel replenished. Give yourself and your followers opportunity to escape." He held out his hands. "There were four of us. Now there are three. This isn't forever anymore."

Chief nodded. "Thank you for your words of caution. I appreciate your concern. It is unfortunate that I find myself in this weakened state, otherwise I would postpone. As it stands, I must play."

"And I respect that."

"Will you attend?"

"That would be my wish. However, I find my spirits are low."

"You miss her."

"Very much so."

"I will endeavour to make a fitting dedication in her honour. The event will not pass without tribute, I assure you."

"I trust that you will, and I am grateful for that." Bend Sinister bowed. "I have taken up much of your time. You have a show to prepare for. I shall bid you farewell." He bowed once more, stepped back, then turned and left the cave, his shadow trailing in his wake.

Chief watched him depart, then knelt on the floor, her head raised to the ceiling. Cobalt eyes stared into the gloom, unblinking. Her shoulders sagged and her hands lay spent in her lap. "We are our every need," she whispered. "We are the hunger that defines us. We are the very dependency on to which we cling, powerless to let go."

She imagined the scene overground. Experience lent the images a terrifying clarity. Troopers marching through the city, weapons in hand; Allears poised like hungry trigger fingers; citizens cowering in shadow disguises. She could feel their fear permeate the two hundred metres of rock above her head.

"Oh, to be free of that which will destroy us."

—

Overground, the Exchange basked in the sun – a vast grey beast formed of windowless towers and jutting balconies suspended above a paved precinct. It was a bleak, imposing structure that epitomised the building's function.

Wulfwin hurried up the steep stone steps that led to the precinct and the gaping maw of the main entrance. He glanced to his left, at the ever-expanding Wall of the Missing. A wry sneer shortened his scar. He found the juxtaposition of the Wall and the building it abutted to be an irony that validated the stupidity of the crowd. *As if validation were necessary*, he thought, before striding through the open doors.

Inside, the space was cavernous, the air filled with echoes of footfall as people crisscrossed the expanse of the central hall. All around the perimeter were closed doors, with a number painted in white on a board above. Rooms one to twenty were for trade in health and social support. Twenty-one to forty were for cash or commercial arrangements, such as lump-sum swaps or fixed-term tax relief. Rooms forty-one to eighty were reserved for trade in dependencies, principally Meezel.

Meezel was a synthetic drug, widely available in the city, despite being technically illegal. Its correct name was Cordexafed, but it earnt the tag 'Meezel' on account of the itchy rash that was the drug's predominant side effect. A growing number of citizens, across the demographic spectrum, were turning to the drug as a means of escape.

Rooms forty-one to eighty proved the most lucrative from the Authority's perspective, having passed amendments to legislation that allowed for medicinal dispensation of the drug. Wulfwin marched towards number forty-six, sweeping past cowering citizens who scurried out of his path.

He walked through the doorway, entering a small room reminiscent of a neglected cell. In the centre was a desk and a chair occupied by a scrawny man, who shot up to attention on Wulfwin's entrance. To its left was a wooden bench, on which huddled a child.

"Is this the boy?" Wulfwin said to the man.

"Yes, sir." He stooped and held out one arm, gesturing to the child by way of introduction.

Wulfwin stepped up to the boy, towering over him in his long leather trench coat. "Name," he boomed.

"Wasif—"

"How old are you?"

"Nine." The boy cowered, not daring to look up.

"Tell me what you told this man."

"Sir... I heard rumour, sir. Talk of a show..." He gulped, wringing his trembling hands.

"Go on."

"Tomorrow night."

"Where?"

"I don't know. Honest to crow. That's all I heard."

"Who told you this?"

"I hears it. On Second Went. Two men whispering. But I still hears them. They cuss, sayin' it ain't right."

"These men, do you know them? Would you recognise them?"

The child shook his head. "No. Don't know them. Don't recognise."

"We'll see about that." Wulfwin stepped back and crossed his arms. Leather creaked. "Tell me. What does a nine-year-old kid want with a wrap of Meezel?" He looked to the man who was still hovering behind him. "That's the swap, isn't it?"

The man sneered. "Yes, sir. The kids are starting young these days."

"Not for me…" said the child.

Wulfwin spun back around. "Is that right, now? In that case, who are you trading for?"

"My mum. She needs it. She's poorly. Meezel helps."

"Well, aren't you a brave boy. Picking up secrets from the streets and coming to the Exchange. I'm afraid the price for a wrap just went up."

The child looked up in horror, his mouth open.

"Tell me who those men are, then we trade." He pulled a cosh from inside his coat and turned back to the man. "Leave us alone," he hissed.

—

"Let's just say I helped the boy understand the benefits of sharing." Wulfwin stood opposite Governor Blix, who was sat behind her desk in her office. He rubbed hand over fist, his sneer pronounced. "A little persuasion can go a long way on one so young."

"He gave you their names."

"No. Turns out he genuinely doesn't know them. But he did, eventually, give a good enough description for us to find the men and bring them in. We're holding them in C-Block."

"Excellent." Blix leant forward. "I trust you've made a start."

"They're being treated to a warm-up as we speak. I came straight here to appraise you. I will head over there next – encourage them to open up."

"The boy."

"Aside from a few breaks and bruises, he got what he came for. I released him."

Bix nodded. "I understand his mother's an addict. Keep the child on side. He could prove useful. And maybe hold back on the physical. We don't want him too afraid to trade."

"As you wish."

Blix stood up and walked to the window, gazing past the Complex to the city beyond. "If the rumours are true, this event could not come at a worse time. There is an unease out there, latent yet tangible. Despite our messaging, the swallow hole has caused a contagion. I've read your latest report. The citizens are becoming infected by irrational fear, the influence of which is destabilising, more so on the multitude than the individual.

"This is textbook mass psychogenic hysteria. The hole is the common trigger – a shared terror. The disease is spreading rapidly, a virus sustained by anxiety and the fear it will happen again. We're not there yet, but it could reach epidemic proportions.

"We must be on guard. Whilst the individual citizen is malleable, en masse, they are volatile. And when already vulnerable, as they are now, their propensity for hysterical reaction is manifold. The threat to civil order cannot be underestimated. I witnessed Rideout, remember; I have seen what influence a mobilised crowd can achieve." She turned to face Wulfwin. "And let us not forget, the Music Makers are still out there."

Wulfwin spoke in a deep, controlled voice. "With the intelligence we now have, coupled with the fact the Allears are already deployed and listening, we will locate the event before it gets out of hand."

"That being so, we are wise to be prepared." Her sharp, crisp suit contradicted the fluster in her voice. "Commander Lore. His last report to you."

"First thing this morning. His men are on rotation. All dishes are attended around the clock. Other units are on patrol. I'm satisfied they are on point."

"Good." Blix hesitated, then returned to her desk. She perched on its corner, hands in her lap. "I have confidence you have this under control, Wulfwin." If she knew how to smile, she might have done so in that moment. Instead, a deep breath and raised eyebrows punctuated the change in subject. "On to brighter matters. An update on Project Alpha."

A year ago, a citizen had offered a lump of iridescent rock for trade at the Exchange. Information regarding its source was duly extracted: the man had found it beside a recent rock fall on the north face of Lyun Mountain. Thoroughly gagged by non-disclosure contracts, a trusted state geologist investigated the site. His report confirmed the presence of opal deposits in a seam of crystallised rock.

Wydeye functioned within its means, but there was no margin to absorb a deficit and no scope for fiscal growth. Ever ambitious, even at the top, Blix sought opportunities to diversify. With the prospect of a wealth source to elevate her legacy, Blix had launched Project Alpha.

"A second deep seam has been found," said Wulfwin. "Engineers are sinking further shafts to intersect the layer. They're trying to determine the extent of the field before scoping the next phase of the project."

"All according to plan. Most pleasing." Blix's eyes glazed momentarily, before snapping back into focus. "It is imperative they remain discrete. Word must not get out."

"They have signed the necessary agreements and are fully appraised of the consequence of reneging."

"Good. Progress is reassuring." She moved around her desk and slid into her chair. "This is good news for the city, Wulfwin. It's a game-changer." She looked into his eyes, betraying a trace of excitement in her own. Finding no reciprocation, she said, "That is all. You may go."

As Wulfwin turned and left her office, Blix picked up a small cabochon of polished opal, revolving it in her long fingers, catching the play of colour. The object was solid, tangible, held firmly in her grasp. Its surface was smooth, faultless. The rippling colour hinted at reward.

Possession, she thought. *You delicate dominion. Why can't it all be this way?*

—

"You don't have to go through with it, Chase," said Naylor. "Ursel said she'd go on her own."

It was Sunday evening. Naylor and Chase had caught the railmotor to Five Wents and were walking beneath the Elevated on First. The underpass was crowded. Authority motorcycles jostled with carters, citizens skirted begging Wethers, stray goats searched for scraps. All were headed towards the Pentagon, a huge, paved space from which spread the Wents – a giant starfish laying prostrate in the city's centre.

Chase pulled at his strap shirt, which clung to the sweat on his back. "You heard her. I don't understand, apparently."

"So, what, you take the risk to prove a point?"

"No. I take the risk to find Wella."

"But there's no need. We keep up the search here and leave Ursel to check out the show. She's part of the Scene, presumably she'll be going anyway. If she's right and Wella's there, then great. If she's wrong, you haven't wasted time, nor risked arrest by going to something you know you should stay well clear of."

"Were it that easy."

"I don't see why…" A railmotor trundled overhead. The screech of steel against rusting iron and the groan of the Elevated under the sixty-tonne weight drowned out Naylor's voice. The locomotive slowed as it approached the Pentagon stop. He gave up trying to compete with the din. Instead, he hurried behind Chase, who had stepped up the pace.

They broke away from the underpass and entered the Pentagon. It was early yet, but already the cafés, food carts and brewery tents were packed. With so much of the city declared a curfew zone from sundown, any citizen who sought escape from the confines of their quarters come evening was forced into the Hundred of Spire Wells or restricted to the limited entertainment available in the surrounding residential districts. A significant proportion of the city's population descended on the same nine square miles – a reliable spike in trade that the proprietors, landlords and stall holders took full advantage of.

"I told Weldon and Tinashe we'd meet them in the Brew," called Chase over his shoulder. He led the way through the crowd, towards a large makeshift bar. Casks were stacked on wooden carts, forming a wall along two sides. Before these stood the bar: two long trestle tables, laden with pint jugs and gill glasses. In the central space were around fifty hay bales, serving as makeshift benches and tables combined. People either sat on the bales, on the floor, or milled around, sipping their Kitson or Pyncher, the only drinks on sale. "There they are." Chase pointed at two people standing by the bar.

Tinashe was tall and dark-skinned, with braided hair and bright eyes. She was laughing at Weldon, a slight, pliable man, all arms and legs. He was performing some sort of impression, contorting his face and gesturing with his hands. Tinashe caught sight of Chase and Naylor as they approached. "Hey, guys. About time."

"Sorry," said Naylor. "We got held up. How long have you been here?"

"Long enough for Weldon to act the fool and still not get a round in." She elbowed Weldon. "Your shout. We'll find somewhere to sit." She turned and headed for a vacant bale before Weldon had the chance to respond.

Chase and Naylor followed Tinashe and sat down beside her. Chase rubbed the sweat from his forehead with the back of his arm and downed the last dregs of water from the canteen strapped to his belt.

"So, what've you been up to today?" said Tinashe. "Why so warm and weary?"

"Wella's gone missing," said Chase. "We've been looking for her."

"Oh, crow. Since when?"

"Sometime between Wednesday and Friday morning. I take it you haven't seen her? I tried to call you and Weldon at the sports centre, left a message there."

"I've had a double shift at the tramways. Sorry, mate."

Weldon appeared with four pints of Kitson. "Here you go, ladies." He sat cross-legged on the floor in front of them. "What? I buy you a beer. Why so glum?"

"Wella's disappeared," said Tinashe.

Chase filled them in on their search so far. When it came to telling them all about Ursel and her theory on Wella's whereabouts, he leant in and lowered his voice. They sat in a huddle, faces close.

"I'm not saying I know your sister well," said Tinashe, "but I doubt she'd get involved in all that. Not after…"

"That's what I said. But Ursel says they're close friends and she seems convinced."

"He's thinking about going with Ursel," said Naylor.

Chase shot him a pointed glare.

Naylor raised his hands. "What? If I can't talk you out of it, maybe these guys will have more luck."

"Seriously, man, don't risk it," whispered Tinashe. She tipped her head to the left. "Have you seen them? They're manning the dishes twenty-four seven. Allears everywhere. It's too dangerous."

"They're for the holes, though," said Weldon. "I'm not saying it's not dangerous. You know what I think about Users. Selfish troublemakers, stirring up shit for the rest of us. But the Allears now, they're listening for more holes. It's a good thing they're doing." Weldon sat back, raising his voice from a whisper. "Have you been over to Glos? You seen how close the swallow hole is to where I live? The thing is huge. I've had nightmares. It's seriously freaked me out. I'm not kidding."

Naylor glanced at Chase, saw his shoulders tense. "No, we've not been out that way. Wella wouldn't have been there." He caught Tinashe's eye.

Tinashe grasped the look. "I agree. She'd have no reason to. Try not to think about that, Chase. There's got to be another explanation." She shrugged and raised her eyebrows. "Maybe this Ursel is right?"

Weldon looked up in alarm, Naylor with a glare of caution. It was only Chase whose eyes revealed the spark of interest.

"I'm not saying that's a positive thing," she added. "Messing with music is dangerous, we all know that. And I'm not just talking about the risk of a beating at the hands of the Deaf Squad. If Wella is involved, then she's in serious shit. But at least we'd know that and we could help her." She looked to Chase. "If Ursel finds her, she can bring her back and we can help her get clean."

"Ursel said she might not be able to persuade her to return," said Chase. He turned to Naylor. "But if I go, I believe I could."

CHAPTER SEVEN

Dent Lore knelt at the base of a towering whisper dish, eyes level with an adjusted Allear. Rigid, breath held, they delved deep into buried frequencies.

Dent sighed. "False alarm," he said, and stood up, leaving the trooper on all fours, blind to the frightened stares of passers-by.

Shielding his eyes from the sun, Dent looked across the Pentagon to a clocktower in its centre. Midday. Twenty more dish sites to inspect before dusk, when the rumoured event could start. He shook his head, cursing the size of the city.

He was about to walk back to his Ops truck when he saw the Chief of Command approach, his black leather trench coat swaying at his heels. Dent stood to attention and awaited the inevitable.

"Update me," demanded Wulfwin as he halted in front of Dent.

"Unit inspection underway. All dish sites are operational, with a three-man detail. Shift change scheduled for sixteen-hundred hours, giving us fresh ears for the evening."

"And the mobile units?"

"Twenty-six dispersed across the city. Density presence in Spire Wells, Creaser and Coxen Lyme."

"Men per unit?"

"Three."

"For fuck's sake, Lore, you can't respond to intel on a piss-all crew. We haven't had as good a lead as this in years. You were under orders to recruit. What happened?"

Dent stared at Wulfwin, shoulders back. "We have a strong class of new entrants in the final stages of training. Once graduated, they will provide a valuable boost to numbers."

Wulfwin sneered and stepped forward, bearing down on Dent. "That ain't gonna help us tonight," he hissed. "Get them in the field, now. Call it work experience."

"But they're—"

"Already I don't care. I want them out."

"Yes, sir."

"Let's get this straight, Lore. We're gonna catch the Music Makers. I don't give a shit what it takes. We will catch them and we will make them suffer." He walked slowly around Dent, interrogating him with his eyes. He stopped, inches before his face. "Tell me, Lore. What are your feelings about the Music Makers?"

Dent stood tall, unwavering. "They are a threat to the city. It is the Authority's priority to capture them. My job is to play an integral role in achieving that mission."

"What? You sound like a fucking textbook." He jabbed his right fist into Dent's stomach.

Dent bent forward, but did not buckle.

"Talk from the gut," Wulfwin growled. "I asked you what your feelings are."

Dent looked squarely at Wulfwin, his jaw clenched. "The Music Makers are dangerous. Therefore, they must be captured, through whatever means necessary."

"This is what I don't get about you, Lore. No fucking feelings. Where's your anger?" he shouted, punching him in the abdomen. "Where's your rage?" He stood back, waiting for Dent to right himself and recover. "That would stop you from pissing about with recruitment. You're too fucking soft. That's why you don't recruit enough. That's why we're short on the ground when we're dealing with a high-stakes exchange." He grabbed Dent by the collar and hissed in his face, "If you balls this up… If we lose them because you're too gutless to get enough bodies to do your fucking job…" He let go and spat in the dirt beside them.

Dent straightened his collar and looked into Wulfwin's eyes. "The objective of the Allears and the will of the Authority is all that matters. I shall succeed."

Wulfwin hesitated for a moment, staring into unreadable eyes. "I'm on your case, Lore. Now, get the newbies out and on the ground. Then I want you breathing down the neck of every one of your blind little sound hounds. The Deaf Squad are ready and up to the job. Unfortunately, they rely on you to do yours." He snorted, then turned on his heels, marching back the way he had come.

Dent was left standing in the centre of the Pentagon, watching the receding trench coat, breathing evenly. He thought about the young men and women, barely adult, up at the Adjustment and Training Centre in the Authority Complex.

He had been forced to increase recruitment three years ago following a failed raid and another of Wulfwin's outbursts. They had been taken from their homes, from their Education Centres, from a climbing frame in Glade Park. Children. Young lives, denied of their freedom because they passed the Test.

The Test was another initiative devised by the vengeful Governor Wallace. It was undertaken annually by every fourteen-year-old in Wydeye, along with retakes from the previous year. Education Centres across the city interrupted their curriculum on the same day, on a given date, while their students sat the Test. No one knew what it was for – not the young students who had to endure five hours of rigorous, relentless tasks; not their Centre instructors, who were required to invigilate without knowing what they were observing; not the parents, who trusted the state education system and who knew better than to question the Authority.

The Test appeared to assess everything, from general knowledge to applied mathematics, from physical fitness to spatial awareness, from lung capacity to aural sensitivity. Everything was marked. Only the results of the listening test were recorded.

The listening assessment was designed to detect a heightened capacity for hearing, including the ability to hear sound at frequencies above and below the normal human range. Although such cases were rare, in a growing population with a high birth rate, the frequency of hits slowly increased.

Then, as the procedures for adjustment were introduced, the pass mark became more accommodating. Surgically induced blindness and anosmia meant that those who marginally missed the grade could, through a programme of retraining, find their hearing intensified. This, coupled with the systematic doping of recruits with a psychoactive depressant called Chromatofen, which modified behaviour to ensure conformity within their new world order, resulted in a healthy boost in numbers.

From the results of the annual test, the Authority compiled a list. The top-ranked candidates were the rare few who had proved themselves naturally gifted with acute auditory sensitivity, as in the case of Dent Lore. The second-tier candidates were those who demonstrated capability for acute sensitivity with the aid of sensory adjustment. Students ranked third were required to retake the Test the following year, to pick up cases of natural improvement.

The final list of names, on average between five and ten each year, became the Authority's targets for recruitment.

As Dent strode towards his Ops truck, he considered Wulfwin's words. He had been right: Dent had made a token gesture in response to his last orders to increase recruitment. He recalled the terror on the faces of the children presented to him – had seen their pictures posted on the Wall of the Missing outside the Exchange.

He cursed under his breath, knowing he would not be able to swerve the order again.

–

Meanwhile, across the city, his qualified Allears listened. They crouched beside whisper dishes, or held their heads to walls, splayed fingers feeling for vibrations. They were trained to control their heart rate, slowing it down to an idle tick-over so their rhythm-section pulse did not interfere with detection. Blank faces froze in concentration. The sockets beneath their sealed eyes were miniature swallow holes, draped in shadow.

Dent knelt beside the outer wall of a blast furnace in Coxen Lyme, struggling to quell his racing heart. Fresh intel had provided a solid lead. Now, the enormity of the situation had escalated beyond compare.

Wulfwin had just radioed him. The initial rumour had been substantiated.

A sleeper in the field had made contact. Details correlated. Date and time. The only missing piece of intelligence was where.

Dent could not recall an opportunity so vital, so pivotal to achieving the ambition of Governor Blix. He bowed his head, closed his eyes and listened.

—

On the Pentagon, Wulfwin marched between files of men, dour-faced and glaring. "Where the fuck have you been?" he boomed at a trooper who came running towards him.

"The Complex, sir. Technical problem with the transmitters. Had to speak to Telecoms Division to alter the frequency."

"You're fucking joking, right?"

"No, sir. But it's sorted now."

"The first corroborated lead in decades and Telecoms cock up the radios. How are we supposed to know if the Allears hear anything?"

The man cowed. "As I said, sir. All sorted now."

"It'd better be." He grabbed hold of the man's collar, all but lifting him off his feet. "I'm holding you responsible for this. If something goes wrong with the radios, it's your fucking fault." He let go and pointed ahead. "Now, get in line. We're supposed to be ready to move the moment we get the signal. And put your ear defenders in position, unless you want to lose your mind to the sodding freak show."

The trooper took a pair of modified military-grade ear defenders from around his neck and clamped them onto his helmet, directly above his ears. The ear defenders were the single most crucial piece of their armour. The Rideout Rebellion had demonstrated that no amount of loyalty or training could protect the military and police from the influence of the music. Hence their name. The Deaf Squad were the only unit in Special Forces sufficiently protected to storm an event and emerge unscathed.

The men, around two hundred in total, stood to attention, defenders clamped just above their ears. Their bodies were rigid, their grim expressions motionless. Only their eyes moved, watching the brooding figure of their leader march back and forth.

Finally, Wulfwin came to a halt and faced his men. All eyes shot forward, staring at nothing.

"Soldiers of the Deaf Squad," he roared, "tonight is your time to shine. All your years of training have been for this moment. If we succeed in our mission, this may well be your swansong. Be hungry for the glory and turn that hunger into rage. The Music Makers have mocked the rule of the Authority for too long. They have flouted the laws set down to safeguard the vulnerable citizens of Wydeye. Our duty is to protect. To protect is to destroy that which threatens harm. We will capture the Music Makers and eradicate the Scene. There are no limits to the efforts to which we will go to achieve this end. No boundaries are deemed too sacred to cross. Reasonable force means the necessary force to succeed. Therefore, relish your rage. Let it rumble in your chest – a pressurised fury fit to explode. Then unleash it upon those bastards who challenge our rule and threaten our peace. Be ready, my men. Our time is nigh."

CHAPTER EIGHT

Klaxons blared like air-raid sirens. Dust-covered and lead-limbed, Chase joined the file of weary drillers and blast hands as they shuffled to the convoy of trucks that would ship them from the quarry, back to Coxen Lyme and the tramway stop at Ulden Cross. Dirt clung to their sweat-drenched bodies. Lungs, desperate for clean air, ached under the weight of humidity. No one said a word.

Chase had worked twelve hours with a half-hour break. His body felt bruised and broken, yet his mind raced. In a few hours' time, he would be meeting Ursel and they'd be making their way to the event to find Wella.

He was glad the window was closing. All day his mind had bounced back and forth, torn between the advice of his closest friend, concern for his sister and the gauntlet laid down by a stranger. Soon the time for doubt would run out and the opportunities to flick the points and switch tracks would be over.

He rode the railmotor through the city, up to his quarters in Creaser. A cold shower and a change of clothes helped to revive him. Then he caught his reflection in a cracked mirror hanging from a door. He ran a hand through his hair, tangled and wet from the shower, and pulled at his black strap shirt and trousers. Having never been to an event before, he regretted not asking Ursel about the dress code. Shrugging his shoulders, he laced up his boots, filled up his canteen with water and headed back out into the heat.

He was early. To kill time, he walked the short distance to Naylor's place in the Wallace Estates.

Looking down from the seventy-eighth floor of tower block twenty-one, the city appeared compressed, partial. Ground level had disappeared entirely. No sign of the underpass, or the limestone buildings, shacks and stalls that hugged its kerb. No trace of the carters cursing the slow plod of their goats, of citizens sheltering in pockets of shade, of Wethers begging for alms. All you could see were the rails and rolling stock of the tramway – a network of tributaries looping through the city, weaving between solid blocks of concrete. Irregular tombstones in uniform grey.

"Quite a view, eh?" said Naylor, joining Chase at the window. "I still can't work out if it's beautiful or thoroughly depressing."

"Depends if you think about above or below, I guess."

Naylor nodded, then moved away to sit in an armchair. The room was small, functioning as living room, dining room and study. Books lined the walls on makeshift shelves. Off the main room was a closet kitchen and bathroom and two cramped bedrooms – his and Clo's, his sixteen-year-old daughter.

Naylor poured lime leaf tea from a steel pot. He held up a glass to Chase. "Here you go. Sorry I can't offer you anything stronger."

Chase accepted the glass and sat at a small table beside Naylor. "I won't lie, I could use a stiff drink."

"It's not too late, you know." When Chase didn't respond, Naylor cleared his throat and added, "It feels like Ursel's persuaded you to go, even if she didn't mean to."

"Why do you say that?"

"I don't know. Just surprised you'd do it, I guess."

"It's nothing to do with Ursel. I've spent three days looking for Wella. I don't know where else to try. And, if Ursel is right and she's there, I want to see her for myself. Even if I can't persuade her to come back, I want to hear it from her – that she's okay and she's chosen to stay." He looked up at Naylor, deep lines across his face. "I know we're not close, but I'll be able to tell if she's on something, or if she's being coerced. Because it doesn't stack up. She knows first-hand how dangerous the Scene is. Ursel makes out she's safe there. That's bullshit."

A silence fell between them. A murky gloom began to fill the room as the sun sank low in the sky.

"Promise you'll send word," said Naylor. "Tonight. Doesn't matter how late. A message to let me know you're safe. And Wella. Promise me."

—

Back outside, Chase climbed the Elevated and caught a railmotor destined for Old Wydeye Town. He got off at the penultimate stop on Standings Cross and looked over at the big top, its orange and green stripes an effective lure amid its drab surroundings. As he approached the gates, a steady stream of citizens filed out past him. Their faces were placid, their movements fluid. Around them hung a murmur of voices, hushed chatter as they discussed the show. Chase caught himself envying their air of temporary relief. He had never once attended a performance. It occurred to him he had no idea why and, for the first time, he felt a flush of curiosity.

Security nodded him through without question. He walked around the big top, resisting the urge to part the canvas and peer through. When he reached Ursel's yurt he hesitated, thrown by the lack of means to knock. He cleared his throat with awkward exaggeration. "Hello? Ursel. It's me. Chase."

A muffled voice from within called out, "Just a moment…"

Chase glanced around. Performers milled between the caravans and tents, still in bright costume and heavily made up. Beneath the warm glow of festoon lamps, the colourful enclave appeared incongruous with the palette of life beyond the boundary fence.

Ursel stuck her head through the flap that constituted her front door. "Okay, you can come in." She held back the canvas and gestured with her head for Chase to enter.

"Good show?" he asked.

"I guess." Ursel wore a short black tunic, around which she was buckling a belt with her one hand. Her movements were swift and effortless.

"I don't know how you manage."

Ursel glanced up, confusion in her frown.

"One arm…" he added, flushing.

"I manage the same as you do." She knelt down and fastened the buckles on her boots. "Take a seat. I'm almost ready."

Chase knelt on a cushion and tried to think of something to say. He hadn't expected to feel this way: awkward and out of place. Taking a deep breath, he looked around him. The space was cluttered with piles of books; charcoal sketches were nailed to the yurt's wooden framework; brightly coloured fabrics were draped from the walls. There was a single bunk, a small table with two chairs and a bookshelf. "Where do you cook?" he asked, forgetting his embarrassment.

"We all eat together. There's a catering tent on the other side of the top." She sat down beside the table in front of a small mirror. Chase watched her as she put an earring into her left ear. It was a silver loop, from which hung delicate silver threads like a miniature dream catcher. She turned and studied Chase for a moment, then cocked her head slightly. "Why are you coming?"

Thrown by the question, Chase rubbed the back of his neck. "Well, you said yourself you doubted you could persuade Wella to come home."

"But you don't even know she's there."

"True."

"You could let me go on my own. Find her. Then you could come next time if you still want to try and convince her to come back."

"That's also true."

"So, why come? Why risk it?"

Chase thought for a moment, juggling conflicting motives. "If she's chosen to stay there, I need to see it for myself. You were right, I don't understand. I have to go there to stand a chance of changing that."

Ursel nodded. "Let's go then."

"Hold on. What about you? Why are you helping me?"

Her eyes flashed and she smiled. "You'll know the answer to that once we're there."

—

Their route was circuitous, taking the tramway south through Crow, then west, to Darlem Fields, via a loop around Spire Wells. They changed lines three times.

"Is this necessary?" asked Chase.

"The onus is on everyone who attends to ensure we don't lead the Deaf Squad straight to its prize. The risks don't diminish just because we choose to attend. Secrecy is our collective responsibility."

"And yet you're showing me the way?"

"I trust you." Ursel looked out of the trailer at the concrete cityscape as she said this.

Chase, bemused, fell silent.

They travelled the rest of the way without talking, until they reached the final stop before Wakenfold. "It's too risky taking the tramway any further," said Ursel. She pulled out a compass from a pocket in her tunic. "We head west, out of the city, then north into the Nanso Heights. I reckon we've an hour or so hike ahead of us."

Sundown had been followed by a warm, still dusk. Crickets chirped at their heels, while small red and green birds flitted overhead, preparing to roost. The air was close; oxygen, low. The long climb was gruelling. Chase bent forward, his hands on his knees. "Can't we stop for a bit?" he said, breathless.

"We haven't time. They'll be on soon."

The coordinates encrypted in the cut-and-paste pages of *Bluemantle* finally led them through the Heights and up to a vertiginous wall of rock. Ursel checked their surroundings, then held her hand against the stone. "This is it."

"What?" Chase looked around him. "But there's nothing here…"

Ursel stepped back and appraised the edifice before them, studying the surface from right to left. "Over there." She walked up to what appeared to be a line of shadow, cast at an angle. She held out her arm; half of it vanished. Turning to Chase, she smiled, then the rest of her disappeared.

"Ursel?" Chase ran over to where she had stood, discovering that the shadow was, in fact, a narrow crevice roughly five feet high. "Ursel, wait!" he called, squeezing his body into the gap and forcing himself through.

On the other side was a narrow passageway, cool and dark – a disorientating contrast from the warm gloaming outside. His eyes struggling to adjust, Chase edged forwards, arms outstretched, blindly feeling his way. All around, infinite echoes of trickling water. The sound reverberated, growing louder as he descended deeper.

As his eyes adjusted, he could see by a pale, washed-out light. Black faded to grey beneath a ghost of illumination. It revealed a path before him, snaking past stalagmites and beneath weeping soda straws. The air smelt damp, yet it held a freshness, pure and stone-still.

Following the path, Chase turned a corner. The light changed in a seamless spectrum-shift from grey to faint orange. The colour danced, rippling across rock. As he moved forward, the orange intensified, no longer a suggestion. The sound changed too: dripping taps drowned out by a pulsing beat. Sensing the vibrations beneath his feet, Chase imagined the beating heart of the mountain. Colour and sound conspired, conjuring an illusion that transformed his surroundings. The mountain became alive, its inner flesh pulsating. Warm blood pumping through moist tissue. Chase, a parasite coursing through the arteries of his host. "Ursel?" he called, his own heartbeat racing.

The narrow passage ended, spilling into a cave around four metres in diameter. Gas lamps were attached to the walls, trailing rubber tubes that led off through a further passageway. In the centre of the opening stood Ursel, circled by the intensified sound. It poured in from behind her: fervent chanting, over and over. "Chief! Chief! Chief! Chief!"

Ursel looked radiant, her eyes alight. "Welcome to the Underground Scene," she said. "Forget your fears. Abandon your assumptions. Embrace the moment with a mind free of preoccupation."

"But Wella—"

"I will find her." She held out her hand. "You must watch Chief."

CHAPTER NINE

"Chief! Chief! Chief!" The chant was both a demand and a conjuring of promise. As Ursel led Chase by the hand towards the sound, the air grew dense, pregnant with noise and heat and the weight of anticipation. They stepped through the passageway into a vast, illuminated cave. Before them, a large crowd of men and women, old and young, calling in unison, "Chief! Chief! Chief!"

The crowd were impassioned, expectant, hot. Black strap shirts were wet with sweat. Exposed flesh and ornate tattoos glistened. A faint haze hovered above heads as steam rose to replace the cooler air above. The ceiling of the cave oozed condensation. Every face was turned to a platform at one end, on which stood a drum kit, microphone stands, amps, monitors and other gear. The skin of the bass drum was emblazoned with a thick band running horizontally across the top.

Kohl-lined eyes stared ahead, searching. Waiting. Faces were frozen, their expressions a universal language: joy, excitement, ardour, need. Chase looked at Ursel and found the same. She knew what was coming, what to expect. Chase himself had no idea, yet he could feel the anticipation electrifying the air. His chest tightened. A raw, adrenalin-fuelled excitement rose from his stomach and flushed his cheeks.

"Stay here and watch," shouted Ursel. "I'm going to look for Wella." She let go of his hand and slipped through the crowd.

At that same moment, the gas lamps dimmed. Arms were raised into the air and the chant became a roar as four figures emerged from nowhere. Chief and her players took to the stage and surveyed the crowd, not saying a word.

The amps crackled to life. The event began.

Chase could not take his eyes off the stage. The centre was filled with a tall, slim woman dressed in patches of grey. Silver dreadlocks flowed over her shoulders. Her piercing blue eyes were locked on to the crowd. Around her were three other people, also dressed in grey – possibly men, but their androgynous appearance raised the question.

Then there was the music. A powerful blend of avant-garde and alternative rock, mesmerising with its minor keys and compelling rhythm. The singer's voice was deep and powerful: the sound of an earthquake heard from the ocean floor.

Feeling a strange lure and dizzy from the effect, Chase tore his eyes away from the stage and let them dwell on the crowd around him. Despite the dim light, he could see their faces. Everywhere, the same expression of ecstasy, of unbridled joy. Some danced to the music, others jumped or swayed. Some stood motionless, transfixed. All were moved. Moved in a way that Chase could not fathom yet could feel the first trace of within himself. A spark had ignited inside him. He could sense its warmth as it coursed through his veins and embraced his heart. Looking back to the stage, he surrendered to the music.

–

"Damn it, get those kids away from here. I can't hear a thing." Dent Lore had raced across the city in his Ops truck, having received word from one of his units in Cinder Hill.

Allears ushered a group of daring children away, clearing an area around the whisper dish. Dent knelt down beside it, ears straining, eyes closed.

Faint. Barely a sound at all. But there, in the distance, was the trace of a note. A filigree murmur from the depths of a bottomless well. His sense locked on to the prize. Shutting everything else out, Dent honed in on the sound, amplifying it by micro degrees through the sheer force of his will. He imagined the wave form, felt the frequency.

He opened his eyes and nodded. "Detection confirmed."

—

Resurfacing from the depths of enchantment, Chase came to and found Ursel standing beside him. "Wella...?"

"She's okay. I'll explain after." She smiled, then turned to look at the stage.

Watching her profile, Chase saw in her eyes the same joy that radiated from all the faces around them. Her expression was one of release, of a reprieve from all the strain and hardship that was the corroding rust on life. Beads of perspiration clung to her temples. Her cropped black hair was damp around the edges. A smile played on her lips.

The music demanded Chase's attention, drawing it back to the stage. Its influence was undeniable now. The initial spark within him had caught, growing into a consuming fire in his chest. He found himself grinning at the players, swept up by the infectious euphoria around him.

In that moment, he felt Chief's cobalt eyes upon him. He looked at her, could feel her electric gaze as a connection was made. The contact was mesmerising, intoxicating. Their eyes locked in a unifying exchange. He felt her touch penetrating his core, pulling at his chest. Yet the moment was all too brief. As he revelled in the instant, she blinked and looked away. Chase felt himself released.

Ursel touched his arm. "Have you seen enough to understand?"

"I don't know that I understand…" He smiled and raised his shoulders. "You say Wella's alright?" Ursel nodded. "Then let's stay a while longer."

—

Within a matter of minutes, Wulfwin and his men were on Cinder Hill. He marched up to Dent Lore. "Where's it coming from?" he hissed.

"The Nanso Heights."

"You're kidding me, right?"

"That's the direction."

"But there's nothing up there. Where would they rig up a stage? If it was outside, even I would be able to hear it from here."

"There's something about the timbre of the sound…" said Dent, scratching his beard, frowning.

"What? Come on, man. What is it?"

"I don't know. I can't work it out."

"Not good enough, Allear."

"It's definitely north from here. Beyond the Nanso Trail. My men will stop and listen along the way. We will find the source."

"Yes, you will." He glared at Dent, then turned to bark into his radio, alerting Comms Control and Operations HQ of their imminent mobilisation. Within seconds, a dozen WatcherCams appeared, hovering high above them – surveillance drones controlled from Operations HQ.

Wulfwin turned to his men. "Okay, listen up. We're heading into the Heights. Pair with an Allear. Stay close. Ear defenders on. Watch for my signal and keep your in-ear radios on open frequency." He turned back to Dent. "You and your blind gimps had better hurry. Don't fuck this up, Lore."

Dent called his Allears to attention. He had assembled ten units; the remainder he had ordered to remain in position across the city. "The source is in the Heights," he said to them. "Spread out; we've a large area to cover. Those of you who are adjusted, you'll have a Deaf Squad trooper to be your eyes. They'll be wearing defenders; sign to them if you need to communicate. Responsibility rests with us. We will not let the Authority down."

The troopers dispersed, the deaf leading the blind towards the looming silhouettes of the Nanso Heights.

—

Blix paced the Comms Control Centre, her hands wringing. The room was a vast, windowless concrete box. Operators sat in rows of desks, headphones on, torsos stooped over transistor radios. They scribbled frantically on notepads, occasionally tearing off a page and waving it in the air as if in surrender, calling out, "Incoming." Runners patrolled the aisles, collecting the paper flags and delivering them to a bank of raised desks at one end, staffed by Comms officers. Lining the walls were humming machines, lights blinking, reels of magnetic tape whirring. Among the machines was a huge switchboard, its wires looping in a tangled web of chatter.

Blix marched back and forth before the raised desks, freezing each time a message was delivered. It had been ten minutes since the last communication. As the interval yawned, Blix flipped between interpreting it as a positive sign, that the raid could be in progress, then rereading it as disaster. The Comms officers kept their eyes low, intent on avoiding her stormy glare. "Come on," she hissed under her breath, scratching her neck. "What's taking so long?"

"Incoming." A hand shot up. A runner collected the piece of paper and trotted over to his superiors at the raised desks. He handed it to a woman in wire-rimmed spectacles, who scanned the note.

"Tell me what it says," demanded Blix, immediately at the woman's side.

"Communication from Chief of Command, Governor. He says, '*Close to source. Preparing to move in.*'"

Blix gripped the table. Her heart raced. "Right. Good," she said, her voice trembling. She turned slowly and closed her eyes, picturing the scene. Wulfwin and his men running in formation, storming into a building, shouting orders at the startled crowd. The violence. The terror. She tried to imagine the victory, but the scene kept dissolving before the moment of capture.

—

Deep in the bowels of the mountain, Chief played on. She surveyed the crowd before her, drinking in their euphoria, feeding off their joy. It had been so long, so very long. She had almost forgotten how good it tasted.

In a brief pause between songs, she stepped up to the microphone, arms outstretched, and said, "Tonight, we remember Saltire. Tonight, we mark their passing. So great is the loss that all words have decayed to empty husks. They fail to convey our sorrow, the hollow in our hearts. Instead, let music speak for our souls; let melody cry grief and love. We sing in remembrance and salute the departed. Saltire; in your honour, we play."

The crowd, silent while she spoke, now roared. Chase turned to Ursel, shoulders raised, shaking his head slightly. Before Ursel had chance to explain, there was a drumstick cue and the amps erupted. De-tuned guitar and a low, urgent bassline pulled their attention back to the stage.

Chief dominated the space. Where she had felt herself fading, her body weak, she now possessed the strength of an army. Her long, slender limbs were invigorated – muscle, tissue and bone super-charged with an electrifying energy. Her spirit was satiated on the feast of her followers. Wonderfully replete, she knew she should bring the show to an end. Yet the taste was so sweet; it had been so long in coming. She recalled Bend Sinister's words of caution but felt unable to resist. As the song drew to an end and the guitar's sustain faded, the calls for "More! More! More!" engulfed her, spellbinding. The demand became her justification, the scapegoat for her greed. *One more*, she told herself, then gave the signal to her players.

Cole caught the signal and hollered, arms in the air. It had been a difficult parting with Evan. Not that Evan ever put pressure on him not to attend. But that just made it harder, Cole felt. The two most important things in his life pulled in a tug of war that could tear him apart. In the end, Evan had encouraged him to go, unable to bear the torment in his partner's eyes.

Gently placing Evan at the back of his mind, Cole had watched the entire performance from the foot of the stage, revelling in the music. His allegiance would always be to Bend Sinister, but he still loved a Chief show. The atmosphere was infectious. A timely antidote to the stress of producing and distributing a thousand copies of *Bluemantle* in under forty-eight hours. He beamed at Chief, all conflict forgotten.

Someone pulling on his arm broke the hex. He turned to find a young man breathing hard, his eyes bulging, mouth agape. Cole let himself be dragged away from the stage, to one side of the cave. The young man cupped his hands around his mouth and shouted into Cole's ear. "Deaf Squad. Up top. Loads of 'em. They're closing in."

A commotion began to stir around Chase as word spread. Oblivious of the cause, he tried to block it out, staring at the stage, not wanting to miss a note.

Beside him, Ursel spotted Cole and read his expression. She grabbed Chase's arm. "We've got to get out of here."

He looked at her, bewildered.

"We have to go," she cried. "Now!"

—

"I'm telling you, it's here," snapped Dent Lore, squaring up to Wulfwin.

"We're on the side of a fucking mountain," roared Wulfwin. "I see no sodding show."

Deaf Squad troopers and Allears surrounded them, wary of the tension between their leaders. The WatcherCams hovered in loose formation. Wulfwin had removed his ear defenders, ordering his men to keep theirs on. They couldn't hear what Wulfwin was shouting, but they had become deft at lip-reading.

"The terrain is messing with the frequency," said Dent. "The mountain's affecting the acoustics. There's something strange about the sound. I can't work it out."

"Don't invent excuses, Lore. You said it was up here. Where the fuck is it?"

Dent stood his ground, breathing even. "We're still hearing it. The source is nearby, I'm absolutely certain. But we're getting too close for my team. I'm pulling them back. It's over to you guys."

Wulfwin glared at Dent. This was protocol; he knew Dent was right. The Allears' job was to find the source, but they were highly vulnerable to the influence of the music. Once they made a positive detection and located the source, they were to fall back and let the Deaf Squad, fully protected, step in.

Wulfwin squirmed, fury and frustration contorting his face. He turned to his men and signalled for them to stand to attention. The men gathered in formation before him, leaving their Allear wards stranded without their sighted guides. Wulfwin spoke into his helmet's mic. "It's down to us to finish the job and bring this home," he said. "The sound is coming from somewhere around here. The area's huge. Spread out. Let's find those fuckers."

They saluted and shouted, "Yes, sir," in unison.

Wulfwin turned back to Dent. "You'd better hope to crow it's out there, Lore. If you've called this wrong, you're going to suffer. I'll personally see to it. And I don't care what Blix says. You won't get away with this." He snapped on his ear defenders before Dent had the chance to reply.

Wulfwin led his men forward. Dusk had long since surrendered to darkness. A full moon graced the ground with silver, illuminating the way by welcome chance, more effectively than the troopers' headlamps and hand torches. Yet the shadows caused by jutting rock and leaning boulder played games with their straining eyes. The Deaf Squad scoured the moonscape, climbing and sliding over rock, up, over and around walls of impenetrable obstruction, hunting ever closer.

Meanwhile, trapped beneath their feet, their prey cowered.

—

The enchantment in the cave had collapsed.

Players and followers alike froze in terrified silence, dreading the rumble of combat boots.

Chief cut the power to the stage and addressed the crowd, at pains to speak softly yet still be heard. "You must flee. But take heed, remain calm. Make no sound. Escape is possible, but through cunning." She gestured to Cole, who made his way through the anxious crowd to her side. She spoke quietly in his ear. He nodded, bowed discretely, then retreated to the far side of the cave. "Follow that man," continued Chief, pointing towards Cole. "He knows of a different route out. He will lead you. But it is dangerous. There are many caves – echo chambers that could betray your escape. Move with caution and have consideration for each other. Under this threat, you are as one. Any sound will alert them to you all."

"What about you?" someone said from the front.

"We will withdraw, but we cannot go with you. I…" She hesitated for a moment, then said, "Hurry. And be safe." She turned and walked to the back of the raised platform, her players following in her wake. They slipped between two gas lamps, disappearing behind the lights' bright glare.

Ursel kept her eyes trained on Cole, while Chase glanced around in a state of panic. "We've got to get out," he hissed, eyes wide.

"Try to stay calm."

"Calm? Are you serious? The Deaf Squad are about to raid us."

The crowd had begun to push towards Cole, who stood poised at a narrow crevice in the cave's wall. Their faces were tense, eyes alert; sweat gleamed on their pale skin. No one spoke, yet there was a growing sound filling the chamber like a slowly rising tide. The deep hum of a distant, whipping gale. The heavy breathing of fear.

Bodies crushed together as the bottleneck backed up. Chase and Ursel stumbled forward, holding hands to avoid separation. Chase tried to pull himself closer and whispered, "Wella!"

Ursel shook her head.

"We can't leave her here," he said.

"I don't know where she is."

"You said you saw her."

"I didn't. I said she's okay."

"What? If you didn't see her, we still don't know that. I've not risked everything by coming here, only to run away without knowing." Chase let go of her hand and turned, attempting to move against the flow.

Ursel managed to catch hold of him, grabbing him by the shoulder. "You're risking your life if you stay, Chase." She glared at him, eyes pleading. "We have to get out. There's no time to look for her. You'll get caught. They're already close." She read his expression: the torment of an impossible decision. The crowd pushed past them, almost knocking her off balance. She held on to his arm and said, "The Troubadours know these caves. This is their home. Their world. They know where to hide to be safe. Wella's with them. She'll be safe too. But we can't hide with them, so we have to leave. It's the way it works here."

A rumble echoed through the cave. The crowd froze, simultaneously catching their breath. They held it, straining to hear. Another rumble: distant, yet louder than the first. They stood motionless, waiting for the sound they feared the most. The echo died around them, leaving silence and a terrifying anticipation. The heavy breathing resumed, the push forward now propelled by a growing panic. Followers filed through the passageway, disappearing into the depths of the mountain.

Chase dropped his head and ceased his resistance. Ursel led him away, joining the crowd and the desperate bid for escape.

—

Static crackled in Wulfwin's earpiece.

"*Delta-Charlie-One, this is Oscar-Charlie-One. Do you read? Over.*"

"Oscar-Charlie-One, copy that. What have you got for me? Over."

"*We've picked up something from a WatcherCam. Position approximately one point six miles due south of your current position. The image shows movement, sir. People. Over.*"

"The event? I don't understand… I would've heard it." Wulfwin stared into the half-light. "More specific. What do you see? Over."

"*Poor resolution, sir. Hard to make out. But it looks like a crowd of people, running. Heading south south-east. Towards the city. Over.*"

"Give me the exact coordinates. And get all eyes on their descent. Update Comms Control. We're going after them. Over."

—

Wulfwin cursed and kicked. His men kept a wary distance.

They had reached the coordinates and found tracks but no sign of life. Stomping down the stone pass, he squinted into the distance, straining to make out movement in the darkness. His eyes fell to the floor and were drawn to a glinting object to his side. He bent down and picked it up. A silver earring: tassels dangling from a hoop. He threw his head back and roared.

Regaining a trace of control, he barked into his radio, "Oscar-Charlie-One, this is Delta-Charlie-One. Read? Over."

"Delta-Charlie-One, this is Oscar-Charlie-One. Copy that. Over."

"Have you still got eyes on the prize? Over."

"They've dispersed. We've got visual on some. Others have taken cover in the woods west of Glos. Over."

"The ones you've got. Where are they now? Over."

"Approximately three miles due west of Westgate Arch, heading south. My guess is they'll re-enter the city via Westedge. Over."

"Copy that. Over and out."

Wulfwin fumed, fighting the urge to hit out at anyone or anything in his path. He saw the expectant faces of his Deaf Squad troopers, their breathing heavy following the treacherous pursuit. Fury raged in his chest as he processed the situation. One chase was over; another was about to begin. "Charlie-Charlie-Zero," he said into his radio. "This is Delta-Charlie-One. Get me Golf Sierra. Urgent. Copy? Over."

"Delta-Charlie-One, this is Charlie-Charlie-Zero. Copy that. Standby. Over."

The radio fell silent. Then came, *"Commander, this is Governor Blix,"* her fraught tone disguised by distortion. *"Tell me what's happening."*

Wulfwin dispensed with radio protocol, knowing that Blix refused to observe it anyway. "We've lost the trail."

Static.

"Request permission to revise objectives."

"You've lost the trail—"

"Governor, there isn't time. The Music Makers have escaped. Permission to continue the raid, but in the city. If we move fast, the scum who attended will still be making their way back. Ops HQ have got eyes on some. Soon they'll be moving through Darlem Fields during curfew. We see anyone, we arrest them. Then we'll target Spire Wells. Raid tea bars and taverns. Take anyone we suspect may have attended. Full-scale sweep of the city."

"*The objective, Commander. The Music Makers are still at large.*"

"And the Users are our ticket to finding them. We haul them in. Make examples of them. Send a message about consequences. Then we get to work on the captured. Encourage answers. Make them talk."

Another moment of static, then, "*Do it. I confirm your orders have changed. Raid the city. Use the necessary force. Bring in as many of the rats as you can. Meanwhile, you'd better come up with a damn good explanation as to why you've failed.*"

CHAPTER TEN

The descent was rapid; the raids that followed, brutal.

Wulfwin and his Deaf Squad tore through the sleeping city, striking it awake with blows of havoc. Citizens were plucked from curfewed streets and hurled into the backs of waiting trucks. Where lamps were spotted in dim backrooms, quarters were raided and startled tenants taken by force. Women wept as men were shackled and dragged, their faces bloodied from a taste of physical coercion. Children cried in terror as they witnessed their parents' violent removal, cloth sacks tied over their heads. The night's peace was destroyed by a choir of sirens and screams.

In Spire Wells, where no curfew was in place, the arrests were more erratic. Riat's, the noodle bar, was stormed by a unit of snarling troopers. They smashed the glass serving counter and hurled ceramic bowls against the walls, shards of china puncturing the arms of cowering customers as they tried to shield their faces. Troopers kicked over tables and raised stools over their heads, threatening to 'crush the skulls of User scum'. They grabbed people at random, strapped their hands behind their backs and frog-marched them out onto the street and to the Pentagon: the holding ground for the Authority's examples and a blatant display of consequence. Beaten and terrified, citizens were made to stand in silent lines until trucks came to transport them up to the notorious detention centres in the Authority Complex.

Drayloc Market was partially demolished, the ramshackle stalls presenting light work for point-proving troopers. The Raven was another prime target, its floor promptly covered with smashed glass, pooling Pyncher and blood. The Authority had long since suspected the tavern to be a popular haunt of radicals and subversives. Near enough everyone who was inside when the Squad kicked open the doors was arrested and dragged to the Pentagon.

Citizens didn't need to spread the word. There was no call for messages to be sent warning loved ones of the dangers to come. Within an hour of the revised objective, the police and Special Forces had hit the principal targets across the city. Sirens wailed in all directions as Authority vehicles raced beneath the Elevated, commandeering the underpass. Fires burnt in Drayloc Market and along the arms of Five Wents.

Over a hundred and fifty men and women, young and old, were beaten, shackled and gagged.

Accounts of the Deaf Squad's brutality spread. The police were harsh, but they had rules, restrictions that observed fundamental human rights. The Deaf Squad, however, had a free pass. Reasonable force was a subjective judgement. It had been a long night already. Anger and frustration at the failed raid had stoked tempers. Wulfwin's unbridled fury had influenced impressionable minds. Excessive, barbarous force was deemed justified by those who wielded it.

Questioning of citizens could come later. There would be time to consider alibies. But not then, not in that moment. It was a period of demonstration. As far as the Authority were concerned, it was a time of learning lessons. Of proving a point. Of reasserting the notion of what it meant to disobey.

The Music Makers had evaded capture once more. Others had to pay the price. Governor Blix and Commander Wulfwin, their fury matched, demanded a fortune.

—

Despite the odds and terrifying close calls, Cole had made it back to Tempur unscathed.

He climbed up a rope he had left suspended from an aperture in his apartment. He teased open the shutter and crept through the aperture into the living room, trying not to knock over the books and ornaments that littered the sill.

The room was dark, not yet touched by the creeping light of dawn. He tiptoed, struggling to control his breathing after running halfway across the city. He froze in the centre of the room. A silhouette hovered at the far end. Terror seized him, his nerves frayed from a night on the run. Then he realised and gulped, almost choking. "Evan…"

"Cole," said Evan, stepping forward into the half-light. His face was wet, his eyes swollen. "I thought they had you." His voice broke and he wept.

Cole hurried forward and embraced him hard, holding his head. Fighting back his own tears, he said, "It's okay. I'm here. We're safe."

—

Chase gave Ursel a leg-up over the chain-link fence that formed the outer perimeter of the Telltale Circus. They both crouched down either side of the fence, their faces almost touching.

They had run for miles, skirting the city centre, sticking to backstreets and the cover of darkness. At one point, Chase's lungs had burnt so hard, he thought he wouldn't be able to keep going. Then they had heard the footfall of a Deaf Squad unit and the roar of Authority motorbikes. Survival instinct kicked in and he kept on running.

Finally, as the rising sun bled light onto the broken city, they had reached Standings Cross and the relative safety of the Circus compound.

"Why don't you hide here too? Creaser will be crawling with the A. There's no way you'll make it home," said Ursel, her hand gripping the fence.

"I have to get back. I promised I'd get a message to Naylor. He'll be worried sick."

"He wouldn't want you to risk getting caught."

Chase shook his head. "I promised. And besides, I know what a state he'll be in. He lives on the seventy-eighth floor. He would've seen the fires. Heard the sirens. I can't leave him fearing the worst."

"You're a good friend. And a good brother. I'm sorry I judged you at the start. I got you wrong."

"No. I think you got me about right. But I'm working on it."

He was about to get up, then hesitated. His fingers curled around the wire fence close to hers. "Despite everything, I'm glad I went. You were right. I needed to see it to understand."

"And do you?"

With a faint smile, weary yet warm, he rose and crept away.

—

It took Chase another hour to loop east, beyond the city limits, back into the edge of Creaser and the towering

Wallace Estates. It was now light. His clothes were torn and drenched in sweat. His face and arms were covered in dirt and his hair hung tangled and damp. Blood oozed from a wound on his shoulder – raw flesh exposed through a jagged gouge. If he was caught now, there could be no denying where he had been all night. Creeping between the towers' shadows, he hurried to block twenty-one. Too afraid to call the elevator, should the squeal of rusting steel draw unwanted attention, he climbed the seventy-eight flights of stairs.

Naylor stood by the window, where he'd remained all night. Smoke signals rose across the city, conveying the night's carnage. The sirens had ceased a few hours earlier. Daylight meant he could no longer follow the headlamps of Authority trucks as they snaked their way up to Leven Hyder. Yet he couldn't move from the window. He couldn't desert his post, knowing his friend was still out there. Somewhere.

A faint knock on the front door made him start. He knew the raids weren't over. He immediately thought of Clo, still asleep in her room. What little blood was left drained from his stone-grey face as he approached the door.

He looked through the spy hole. There was no one there. His pulse racing, he held his ear to the door. Silence.

Only, there wasn't silence. He knelt down and listened. He could hear breathing on the other side. Low down, almost to the floor.

He inched open the door, peering down through the narrow gap. "Oh no…" he said, finding Chase slumped on the floor. He opened the door fully and grabbed Chase under his armpits, dragging him through. Before locking the door, he glanced both ways down the corridor, fearing a witness.

He pulled Chase into the centre of the room and placed a cushion under his head. Seeing the bloody wound to his shoulder, he found a cloth and held it firm against the gash. "Chase, wake up," he said, lightly patting his cheek with his free hand.

Chase's head lolled, his mouth half open.

Naylor hurried to the kitchen and poured a glass of water, which he held to Chase's mouth. The first few drops spilt out and poured down his chin. Then the cold liquid on his tongue revived him. Naylor held Chase's head still, trying to get more water into his mouth.

Chase swallowed, then swallowed again, then grabbed the now-empty glass.

"Wait. I'll get you some more," said Naylor.

Chase regained consciousness, dizzy and confused. After two more glasses of water, he looked up at Naylor. "Sorry I took so long to get back."

"I was worried."

"I know you were."

"What happened to your arm?"

"It's nothing."

"It's a bloody great hole, Chase. You need sutures. Did the A do it? Did they get you?"

"I fell, that's all. There was glass everywhere. It's nothing." He waved a weak hand in dismissal.

Naylor hesitated, afraid to ask. Yet the not knowing was worse. "Ursel?" he said. "Is she okay?"

"Yes. I left her at the Circus."

"Thank the Deep. And Wella? Did you find her?"

"No." Chase struggled to sit upright. He rubbed his temples, eyes closed. "No, but Ursel's convinced she's there."

Naylor slumped back, sack-like.

"What?" said Chase.

"All of that... For nothing."

"No, it wasn't."

"But you didn't see Wella." His whole body sagged. "All night. I stood by the window, watching. I never moved. I heard the sirens, imagined the screams. There were fires: blisters dotted across the city. I saw the convoys shipping people away. I was terrified you were among them. I should never have let you go."

Chase saw the residue of terror in his friend's expression and realised he felt no fear himself. Instead, an unfamiliar peace warmed his chest. The adrenalin that had propelled him across the city was spent; the exhaustion left in its wake was superficial. Overriding all else was a peculiar calm. "I'm glad I went."

"You're what?"

Chase sat forward, the warmth spreading. "Something happened at the show. I don't know what it was. I don't pretend to understand. But I felt something. Something incredible."

Naylor stared, mouth agape.

"I felt this powerful connection with the music. I was drawn to the woman singing. It was as if there was an electrical charge flowing between us, captivating me. I felt euphoric. That's the only way I can describe it. Euphoric."

"Did you even look for Wella?"

"Ursel did." Chase read the incomprehension on Naylor's face. "She told me to watch the show."

"So, what? You just relaxed and enjoyed yourself? Forgot that you were risking your life to find your sister?"

"I'm trying to explain—"

"All I'm hearing is that the A is fucking right. It's like you were drugged. Did they give you something to drink?"

"No. It wasn't like that."

"Then tell me, Chase. I've heard the radio. I witnessed the attack on the city. Tell me. What *was* it like?"

CHAPTER ELEVEN

Governor Blix stood behind her desk, white-knuckled fists pinning down its surface. She leant forward, her face contorted, bereft of its characteristic composure. "Tell me there is a sound explanation for this monumental fuck-up."

Wulfwin stood to attention before her. His face was streaked with sweat and dirt; his eyes, bloodshot. He gritted his teeth, knowing there was more to come. Biding his time, he met her stare.

"We had solid intel," she hissed. "The best lead in years, squandered. Someone is responsible. Someone who clearly does not grasp the severity of the situation. That someone is about to pay dearly for their utter incompetence. I demand a name, Wulfwin. Not a scapegoat. I want to know who thinks they can fail my will."

"I want those damn Music Makers as much as you. Believe me, if there was someone who failed to follow orders, I would be dragging their tortured body here to await their official punishment."

"Someone is to blame," she said, her voice low and laced with threat.

"You have my report, Governor. There are lessons to be learnt. Steps we can take to make sure we're able to succeed next time. Meanwhile, we have the detention centres bloated with User scum. We'll make them talk, beat them until they tell us where the Makers hide. We failed to raid the event, but it's not over yet. I give you my word."

Blix stood up straight and pushed her shoulders back. She grabbed a sheaf of papers from her desk. "Yes. Your report." She flicked the pages without looking down. "You mentioned inadequate numbers of Allears. Explain."

"Although they declared a positive detection from a source in the Nanso Heights, Commander Lore ordered the majority of his units to retain their positions across the city, taking ten units with us to pursue the source. In my opinion, he made the right call to split resources. Had he achieved his recruitment targets, as he was ordered to do, we would have had more bodies on the Heights. This would have enabled us to trace the source sooner, giving my men more time to locate the target."

Blix glared at Wulfwin, her hands twisting the crumpled report. "Tell me straight."

"Lore was under orders to recruit. Let's say his efforts fell short of par. Numbers should be higher. As it is, resources are stretched."

Attempts at composure were abandoned. Blix's alabaster skin flushed pink. The twisted report became a baton that she held forth as if poised to duel. "Subpar performance. Failure to follow orders. You knew about this, yet it is only now that you think to inform me. Explain."

"I take full responsibility. He had recruited, but I had not monitored numbers as closely as I should. He followed orders, but only through dragging his heels. This is unlike him and his impeccable track record. I should've kept a closer eye. The issue came to my attention yesterday morning; hence raising the point in my report." Wulfwin paused, then said, "With regard to his loyalty, I am in no doubt. He regurgitates textbook commitment which, until now, he has consistently delivered. I find no cause to question it. I am certain the reluctance is motivated by something else."

"Then find out what it is. And Wulfwin, if you're wrong about Commander Lore… If I hear of any cause for doubt, the slightest mote of suspicion that his loyalty to the Authority is anything other than two hundred per cent, I hold you directly responsible. You will both be charged with treason. I trust I make myself clear."

Wulfwin held her eye contact like a challenge accepted. "Yes, Governor."

"And from now on, you are responsible for Allear recruitment. I want numbers doubled. I don't care how it's achieved. Get them in training and fast-track the best. We will not fail again."

—

His feet pounding baked earth and stone, Dent Lore ran the Nanso Trail.

It was dusk, approaching twenty-four hours after the raid. Dent still hadn't slept. His limbs were deadweights and his chest burnt, yet a passion numb to pain propelled him onwards. Although the light was fading, the route was an exercise in muscle memory. He ran the Trail every day – in part to maintain his fitness, but also through compulsion to search for something long since lost. He had no idea what this might be; for him, that was beside the point. He craved the movement, the travel. Never running away, but always forwards, towards an answer for which he did not know the question.

He pushed hard, snaking up Cinder Hill, winding through limestone outcrops and up barren inclines. The track twisted and climbed until it reached the foot of the Nanso Heights, only to loop and drop back down again as if intimidated by the prodigious mountain range. A stone-strewn descent led to gradual signs of civilisation, culminating back at the start on the suburban fringes of Wakenfold.

Reaching the highest point before the fall, Dent stopped running and bent double, his hands gripping his knees. Having caught his breath, he stood upright and gazed at the view.

Wydeye lay before him, a sprawling blur in the half-light. Sections of the city appeared to be greyscale wastelands: the less populated Hundreds of Wickerwood and Hole. Other areas glowed amber, illuminating the vast concrete structures beneath the darkening sky. Single bright lights snaked through the city, pausing intermittently as if caught by indecision: the headlamps of the steam railmotors as they rode the Elevated. To his left, the cold lights of the Authority Complex formed silhouettes of three vast detention centres and the featureless box that was the Allears Training Centre.

He stared, despondent. Achieving the ambition of Governor Blix and the Authority was his sole purpose in life. He shared the determination to achieve the long-sought end of catching the Music Makers. Yet the sheer brutality and arbitrary violence of the raids appalled him. He did not share Wulfwin's pleasure in the suffering and cruelty that occurred through the course of avoidable action.

All that pain. Immeasurable hurt. And more to follow.

His mind turned to the detainees, crammed into squalid cells, awaiting interrogation. He knew it would be a protracted process – a message to others as much as method. Then he thought of the Allear recruits. He dwelt on the children who passed the Test, on the families they were taken from, on their adjustment.

The Authority depended on him and his command of the Allears. He relished the responsibility, honoured the cause, but deplored the cost.

The sun had dipped below the skyline. Darkness flooded the view, reducing the city to a sea of bobbing lights. Dent turned and began his descent.

—

"Blix is all out for scalps and she's got her eye on yours," said Wulfwin. He walked slowly around Dent Lore, who stood to attention, eyes front.

They were in Dent's office inside the Allears Training Centre, a windowless concrete box that constituted Dent's work-life imbalance. The room was small and featureless: a desk at one end, a few wooden chairs against one wall, a large, pin-filled map of Wydeye pasted on another.

Wulfwin spat the words through grinding teeth. "Now, just so you know, I've stuck my neck on the line for you. Fuck knows why because right now I think I'd rather sacrifice your scalp to get her off my case." He stopped in front of Dent and leant in towards his face so their noses almost touched. "Tell me I didn't make an error of judgement. Tell me I don't need to doubt your loyalty to our respected Governor and the mighty Authority, of which she is supreme leader."

Dent's eyes widened and looked directly into Wulfwin's. He leant his head back so he could focus, given the close proximity. "No, sir. You did not make an error of judgement. I am and have always been loyal to Governor Blix. I serve her will and the rule of the Authority."

Wulfwin twisted his face, his scar extending the sneer that had crept across it. "That's what fascinates me about you, Lore. Textbook allegiance, but with all the passion of a dying goat." He stepped backwards to appraise the full extent of his subject. "I've just informed you that Blix is considering charging you with treason. Me too, as it happens, if I've judged you wrong."

"And I swear my loyalty is unwavering. She is a fair leader. I trust that she will believe in my dedication if there is ever call for me to prove it."

"Such a time has come, so let's hope you're right."

"What do you mean? She has found cause to doubt me?"

"One word, Lore. Recruitment."

Dent looked ahead, adjusting his breathing to maintain his poise.

"Or," continued Wulfwin, "to be more specific, lack thereof. I put it to Blix that our mission was compromised, that it may have been a success had you recruited enough gimps to do the fucking job." He resumed his slow circumambulation of his charge. "In my infinite wisdom, I assured her that it was not, as she suspected, a lack of loyalty that had compelled you to pay sod-all regard to the plain-as-day orders I had given you. Instead, I intimated that it was something else that resulted in your piss-poor effort." He stopped directly behind Dent, locked his arm around his neck and bent it back so that his bulging eyes were forced to stare at the ceiling. "Enlighten me."

Dent was released only after he'd turned crimson and had begun to choke. It took him a few moments to recover, affording him time to consider his response. He knew he couldn't tell Wulfwin the truth. For a man who relished cruelty as an occupational perk, a confession on the influence of compassion would not be well received. He had to think fast. When he could drag out his coughing no further, he said, "I've been working on the Test. I believe there's scope to assess potential for high-functioning aural capability with less severe adjustment."

Brows raised, Wulfwin nodded slowly. "Okay. Elaborate."

"The current measures of adjustment are effective, but the consequence of some have a negative impact on performance. Not the surgically achieved anosmia – that works well and I maintain it's an effective intervention. I'm talking specifically of the adjustment to achieve blindness."

"That's been policy from the start. We know for a fact it heightens aural functioning. What's the issue, Lore?"

"The issue is that the majority of recruits undergo the surgery because they don't currently achieve the benchmark score for a sighted Allear. At present, seventy-eight per cent of my resources can't see. As I'm sure you appreciate, this inevitably has a detrimental impact on performance in the field." Gaining confidence in his off-the-cuff theory, Dent spoke with conviction. "If more of them could see where they were going, the Allears would do a faster, better job."

"An observation that is blindingly obvious."

Dent didn't respond. He could see he'd sown a seed of intrigue in Wulfwin's mind. He remained silent, watching, waiting for it to take root.

Wulfwin walked over to Dent's desk and sat behind it, leaning back, feet up. "Go on then, hit me with it. Where's this mysterious scope in the Test?"

From there, Dent knew he was on safe ground. Wulfwin's expertise was all about muscle and mayhem. He didn't understand the science. Knowing this, Dent peppered his explanation with incomprehensible terminology, whilst ensuring Wulfwin would grasp enough of the gist to be won over. He concluded by saying, "I've almost completed the proposed enhancements and was on the verge of presenting them to you. If you are happy to approve them, I can implement them in time for the scheduled assessment date."

Wulfwin stared at Dent, piecing together the parts he could understand, assimilating the results. Then he slowly nodded his head. "I believe you've just saved your scalp," he said. "I'm on board. You're authorised to go ahead."

Relieved that his ploy had paid off, Dent's mind went straight to work on how to create the fictitious changes within the timeframe. He calculated he had just under two weeks – challenging, but plausible.

Wulfwin stood up and headed towards the door. At the threshold he turned around and said, "By the way, Blix has put me in charge of recruitment, so you're relieved of the burden. Assessment and training remain your responsibility. No need to present the changes to me. Proceed with their implementation. I'm bringing the Test forward. You've got three days."

CHAPTER TWELVE

Deep underground, a gas lamp flickered. Before it danced three shadows, seeping from feet unmoving. The Troubadours stood a few paces apart, heads almost touching the cave's low ceiling. Somewhere, water followed its path of centuries, carving space from stone.

"I hope it was worth it," hissed Pale Dexter, a flint edge to his voice.

Chief flicked back her silver dreads and crossed her arms.

"What's done is done," said Bend Sinister. "They did not find us. Ourselves and our players remain safe."

"That does not excuse the cost." Pale Dexter turned to Chief. "Spare a thought for the captured. You have their suffering on your conscience. Can you feel the weight of their pain? Or are you still high?"

Chief stepped forward, fury in her stride.

Bend Sinister held out an arm to bar her way. He turned to Pale Dexter and said, "Enough. She had to play. You will too, in due course. This is who we are."

"Survival demands we lack the luxury of choice. You know that," said Chief to Pale Dexter, her tone trip-wire tight.

"To witness the fear in their eyes when we heard the troops approach. To know what they risk in order to attend. This is not something I choose."

"I said we should delay."

"And I maintain I could not."

The walls of the cramped cave appeared to close in as tension pulled at the space between them. Pale Dexter took a step backwards as if to counter the pull. "This is why we must resolve the question of succession. How can we proceed without a leader? Our stalemate sounds petulant; it is beneath us."

"I agree," said Chief. "We cooperate best under leadership. The sooner we agree a strategy, the better."

"I still maintain we would do well to trial a more collegial model," said Bend Sinister. "Although, I acknowledge the unfortunate irony in that. Two against one. I am out-voted. Pale Dexter, you've clearly given this much thought. How do you propose we address the issue? We've found ourselves in this situation only once before. That particular method of election is problematic in the light of recent events."

"Regardless of that, I would be in favour of a Contest, as before."

"What?" Chief glared at Pale Dexter. "Not a moment ago you had the mind to accuse me of putting my needs before the safety of others. You suggested the risks of performing outweighed my requirements to survive. Now you want to escalate that risk tenfold with an event that will undoubtedly lead to our capture? An interesting contradiction, wouldn't you say?"

"Chief is right," said Bend Sinister. "A Contest is far too dangerous. There is no way we would be able to contain the sound. It was different before. We were free to play where and when we chose. Such an event is out of the question."

"Out of the question? Where's your democracy now?" said Pale Dexter.

The two Troubadours squared up to each other, eyes locked in defiance.

Bend Sinister broke away and sat on a rock, his right hand touching the small tattoo on his cheek. "We should at least explore alternatives. There must be other methods for selection."

"What might they be, exactly? A dubious campaign pledging the predictable? Fair rule. Equal opportunity to play. Protection from the powers that be. Then what? The three of us vote on it?" Pale Dexter sneered. "I've a good memory, you know. You two share a history of joining forces."

Chief looked to the ceiling and spoke as if thinking aloud. "We are without an objective judge. Our players and followers bear allegiance to one of us. Those not already bound by loyalty are, by definition, not part of the Scene." She sighed and shook her head, dreads swaying like charmed snakes. "The magnitude of risk should preclude it, but I can think of no other way." She looked at Bend Sinister, shoulders raised.

Bend Sinister remained silent, his fingers tracing lines along the limestone rock on which he sat. His mind searched for a solution. Possibilities appeared like oases in an arid desert, only to reveal themselves as illusory mirages once examined from all sides. His efforts proved fruitless, yet he would not surrender.

Eventually, he stood up and addressed his counterparts. "I admit, I am unable to propose an alternative. However, I maintain that a Contest is too great a risk. While we still have the luxury of choice, let us take a while and reflect further. If, after a week, we are unable to suggest a viable alternative, then we open dialogue on the Contest. Are you both agreed?"

"Yes," said Chief.

Pale Dexter snorted and held up his hands.

"I'll take that as unanimous assent. Meanwhile, the fact remains we have to be able to perform, regardless of the outcome of our deliberations. In a few months' time, it will be your turn, Pale Dexter. I say we concentrate on working together, find ways to make conditions safer. Unfortunately, this is one area in which we have no choice."

Pale Dexter's face twitched. He turned to Bend Sinister, arms wide. "Make the conditions safer? How exactly? We have already sacrificed daylight for a life underground. As the years have passed, we've retreated deeper into these caves. We live like bats, afraid to emerge into the light. Buried fugitives. What life is this?"

"What are you saying?"

"That we've hidden ourselves away for long enough. There will come a point when we can retreat no further. So why not leave? Start again somewhere new? And, in light of our leadership debate, perhaps depart and go our separate ways."

Chief stared at Pale Dexter, eyes wide.

"You know we can't do that," said Bend Sinister.

"We haven't tried for two centuries. Times change. For all we know, our chances could be different now."

—

TWO HUNDRED YEARS AGO

On a sun-scorched day, two hundred years ago, four groups of strangers entered the humble settlement of Wydeye. The townsfolk regarded them with caution, wary of their bizarre attire and foreign features. The strangers had appeared from different directions: one group from the north, one from the south, one from the east and one from the west. Although they entered the town on the same day, at the very same moment, they were not known to each other. Each of the groups looked to one among them: a Troubadour, who stepped forward and spoke on their behalf. Their names were Bend Sinister, Pale Dexter, Saltire and Chief.

Recognising that the visitors posed no threat to the peace of the town, the Chief of Wydeye, Headman Glade IV, welcomed the strangers and bid them tell their tales that had led to their arrival. To the wonder of the strangers, as much as to the townsfolk who had gathered to hear them speak, their stories were identical.

The Travelling Minstrels, as they henceforth became known, had traversed the four corners of the world, playing music to anyone who would listen. They each described a quest of sorts, forever moving on in search of an audience with whom they could connect. When pressed on what this meant, the strangers each appeared coy, reluctant to elaborate. Whatever it was, the desire to connect was sufficient to drive them to journey for years on end, often through harsh terrain and with little in the way of adequate food and shelter. When they appeared before the citizens of Wydeye, the strangers were weak and weary, yet wholly committed to their quest.

Headman Glade IV, a lover of stories, was delighted by what she heard. To her mind, the bizarre coincidences of both the shared quest and the simultaneous arrival of the strangers, added a certain magic. She declared the Minstrels guests of Wydeye and announced that there would be a feast in their honour, to which the whole town was invited. In return for the generous hospitality, Bend Sinister, Pale Dexter, Saltire and Chief each offered to perform their music during the feast.

The citizens of Wydeye were a trusting community, raised in the belief, held by many generations before them, that the watchful eye of Wydeye Deep would provide for and protect them. Some of the more superstitious among them believed that the arrival of the Travelling Minstrels was a gift from the Deep, to lift their spirits following the hardship of a long, sweltering summer, during which their crops had failed. All welcomed news of the feast, hoping for a day of celebration in which they could forget their struggles and regale their foreign visitors.

Preparations were carried out by all with joy and eager anticipation. Although food was scarce, resourcefulness was second nature. The townsfolk added crushed spices to their flat bread dough; foraged for mushrooms and garlic in Wickerwild forest; picked sorrel, burdock and clover, to add flavour to their simple stock; set traps for rabbits and stoats in the pastures beyond the Deep. A few of the more successful farmers donated a cow or a pig for slaughter. The majority, who had no food to spare, donated their time. They stitched and draped flags from their lowly limestone dwellings; mixed pigments into lime wash and painted the buildings around the town square; picked meadow flowers and hung them from every archway, porch and pillar. At one end of the square, a platform was erected. It was from there that the Travelling Minstrels would perform following the sharing of food.

The day of the feast was, indeed, a day of celebration. A cool breeze tempered the scorching sun. The air above the trestle tables in the centre of the square was filled with laughter as the food was passed around. Every man, woman and child ate their fill, yet there was still plenty to spare. As dusk fell, the Troubadours each took to the stage in turn and performed their unique music. Headman Glade IV and her people listened in wonder. Whether it was their full stomachs, or the effect of the nettle wine, they found themselves lulled into a blissful stupor, breathing in the music along with the cooling night air.

In the days and weeks that followed, the four groups of strangers played their music in the sparse taverns across the town. The townsfolk felt a compelling desire to see and hear the Minstrels play. The music did, indeed, lift their spirits. Morale blossomed, as did a keenness of faith in their own resilience. The recent hardships were soon forgotten.

Meanwhile, the players themselves relished the reaction of their hosts, sensing a connection had, at long last, been made. With each performance, their audiences grew. The players soon recovered in strength and health. The four Troubadours began to believe, after untold years of searching, that their quest was finally over.

The Travelling Minstrels had arrived at exactly the same time. They had all faced the same arduous journey, motivated by a common need. There was no claim to be territorial, which they fairly acknowledged. Instead, Bend Sinister, Pale Dexter, Saltire and Chief recognised their remarkable good fortune, settling into a harmonious arrangement sustained by mutual respect. They each enjoyed sufficient support to survive. It did not occur to them to seek more than their fair share.

The relationship was symbiotic. When the Minstrels performed, their audience experienced pure joy, a euphoria that lifted their spirits for days. This enabled them to better cope with the hardships of labour and the perennial struggle to survive. At the same time, the players fed off this euphoria, empowering them through the exchange, providing the sustenance on which they thrived.

Players and townsfolk alike continued in this way for many decades. During this period, prosperity graced the town. Again, the more superstitious among them attributed the time of plenty to the presence of the Minstrels, timely manna from the grace of Wydeye Deep.

As the decades passed, no one seemed to notice that the players showed no signs of ageing. While the elderly citizens retold the *Tale of the Travelling Minstrels* to their children, then their children's children, the players retained the full glow and vigour of youth. Or, at least, if anyone did notice, no one dared give voice to their observation for fear some spell would be broken and the prosperity would end.

Over time, the townsfolk formed an allegiance to either Bend Sinister, Pale Dexter, Saltire or Chief – a fealty they paraded with pride. An emblem was designed for each Troubadour, which was woven into badges and sewn on tunics and cloth caps. The emblems were incorporated into colourful banners, used to herald a forthcoming show. Pennants bearing the insignia adorned the taverns in which the players performed.

When Headman Glade IV passed away and was replaced by her son, Headman Glade V, and by his daughter in turn, the Minstrels were always made to feel part of the community. The Troubadours' itinerant past had been a necessity of circumstance. With no reason to leave, Wydeye became their home. Thus, the harmony remained for 152 years.

Then came the unexpected death of Headman Glade VI. With no natural heir to assume her position, the Glade dynasty, which had led the Court of Wydeye by the principles of fairness and equality for over a quarter millennium, came to an abrupt end.

When Councillor Morgan Wallace orchestrated a contentious election and declared himself State Governor, life in Wydeye changed beyond compare.

One of the more significant changes was the impact of his migrant workforce scheme, which led to a steady growth in population. This, coupled with his Three Child Initiative, ensured the headcount would continue to grow.

For the Troubadours and their players, a delicate balance had been disturbed, the harmony challenged. After the fair share over the last 150 years, there was now more than enough to go around.

Rejecting the ideal of balance based on equal measure, Saltire and Pale Dexter recognised an opportunity to seize control. They stepped up their efforts, enhancing their shows to attract the attention of newcomers to the city. This concerned Bend Sinister and Chief, who strived to restore harmony. Recognising their efforts were failing, Chief abandoned the attempt and began to compete. In time, and in the interests of his players, Bend Sinister felt compelled to do likewise.

Tension between the Troubadours grew, aggravated further by Governor Wallace and his new Authority's cuts to arts and culture. Popular music venues were destroyed to make way for concrete high-rises, built to house the burgeoning population. Theatres were razed to the ground, clearing the way for vast furnaces and processing plants in what became the sprawling industrial Hundred of Coxen Lyme.

Scrabbling for places to perform and faced with citizens increasingly jaded by a creeping oppression, the dynamic of the Scene shifted. The Troubadours began warring among themselves. Meanwhile, they each knew they could not risk leaving Wydeye. It had taken them untold years to find an audience with whom they could connect; they doubted they would find such a home again.

With their harmonious balance destroyed, the Troubadours recognised they needed a leader among them to control the Scene. They agreed to compete against each other to determine who this should be. It was decided that the Troubadour who attracted the largest audience and, therefore, possessed the greatest influence, should become leader. A formidable Contest was held.

Victory fell to Saltire.

Over the decades that followed, resentment would rumble and the tension return. Periodically, Pale Dexter attempted to take advantage of the still-growing population and increase his influence. Each time, his efforts failed and Saltire retained her rule. She upheld the principle of fairness, long since lost from the Glade dynasty and the Wydeye of old.

Then came the Rideout Rebellion, the outlawing of live music and the Authority's proclaimed hunt for the Music Makers.

The Troubadours knew they could not leave and risk losing the connection that was essential to their subsistence. Instead, the Scene was forced to retreat into the shadows and then, in time, to a life underground.

Mindful of the great risk to player and follower alike, Saltire declared that they each take it in turn to perform and that frequency should be determined according to the absolute minimum required to survive.

Then, one night, a vast swallow hole opened its maw, sucking Saltire and her players into the depths of the earth, lost forever.

CHAPTER THIRTEEN

The City was suffocating. The sultry air had become pea soup-thick. Fine sand hung heavy, creating a dense desert smog. Visibility was a measure of arm's reach.

A dust cloud was forming. The citizens recognised the signs and dreaded the inevitable. Such a phenomenon was rare, but experience of the extreme left scar tissue. The exceptional felt wearily familiar.

Yet it wasn't the dust cloud that compelled the citizens of Wydeye to draw closed their shutters and seek shelter in dark quarters. It wasn't the clogged air that caused them to keep their heads down, eyes trained on the ground. They shuffled in silence, seeking anonymity through stealth like paranoid prey.

They knew the cross hairs could be trained on any one of them.

As the days following the raid passed, a lingering echo haunted the city. Deaf Squad troopers maintained an unequivocal presence, patrolling the underpass and loitering on street corners. Active Allears were up in number, raising questions as to whether they genuinely were listening as a precaution to avoid another Glos hole tragedy. Occasionally,

Special Forces troopers would storm a café or kick down the door of a terrified family. Individuals were either arrested or beaten before petrified loved ones. They were the unlucky examples, randomly selected to demonstrate a point. The Authority was in control.

Relentless mandatory broadcasts reinforced the message in their motive: *"Citizens of Wydeye, rules are for a reason. Those who break them must face the consequence. If you're not with us, you're against us. Think about it. Sharing is caring; visit the Exchange today if you know something we don't. There's something in it for you. Trust us. It's the right thing to do. Workers of Wydeye…"*

Murals were painted on the sides of buildings: huge concrete canvases, eye level with the Elevated, transformed into persuasive visual aids that proved impossible to ignore. A limited colour palette was maintained: red, white and black. Pointing fingers, accusing stares. Guilty secrets portrayed as rats. The script was consistent.

Outside the Exchange, the Wall of the Missing was extended by a new montage of photos. Citizens pinned ID card thumbnails of those detained by the Authority, along with statements declaring the innocence of the man, woman or child depicted. It had started with a handful of daring posts, demanding the release of whomever had been arrested. These demands were promptly removed by Exchange officials, although they left the accumulating pictures – an unintended source of pride. Over the subsequent days, more and more photos were added, along with more judicious statements asserting alibis and innocence. For the families who wrote them, they became the only way to present a defence case in the absence of a trial.

Weldon and Tinashe walked past the Exchange in silence, pausing briefly to take in the expanding court-by-proxy.

Tinashe gazed at the headshots of haunted faces, lingering to read the pleas for mercy.

"Come on," said Weldon, taking her by the arm and coaxing her away.

They walked the length of First Went and entered the Pentagon. It was Friday afternoon; most citizens were at work. Even taking that into account, the open expanse was unusually quiet, made more eerie by the desert smog that robbed the space of horizon. Weldon and Tinashe didn't speak until they reached the shelter of the Brew tent on the opposite side. This, too, was uncharacteristically quiet.

Weldon walked up to the table-top bar while Tinashe had a rare pick of hay bales from which to select a seat.

"Got served straight away," said Weldon, handing her a brimming glass of Kitson. "When's it going to get back to normal?"

"What is normal?"

Weldon huffed and sat down on a bale opposite. They sipped their drinks in silence, glancing around the near-empty tent. Eventually Weldon said, "They're building new whisper dishes. In Wakenfold and Darlem Fields. Some are twice the size. And they're not to listen for holes." He leant forward and lowered his voice. "Maybe the bigger ones are to hear conversations. Do you reckon they can do that? Eavesdrop with concrete ears?"

"Wouldn't surprise me."

"I don't remember it ever being like this. Never this bad."

"I spoke to my old man. He said it reminded him of after Rideout. He said they were too afraid to go out for weeks. And he wasn't even at the stadium or the protests." She sighed and shook her head. "All this because of some stupid festival."

"But it's not, though, is it?" Passion sharpened an edge to his voice. "It was the music. The crowd. The drug. That's why it's still going on, why the selfish bastards still insist on going to the shows. They're addicted."

"According to the A."

"According to anyone who's got eyes and can see what's happening. Why else would they do it? Why else put their lives, and the lives of everyone around them, at risk? They're Users, worse than the fucking Meezels. They do as they damn well please to get their fix, then they're too high to give a shit about the rest of us."

"But we don't know that. You heard what Chase said about that woman – Ursel. She doesn't sound like some messed-up addict. And if she's right and Wella is involved, then we both know Wella. She's a good person. Strong."

"When did you last see Wella? I know I haven't spoken to her for months. Drugs change a person pretty quick. You don't know what she's become."

"I think you're wrong."

"And I think you're missing the point. What about the swallow hole?" he said, frustration flaring.

"What about it?"

"It could happen again, at any time. The Allears were out listening for signs. They were protecting us, to save lives. And now they're back on the hunt for the Music Makers. If another hole does open up, they won't hear it to give the warning."

"I'm sure that—"

"Have you been to Glos recently? Have you seen what they've done?"

Tinashe shook her head, shoulders sagging.

"The hole," said Weldon. "They've filled it in. All twenty-seven million cubic metres of it. Plugged the entire thing and relaid the Westway Road. Carts and trucks going over it like the hole never existed. And still they never found a single body. What if there was an air pocket? Where survivors were waiting to be saved? What if Ursel's wrong and Wella's down there?"

"Shut it," hissed Tinashe, grabbing Weldon's wrist. "Don't you ever go saying that to Chase."

Wide-eyed, Weldon pulled back, his free hand held up. "Okay, okay. I was only making a point."

"And your point is?"

"The Allears were trying to save lives. Now the A's back to taking them. You saw the Wall outside the Exchange. How many? Hundred and fifty? Two hundred new photos? All because selfish fucking Users can't kick the habit and stay away. If they did, the Scene would die out and we wouldn't have to live in fear. This," he said, sweeping his arm to encompass the deserted beer tent, "this isn't because of the weather. No dust cloud has stopped people escaping their shithole quarters before."

"I just think there's more to it. You know better than to trust the A. Don't believe everything they tell you."

"Give me some credit, Tinashe." Weldon stood up.

"Where are you going?"

"To get some air."

Tinashe watched Weldon as he stormed out of the tent. She remained seated, plucking strands of straw from the bale, processing his words. *It's not like him to become so fired up*, she thought. He was usually the one providing light relief from the daily strains of life under the Authority. That was why she hung out with him. He reminded her to laugh every once in a while.

She glanced around the tent, at the huddles of people keeping close, repelling the space around them. Some whispered; others sat in silence. Their heads drooped and their bodies barely shifted. The atmosphere was heavy like the dust-clogged air outside.

The two young boys serving behind the bar stood idle, waiting for custom. No one entered.

The only thing to move freely was a brown, long-haired dog. Tinashe watched it play with a moth that fluttered above its nose, inches out of reach. The dog's motion was light and unconscious. Its tail whirled in a blur while its head darted this way and that, tracking the taunting moth. The playful scene struck her as incongruous. The joy in oblivion. Carefree abandon.

Rising slowly, her spirit strained under the weight of the city. She weaved through the empty bales and out into the glare of the Pentagon.

—

That same afternoon, Chase stood before the Telltale Circus, watching the trickle of wary citizens drain from its exit and disappear into the fog.

He hadn't seen or spoken to Ursel since their flight across the pummelled city.

The euphoria he had experienced at Chief's show had long since faded from his consciousness. There was no lingering impression, no aftertaste that could serve as memory. Now, the ephemeral sensation felt like a dream too vague to recollect. He clung on to its ghost, bemused and hungry for explanation. It had felt a long wait to see the only person he believed could provide him with one.

"Come in," said Ursel, holding open the flap to her yurt. She gestured to a cushion on the floor. "Take a seat. Can I get you water?"

"No thanks." Chase stood for a moment, his eyes adjusting to the change in light, then knelt on the cushion. "Low turnout?"

"Numbers haven't picked up since the raid. We'd hoped to get a crowd in today; the performance is our most popular. It's usually sold out. *The Travelling Minstrels*. Have you seen it?"

"No. No, I haven't."

A silence swelled in the space between them.

Ursel knelt down opposite Chase, her calm, collected expression a stark contrast to his. "You have some questions," she said in a voice like still water.

"Yes." He hesitated, absentmindedly touching his shoulder, feeling the dressing beneath his strap shirt. After days of deliberating, he now felt unsure where to start. He cleared his throat and rubbed the back of his neck. "Wella," he finally said. "You said you didn't see her."

"No. But I spoke to someone I trust. They said she's joined one of the other groups of players: Bend Sinister. She's working for them. Some followers do that. Not many. But some do. They choose a new life in the Scene. I guess things got too bad for her overground."

"What sort of life is that? Trapped in a cave."

"As I said, not many people make that choice. A handful at most. The rest of us run the risk and balance the two. But from what I've been told, and I've no reason not to believe my source, Wella has made that decision. She's not trapped, as you put it. She can change her mind at any time. The fact she's chosen that path suggests to me she's okay."

"Until the next raid and she's captured."

"All of us who follow run that risk."

"Whatever. I still don't accept she's safe there. I've got to find her. Persuade her to come home."

"Even if she's found a new home?"

"Yes," he said, looking at her squarely.

Ursel matched his stare, her eyes searching his. A slight

frown broke the stillness of her face. "You felt something down there. I know you did. But that's gone, hasn't it?"

"What was it?"

"Why don't you start by telling me how you felt?"

Chase looked away, searching the room for the right words. He felt the ache in his shoulder, the itch of the scab. His experience of the event had left such a nebulous impression, it felt like recalling the tales of others. "When I made it back to Naylor, he said I described it as euphoric. I can remember a wonderful warmth. A joy. She looked at me, the woman on stage."

"Chief."

"It felt physical. Like she was touching me. In my chest. Inside my stomach." He dropped his head and shook it, trying to free the memory from where it lay hidden. "It's gone now, but at the time it felt so strong. All-consuming." He looked up, into Ursel's eyes. "Tell me. What was it? What happened?"

"You experienced the reason why I, and Wella, and hundreds of others, are prepared to risk what we do in order to attend. That wave of emotion, that sensation of connection, is what we all feel."

"Were we drugged?"

"No. Reject the A's rhetoric and trust your feelings. They were real. The State's propaganda is not. You responded to Chief and their music. That response, the intensity of that feeling, is why we follow the Scene – why we keep going back, despite the risk."

"I still don't get it."

"It's difficult to explain in abstract terms. That's why I wanted you to experience it for yourself. Contact, as strong as life. I felt sure it would touch you. The feeling has gone from you now, but the more you attend, more of it lingers. Sure, there's always a come-down. But then we know there will be another show, another chance to experience the joy that makes us stronger. We can't wear our hearts on our sleeves. But I bet you that followers of the Scene are the happiest people in this miserable city."

"What about Chief, then? And the others? Enemies of the State, yet the bands play on. What's in it for them?"

Ursel smiled. "Few of us get to know them well enough to know for sure. But I've been following for several years now and I think I understand. I see it happen at each event."

"What?"

"How they respond to us. When she's on stage, I see Chief connecting with us. Same with the others. Bend Sinister and Pale Dexter – Saltire too, in her time. I've seen them all and their reaction is the same. They need us as much as we need them."

"I don't get it. We didn't even pay for tickets. Oh…" he said, brows raised in the moment of dawning. "Unless you did? Sorry, I didn't even think to ask. How much do I owe you?"

"It didn't cost anything. It never does. Again, leave your preconceptions behind. It isn't a commercial transaction. They're not risking their lives to scrape together a living."

"I'm sceptical about anyone who claims they do something for nothing. There's always a price."

"But that's what I'm saying. They do get something out of it. I don't know what exactly. Something to do with the crowd's reaction. Maybe it makes them feel the same way I feel when I'm there. I'm not sure. Not that it matters."

"Of course it does." Chase realised afterwards that he'd raised his voice. He suppressed the frustration. "Sorry. I mean, surely it matters."

"Why?"

"Because it's got to be more than a feeling to do what they're doing. Breaking the law. Living the life of fugitives.

Weren't they at Rideout? Aren't they the cause of all this?" He waved his arm to gesture but realised the spatial context was wrong. "Deaf Squad. The Allears. The raids, for crow's sake."

Ursel sighed.

"What?" he said.

"When we were there, I saw it in you. Even afterwards, back here. Before you left."

"What?"

"You didn't understand. But you didn't need to. And that's because you felt it. You knew it regardless."

—

As Chase rode the Elevated, the clatter of steel on steel drowned out the white noise in his head. His eyes itched, unable to focus on the murals that now dominated the view, their paint still wet. His nerves were a clenched fist, ready to strike.

The frustration he felt when he had spoken to Ursel the previous day still rumbled within him. Time was not helping. Now he was on his way to see Naylor – the first meet up since he'd collapsed on his doorstep following the raid. The prospect knotted his stomach.

When they were last together, Naylor had been angry with him. Now, having regained the headspace of sobriety, Chase appreciated how his claims of euphoria must have sounded. With the sensation long since absent, he could no longer recall the feeling, let alone argue its merit. Still, whatever anger he had provoked, he knew their next conversation would be no more palatable for his friend.

"Come in," said Naylor, holding open the door to his flat. "I've just boiled some water. Tea?"

"Yes. Thank you."

Naylor disappeared into the kitchen, leaving Chase to loiter in the living room. He instinctively approached the window, always captivated by its bird's-eye view of the city. Now the view was lost, drowned by a sea of dense orange fog. The only things visible were the tops of the taller concrete structures, emerging through the dust cloud like boulders in a mist-covered bog. He turned away and caught sight of Naylor's daughter, peering around her bedroom door before silently closing it.

Naylor returned with the tea, handing a glass to Chase. They both sat at the table with their backs to the buried view.

"What's wrong with Clo?" said Chase.

"She had the Test yesterday."

"Ah…"

"It's the second year she's had to retake it. She's the only one in her group of friends who has to."

"That's got to feel tough for her."

"She keeps failing but doesn't know why. I hope she passes this time, for her sake. It's knocking her confidence. I hate to see her so low. She's due to spend the weekend with her mum but she's refusing to go. Not that I blame her, but I can hardly say that."

"I thought they got on."

"What can I say? She's growing up fast and becoming a good judge of character." They both smiled, faces relaxed – ice broken. "So, how's your shoulder?"

"Healing nicely, thanks."

"That's good." He hesitated, unsure whether or not to ask, deciding he couldn't not. "Any news?"

"Still no sign. Every day after work I've searched a different area of the city. She's not even contacted the furnaces, let alone shown up for work."

Naylor's expression softened. "I'm sorry, Chase."

"I've decided. I think Ursel's right."

Naylor sighed.

"What?" said Chase. "I've looked everywhere. And Ursel's convinced."

"I know, I know. I hear what you're saying. I just wish there was another explanation."

"Tell me about it." Chase sipped his tea, fighting the urge to go on the defensive. He needed Naylor on side.

"I know it's farfetched, but maybe she's left Wydeye?"

"I've looked into that. The furnaces still hold her papers. She can't go anywhere without them."

"Dare I say it, have you asked at the Exchange?"

"No," he replied – a little too quickly, he thought. Flushing, he cleared his throat and added, "I've nothing to trade. And besides, if she's involved in the Scene, I don't want to raise her profile with the Authority."

"But if they've got her in custody, at least you'd know. Can't you just ask them that?"

"They would never tell me. The Wall of the Missing exists for a reason. You know that."

"I take it you've at least posted her photo there?"

"No."

"What? You're joking, right? People look at the Wall. Someone must know something. I can't believe you didn't do that right from the start."

"Look, it's too risky, okay?" He took a deep breath and tightened his lips. Then he said, "I can't get my head past those copies of *Bluemantle* hidden in her rooms. And with everything Ursel's said, it's fairly clear Wella's involved with the Scene. That being the case, I don't want to attract any more attention to her than I have to. It's bad enough I've had to ask questions at her work. They're ruthless at the furnaces.

They've probably reported her for absence. I know they've terminated her worker's contract."

Naylor straightened his back and looked squarely at Chase. "It sounds like you've got a plan in mind."

"I'm going back to look for her. Underground. Ursel says that I have to wait until there's another show; I can't just search for her there. So, whenever that is, I'm going to attend."

"What? Why?"

"Because it's the only way."

"But after last time, the raid on the city—"

"I have to take the risk."

"No, you don't. Ursel goes anyway. Get her to take a message to Wella. If Wella doesn't come back with her, then that's her choice. Why risk your life while there are options?"

"I can't rely on Ursel. I need to see Wella for myself."

"Why? You think you're the only one who can persuade her? Come on, Chase. You guys aren't even close. If she's already taken the risk and chosen that path, she's not going to change her mind and come back just because big brother tells her to." He cocked his head and squinted. "Or perhaps you need to see a show again. Is that it? They've got you hooked already?"

"No."

"What was it you said? *Captivating*, I think it was. *Euphoric*. Need another dose now that the buzz has worn off?"

"No!" He felt the frustration rise, fought to keep it in check. "Look, I've been thinking about the last time we met. You were right to be angry. I don't blame you. I wasn't talking sense. My mind was all over the place. Probably the adrenalin and dehydration. I was a mess. Ursel has tried to explain it to me since and none of it makes sense. The Scene's trouble; I'm with you on that. So, it's not because I want to see another show. Honest to crow. It's not that at all."

"Then what is it? Because it doesn't stack up. Not when

there are options. There's got to be more to it."

Chase dropped his eyes and toyed with the edge of the table. He took his time to choose the right words – weighing them out, then arranging them in order, constructing sense. "It's because of Brann. Because of what I couldn't do for him. I felt helpless then. Powerless. I swore I'd never let myself be in that position again – standing by, unable to intervene. You're right. This time I have options. Whether or not it's the right thing to do, I have the opportunity to act, to have some control over things. I can go there, speak to Wella, try to bring her back. If I don't at least try and the A takes her, I'll never forgive myself." He stood up as if to leave. "I came here to explain my decision. I have to do this, Naylor. I hope you understand."

Slowly, Naylor rose. He said nothing. He just put his arms around his friend and held him close.

—

As night drew in, the dust cloud turned a darkening grey. The streets in the curfew zones were deserted. The arms of Five Wents and the expanse of the Pentagon, ordinarily packed late on a Saturday night, were equally desolate. Silence cloaked the city, broken only by wails from fighting feral cats and the bleating of sleepless goats.

Gas lamps burnt on the Pentagon's periphery. They flickered behind shuttered apertures of cowering quarters and glowed through the glazed windows throughout the Authority Complex.

Sleep overcame the work-weary. Between dreams came moments of peace.

By dawn of the new day, eight children had disappeared from their beds.

CHAPTER FOURTEEN

"It has been a week," said Bend Sinister. He stood before Chief and Pale Dexter, forming a wide triangle in the centre of one of the mountain's deepest caves. The air was cold – a sympathetic companion to the chilled relations between the Troubadours. Behind each of them stood their players. "We have each had time to reflect on alternative options for determining Saltire's successor. Have either of you a proposal you would like to share?"

Pale Dexter spoke first. "Despite what you might assume, I have given the matter much thought. Whilst I acknowledge the severity of risk involved, I still maintain that a Contest is the only appropriate and meaningful method of determining a new leader."

Behind him, his players nodded their assent.

Chief cocked an eyebrow. "When we last discussed the issue, you made reference to the option of departure. Does leaving no longer appeal? Are you not tired of *living like bats?*"

Pale Dexter winced. "As I have said, I have given due consideration to all alternatives, leaving Wydeye among them. I have ruled this out."

"On what grounds?"

"You know full well."

"But times change, do they not?" said Chief, suppressing a sardonic smile.

"Enough," said Bend Sinister. "I think we can all agree that leaving, however desirable, is not an option we have the luxury of pursuing." He raised his eyebrows. "Chief. Do you have any viable alternatives to the option of Contest?"

Chief looked from Pale Dexter to Bend Sinister. "I believe we came close to capture when I last played. The safety of our players and our followers is the greatest responsibility we bear. Yet, truly, I can conceive of no other way. We must all have trust in the process in order for the outcome to be meaningful. If I am to respect and obey a leader, then a Contest is the only way that individual can be determined." Their faces grave, Chief's players nodded their support. "And what of your thoughts, Bend Sinister? You were the one opposed to the motion."

Bend Sinister looked behind him at his bassist, guitarist and keyboard player. He met their eyes in turn and found what he sought. He turned back around and addressed his counterparts. "I am without a solution. I maintain that we would do well to refrain from establishing a successor. I have faith we have the intelligence and mutual respect to cooperate in harmony without the need for hierarchy. However, I touch on old ground here; you have both made your position clear. Therefore, it is with reluctance and trepidation that I concede to the proposal. Election by Contest would seem the only method with the required integrity." He dropped his head and stepped backwards, his players by his side.

"It's decided then," said Pale Dexter, unable to hide a triumphant smile. "While our players are here, we should agree on a date. I see no value in delaying. The sooner the better, as far as I'm concerned."

"I agree we should set a date," said Chief, "if only to give Bluemantle sufficient time to disseminate the message. We need word to reach as many followers as possible, including those loyal to Saltire who are yet to form a new allegiance."

"And I see no benefit in rushing when the cost of haste could be the end of us all," said Bend Sinister. "There is more work to be done on our defences, deeper caves to be explored."

"We've spent the last week doing exactly that," said Pale Dexter. "We've blocked old entrances, excavated new. We've retreated deeper than ever before. We've established new performance caves with multiple escape routes. That's if they even detect the sound. We are so deep, the rock so dense. What more do you propose we do?"

"Pale Dexter is right," said Chief. "We've worked hard and accomplished much. I am confident we can compete with less danger of detection." She looked behind her to find expressions of support. She turned back around, arms crossed. "My players and I are agreed. We are ready to compete at the earliest opportunity."

Bend Sinister sighed. He looked to his players beside him, who each reached out and briefly touched his shoulder. "Then it is agreed. The Contest is on. We must each nominate an adjudicator. It will be the responsibility of the adjudicators to collaborate on the recording and verification of audience attendance. The Troubadour who attracts the largest number of followers over a sustained period of time will be declared leader. As in the past, we shall have a long week's grace in which to prepare. We play eight days from tomorrow."

"I shall bid our messenger come," said Chief. "Bluemantle will call our judges forth."

—

Having withdrawn, Bend Sinister sat on a rock in the centre of a small, dimly lit cave, his three players seated around him. They had been silent for some time. The enduring flow of water that, for centuries, had carved caves in stone, trickled in the distance. Beyond the ochre glow of gas lamps, darkness drenched the space, blending rock and hollow into a backdrop of perpetual night.

"I won't lie to you," he said eventually, his voice soft and low.

"And we trust you," said the bassist. "We ask the question because we know you will speak plainly."

"Then I will answer. Yes. I am afraid."

Silence returned, seeping into the space between them, adding weight to the admission. The players waited for more but were denied.

The guitarist cleared his throat and said, "When we agreed to the Contest, it was because we could think of no viable alternative. But there is one option we did not, between us here, consider." They all looked up, curious. "We could choose not to compete."

"And let Chief and Pale Dexter fight it out between themselves?" said the keyboardist in alarm. "Are you serious?"

"Why not?" said the guitarist. "We've been content under the leadership of another for over forty-five years. Why the sudden need for control?"

"But Pale Dexter—"

"He wouldn't be my preferred choice, granted."

"Besides, it's not about desire for control. It's wanting what's best for the Scene. If there has to be a leader, only under Bend Sinister could our situation be improved. And by that I mean the whole Scene, not just us. Pale Dexter would care only for his own."

At this, the three players looked to Bend Sinister, their curiosity begging a response.

Bend Sinister studied the guitarist's face. "I admire and respect your thoughts, my brother. And if it were a case of relinquishing our right to compete so that Chief may claim the title, then I would even go so far as to agree with you. However, as our keyboardist has indicated, Pale Dexter is the issue here. I fear life under his stewardship would feel in stark contrast to the harmony we enjoyed throughout Saltire's reign." He looked at his players with an expression both sad and kind. "Alas, our hand is forced, if only to prevent Pale Dexter from achieving his ambition. And this I concede in the context of the fear that I have admitted to you. I am afraid. But I will not let that influence my thoughts or deeds. It is a feeling I acknowledge and manage. I simply had not shared it with you as I did not want the emotion to assume an influence over your own. And I will not ask the same question of you. I can see the answer in your eyes."

The keyboardist and guitarist dropped their gaze to the floor.

"Do not let it cause you shame," he continued. "We have good reason to be afraid, have we not? Far more so than the others. For we know what it means to lose one of our own." Bend Sinister hesitated, affording the subject space. "We so rarely talk about him. But perhaps this is one of those moments when we should, however painful, because his absence is always with us. His place among us remains empty; the hole that remains is *something*. A permanent lacuna that will never be filled. So, let us remember our drummer."

The guitarist slowly rubbed his arms. "When the Authority raided our show and took him away," he said, "we didn't know what would happen to him. And we still don't. That was twenty-six years ago." He shook his head, his voice breaking. "For me, the not knowing is the hardest part. That and the image I have of when he was captured. I remember it as if it were yesterday. He knew. He knew he would never see us again. That's why I'm afraid. I couldn't bear that happening again."

Bend Sinister reached out and put a hand on the guitarist's shoulder. "We are family. Closer still. I share your fear."

The bassist nodded. "We are the sum of our parts. To lose one is to lose part of ourselves, part of who we all are. Like you, I couldn't endure another loss."

"This is why we never talk about him," said the keyboardist. "Because it's not over. All the while we don't know what happened to him, all the time we face the real and present danger of the same thing happening again, it can't be over. Unless we leave here, that threat will remain."

Bend Sinister looked up at her. "But you understand why we can't leave. Don't you?"

"I understand why we haven't left before now. But we've never actually tried. I just wonder if there is a tipping point, where the conditions we endure here and the danger we face every time we play are worse than the prospect of leaving."

"I appreciate that the perils of leaving may appear a more nebulous threat, but they're not. To my mind, they are as dangerous as the risk of capture. We depend on our followers. We cannot survive without them. If we were to leave Wydeye, we face the real, catastrophic risk of failing to connect elsewhere. That is a scenario informed by experience, not speculation. I know I don't need to remind you of what we endured, how close we came to expiring, before we found Wydeye. We must continue to have faith that one day the regime will change. It has done so once before. The Wydeye of old was a peaceful, halcyon era. I reject the argument that such harmony can never be achieved again."

"It was different then," said the bassist. "We can't get it back."

"My hope lies not in the past, but in the future. In the potential for change." He sat upright, pushing his shoulders back. "I say this with conviction. I absolutely believe leaving Wydeye poses the greater threat. And abstaining from the Contest is not an option, despite the danger it puts us in. Absit omen. We can only hope the event will pass without incident and we can all move beyond the question of leader."

"But we still need to play to survive. The danger won't end with the Contest."

"That is why we must each manage our fears. When they claim constancy in our lives, we must live beside them, yet not be controlled by them. I look to our followers and think of the danger they, too, are in when they come to see us play. They risk everything. Yet they still come back."

At this Bend Sinister rose, opening wide his arms. "So come, let us be led by their example. There is much to do. We have a Contest to prepare for."

—

Overground, Ursel weaved through Drayloc Market, bound for The Raven. She had only walked a few hundred yards from the tramway terminus, but already the bandana tied over her mouth bore a dark, damp circle. The dust cloud was thickening.

Drayloc Market looked unearthly in the dense desert smog. Citizens were reduced to hunched shapes and shadows. Determined barkers hollered their wares through scarves, their spiel muffled and remote. Smoke from food-stall braziers formed a smudge of grey upon orange. Goats hung their heads, eyes closed, sneezing.

An Allear Unit marched past, the majority accustomed to the lack of visibility.

The rare weather conditions exacerbated the discomfort already felt from the sultry heat. Skin, damp from perspiration, was perpetually gritted with fine sand. Many citizens had resorted to shaving their heads, unable to endure itching scalps from dust-clogged hair.

It was late afternoon. Ursel had just finished her shift at the iron refinery in Coxen Lyme. With a brief window of freedom before her evening performance, she had decided to stop for a drink at The Raven, recently reopened after extensive post-raid repairs. As she approached the bar, she noticed a familiar face to her left, seated in a dark recess. "A Kitson and a lemon seltzer, please," she said to the barman. Once served, she carried the drinks over to the man in the shadows. "Mind if I join you?" she asked, with a kind, familiar smile.

Cole looked up, surprised. "Ursel. Good to see you," he said. "Please do." He pulled out a stool opposite him. Ursel placed the Kitson beside his near-empty glass. "That's kind. Thank you."

"I figure you've earnt it," she said in a half-whisper. "On your own?"

"Yes. Need to muster some courage. I've just received news that Evan's not going to like."

Ursel raised an eyebrow.

Cole switched tracks. "It's dead in here. I think people are still staying away."

They both looked around the room, which was short of a few tables and chairs lost to unreplaced breakages. The place was quiet; a dozen or so people perched in corners or shadowed alcoves.

Maintaining his idle observation of their surroundings, Cole dropped his voice and said, "I'm glad you made it back okay. I know a lot who didn't."

"Any word on them?" she asked, mimicking his feigned nonchalance, a counterpoint to the strain in their voices.

"Only rumours. Interrogation, torture, no trial. The usual."

A silence pooled between them, thoughts having turned to all-too-familiar impressions of horror. Followers knew the score, knew the risks and the high price they commanded. The fact they believed the risks were worth taking did not make the consequences bearable. They just mutually acknowledged there was nothing meaningful to be said in such moments. Cole and Ursel sipped their drinks in silent outrage.

Eventually, Cole spoke. "It won't end there."

"What do you mean?" said Ursel, unable now to resist looking straight at him.

"I guess I'm as safe to tell you in here as outside." He rested his chin on his hand so that his fingers almost covered his mouth. "I've just been underground. I was summoned." Ursel stared, struggling to freeze her face to mask her reaction. "There's going to be a Contest. To elect a new leader. I'm to start work on *Bluemantle* straight away." He looked into her eyes. "We need to put the word out. People aren't going to expect an event so soon; they might not think to look out for a drop. But the news has to reach every single follower of the Scene. This is the most important event the Troubadours have ever held. We can't have followers too afraid to attend."

Ursel swallowed hard and nodded. The original Contest was the subject of legend – a dramatic climax immortalised in *The Travelling Minstrels*. No follower ever imagined such an event would ever happen again. Then came Saltire's death. Ursel realised that it hadn't occurred to her Saltire's position would need to be filled.

The implications flooded her mind in a riptide of realisation. *This is huge*, she thought. And, in the wake of the raid, the risks were higher than they had ever been. The Authority's anger and frustration were not a matter of speculation; the radio broadcasts and ubiquitous murals reinforced the fact.

"I take it you can't tell me when and where?"

"SOP, you know that. I'll distribute on Saturday. Then you'll find out."

"What can I do to help?"

"Spread the word. Tell them to look out for *Bluemantle*. Don't tell them what it's about. Just tell them it's coming."

CHAPTER FIFTEEN

Inside the Allears Training Centre, Governor Blix glided down a concrete corridor, torso erect, her sharp grey suit marble-rigid. Her eyes glared from left to right, catching glimpses of brightly lit rooms through glazed letterbox apertures. Wulfwin walked one step behind her, hands behind his back, his leather trench coat reflecting the strip lighting above.

Blix stopped beside one of the oblong windows and stared at the scene beyond. "Progress," she said. "Talk me through."

Wulfwin stood beside her, shoulder to shoulder. "Eight made the grade. None in the first rank. They all require adjustment." He looked through the window at a small form lying on an operating table, grey cloth covering all but a strip of face where eyes once belonged. A woman in a white gown was leaning over the body. She trimmed a suture, completing two lines of stitches side by side: gentle half-moons, mirroring the brows above. Blix and Wulfwin watched as the woman picked up a razor and gently ran it over each brow, erasing them with a single swipe.

"Commander Lore made a number of changes to the Test," said Wulfwin. "They are designed to reduce the instances of surgical intervention to achieve a higher proportion of sighted Allears. However, the modifications will take time; we need more resources now. All eight have had the procedure."

"Timescales," said Blix, her eyes fixed on the child.

"Ordinarily, six months. I've manipulated the programme to fast-track this cohort, as per your orders. We usually begin with Chromatofen ingestion and a period of attitude retraining, modifying their established ideologies until fully aligned. I've brought their physical adjustment forward so that their aural sensitivity can adapt to the changes while we work on their minds. They should be ready to enter the field in four months."

"I want them ready in three." Blix turned away from the window, her eyes as cold and unyielding as the concrete that surrounded them. "Show me the latest graduates."

Wulfwin led Blix through a maze of corridors, punctuated occasionally by solid steel doors. Eventually they reached a door left slightly ajar, through which a low, expressionless voice could be heard. "Wait," said Blix as Wulfwin went to push it open. "I want to observe unnoticed."

Without a word, Wulfwin turned and led Blix further down the corridor, up two flights of formed concrete stairs and into a small, windowless room. A uniformed officer was seated behind a monitor, her startled face luminescent in the screen's blue glare. Recognising who stood in the doorway, she jumped up and saluted.

"We need this room," said Wulfwin. The officer began to gather some papers and a notebook from the desk. "Leave everything. Wait outside." The officer did as instructed and scurried out, saluting once more as she passed Blix on the threshold.

Wulfwin gestured for Blix to sit in front of the monitor. On the desk was a bank of switches and dials. As he operated the controls, the image on the monitor jumped to different scenes: training rooms, laboratories, wards and dorms around the Centre. He stopped when the screen showed a top down view of Dent Lore addressing a group of recruits in Forces-issue coveralls. He flicked a switch and Dent's voice crackled from speakers either side of the monitor.

"...*training have led to this. You bear a great responsibility, on which the Authority depends,*" came Dent's voice, low and level.

Blix spoke over the monologue. "You have vouched for Commander Lore. You are confident of his loyalty, but you acknowledged a reluctance to recruit. I've yet to feel reassured."

"I find his lack of passion strange. There is evident commitment, but no fire. No fury. It frustrates me, but it does not concern me."

"And that is supposed to reassure me."

"His motive for temporarily limiting recruitment was sound in theory. His proposal to modify the Test to achieve more sighted Allears bears merit. If his plan succeeds, I will even be impressed. It will improve performance significantly."

"Your conclusion."

"His rationale was laudable. He did not consider timescales and the need to increase resources. Since I raised the issue, in the context of your displeasure, he has responded positively. He is keen to start work on the new recruits the moment they recover from surgery."

Blix stared at the screen, scrutinising the top of Dent's head and his broad shoulders. The angle of the camera meant she couldn't see his face. His address continued: "...*in service to the Authority and its ambition to apprehend the Music Makers. Failure will not be tolerated...*"

"I've seen enough," said Blix, standing up. "We are done. I must return to my office."

"Before you leave, there's something else you should know."

"Continue."

"We have a sleeper in the field. Sent us a Code S."

Blix stared at Wulfwin, eyebrows raised, her breath quickening.

"I've met with him," he continued. "He's become active. It was he who corroborated the intel from that kid from the Exchange, the lead about the last event. He says he has integrated with a high-value source."

"This is positive news. We should arrest his source."

"If I may offer my opinion, Governor, we would do well to wait. It is likely we will learn more through covert means. The sleeper in question has proved a reliable informer in the past."

"I couldn't care less about your sleeper. Tell me more about his source."

"That's all I know. It's a new development."

"Then find out," she said, failing to suppress a tremble in her voice. "And if you can't, we step in. I don't have time for games."

Wulfwin watched Blix with a calm, steady stare. He had noticed a tremor in her hands, which she now held behind her back. "May I offer counsel, Governor?"

"You may."

"I strongly recommend we hold off intervening until his source proves unreliable or has gone cold. I see no risk in doing so. Instead, there is potential for us to learn vital information that could lead us directly to the Makers. I believe patience will reward."

She looked away from him, touching the side of her neck with her long, pale fingers. Beneath her skin, she could feel her flesh pulsate in time with the thudding in her chest. Taking a deep breath, she said, "I hear your counsel. We hold back. For now. In the meantime, I demand regular updates. Everything you know, I must know. Immediately."

"As you wish, Governor."

Back in her office, alone at last, Blix collapsed in the chair behind her desk. She had locked her door and drawn the blinds, blocking out the orange glow from the thickening dust cloud. Fumbling to open a drawer beside her, she pulled out a small, silver box. With trembling hands, she opened the box and tipped out two white pills. She put them in her mouth, wincing as she swallowed.

A sheen had formed on her face, dampening the edge of her hair where it was scraped back into a bun. Her neck had flushed from pale to pink where her clipped nails had attacked the creeping itch. Anxiety wracked her body, agitating every nerve, causing her heart to race.

What had begun as a commitment to Governor Wallace's legacy had grown into a dark, consuming obsession. She had expanded the Deaf Squad, strengthened the Allears, built countless more whisper dishes. Yet, in twenty years of being in power, she had failed to claim the life of a single Music Maker. She felt their very existence to be a perpetual taunt, a pervasive threat to her control of the city and its impressionable citizens.

She would not rest until they were destroyed.

She gripped the edge of the chair and struggled to slow her breathing. Her eyes fell on the latest Project Alpha report, which lay on the desk before her. She picked it up and flicked through the pages until she found a table densely filled with numbers. Below this were charts in various format. As she ran a finger along lines of data, her breathing gradually slowed and the faintest, most diluted hint of colour returned to her cheeks.

She had read the report several times already. The project was ahead of schedule and achieving positive outcomes. Her ambition for export diversification and wealth generation was one step closer to becoming a reality.

Closing the report, Blix leant back against the chair and closed her eyes, relishing the calming effects of order, success and the five hundred milligrams of Meezel dissolving into her bloodstream.

—

Dent Lore stood before the glazed aperture, silently observing the scene within. The room was like a small hospital ward, with two rows of four beds facing each other. In the beds lay eight small bodies in striped pyjamas. Bandages were wrapped around their heads, covering their eyes and nose. Tubes ran from raised pouches of opaque liquid down to limp arms. A man in a white lab coat moved from one bed to another, administering an injection into the upper left arm of each occupant, then scribbling something on a clipboard at the end of their bed.

It had been five days since the children had been taken, two days since their physical adjustment. They were now receiving their first dose of Chromatofen. Dressings would be removed tomorrow. Training scheduled to commence the day after.

The man in the white coat injected the last child. As he moved around the bed to pick up the clipboard, he caught sight of Dent through the window. Their eyes met.

The contact was fleeting, but it was enough for Dent to read the man's expression. The faintest trace of accusation, laced with muted disgust. Then the man looked down at the clipboard and jotted something. He replaced it, checked the child's pulse and left the room.

Eight minors, aged between fourteen and sixteen. Five girls, three boys. In twenty-four hours, the remainder of their adjustment would become Dent's responsibility. Aside from the daily dose of Chromatofen to ensure compliance, it would be his own devised programme of training and re-education that would transform them from civilian minors into an elite Special Force. And his time to achieve this end had been reduced by half.

When Wulfwin had told him about the deadline, he had believed it impossible. Then he refocused, summoned resolution. If the Governor willed it to be done, then it must be done. If the timescale was required to serve the Authority's needs, then he had to do everything in his power to achieve success. This was his motivation, his sole ambition.

Despite his ploy to minimise their suffering, the damage had already been done by hands not his own. The children had been forcibly taken, their bodies unnecessarily mutilated. He could not undo the violence. What else, then, but to endeavour to ensure it wasn't all for nothing? The logic salved his conscience. The look in the man's eyes was a passing stab at an already tender wound. Dent repressed the hurt with faith that it wouldn't last.

Submerged in his thoughts, he failed to hear footsteps approach. A voice directly behind him, close to his left ear, brought him rushing to the surface. "Tell me what you see," it said.

Dent spun around and came face to face with Blix. "Governor—"

"Look at them, not me," she said in a cut-glass half-whisper. "I repeat. Tell me what you see."

His heart pounding, Dent grappled with composure. Taking deep breaths, he surveyed the scene through Allear eyes. "I see potential, Governor. Latent talent that is my responsibility to make manifest and maximise."

"Interesting. You say it is your responsibility. I am curious to know your will."

"My will is to serve you, Governor Blix, and the Authority. I am loyal to the cause."

"You mention loyalty. I did not." She stepped back. "Turn and face me." Dent obeyed, looking ahead in the poise of salute. "Look at me." A moment's hesitation, then Dent met and held her piercing stare. "Now respond in a way that isn't textbook arse-licking."

Faint lines crept across Dent's brow as he struggled to reformulate his response. Wary of how hesitation may appear, he said, "I speak the truth as plainly as I know how. My will is committed to serving your own. In the context of my function as an Allear, it is to assist the Authority in the detection and capture of the Music Makers. It is what I am trained to do; it is all I want to do. Your goal is mine."

Blix studied his face, intent on reading expression in his eyes. Then it occurred to her why it was, indeed, such a struggle. She recalled what Wulfwin had said to her, how he lacked passion. No fire and fury. That was it, she realised. It was like gazing into glass marbles – lifeless orbs. Satisfied for the time being, she nodded once, then looked away, into the dormitory. "They are here because they passed the Test. If they fail to pass the training, it is because you have failed to realise their potential. If you like, their training is your Test. You are thoroughly expendable. You'll do well to remember that." She turned and walked slowly down the hallway.

Dent stared at her retreating form. Beads of sweat broke ranks, forming and falling down his brow. His mind scrutinised the exchange. He believed he had spoken in all honesty, expressing genuine commitment. *So why do I feel like I've already failed?* he thought.

CHAPTER SIXTEEN

Chase shuffled along with the crowd, emerging into the murky haze of dusk. Somehow, the space inside the big top had remained clear of the otherwise pervasive airborne sand. Stepping into the dust cloud was a sudden, unpleasant reminder of how difficult it had become to breathe.

"Chase?" called a voice from behind him. He turned around to see a shadow enlarge as someone approached. "I thought it was you."

"Oh. Hello, Ursel."

Ursel was still in costume, heavy face paint making her appear strangely unfamiliar. She had removed the long, white wig that had made her almost unrecognisable on stage. Smiling, she ran her hand through her hair, which clung to her temples, damp and compressed. "I thought I saw you in the audience. You didn't tell me you were coming."

"It was last minute." He faltered, thrown by a strange disorientation.

"Have you got time for a drink? We can go to the catering tent. I'll shout you a Pyncher."

Chase hesitated, grappling with the unexpected. Then he said, "Sure," and followed Ursel away from the departing crowd.

She led him first to her yurt, saying, "Wait out here. I'll be five minutes," before disappearing inside. To Chase's relief, she emerged looking like the Ursel he knew: stage make-up and costume removed, replaced with a simple grey tunic and a touch of eyeliner. "Come on, let's get that drink," she said.

The catering tent was little more than a large awning spanning several long trestle tables, banked by benches. Mismatched lengths of fabric had been pegged to the awning's edge, creating makeshift walls, in an effort to keep out the cloud. Inside and at one end was a wooden caravan, its side opened up to reveal a basic kitchen. Before it stood a long table, behind which a man and a woman served bowls of steaming soup and fist-thick chunks of bread. Ursel walked up to the far end of the table, to a large pitcher and stacked glasses. She helped herself, filling two glasses. "Here you go," she said, handing one to Chase, who hung behind her.

Many of the performers who Chase had just seen on stage began wandering into the tent, chatting as they queued for soup. Ursel led Chase to a corner furthest from the kitchen. They sat down, facing each other. "What did you think of the show?" she asked.

"I enjoyed it. I was surprised how much."

"You've not seen *The One-Legged Crow* before, then?"

"I've not seen anything at the Circus. Although, I know the story. Everyone does."

"Well, I hope you think we do it justice. It's important we capture the essence. That's the whole point. Our efforts are redundant otherwise."

"What do you mean?"

"The whole idea of the Telltale Circus is to enact the crux of the tale, the kernel of truth at the heart of the story. The founders believed in the oral tradition, spreading the word to keep it alive. They recognised that the message of a folktale is just as relevant outside of the community it came from."

"Then why did they stop travelling?"

"That's the question."

Chase frowned, bemused. "And?"

"I've yet to know the answer." A smile crept into her eyes. "But that's okay. A question only becomes a problem if it's not addressed." She tipped her head towards the tattoo on her shoulder. "As long as we keep asking 'why', we'll discover the answer eventually."

"Don't you ever want to move on?"

"This is my home. Despite my travelling forefathers, I've only ever known Wydeye. And besides," she added, lowering her voice, "there's more than stories to keep me here."

Chase noticed a subtle change in her expression. Her eyes turned from ebony to onyx; her lips were tight yet shaped by the faintest upturn at either end; her long, pale fingers grasped the shoulder above her absent limb. This change reminded him of the night underground – the look on her face as she watched Chief perform. At the time he, too, experienced the joy that held her in raptures. Now, sitting before her, he wished some trace of it still lingered inside him.

As if reading his mind, she said, "I know you felt something that night. It's gone now, but I wonder if you remember what it meant to you. Even if there aren't words to describe it."

"I—"

"Wait, that wasn't a question. There's something different I want to ask you. If you can recall something of how it felt, has it changed your perception? Even if you wouldn't do the same yourself, can you now see why some choose to participate in the Scene?"

"It…" Chase faltered and looked away, staring at a distant nothing. "It's hard. The feeling was so strong at the time, yet I feel nothing of it now."

"But a realisation? Of why some choose to follow?"

Chase dragged his eyes back to the space between them. He stared at their glasses, avoiding Ursel's searching expression. "I think so. Yes."

"Look at me."

Chase hesitated, then looked up to meet her gaze. Something jolted inside him.

"I trust you," she said. "But I need to be sure. If what you felt has changed your impression of the Scene, then I know I'm right about you."

Chase closed his eyes and saw himself on the edge of a precipice. He couldn't tell which direction it would mean to fall. He opened his eyes and looked into Ursel's. "What I felt has changed everything."

Ursel let out a deep breath and released her shoulder. Her whole body relaxed, like overstretched elastic. Taking a moment to regain her composure, she said at last, "There's something I need to tell you." She swallowed and reached out, touching his hand. "I've heard news. There's going to be another chance to find Wella."

—

"…so the old guy says to the barman, 'You can keep your donkey. My chain's too old for the pulling,'" at which Weldon cracked up, bent double with laughter.

Despite herself, Tinashe laughed too. The joke didn't need

to be funny; she felt Weldon had a way of telling them which made his own good humour infectious.

It was early evening. They had been playing leicon for an hour at the Bayley Road Sports Centre on the edge of Glade Park in Spire Wells. Having just finished a match, they were packing up their gear, red-faced and breathless.

The tension from their argument a week ago had been short-lived. Tinashe knew Weldon to be sensitive; his reaction to the swallow hole didn't surprise her. His rant against 'Users', however, troubled her. She feared the degree to which he was influenced by the Authority's escalating campaign, with its graphic demonisation of the Scene. Yet she knew Weldon's response was the prevailing reaction. The murals made it easy for citizens to blame the Scene: a simple target and a plausible scapegoat.

He nudged her with his elbow. "Listen to this. I've got another one—"

"Save it for the journey." She pulled out a pencil and a scrap of paper from her kit bag and scribbled something down. Folding the paper, she handed it to Weldon.

"What's this?"

"Today's score."

Weldon unfolded the paper and read, "*Weldon – twelve. Tinashe – twenty-one.*"

"I noticed you failed to bring our score pad. Don't want you forgetting the damage on the rare occasion I actually beat your bony arse."

Weldon laughed and shoved the piece of paper in his wallet.

"Come on, let's go," she said. "We're already late."

They had arranged to meet Chase and Naylor at Su-Lin's, a café on Third Went that specialised in traditional Wydeye street food. The café was little more than a timber shack, recently reinforced with recycled paper pasted to the walls to keep out the cloud. Inside, smoke-spewing braziers stood in the centre. A large hole in the roof allowed the smoke to escape and the patrons to breathe. Circling the braziers were an assortment of pallets and packing crates, roughly modified to function as tables and stools. Citizens perched, holding foil parcels in one hand, picking at the contents with the other. The menu was limited yet popular: kobbos, a spiced lentil cake, and balkra, cold curried meatballs, finished off with mishi, fried rice balls dipped in sugar syrup.

By the time they reached Su-Lin's, Naylor had already arrived and was stood in the queue. He gestured with raised arm and a stabbing index finger towards a vacant table. Weldon responded with a thumbs-up and weaved a path over to the table, followed by Tinashe.

It had been nearly two weeks since the raids. Fear continued to loom large, with Special Forces maintaining an intimidating presence. New pictures appeared on the Wall of the Missing, including those of a number of children. No one dared to ask questions, or even to speculate. Citizens were well aware of the consequence of paying uninvited attention. And when any neighbour, work colleague or cousin could be an informer, talking in confidence required a high-risk faith in trust. Wary of threat from all sides, most citizens felt they had no choice but to hold their tongue.

Despite the air of fear and intimidation, the size and condition of most quarters, particularly in Rader, forced the issue of venturing out. As a result, the café was fairly busy.

Having queued for food, Naylor approached, arms loaded with parcels of wrapped foil. He let them tumble to the table and sat down. "Dig in," he said, with a smile that didn't appear to belong.

"Thanks," said Tinashe, reaching for a parcel and teasing it open. "Where's Chase?"

"I don't know. He said he had to go somewhere but that he'd come after."

Eyes down, they tasted the food in silence.

Tinashe glanced at Naylor. His fraught expression betrayed a mind elsewhere. "So, anyway," she said, attempting to sound more casual than concerned, "how's things with you?"

"Oh, you know. Head low, wings like the crow and all that."

"And Clo?"

"Not so good. It's that time of year again."

"Oh yes, the Test. How did she get on?"

"Bad news. She has to resit." Naylor shrugged, raising his eyebrows. "Oh well, there's always next year."

"That's tough for her. Same thing's happened to the son of a friend of mine. It's not like it's something you can revise for. And he's one of these competitive types; he has to know where he went wrong so he can improve. But they don't tell you, do they?"

"No. They don't tell you anything. She's the only one left in her grade that has to retake. It's really knocked her confidence." He let out a deep sigh. "Hopefully next time."

Weldon reached over and picked up the remaining foil parcel. "I take it this is Chase's? He's too late. I'm claiming it." He ripped open the parcel and tucked in.

"Actually," said Naylor, "while he's not here, there's something I wanted to flag with you both. Not necessarily for you to do anything about. Just in case it, you know, comes up."

Tinashe sat up straight, expectant. Weldon watched Naylor whilst eating.

Naylor cleared his throat and lowered his voice. "I'm worried about Chase. He's got wind of another event. He's determined to go again."

"What the...?" said Tinashe, eyes wide.

"You're joking, right?" said Weldon.

Naylor shook his head. "He dropped by my place late last night. He'd been with that woman we met. Ursel. Apparently, she said there's going to be another show and she's convinced Wella's there. Chase is insisting on going to find her."

"Even after what happened last time?" said Tinashe. "He was lucky to escape arrest. Plenty of people didn't. What's he thinking of?"

"What are *they* thinking of, more like," hissed Weldon, pushing his food aside. "Users and their fucking Scene. Why can't they see what they're doing? The danger they cause for the rest of us? Haven't they seen outside the Exchange?"

"I know, I know," said Naylor, trying to keep his voice down. "Look, I'm with you on this. I've seen enough of the fall-out. Nothing's worth the suffering it brings. But, if Ursel's right about another event, it would suggest the Scene doesn't view it in quite the same light. And my problem right now is trying to persuade Chase not to go. I know it already; he won't listen to me. He's too stubborn. But he might take more on board if it's coming from all sides."

"It didn't stop him last time," said Weldon.

Tinashe shook her head and sighed. "I can't imagine he'll listen to us either, but we've got to at least try. Maybe we should change tack. Focus on what Ursel's told him before, that Wella's made a choice. She's where she wants to be."

"As much as I worry for Wella, you could be right," said Naylor. "He could risk his life, only for her to insist she wants to stay. But he won't even consider that. He's just got this big brother protection thing going on. It's like he thinks he can somehow make up for Brann by bringing Wella back."

"For crow's sake, listen to yourselves," said Weldon, his voice wavering.

Tinashe and Naylor looked at him, bemused.

"Both of you. All softly softly, balancing on eggshells

around him. Chase is a grown man. He's capable of making his own decisions. And when he went last time, it was the wrong decision. Now he wants to go again. He knows the risks. He's just proving he's as selfish as the rest of them."

"That's hardly fair—" said Tinashe.

"No. You're missing the point here. While you're debating how best to mollify Chase, you're missing the actual fucking point." He leant in, face flushed, and whispered through gritted teeth, "There's going to be another event. It's all going to happen again." He could feel tears welling and fought to push them back. "The A are right. It's the Scene's fault. Users are the cause. All the terror, all the violence that comes with the raids; we can't blame the Deaf Squad. It's all because of the Scene, so why won't they stop playing? It's all their fucking fault." He stood up, hands shaking. "Say what you like to Chase. I don't care if he goes. If he gets caught, that's his problem. That's the score." He turned and left, bumping into startled diners in his path.

Stunned, Naylor stared in his wake.

Tinashe reached out and touched his arm. "Don't mind him. He's got himself wound up over all this. You know what he's like."

Naylor nodded and dropped his eyes.

"I know you're worried for Chase," she said. "I am too. When he arrives, I'll find a way to raise the subject. We can both speak to him, try to make him see it differently. He's stubborn, but he also respects you. If we're both on the same page, hopefully he'll at least think about it. I'm with you. It has to be worth a try."

Naylor was about to speak but then looked up. He pulled his arm from under Tinashe's hand and sat upright, swallowing hard. "Chase is here. He's coming over."

—

Preoccupied by what was to follow, Chase had forgotten he'd arranged to meet everyone at Su-Lin's. It wasn't until Naylor had called in after work to travel over together that Chase realised the clash. He had tried to duck out of it, scavenging for some plausible excuse, but Naylor had pressed. "Okay. You win," Chase had said. "But I have to go somewhere first. It won't take long. I'll meet you guys there."

Appeased, Naylor had left him and caught the tramway to Five Wents.

Chase had loitered in his quarters, balancing the need to give Naylor a head start, with the knowledge that he couldn't be late for his appointment. After several tense minutes, he set out on his way, tracing a circuitous route through Creaser, heading west into the Messam.

It was past six in the evening; offices had closed for the day. The Messam was a curfew zone; citizens did not loiter on their homeward journey and there were no bars, cafés or stalls to distract them en-route. The only signs of life were office cleaners and street sweepers: stooped shadows in the dust cloud, intent on completing their tasks before the fast-approaching sundown.

With a little time to spare, Chase stepped into a recessed doorway, disappearing under the cover of shadow. His mind flipped between the task at hand and his last conversation with Ursel, all her talk about changing perspective on the Scene. *Yes*, he thought, *something happened at Chief's show*. Something had touched him. But it didn't alter his opinion of the Scene. After what happened to Brann, he doubted anything could change that.

Then his mind flipped forward, to the now, to the coming moments. The moment of choice before the fact of consequence. It sometimes gave him a sense of power. But that wasn't what he sought. It wasn't his motivation. And now, the thought of such a feeling revolted him.

Instead, he kept his mind trained on what he knew to be true. He grasped that belief like a totem. Confidence flourished; self-assurance squared the last remaining circle. It was always the same; this time was no different. Nothing had changed.

Conscious of time, Chase crept into the dying daylight. He ducked down a side street, dwarfed by towering concrete blocks – a soldier ant scurrying to perform its duty. He turned left down a narrow alley and stopped before a solid steel door.

The door opened onto darkness. Stepping inside and closing the door behind him, Chase waited for his eyes to adjust. Shafts of dusty light fell from grilled apertures high above his head, illuminating rectangles of dirt and debris on the cold, concrete floor. A rat darted through one of the patches of light, visible for barely a second, as if the light was a projection and the rat merely frames spliced into footage of nothing. Real, but not real.

The scrape of boot sole against stone killed the silence. A shadow that might have been a pillar before, moved forward. A broad silhouette loomed large, shifting from black to greyscale down one side as it intersected a shaft of light. Chase could make out one side of a man's face, one eye glinting, and one side of a leather trench coat.

"What have you got for me this time?" said Wulfwin.

CHAPTER SEVENTEEN

"You advised me that patience would pay off. It appears you were correct in your counsel." Blix sat bolt upright in her office chair, her long, pale fingers tapping the desk in rapid rhythm. Her eyes scanned Wulfwin's report. "And the news itself…"

"I was surprised, Governor," said Wulfwin. "I had not expected it. Not so soon."

"And this man… Chase Newell. Your assessment of his reliability."

"He's informed for us for some time, albeit in a sleeper capacity. When he has provided us with intelligence, it has proved to be accurate and of value. I have no cause to doubt what he told me last night."

"It has taken you until this morning to inform me. Explain."

"The intelligence, if bona fide, is significant. Whilst I have no cause to query the source, I wanted to cross-check in case we have other information that could verify or falsify it. And, while you were out of sorts when I returned from the meet," he refrained from glancing at the silver pillbox that sat half-hidden by a sheaf of paper, "I thought it best to let you rest and deliver the news, verified, this morning."

Involuntarily, Blix smoothed her hair where it was scraped back into a bun. Not a single strand was out of place. "Judgement approved." She sipped from a glass of water. "This gives us an unexpected and valuable lead. However, we need more. I want details. Specifics. This man, Chase. He must have pressure points."

"They've not been required for some time. Initial cooperation was reluctant. Following a period of re-education and with the influence of his implant, he's been consistently compliant. In recent years, we've not had to apply any pressure at all. He uncovers intelligence, triggers a Code S and comes straight to us."

"Still, everyone has a weakness."

"That's if he knows more than he's told us already."

"Find out. And meanwhile, the Exchange. We've used incentives before."

"We have. But the quality of intelligence has deteriorated of late. I've taken steps to address this."

Blix raised her eyebrows. "Elaborate."

"In the past, we've traded with low-grade intel to stimulate business. The fact that citizens autonomously elect to betray each other in order to obtain something in return holds an intrinsic value that we've sought to manipulate. Everything comes at a price. However, as a result of enticement, we've become too generous with the needy scum who come begging. Citizens are daring to proposition with hearsay and expect something in return. They're taking advantage and we've been rewarding them, undermining the purpose of the whole enterprise.

"Therefore, I've ordered the withdrawal of trade for anything that isn't grade A. This way, the scum will work that bit harder to find us information that's worth us giving a damn. I'm confident the addicted among them will establish ways of obtaining information, even if it means crossing some sanctimonious personal boundary by betraying friends and family. A little push in the right direction. I trust you approve."

"Good work. Forget incentives. Your intervention sounds effective. I look forward to hearing results."

Wulfwin sneered. The cultivation of a society webbed with betrayal; its potential for debasement appealed to him.

"In the meantime," added Blix, "put pressure on your sleeper. If he doesn't know more, I want him to proactively learn more. If what he has told us so far is true, this could be the beginning of the end. And, if that's the case, I demand we know everything there is to know in order to succeed." She rose from her chair, steel-rigid. "The beginning of the end. A hard-fought victory you want as much as I. You are my Chief of Command. Deliver me the Music Makers and destroy the Scene. No matter the cost."

—

"The crow flies low over Glade Park." Evan struggled to get the words out, despite the countless times he had uttered them over the years. It had been an emotional journey over to Old Wydeye Town, to the familiar squat building hiding in its cobbled alleys.

Evan didn't wait for the old man to say anything; he couldn't see the point. Instead, he stepped past him with a nod of fond acknowledgement and approached the wooden cupboard that concealed the basement's hatch. The old man clutched his crooked cane and slowly retreated to his armchair beside the front door and resumed his watch.

Kneeling beside the trap door, Evan was struck by a wave of nauseating doubt. He was about to do something he had considered so many times before but had never dared to follow through. To do so would have been to risk destroying a bridge that led to the only route home. He imagined the bridge stretching before him now, embodying the stakes. Yet this was no gamble; how could it be when he already knew the outcome? *So why go through with it?* he thought, his finger in the lip of the trap door.

He pictured Cole below, hunched over the typewriter, ink-stained fingers pecking at the keys. He imagined Cole's face, the feeling in his stomach whenever their eyes met. The way Cole's expression transformed into light when he laughed. The scar across his back, which he called his 'reminder'. His slight frame, at odds with his strength of character and purpose.

This brief cut-and-paste montage of the man he loved provided the answer. *He is the reason*, he thought. Gritting his teeth, he lifted the hatch and descended into the basement.

Cole looked up from the desk, beamed at Evan, then looked back down. "Almost finished," he said, cutting out a square of printed text and carefully gluing it onto the master.

Evan hung back, watching him work. The space was cramped and poorly lit. Cole worked with an intensity and focus that eclipsed his surroundings. Evan hovered on the periphery, excluded from Cole's sphere of existence, yet pricked by the tension that hung heavy in the air.

Finally, Cole stood up, hands on hips, smiling down on his creation. "Done," he declared. "I'll just get the generator going so I can start copying." He disappeared behind a dresser that formed a partition of sorts. There came a click and a muffled whir. Then another sound, repeated over and over. Cole returned, deftly folding a printed sheet of paper, this way and that, until it formed a ten-page pamphlet. "Here you go. Hot off the press. *Bluemantle*. Contest edition," he said, grinning with pride, as he handed the fanzine to Evan.

"Cole, listen. We need to talk."

"What's wrong?"

Evan stalled, prolonging the moment before he struck the match and held it to the bridge.

"Hey, come on. It's alright," said Cole, approaching Evan and placing a hand on his shoulder. "Talk to me."

"I can't do this anymore. I can't watch you risk your life. I've got a bad feeling about this time. You're not going to make it. I just know it. And I can't bear to lose you. I couldn't live if something happened to you." The words tumbled out of his mouth like lava, engulfing the pass. "I know what *Bluemantle* means to you. That's why I've never pushed you, never put pressure on you to stop. But this time it's different. I'm letting you down and I'm sorry for that. More than you know. And making you choose is pointless. The choice has already been made. I know I can't stop you. But neither can I stand by. I can't wait at home, wondering if they've caught you, knowing what they'd do to you if they do. *When* they do. Because they *will* catch you. One day. And after last time, it feels like you've used up all your lives. No one's that lucky. Not even you."

Cole stood motionless, staring at Evan, his eyes red and welling. A tear breached the lower lid and ran down his face, coursing a route for others to follow. "What... What are you saying?"

"Do what you feel you have to do, but if it's making the drops and attending the Contest, I can't be part of your life anymore. Because while I wait for it to kill you, the fear of losing you is killing me. This isn't an ultimatum. I'd never do that to you. I already know you'll choose *Bluemantle*. And despite everything, I understand why." Crying now, he stepped forward and embraced Cole.

"I won't go," said Cole, holding on to him as if he might drown otherwise. "I'll make the drops, but I'll not attend."

Evan broke away, stepping back. "I think you will."

"I won't. I promise. I don't want to lose you."

"Don't make that promise because then you'll feel worse when the time comes."

"Please—"

"If you decide not to go, I'll be waiting for you. But before now, you've not had to choose. You've always believed you've had to do the things you've done, despite the consequences. And I get that. Which is why I won't stand in your way. But I can't stand behind you anymore, waiting for what I know will come."

"Evan—"

"I love you, Cole. Don't promise you won't go. Just promise you'll survive." Evan dragged his arm across his face, smearing tears. Trembling, he turned and climbed the ladder. He didn't look back.

Cole's legs gave way. He knelt on the floor, head down, his back heaving. The freshly printed copy of *Bluemantle* lay in the dust before him – contraband of the unexpected trade.

He couldn't move, couldn't think. He felt as if half his life had been obliterated before his eyes, leaving the other half in a giddying tail-spin. He remained on the floor, head in his hands, waiting for the whirlwind to stop.

Then he heard a familiar noise above him: the creak of hinges as the trap door was lifted. "Evan...?" he said, hope reigniting his spirit. He dropped his hands and opened his eyes, squinting.

"Is everything okay? I just passed Evan in the street. He looked a wreck." Ursel climbed down the ladder to find Cole crumpled on the floor, his face chalk-white in the half-light. "Cole... Are you alright? What's happened?" She knelt down in front of him, her hand on his shoulder, peering into his tear-streaked face.

Struggling to recount what he could barely comprehend himself, Cole told Ursel what Evan had said.

"Maybe he'll change his mind," offered Ursel, unsure if hope, false or otherwise, would help.

"No. He won't. I could see what it meant for him to tell me."

"What will you do?"

"I don't know." Cole stared at his ink-stained fingers – the undeniable blood on his hands. "In the twenty-five years I've been making *Bluemantle*, we've never needed it as much as we do now. It's never felt so vital."

"Because of the Contest?"

"No. I mean, the Contest is important. Of course it is. Followers must be told. But it's so much more than that. The A have stepped up their campaign, even by their standards. And it's working. You've seen the murals: images of raised fists and jackboot-trampled rats. They're engendering resentment and reinforcing division. I've heard people talk. Even in The Raven. They're soaking up the A's fiction and regurgitating it as fact. They're no longer simply wary of the Scene. There's a hatred brewing, fuelled by the lies the A feeds them. What chance has the Scene to counter the message? How can it compete other than to prove the truth?

"When I started out, all I wanted to do was to share what I had discovered. To grow the audience so that others could experience what I had felt at that first Bend Sinister show. I was sixteen, yet I remember it like it was yesterday. The experience changed my life. I knew others would feel the same, if only they had access. I believed more would be prepared to take the risk if they knew the reward. My hope has always been that the tide might then reverse. If enough people overcame their fear, despite the risks, then there's hope for a movement to challenge the A. Deny the fiction. Growing the audience – that's always been my aim."

"And you're achieving that," said Ursel. "There are hundreds of us. I see new faces each time I go. You're still reaching people; it's still working."

"But it's not enough. It's not happening fast enough. I'm afraid the Scene is close to collapsing. *Bluemantle* can't compete anymore. It can't counter the growing force of prejudice. Hatred and blame are a disease that citizens are too weak to resist. Fear has left them too blind to challenge."

"But that's what you've always responded to. *Bluemantle* invites the challenge. I appreciate progress may feel slow. But it can't be about pace of change. Because what's the alternative? Do nothing and let them win?"

"No, of course not. But at this rate, popular sentiment will overpower us. They portray us as vermin. I can see us becoming drowning rats."

"I don't think you believe that."

He shook his head and sighed. "No. I don't."

Ursel reached out her hand and held his. "You're upset. What's just happened with Evan, that's terrible. I know how close you guys are. And I don't want to say anything now that encourages you to act one way or another. But on the question of *Bluemantle*, I will say this. It has to stand firm. It's the only invitation. It's our only chance."

Cole nodded. "Yes," he said. "You're right. It has to keep going. I have to keep it going. It's just that now, on top of everything, I risk losing the only other thing that means anything to me."

Wary of interfering, Ursel hesitated, then said, "Was it specifically about attending the Contest? Or was it also about making the drop? If he's asked you to choose, is making the drop part of it too?"

"For him, yes, I believe it is."

"And for you?"

Cole sighed and slowly stood up. His shoulders sagged; his arms hung limp by his sides. "The Contest is less of an issue. However important it is, however much I long to be there and have my vote counted, I guess it can happen without me. But *Bluemantle* is different. Making the drop. That's where I don't have a choice. I've made a commitment. I have to…" He broke off, noticing the silence surrounding them. "The copier…" He disappeared behind the dresser. A few moments later, the whir of industry resumed. He reappeared, holding a wad of printed sheets. "I'd best get folding. Excuse me."

"I came by to help. I know you normally manage on your own, but I figured they'd want you to print more. I can do some of the folding. Singlehanded," she added with a smile. "I can help with the drops too, if you like."

Cole hesitated, staring at the spot where Evan had stood. Then he nodded once and placed the copies on the desk. They both stood in silence, pressing fold after defiant fold.

After two hours' work, the fanzine was ready for distribution. Copies were packed into tight, brick-like bundles, wrapped in brown paper bags and stacked tall like a sandbag wall. Ordinarily, Cole would then work his way around the city, hiding bundles in secure locations familiar to followers. This time, however, he had been asked to double the quantity. He knew he couldn't carry too many at a time and still remain inconspicuous. The job of distribution would take several days.

Cole noticed Ursel surveying the wall of bags. "I can manage," he said. "You've already saved me hours on the prep. I can handle it from here."

"I know you can. But you don't have to do this alone."

He brought his fingers to his eyes and gently rubbed.

"But I don't want to interfere," she added, unsure of how to read his hesitation. "This is your deal. I'll do whatever you want. Just know that I'm happy to help."

It was only then that Cole realised what felt odd. Usually by now he would be high on adrenalin, having worked flat out to produce his prized creation. The job of distribution was fraught with danger, yet it was such a crucial part of the whole operation that it usually rewarded him with a deep sense of accomplishment – a rare moment of humble pride. This time it was different. He felt detached from the process, numb to the purpose and what it represented. Pride was replaced by guilt. His sense of accomplishment, now a daunting obligation to a promise already made.

He turned around and picked up a long roll of paper that was leant against the dresser. He knelt down on the floor and unrolled the paper, placing makeshift weights on each corner. It was a large, handdrawn map of Wydeye. "If you're sure, then I would appreciate your help," he said, looking up at Ursel.

She nodded and knelt down beside him, listening carefully as he plotted their separate routes to cover the forty hides he had established across the city.

By the time they left the basement, the first batch of bundles carefully hidden inside their clothes and in a discrete satchel slung over their shoulders, it was early afternoon. As they stepped out into the sand-clogged air, they both welcomed the unexpected cover it provided. A moment's pause, a silent acknowledgement, then they parted, disappearing into the folds of the dense dust cloud.

—

The railmotor trundled through Glade, dropping southward and looping through the district of Tempur. Visibility from the Elevated had deteriorated to zero. The cloud trapped the engine's steam, causing it to linger over the trailers like a delinquent mist. As it condensed, moisture caught particles of fine sand and clung to the windows, adding to accumulating layers of caked dust. The trailers rode blind. Early evening and the passengers already sat in darkness.

Chase regretted his decision to take the tramway. He had a couple of hours before he was due to meet Weldon. His intention had been to kill time and avoid the cloud by taking a circuitous route to his destination: Riat's on Second Went. Hunched in the dark, with no view to distract his myopic attention, his plan had failed. Grunting, he alighted at Tempur Main, having decided to walk back the way he had come.

Weldon had put a call through to him that morning, asking to meet up for a drink. When Chase had met Naylor and Tinashe the previous evening, Tinashe had mentioned how Weldon had stormed out shortly before Chase had arrived. Without going into details, Tinashe had hinted at the cause of his frustration. Knowing Weldon to be a man who spoke his mind without precautionary kid gloves, Chase was curious to hear what he had to say.

As he walked beneath the Elevated, his work-weary body laboured under the effort. All week, his shifts at the quarry had been extended to help cover the growing number of absentees. Employers were not permitted to recruit replacements. As hundreds of citizens remained incarcerated without charge, the paperwork didn't exist to legitimately declare their posts vacant. Consequently, those at liberty to work were forced to pick up the slack. Since the raids and the subsequent arrests, Chase's hours had risen from sixty to seventy-two a week, without adjustment to remuneration. His co-workers cursed the Scene, blaming the extended hours on the Users who participated in it. Chase didn't regard the cause and effect in such simplistic terms. However, he sympathised with and shared their rumbling frustration. *Another reason*, he thought.

But the justification didn't break the arris in the way it usually did. His mind dwelt on his meeting with Wulfwin, struggling in vain to pinpoint the cause of a gestating disquiet. The encounter had progressed as it had done so in the past. Information provided in exchange for a deal struck long ago. A deal whereby he would always be in debt. Yet, the enduring terms of repayment had never troubled him. On the contrary, he had become a willing informer, finding an ulterior motive that sweetened the pill. *So, what's changed?* he wondered.

With his mind still preoccupied by the question, Chase found himself on the approach to Tempur Cross, the district's central square. Realising he must have exited the tramway station and turned right instead of left, he cursed under his breath. Turning around, he picked up his pace, hurrying along the underpass in the opposite direction.

A movement to his right caught his eye.

He paused involuntarily, eyes peering through the gloom towards the cause of his distraction. What had appeared to be a bulbous shadow in the throat of an alleyway, now became elongated and hovered towards him. The dust cloud parted to reveal a man, shoulders hunched and eyes darting from side to side. As the man shuffled past him, there was something in his expression that Chase recognised. Baffled, he couldn't place the face. Then recognition struck him. *Ah, that's who!* he thought, smiling at the satisfaction of a mystery solved. Then the reality of the stranger's identity slowly dawned on him. He didn't have a name. The association was enough.

It was the man he'd seen at Chief's show. The man who Ursel knew.

The man who created *Bluemantle*.

Chase watched him merge with the cloud, feeling an odd sense of relief that he hadn't been recognised in return. *But why would he?* he thought. *And why would it even matter?* Then the questions faded, overcome by a compelling curiosity as to what the man was doing. Intrigue, laced with the scent of opportunity, snapped his mind to attention. He hurried after the receding form, afraid that he would lose sight of him in the sandy gloom.

Whilst the cloud gave Chase cover, it also made it far more difficult to follow from a safe distance. Darting between the stanchions of the Elevated, Chase tailed the man on the underpass, heading east, away from Tempur Cross and at right angles to his route back to Bayley Road. He had already decided Weldon would have to wait.

After a short while, the man looked both ways before slipping down a narrow side street. Chase approached, peering cautiously around a dilapidated building on the corner of the junction. He strained to make out the man's nebulous form. Bending down, he appeared to be tampering with something fixed to the side of the building, knee-high from the ground.

The man stood up and headed back to the underpass. Chase ducked into the shade of a building's open porch. Once again, the man walked straight past him, oblivious of his observer, despite his furtive glances this way and that. Confident that the man was unaware of his pursuer, Chase followed.

A few blocks on, they broke away from the underpass, heading down a side street, off which the man turned left then right. Eventually he paused outside a six-storey block of residential quarters. Tiny apertures perforated the concrete, affording a view truncated by identical blocks opposite. Chase hung back while the man entered. After a few moments, a light appeared through an aperture on the fourth floor. Barely visible, yet somehow distinct in Chase's mind, the man appeared, closing the shutters on his home.

Chase made a mental note of the address. Then he turned around and retraced his steps, back to the narrow side street.

The light was fading fast; it was difficult to make out the forms that were reduced to black on grey. Feeling his way, Chase stopped at what he thought was the place where the man had crouched down. Attached to the wall was a water trough, one of thousands installed around the city when the goat population was reaching its peak. The trough was empty, bar a crust of fine sand. He felt along the walls to either side but found nothing untoward. He was about to stand up to investigate elsewhere, when he brushed his fingers along the underside of the trough.

They touched something smooth. Not concrete. Not stone. Something that crackled and crumpled under pressure as he gently teased it out.

A brown paper bag.

—

"Sorry. I got held up," said Chase, out of breath. Having taken a copy of *Bluemantle* from the bundle, he had carefully hidden the package where he'd found it and hurried back to Temple Main and the tramway for Bayley Road. He was over half an hour late.

"Whatever," said Weldon, not getting up from his stool. He was sat in a corner of Riat's, hands wrapped around a half-drunk pint of Kitson.

Come evening, Riat's Noodle Bar was transformed. The food counter was closed down, bowl stacks cleared away. Kegs of Kitson were lined up on the counter beside corked bottles of Pyncher and an assortment of fruit seltzers. Candles were placed on the makeshift tables, flickering over finger bowls filled with spiced corn nuts. The atmosphere morphed from a bustling canteen to a low-lit bar, inviting privacy and quiet conversation.

Chase noted Weldon's fixed stare and pinched mouth. "I've apologised, alright?" Shrugging, he weaved between tables towards the counter.

Weldon watched his back, straining to control his breathing and calm his mind. He had debated for long enough whether or not to ask Chase to meet up; he had deliberated even longer on what it was he wanted to say. Now the moment had arrived, the words became jumbled, his emotions dismantling order. He downed the remainder of his drink.

Chase returned, placing two glasses of Kitson on the table. "I take it I can join you?"

"Sorry," muttered Weldon, standing up and holding out a hand. "Thanks for meeting me." They shook hands with half smiles, then sat down facing each other.

"What's on your mind?" said Chase.

Weldon dropped his shoulders and shuffled on his stool. Taking a deep breath, he said, "Naylor told Tinashe and I that you're planning to go back to… you know…" He lowered his voice. "He told us that there's another event planned." He looked up.

Chase nodded but said nothing.

Weldon continued. "When I left the other evening, before you arrived, they said they were going to try and talk you out of going. But they're so damned wary of pissing you off, I knew they wouldn't say it straight. And correct me if I'm wrong, but I reckon you can cope fine with a dose of straight talking."

"They did spend some time teasing the subject. And, yes, straight talk would be a refreshing change."

"Did they manage to persuade you?"

"No."

"I thought as much."

"Is that what this is about? Are you going to try the hard sell approach?"

"No. You can do what you like. I don't give a toss whether you go or not." Chase raised his eyebrows. "I'm just surprised, that's all. You, of all people."

"I have to find Wella. It's the only way."

"That's bullshit and you know it."

"Well, that's straight alright—"

"You guys have never been close. So what if she's chosen to go with the Scene? Naylor said someone has seen her there, so you know that's where she is, right? It wasn't the hole. Search over. Why not leave her to it?"

"She doesn't know what she's got herself involved with."

"Come on, Chase. Everyone knows what it means to mess with the Scene. That's why Users are scum. They know exactly what they're doing, regardless of the shitstorm it creates for the rest of us."

Chase leant forwards, spitting half-whispered words. "You might be pissed off with me, but we're on the same side. I'm as fucked off with the Scene as you are. The sooner the A puts a stop to it, the better."

Weldon's eyes widened, lit by a glint of comradery.

"That's right," said Chase. "Tinashe told me about your little rant, and I couldn't agree more."

Animated, hands twitching, Weldon spoke in a quiet, tense voice. "It does my head in, you know? We're living at their mercy. If your contact is right and there is another event, the raids will be worse than before. The A won't stand for another failure. The way they responded last time; it was a message. They're so fired up; you just have to listen to the radio to know. I don't blame them, either. Users know the consequences. Not just to themselves. Mates of mine are still banged up without charge. No one's allowed to visit or speak to them. I've no idea how they're doing, if they're coping. And they did fuck all wrong, apart from be in the wrong place at the wrong time."

"I know. More innocent people suffer than those who actually deserve it. Take Brann. How the A reacts is wrong; but, if Users didn't keep the Scene going, the A would leave everyone alone."

"My point exactly. Man, it's so good to know you feel the same. It's become this incendiary taboo, yet it's dividing the city."

"Well, rest assured, I'm with you on this one."

"So, what about that woman? What's her name, who took you last time?"

"Ursel."

"Why don't you report her? She's one of them. The Exchange would jump at the tip-off. You could negotiate a decent deal, I reckon. Meanwhile, they get intel out of her that could lead them straight to the nest."

An image of Ursel flashed across Chase's mind: strapped to a chair, skin torn and bleeding, eyes buried beneath swollen sockets. Bile rose up his throat and he almost gagged. He took a swig of beer to wash it down and buy time to recover.

"I'm serious," said Weldon, oblivious. "It's not like she's a friend. You barely know her. Okay, you might feel bad, knowing what they'll do to her. But if it means leading them to the Scene and an end to it once and for all… Think of all the suffering that'll be avoided in the long run."

The unconscious reaction had receded, leaving behind a wound of recognition, tender to coercion. "No. Leave Ursel out of this."

"What? Why?"

"Because she's trying to help. I know she's part of the Scene, but it's different."

"How, exactly?"

"Because she's Wella's friend. She's helping me in order to help Wella. I can't go behind her back and betray her. Besides,

I need her to take me to the next event. I hear what you're saying about leaving Wella to face the music, but she's still my sister. Unfortunately, blood runs deeper than reason. I have to at least speak to her. And I need Ursel to do that."

"If she knows where and when the next event is, why doesn't she just tell you? She doesn't have to take you there."

"It's some secrecy pact they have. The details are in *Bluemantle* for those who can decipher them. They're not allowed to actually tell anyone."

"That's ridiculous. She'll take you there but can't tell you anything? How's that more secret?"

"I guess it's so that word can't get out beforehand, so the A don't get wind of it."

"She trusts you, right?"

"So she says."

"Then push her. Come up with some excuse. Persuade her to tell you."

"She won't. I know she won't. Besides, she might get suspicious if I start laying on the pressure."

Weldon sat back, arms crossed, eyes small and delving. "Why are you protecting her?"

Again, Chase's chest tightened; his gut rolled. "Look," he said, with more force than he had intended, "I'm protecting Wella, not Ursel." He attempted to reign in the sudden flush of frustration. "Ursel's on our side and I need her to stay that way."

"Everything Users do is a finger up to the rest of us. They don't give a shit, as long as they get their fix. They've given up caring about the consequences, they're that drugged up. Fine, protect her. If that's what you want. But I'm telling you, if the next event is raided, and Wella's captured, then remember you could've done something to stop it. When you're arrested and tortured alongside the hundreds of innocent people who weren't even at the fucking show, then spare a thought as to how things might've turned out different if you'd had the balls to act." Weldon stood up. "I hope I've been straight enough. It's over to you." Denying Chase the final word, he turned and left.

Chase remained, bewildered in the debris of reaction. He had to protect Ursel as his source. He felt sure his rationale had stood up to the pressure. She was his ticket in. Without knowing where and when the event was to be held, she was the only way he'd find it once the time came. Then he'd get word to Wulfwin and the raid would be on. By then, he'd have time to get Wella out. And Ursel too.

He pictured Ursel's face at the Chief show: an image of crystalline emotion that had lodged itself in his memory, reappearing repeatedly since that night. He reached up and touched the scab on his shoulder, suffering its nagging itch. *Ursel's different*, he thought, believing his conviction without understanding why.

—

It was midnight. Weldon stumbled through the Pentagon, propelled by a toxic cocktail of alcohol, frustration and rage.

When he had walked out on Chase, he was too fired up to go home. Cutting through to First Went, he had headed for a Pyncher bar. One gill led to three, then four. Still, his temper would not rest. The arguments kept up relentlessly, stoking the fire of anger and resentment that burnt in his chest. Beside him, pasted onto the wall where he had sat, was an Authority-issued flyer. It depicted a terrified child pressing her hands against her ears, while crotchets and quavers stabbed like bloodied daggers through the walls. Above, the slogan: "*Keep Our Children Safe. Do the Right Thing.*"

Now in the Pentagon, the warm, sand-clogged air did nothing to clear his mind. All he could think about was the children who had gone missing the previous week. Rumours were rife. Stories of infant labour in one of the unmarked factories in Coxen Lyme, speculation about laboratory tests in the Science Centres of the Authority Complex, talk of their use in subterranean excavations beneath a top-secret military base in the Nanso Heights. There was no evidence to suggest their disappearance was somehow connected to both the Authority and the Scene, yet this was the theory that Weldon could not shake. The children's abduction had appalled him. The thought of what might have happened to them filled him with horror.

The Pentagon was deserted. Gas lamps flickered around its perimeter, barely visible through the cloud. He headed what he had thought was west, aiming for Fifth Went and his route to Darlem Fields and home. Instead, he emerged on the underpass of First Went. In front of him stood the monolithic concrete structures of Wydeye's municipal buildings: City Hall, the Civil Museum, Wallace Library, the Exchange.

All night long, the gas lamps burnt on the façade of the Exchange, luring custom towards its insatiable flame. No hour was too late to trade. Weldon felt the pull and approached the steps. He crossed the precinct and walked passively towards its open jaws, oblivious of the other stooped shadows that it sucked in and spewed out.

He didn't know where to go. He stood in the vast hall, blind to the reality of his surroundings, and waited. In time, a uniformed official approached him. "What is the nature of your business?" said a voice.

Weldon blinked and swallowed hard. "I have something to trade," he said.

"What have you got?"

"A name."

CHAPTER EIGHTEEN

"I see my colleagues have worked their powers of persuasion. And yet…" Wulfwin sighed with theatrical exaggeration. He circled the slumped figure on the cell's blood-splattered floor. More blood was smeared at head height on one wall. The cell was small, bare, apart from a waste bucket in one corner. This lone consideration of basic need was redundant; it was clear from the stench and stains that the man had urinated and defecated where he lay.

Weldon was barely conscious. He sensed that someone else was in the cell with him. A man, saying something. Who it was or what he was saying, Weldon did not care. He had moved past the point of caring several hours ago.

During that time, Weldon's understanding of pain had changed. It ceased to be a sensation with definition or parameter. At the start, it had been something physical, excruciating, that was exerted upon him. Then, gradually, it had become all-consuming, obliterating all else. That was when he thought he would die.

But he didn't die. And the pain morphed again, merging with his consciousness to become part of him. Pain had come to define him; he could not feel, think or know anything else. Pain was everything. *He was pain*. And with nothing else to measure it against, nothing beside it to give it form, to demonstrate that this is what it is because this is what it is not, pain ceased to mean anything. And if it meant nothing, Weldon decided he could feel nothing.

His consciousness clung on to the precipice of existence by its trembling fingertips.

Wulfwin kicked the heap of soiled rags with his boot. "What good is this?" he hissed, striding to the cell door. "The idiots have gone too far."

He left the cell and returned a few minutes later with a bucket of water and a wooden chair. He hauled the deadweight body, arms bound behind its back, legs strapped together, onto the chair. He pushed the head back, chucked water into its swollen, purple-patched face and waited.

The shock grabbed Weldon's consciousness by the wrists and hauled it back from the chasm's brink. He coughed and spluttered, head lolling.

"Welcome back," said Wulfwin, standing in front of Weldon, legs astride and arms crossed. "My colleagues can be a little heavy-handed when they don't get their way. And, as I understand it, you haven't played ball. A shame, really. For all involved." Weldon's head tipped forward. Grabbing hair in his fist, Wulfwin tugged it back. "Now, stay with me. We've only just met."

As his consciousness began to take hold, Weldon felt stabs of searing pain in his chest, in his abdomen, across his face. Panic's adrenalin shot through his veins. He had thought it was over; he had so desperately wanted it to be over. And now the pain was back. A tear leaked through bruise-buried eyes.

"But it's your lucky day," continued Wulfwin. "Although, granted, it might not feel like that. You see, I'm more restrained. I'm prepared to give verbal persuasion a fair crack at the whip before resorting to a little arm-twisting. You might be wondering why we didn't meet sooner. Save you some of the discomfort. If you are, I wouldn't blame you. You don't look at all well. Maybe that could have been avoided if we had met sooner. Perhaps. Or maybe if you'd only fucking *talked*." He punctuated the word with a right jab across the face, releasing the hair from his other fist a moment too late so that he was left holding a handful. He picked up the bucket and splashed more water into Weldon's face. "But you seem reluctant to do that. And I don't understand why." Weldon groaned. "Pardon me? Speak, you fucker."

"No more… Know no more…"

"Yes, so you keep telling us. Only, we don't believe you."

"S'true. No more…"

"You give us a name, but you can't tell us her surname. Where she lives. Where she works. What she even fucking looks like. But despite your piss-poor efforts to elaborate, we run a few checks. And guess what? There's no fucking Ursel on state records. As far as we can gather, she doesn't exist. So, either you're playing some sort of ill-advised game, or there's something you're not telling us. Either way, it's not going down well this end.

"So, this is the deal, my friend. You either talk to me now or I finish the job. If this is all some stupid prank, then you deserve what's coming. If, on the other hand, you have more to share about this mysterious Ursel, then I suggest you do so now whilst you're still able to speak. My patience is my greatest weakness. Already it's beyond thin."

"Please…" Weldon writhed in the chair, desperation trumping the pain. "I don't know. I swear…"

"Disappointing." Wulfwin pulled a piece of paper from his coat pocket and slowly unfolded it. "Found this in your wallet, by the way."

Weldon froze.

"Just so you know," said Wulfwin, "I'm a man who doesn't like to lose. So, this is how it's going to play out. I'm going to go and pay your friend a little visit." He made a point of reading from the scrap of paper, despite his audience's inability to see the gesture. "*Tin-a-she*. Is that how you pronounce it? I'm going to call in on Tinashe. See if she can be a little more forthcoming."

"No!" Weldon screamed.

"Oh? You don't like that idea?"

"Leave her. She doesn't know."

"Doesn't know what?"

Weldon howled, wracked by terror at what might happen.

"Last chance," said Wulfwin, sneering at the blind, quivering heap.

Loathing himself, yet torn in despair, Weldon broke. "… Chase… Newell…"

—

Chase had triggered the Code S first thing that morning.

Among the shadows at the rendezvous point, he waited.

He had endured a restless night with little sleep. His conversation with Weldon and the reaction it prompted had rattled him. He had somehow shifted from relishing the upper hand to balancing a house of cards.

Ursel hadn't meant to matter. He was a sleeper because he wanted to bring down the Scene. He hated the Authority; he just hated Users more. That's where he had agreed with Weldon. If Users obeyed the law and stayed away, the Scene would die out. There would be no need for the Deaf Squad and their legitimised brutality. The Wall of the Missing would dwindle, rather than expand on a daily basis. The benefits of the original deal aside, Chase had felt comfortable with the arrangement. His contribution to a desirable outcome suited him.

Now, that comfort had a blade pressed against its throat. Weldon's questions had triggered a reaction he had not anticipated, but which confirmed a suspicion that had crept into his chest when he had witnessed Chief perform. He couldn't articulate why, but Ursel had begun to matter. She was no longer a means to an end. Weldon's suggestion had given intuition an undeniable form.

Whatever other betrayals he was responsible for, he couldn't reveal who she was. He couldn't let her be part of the cost of saving Wella and destroying the Scene.

Hence the precarious cards, poised to topple by his own wrong move.

Wulfwin had already pressed him on the identity of his source. Maintaining a plausible argument for withholding her name was his first hurdle. The second was how to manage the flow of intelligence so that his plan could still work. Wulfwin had trusted him up until now, but he knew that could too easily change. He also knew Wulfwin's reputation; he was not a man to double-cross and expect to survive unscathed.

Inside the dingy basement of a disused industrial unit in Coxen Lyme, Chase waited, his heart racing.

Wulfwin emerged from the shadows, silently appearing as if he had been there all along. His tall, broad frame, coupled with the ankle-length trench coat, made his silhouette huge and imposing. Chase swallowed hard.

Wulfwin stepped into a shaft of faint light, revealing the side of his face that bore the sneering scar. He studied Chase in silence, his mind still processing the morning's interrogation. He had left the man in the Complex Infirmary. There was significant doubt over whether or not he would survive the internal bleeding and punctured lung. It was of no consequence to Wulfwin; he had already won. Two names. It amused him to suspect that the man had little idea of their value.

He stood before Chase, a wry smile on his lips, debating when to play his hand. "What have you got for me?" he said at last.

Chase stepped forward. "I saw a man. In Tempur, yesterday evening. He's part of the Scene, I'm certain. Here," he said, holding out a piece of paper. "An address. I think it's where he lives. You might want to check him out. I believe he's the creator of *Bluemantle*."

Wulfwin raised his eyebrows, now fully engaged. "Really? And what makes you think that?"

"I followed him. Saw him duck down an alley, acting suspicious. I went back later and found a package there, tucked away." He pulled out the fanzine from a pocket in his trousers and held it out to Wulfwin. "*Bluemantle*. He'd been stashing bundles of them."

Wulfwin took the fanzine and glanced through the folded pages. "You have done well, Chase. I'm impressed. And we know what this means, don't we?"

"An event."

"Indeed." Wulfwin nodded slowly, absorbing the implications. "I take it you've read this carefully?"

"Every word. Nothing stands out."

"Meanwhile, we know who can read between the lines." He looked up, his eyes locking on to Chase's so the latter couldn't look away. "Now is the time, Chase. We have to know the date and location in order to pre-empt the show. We can be in position, ready to strike, the moment the Music Makers appear. You have to give up your source. We will make them decipher the code."

"I can't—"

"What do you mean, you *can't?*"

"I, er... We need that person to take me there. The coordinates might not take us all the way."

"The coordinates can take us far enough. Quit bullshitting, Chase."

"I've just given you the address of *Bluemantle's* creator. He writes the damn thing. He'll tell you."

"I'm well aware of that avenue of investigation and I'm looking forward to pursuing it. However, experience tells me some Users can't be broken. If he is, as you suspect, the creator of *Bluemantle* and not just some dope, arm-twisted into distributing it, then it means he's heavily involved. Chances are, he'll go all the way and we won't learn a sodding thing. Your source is our back-up."

"Look, I'll persuade the person to tell me the date and place. That way, we'll know when to be ready and I'll still have them on board. If I give them up now, it burns the bridge for good."

"Nice try."

"What do you mean? I'm serious. We need them on side."

"I'm intrigued, Chase. You seem very protective of a type you've previously branded 'User scum.'"

Chase felt his face flushing. Wulfwin was becoming suspicious, he could tell. He floundered, struggling to come up with a plausible excuse. Then it hit him. Something Ursel had said that first time he and Naylor met her at the Telltale Circus. *"Not quite, but that'll do."* Hoping that he'd interpreted her correctly, he relinquished his forced hand. "Her name's Ursel."

"I know."

"What...?"

"A friend of yours dropped by the Exchange. He betrayed your precious source – not long before he betrayed you." Wulfwin smiled, relishing the reveal.

Chase's mind raced. *Who could've...? Who would...?* he thought. *What else does he know?* The cards collapsed.

"Only, your friend was of limited value. Sure, he told me her name and then linked her to you, but that was it. Turns out she's not on state records. Whereas, you're better acquainted with the woman in question. So, tell me. What's her full name? Where does she live? She must work. Where?"

"I don't know." Chase blinked.

"You're kidding me, right?"

"Honest to crow. They're so fucking paranoid. We meet in public spaces. She's never said anything about herself. All I know is that she's called Ursel and she's a User. She must be going by a false name."

"What does she look like?"

"Short. Fair hair. Late twenties, perhaps."

"Attractive?"

"Not especially."

"Distinguishing features?"

"No."

"How did you meet?"

"Friend of a friend introduced us. The subject of the Scene came up. I feigned interest and she started telling me about it. I lied and said I had a mate who'd gone there and ended up staying, that I needed to get a message to them about their mother being sick. Played for the sympathy vote. Laid it on thick. And it worked. Ursel agreed to take me to the last event. That's when I became active and contacted you."

"You're saying you don't know anything else about her? About where we can find her?"

"Yes."

"So, when you want to speak to her, what do you do? Telepathy?"

"Contact is on her terms. She finds me. She knows where I live and work, where I drink. Now that *Bluemantle's* out, I expect she'll track me down. She'd already offered to take me. She'll want to make sure I'm on standby, even if she doesn't tell me when it is. At least, that's what happened last time." Hope kindled.

Wulfwin stepped forward, peering into Chase's face, breathing heavy. He grabbed him by the neck, almost lifting him off the ground. "If I find out you're lying to me, I will not be held responsible for the pain I will inflict on your sorry, forsaken body. Do I make myself clear?"

Chase nodded, unable to speak, trying not to choke.

"I have myself a reputation. You might've heard about it. Yes?" More nodding. "Let's put it this way, it don't fucking do me justice. Not even close." He squeezed tighter until Chase turned crimson, his eyes bulging. Then Wulfwin let go, stepping back while Chase bent double, holding his neck, gagging for air.

Eventually, Chase stood upright, gathering the remnants of his wits. "I get the message," he said. "I swear, I'm telling the truth. And I've always been good for my word in the past. You know why I inform, why I hate the Scene. Nothing's changed."

"Let's hope so."

"I'll wait for Ursel to approach me. When she does, I'll push for details. I'll make something up, convince her. She trusts me. She might break the rules and tell me."

"And if she doesn't?"

"I'll follow her. Find out where she lives, where she works. Then I'll send a Code S. I'll tell you where to find her."

—

"It's late. This had better warrant my disturbance." Blix stood in the doorway to her private quarters, a grey silk robe wrapped around her angular frame, the bun still firmly in place.

"You gave orders for me to tell you if we learn anything new. Immediately," said Wulfwin.

"Enter." Blix stepped back, inviting Wulfwin in.

Her quarters were as sparse as her office. A single bed was shoehorned into a far corner. A steel desk dominated the central space. The windows were uncovered, revealing a commanding view of the Authority Complex, glowing yellow against the dark night.

Blix stood before her desk, rubbing her arms, her eyes pink and twitching. "Straight to the point."

Wulfwin held out the copy of *Bluemantle* that Chase had given him. "This has just come into circulation. We've yet to decipher the content to determine time and place. But I believe we shall soon have the means to do that."

Blix grasped the pamphlet and stared at its cover, her chest quickening its rise and fall. "Explain."

"Our sleeper has led us to someone who we suspect is *Bluemantle's* creator. My men are preparing. We storm his quarters at dawn."

"If our assumptions on *Bluemantle* are on point, questioning the man behind it will glean nothing."

"I agree. We will interrogate nonetheless. To the end." Imagining the prospect, he failed to resist a creeping sneer.

"Which leaves us without the intelligence we require."

"Other avenues have presented themselves. A rat gave up the name of our sleeper's source. It isn't appearing on state records. However, judging by Chase's reaction, I'm confident the name is the one he knows her by. If we can't trace her, we'll let him do the legwork for us. I'm allowing him a day's grace, then he's under surveillance. We'll know his every move, observe everyone he meets, haul in anyone that could possibly be the source."

"This is uncharacteristic of you, Wulfwin. I would have expected you to command your man to lead you to her immediately. Tell me why not."

"I've reason to suspect he's protecting her. I want to know why. We will still reach the same end. I intend to indulge my curiosity in the meantime. With your permission, Governor."

"As long as we establish the date and location, that's all that matters."

"And we will. You have my word. *Bluemantle* always gives advance notice, so we have a limited window to play with. If Chase doesn't lead us to her in the next twenty-four hours, he will find himself watched and under direct orders. If he resists, he'll be reclassified. He'll find the revised terms of our relationship unendurable. He's already proved himself at ease with betrayal. I'm sure it won't take undue pressure before his desire to protect is compromised."

—

"I know you spoke to Tinashe and Weldon. Tried to get them to talk me out of going," said Chase, his tone abrupt. It was the following evening. He was sat opposite Naylor in The Raven. Naylor had put a call through to him at work, asking to meet there as soon as he finished his shift. "Is that what this is about? Round two?"

"For a start, I did that with your best interests at heart, so drop the attack. I'm worried for you; I don't want you to go. I hoped they might make you see sense."

"You wasted your time—"

"And secondly," he said, cutting in, "no, that's not what this is about."

"So, what's the score then? Why the urgency?"

"I don't know. I was given a message at lunchtime. I think Tinashe had tried calling us both at work, but no one put her through. She managed to persuade the switchboard at my place to message me instead." Chase looked up, the tension in Naylor's voice piquing his interest. "She didn't say what it's about. Just that she had to see us. She should be here any minute."

They both fell silent, feeling a rare awkwardness that rendered small talk an unpalatable pretence. Around them, the mood of the tavern was more jovial than it had been of late. Although far from busy, many of the more frequent patrons had returned, seeking solace in a chilled Kitson and barside banter after a gruelling shift in the furnaces, processing plants and factories of Coxen Lyme. Chase and Naylor idly looked around the room, inviting the ambience to fill the space between them.

Tinashe arrived. She was flustered, breathless, her eyes wide and shifting.

Naylor stood up as she approached. "Tinashe. What's wrong?"

"It's Weldon. Something's wrong. I know it."

Naylor took her arm and led her to a seat at their table. "Okay, okay. Try not to get yourself worked up." He looked squarely at Chase and tipped his head towards the bar. "Chase is going to get you a drink. Now, catch your breath, take your time. Then tell us what you know."

Chase got up and went to the bar, leaving Tinashe sitting rigid. Her braids fell about her face, which was ribbed by deep lines in her skin. "I've been worried about him," she said. "Since he stormed out on us at Su-Lin's. The way he's been talking recently. Getting himself all worked up." She took a deep breath and rubbed at tear-wet eyes. "I saw him briefly on Saturday. He said he was going to see Chase. Wouldn't say what it was about."

Naylor raised his eyebrows and glanced over at Chase at the bar.

Tinashe missed the reaction. "I asked him if we could meet. Explained I was worried. He was fine with hooking up. It was him who suggested getting together for supper yesterday. Invited me over, said he'd cook. When I arrived, he wasn't there. I waited outside for over an hour. He didn't show. I went back, late, then again, this morning. His neighbour said he never came home last night."

Chase returned to his seat and placed a double Pyncher in front of Tinashe. "I didn't know what you wanted."

Naylor turned to Chase and filled him in, then asked, "Did you see Weldon on Saturday?"

"Yes. He'd asked to meet me."

"How was he?"

Chase shrugged. "I don't know. Pissed off?"

"Why? What did you talk about?"

"He tried his own approach at discussing my intention to go back to the Scene. 'Straight talking', was how he put it."

"And did it work?"

"What, as in persuading me not to go? He told me he didn't give a damn whether I went or not. Instead, he tried to get me to give Ursel up to the A. I didn't take kindly to that."

"That doesn't sound like Weldon," said Tinashe, shaking her head.

"So, what happened?" said Naylor.

"Stalemate. I said I wasn't going to betray a friend. He said that, if the event is raided, it'll be my fault for not going to the A. I didn't bow to his petulant demands, so he stormed out. End of story."

"This is why I'm worried," said Tinashe. "Asking you to do that to Ursel. That's not like him. And the anger, the bitterness. I know he's sensitive, takes things too seriously. But this feels different."

"What he said to us," Naylor said to Tinashe, "before he stormed out. The way he's talking about Users. The language is all from the A. You can't escape the posters, the radio messages. But it's like he's absorbed it all. He believes it."

"I know. It's changed him. But that doesn't help… I mean, it doesn't explain."

Chase choked. He recalled Wulfwin's words: "*A friend of yours…*" Truth collided, headlong and crushing.

Naylor stared at Chase, frowning. "Are you alright?"

"I, er…" Chase held his hand to his throat, his face a creeping crimson. "Excuse me." He got up and staggered towards the bar. Holding on to the edge, he struggled to pull himself together. "Water. Please," he croaked as a serving boy approached. He downed the glass handed to him.

Conscious of the others behind him, Chase took deep breaths and closed his eyes. He knew it, without question. It was Weldon who had given Ursel's name – who had also betrayed him. *The bastard*, he thought, fury welling. *What else does he know about her? What else did he tell them?* The realisation he'd felt before, so subtle in its dawning, became iron-strong and undeniable. Panic seized him.

He considered Weldon with contempt. Without a trace of doubt, he knew what would have become of him. Wulfwin's words said it all: "*Your friend was of limited value…*" There was only one way to interpret that, Chase knew. Weldon's disappearance confirmed it. But he couldn't say anything to the others. He gritted his teeth and forced back the fury.

"Sorry about that," he said, returning to the table and sitting down. "Sand in my throat. This cursed cloud. Water helped." He coughed, hand to chest.

"Tinashe was just saying she's tried the sports centre and his work. He's not staying with family. I can't think of anywhere else he'd sleep. Can you?"

"Not off the top of my head." He heard the tone of his own voice. He tried harder to sound like he cared. "If he's got himself wound up, maybe he's just laying low to let off steam." He laid a hand on Tinashe's arm.

"Maybe. Hopefully..." she said.

There was a clatter at the entrance, apologies as a fallen chair was righted. The low sun made the apertures glow bright against the dark silhouette that stood in the doorway. It approached their table, swift with intent. Chase stood up as the shadow faded to reveal features. "Ursel?"

She grabbed his arm and pulled him to one side. Her eyes were wide, her skin glowing. "I've been looking for you everywhere."

"What is it? What's wrong?"

"The fucking A. They've raided Cole's flat."

"Hold on. I don't understand. Who's Cole?"

"The creator of *Bluemantle*. I pointed him out at Chief's show. Evan, his partner, is safe; he wasn't home at the time. But he's pretty sure Cole was. If they've got Cole, they've got *Bluemantle*."

She gripped his arm, her knuckles white. "It's over, Chase. Without *Bluemantle*, the Scene can't survive. It's finished."

CHAPTER NINETEEN

Chief and Pale Dexter stood opposite each other, the small cave's width apart. Pale Dexter eyed his opponent with cool suspicion. Chief maintained her gaze on the archway through which Bend Sinister was due to appear.

"He is late," muttered Pale Dexter. "He calls an unscheduled assembly, then fails to attend on time. He's not one for mind games, but then perhaps he's resorted to desperate measures."

"I'm sure there's good reason enough."

"Rumour has it one of his players suggested not competing. Stepping back and letting us two battle it out."

"Eavesdropping? That's low, even by your standards."

"Echoes travel far in these caves. My player couldn't help but overhear."

"I find that highly unlikely." Chief turned to face Pale Dexter, her cobalt eyes interrogating his. "This must be a fair Contest. Any misadventure will not be tolerated. There has to be trust between us."

"It is you who lacks trust to imply such a thing is even possible. We have shared a code of honour for two hundred years. A little respect at this testing time would serve us well."

"As would privacy."

"It was unintentional."

Chief set her jaw.

Pale Dexter smiled. "Anyway," he continued. "You and Bend Sinister converse from time to time. Do you know why he has called this assembly?"

"No. I…"

Breathless and flustered, Bend Sinister appeared. "My apologies to you both. One of my players was taken ill. I had to attend to him."

Pale Dexter failed to repress his amusement.

Chief caught his look and sought to compensate. "I am sorry to hear that. I trust his illness is not grave? Can I do anything to assist? I have a healer among my players."

"I am grateful for your kind offer, Chief. But no, it is not serious and will pass with rest and nourishment, I feel sure."

"Well, now that we've settled that…" said Pale Dexter, taking up space in the centre of the cave and projecting his voice. "You have summoned us to an unscheduled assembly, Bend Sinister. Please, enlighten us as to the reason."

"The matter is most distressing. I have just received news from a follower overground. Bluemantle is absent, feared captured."

"Oh no," cried Chief, hands to mouth.

Pale Dexter gaped at Bend Sinister. "Are you sure? Can this be verified? You realise what this means… Perhaps they are mistaken?"

"It appears unlikely. The follower has spoken to others with connections to Bluemantle. Consensus is that he's been taken. His work is known to the A. He will not cooperate and they will not let him live. Therefore, we must assume Bluemantle is no more. And, as that appears to be the case, I urge us to take a moment to reflect upon the loss before we dissect the implications."

The three Troubadours bowed their heads and stood in silence. Even the distant sound of water's perpetual course could not be heard.

Eventually, Bend Sinister raised his head and said, "Since his intervention, we have come to rely on Bluemantle. He has been both herald and champion, our bridge to followers both committed and potential. Attendance at our events is due to his actions, conducted at great personal risk. The growth in our following is proof of our great debt to him. Without Bluemantle, we must be prepared for our fortunes to reverse. Without a way of spreading the word, no one will know to come."

"There must be someone else," said Pale Dexter, dropping the posturing to unmask the shock that overwhelmed him.

"Bluemantle was both man and his creation. Such remarkable skill. Unparalleled."

"But someone else could learn the skills; or else establish an alternative means of spreading the word."

"With sufficient security? Don't you see? What made Bluemantle exceptional was the complexity of the encryption. Despite their most determined efforts, the Authority has never been able to crack the code. It took immense skill to bury the information so deeply yet render it decipherable for those eyes intended to read it. We can make enquiries, of course. Consult our followers. Yet, I believe we've always known, Bluemantle's was a unique talent."

"Then what do we do?" said Chief, her voice trembling.

Bend Sinister sighed, shaking his head. "In terms of the future, I'm at a loss to know. But for now, we have a Contest to hold. Bluemantle completed his final commission: word is out. We shall hold the Contest in Bluemantle's memory. Whoever wins will be our leader. It will be their responsibility to safeguard the future of the Scene. They must decide what is to be done."

The three Troubadours looked to each other, inwardly processing this altered prospect of triumph.

—

The district of Aldar Point, skirting the south of Coxen Lyme, was home to a swathe of semi-derelict industrial units – a sprawling maze of crumbling concrete and rusting steel. By day, the state's lowest-grade workers operated machine relics, processing animal feed, tanning hide, threading iron bolts. Most worked twelve-hour shifts, enduring the most dismal of conditions in sullen silence. By night, Aldar Point became a dead zone.

In the basement of a disused factory, buried in darkness, crouched Cole. He held his knees to his chest, arms trembling, eyes wide. It was well over twenty-four hours since the A had stormed his quarters. Cole had not slept.

The images flickered in his mind: jumpcuts of horror.

It had been dawn, the cool grey of first light revealing shapes in the dust cloud. Before then, Cole had ventured home once since the argument – a window of opportunity when he knew Evan wouldn't be home. He couldn't face him at the time, not having just spent the afternoon hiding bundles around the city. Gathering a change of clothes, a canteen of water and a small amount of money, he had returned to his workshop. He spent the night there, surrounded by accidental confetti – the debris of his creation. The following day he completed the drops. By the time he had finished, he still couldn't face his partner – couldn't witness the disappointment and the assumption of a decision made.

All night he had stayed out, hiding on a friend's balcony. Tempur was a curfew zone; he couldn't risk street level. The balcony afforded him cover, as well as full view of the night sky, an infinite canvas on which to think.

By dawn, he had decided. Curfew wasn't quite lifted, but Cole couldn't wait. He knew Evan would be up soon, getting ready for work. He didn't want to miss him, couldn't wait another day before telling him. The impossible was overcome; he had made his decision.

Leaving a note for his sleeping host, he had climbed over the wall of the balcony and dropped the ten feet to the ground. Hugging the shadows, he had hurried towards home. As he crept around the final corner, opposite his block, he saw black-clad Special Forces storm the building. Flashlights blinked through the stairwell apertures. Even from where he crouched, frozen in horror, he heard the shouts, heard the thuds as they kicked down the door. He saw the shutters to their main room fly open. One of the troopers leant out and signalled to two men below, who ran into the building on his command. Cole stared in terror at their flat's other shuttered aperture, the one to their bedroom. Banging, shouting, torches flashing. *No… Oh please, no…* he screamed in his head. He turned back around the corner, collapsed to his knees and vomited.

That was where the looping reel of images stopped. What happened after that was unintelligible white noise.

Eventually, he had found himself stumbling through the ruins of Aldar Point, towards a derelict building. Stepping over shattered glass and the decaying corpses of birds and rats, he had entered the building and descended a stairwell that led to the basement. Cowering in its furthest corner, his legs had buckled. Collapsing to the floor, he sobbed, giving in to the devastation that had burnt in his chest for so long.

That was fourteen hours ago.

In that time, Cole had barely moved. The sobs would come in waves, the tears never more than a moment's thought away. He couldn't get out of his mind the note he had left: *"Thanks *for letting me stay. I've decided. It can only be Evan. I'm going home."* Now, faced with the horror of Evan's fate, the fact he'd taken so long to reach that decision fuelled a guilt that tore at his chest, stabbing his flesh with agonising regret.

He had no plan. No idea what to do next. He couldn't think straight. Not yet. In time, he knew he would have to pull himself together. There were places he knew he could hide, places he would be safe. If he made it across the entire width of the city, he felt sure they would take him in underground.

But this was Evan's time. A time to grieve the life he had loved, risked and almost certainly lost.

—

For Cole had no way of knowing.

Evan *should* have been there. *Would* have been taken.

Yet, Evan had weakened in his resolve, had accepted he loved Cole, no matter what. He could live with the fear. That was far better than living without the man. So, when Cole hadn't returned to their flat on the second night, Evan had flouted the curfew and stole out to find him. Their friend with the balcony was his last place to look. She handed him the note Cole had left.

When he read Cole's words, his world transformed in a rapid blossoming of hope. His soul had been caged by bars of despair. *'It can only be Evan'* released him. He could conceive of a life absent of fear. He had to get home. To their home, which now held their future, rather than the ghost of their past.

Evan ran, impatient.

He reached the street outside their block and froze.

Special Forces vehicles barricaded the road. Cordons had been erected. Troopers stood on guard, hands on weapons, at the block's entrance. At the apertures to their flat, other troopers postured before a gathering crowd below.

Hope collapsed into a black, fathomless hole.

Evan stifled a cry as he screamed inside, staring at the manifestation of his long-feared nightmare.

CHAPTER TWENTY

The situation had changed; the balance of control shifted.

Early that morning, Chase had been summoned to meet with Wulfwin. That had never happened before. Chase knew to be wary, was cautiously on guard when they met in a deserted lot in Brolan. Wulfwin had informed Chase that his time was up: the Authority was assuming control. "Our little relationship has just changed," Wulfwin had said. "You're under orders now. My orders. Do you understand? You've got forty-eight hours to deliver Ursel." Then he had elaborately described the consequence of failure.

As if the threats weren't pressure enough, Chase was convinced he was under surveillance. Since he had left for work that morning, he had felt acutely aware of company. He hadn't actually seen anyone; he didn't need to. He knew too well how the Authority operated. They had the means, the men and machines, to take 'covert' to the letter. Chase himself was a sleeper; he'd never been under the illusion he was one of a select few. Any one of his work colleagues or Creaser neighbours could be on the Authority's payroll. Once you were marked a target, there were abundant eyes and ears to track your every move. Public kiosks were patched, switchboards voiceware-activated, conversations recorded, WatcherCams locked on. Once triggered, surveillance was city-wide.

He knew what the trigger had been. His resistance to giving up Ursel had cost him dear. Wulfwin had pressed him but not as hard as he'd anticipated. At first, Chase had thought he'd got away with it. He now realised it had merely been a matter of time. His leeway had lapsed.

If he was going to protect Ursel, he knew he would have to act fast. It wouldn't be enough to get a message to her. He imagined her reaction, her perennial need to question why. He knew she wouldn't just accept it; she'd need an explanation. Which meant he had to find a way to speak to her.

That meant a trip to the Circus.

As the crowds ambled towards the Telltale's big top, its streamer flags limp in the still evening air, Chase merged with the flow and attempted to disappear. He recognised a friend of Naylor's and ingratiated himself upon her, trusting his instinct that the woman wasn't in the pockets of the A. To his relief, the woman, whose name he fought in vain to recall, remembered him. Hoping he might blend in more if he wasn't alone, he pulled out all the stops and managed to maintain small talk until safely within the sanctuary of the tent. Once inside, he crept around the back of the tiered stands, loitering while people checked tickets and located their seats. Then he climbed a metal stairway on one of the stands and slipped into a vacant seat on the back row.

The time it took for the gas lamps to dim and the space to fall into darkness felt interminable. Spotlights illuminated the stage and the performance began. Chase stepped onto his seat, climbed over the rail behind it and dropped to the floor.

"Are you going to tell me what all this is about?" hissed Ursel, emerging from the shadows. "And why in crow's name the wig? I feel like an idiot."

"Quiet. In here," whispered Chase, ushering her beneath the stand, out of sight.

When he had passed security on the way in, he had handed the guard a sealed envelope. To his relief, it was the same guard who had let him pass when he'd visited Ursel before. Chase had pressed him with a wordless plea to deliver the envelope, on which Ursel's name was scrawled above the word 'URGENT'. The guard had hesitated, then read something in Chase's face and hurried off.

It was only blind desperation that had given Chase hope that his plan might work. Now that it had, with Ursel standing there, white-wigged and altered, he was taken aback. If the rest of his plan played out, he would be able to protect Ursel, find Wella and still give Wulfwin the details he wanted. If it brought about the end of the Scene, then Chase would get what he wanted too; but that was beyond his control. All he had to do was convince Ursel.

"The A," whispered Chase in the shadows. "I don't know why, but they're watching me."

"Oh, crow. Are you sure?"

"Certain. Since this morning."

"I don't get it. Why you? Why now?"

"Like I say, I don't know. Maybe it's linked to Weldon..." He could see the whites of her eyes reflect what little light there was. "Maybe not. But it just seems, you know... I can't think why else. Anyway, it makes no odds. They're watching me. I had to tell you, warn you to stay away. We can't be seen together."

"I don't see why—"

"You're part of the Scene. If they see me with you, they might take an interest. I'd be putting you at risk. It doesn't matter if they see me with Naylor, or Tinashe, or the guys from work. As far as I know, the A would have nothing on them. But you. You're too involved. You know too much."

Ursel let out a deep breath and crouched to the ground. Chase knelt down beside her. He tried to make out her features in the half-light, wishing he could see her eyes, her expression. "And what about you?" she said, her voice soft.

"I'll be okay. They can't know I was at Chief's show. They would've hauled me in before now if they did. So, whatever they think they've got on me, it's bullshit. I'm not worried about me. I'm worried about you." He took a deep breath. "And Wella."

"Right now, she's safer than you are."

"That may be so. But this doesn't change anything. I still have to at least try to speak to her."

"Wouldn't she rather have you alive than on some guilt-motivated mercy mission she doesn't even want?" She sensed Chase recoil. "What I'm trying to say is think about what this means for the future, not the past. Even if you had cause to make amends, which I don't believe you do, this is not the way to do it."

"And what about you? Knowing about your friend, Cole. That's his name, isn't it? You said, if the A have got Cole, the Scene's finished. But you'll still go to the event, won't you?"

"Yes."

"Why?"

"Look, that's different."

"Bullshit. It's the same thing. Come on, you encouraged me to ask the question. So, why? If it's about to end, why risk everything for this one final time?"

"Because I've decided. I'm not going to let it end."

"What?"

"I was up all last night thinking about it. I've thought of nothing else. There's nothing we can do to save Cole. He won't crack and, once they realise that, they've no reason to keep him alive. If they do, he'll be banged up in Itherside Hold. And a trip to the Hold is only ever one-way." She hung her head and sighed. "It kills me to say it because, aside from what he's done for the Scene, he's also a good friend. It sounds like I'm giving up on him, but I have to be realistic. They don't have to kill him to take his life. Either way, we've lost Cole. I can't help him, but I can do something for him. Make it so that it's not over. I've decided. I'm going to pick up where he left off. I'm going to take on *Bluemantle*."

"You can't—" he said, struggling to keep his voice down.

"Why not?"

"You'll get yourself killed."

"Not if I'm careful."

"Careful? What about Cole?"

"Cole was careful. He produced *Bluemantle* for twenty-five years without any trouble. He'd sussed everything. The operation was flawless in its caution, mission and ambition. That's why I'm convinced. He wasn't found out. Someone traded. Some bastard turned him in."

Chase's heart rate spiked; his mouth felt dry.

"And if that's the case," she said, "I won't let that person win. I won't let them destroy everything Cole created, everything it stood for. All for a wrap of Meezel? Or a rent rebate? No fucking way." She stood up, trembling.

Chase stood up too, placed his hand on her shoulder. "Please, don't do this. The risks—"

"There's nothing you can do or say to change my mind, alright?"

Chase let go of her shoulder, his arm falling limp by his side.

"I absolutely believe it's the right thing to do. The Scene is a lifeline for hundreds of people. *Bluemantle* is the route through. Cole didn't just create it to promote the shows. It's a means of challenging the A's narrative. Not with counter-rhetoric but with a map, inviting citizens to find out the truth about the Scene for themselves. He knew, just as I know, that if people discovered the truth, they'd see through and stand up against the lies. Only then can we break down the prejudices, born of the state's drip-fed propaganda, that lead people to label us 'scum' without knowing what actually happens at an event. Growing the Scene was never just about numbers; it was about shifting the sway of opinion.

"I'm an actor, Chase. I was born into a travelling theatre committed to retelling old tales so that others may discover the universal truths behind them. A means to an end – a map to reveal the way. *Bluemantle* is no different. You say you can't walk away from Wella, even though I've told you she's okay? Well, I can't walk away from this. And, I'm sorry, Chase, but keeping *Bluemantle* alive means a damn sight more than one woman's desire to withdraw from overground."

"But why you? There are hundreds involved in the Scene. It's not your battle alone to save it."

"No, but I have the means. I know where Cole's workshop is. I know where all the drops are. He showed me everything. As far as I'm aware, I'm the only one. I also know who taught him cryptography. Cole took it to another level to beat the A. I'm not saying I can match his skills, but at least I can try. All I need to do is approach the Troubadours and seek their permission to represent them. They need *Bluemantle*. I can't imagine they'll turn down my offer."

Despite his objections, Chase listened. And he understood enough to witness his tidy plan unravel. His motives blurred as the startling realisation dawned. *What am I doing?* he thought. Doubt held the hand of hesitation. He had thought he had it all worked out, a neat parcelling of care and attention. Now, in the midst of game change, he had to reorder. He fell back onto firm territory, years of consolidation. *That must be it*, he decided. All that he knew hadn't suddenly changed just because of Ursel's revelation, or the way it had made him feel. He forced that away, saved for another time. Stabilised by the familiar, he sought a route through. If he was lucky, it could achieve the same end.

Taking a deep breath, he said, "Okay. I hear you. I can see I can't change your mind and I think I understand why. I would rather you reconsider, but I respect your motives. If only I were that brave."

"It's not bravery if there are no alternatives. Recognising that, the decision becomes a far simpler one to make."

"Then I won't push you to change it. Just as, I hope, you won't push me to change mine. I know you see alternatives as far as Wella is concerned. For me, however, there are none. It is something I must do."

"And I respect that." There was a pause. Muffled voices from the stage reached them through the gaps in the stand. Chase had almost forgotten where they were, why they were hiding. Ursel hadn't. She itched at the side of her wig and said, "Listen, we haven't got long before the interval. I take it you need to be back in your seat before the lamps come up?"

"Yes."

"And I'm assuming we can't easily meet again while they're watching you?"

"It'd put you in danger."

"Okay, then. Here's the deal. I'm about to break the biggest rule in the book, but I think we understand each other. If we can't meet for me to take you to the event, I need to tell you when and where it is. If you've managed to avoid detection by coming here this evening, I'm trusting you to take tenfold more precaution to get to the event without being followed. I don't need to spell it out to you, but I will anyway. If you lead the A to the Scene, you will not only be risking Wella's life, which wholly defeats the object. You will also be risking your own life, my life and the lives of several hundred innocent people enjoying an evening of harmless music. That's a catastrophic consequence that would put most people off attending in the first place. However, if you're still determined to go, then I'll tell you when and where."

She pulled out an eyeliner pencil from a pocket in her tunic. "Roll up your sleeve," she said. Chase did as instructed. Ursel wrote something on his skin, then covered it back up with his sleeve. "Those are the coordinates. I'll meet you there. Night after tomorrow. The bands are on at ten." Before Chase could respond, Ursel said, "Lights up in one minute," then she turned and disappeared.

—

The work-weary men, women and minors in Aldar Point were down to the dregs of their energy. With an hour left until the end of their shift, they let themselves dream of their pending reward: a shower, a cold Kitson, a hit of Meezel or simply sleep.

In the tannery, next door to where Cole lay foetal in the basement, they poured water onto the concrete floor of the fleshing room. On raw hands and knees, they scrubbed at the blood, torn flesh and fat that had fallen from the rolling machine. The hide detritus and water mixed with the chemicals spilt from the dehairing vats and trickled down waste drains laid into the floor. It spewed out into the Spire, fouling Wydeye's spring-source river.

As the klaxons sounded, thousands of workers punched their cards and filed through the gates of the various factories and processing plants. They merged together in silence and shuffled along the central artery, heading for the tramway stop and their journey to the marginally less squalid Rader tenements. Home.

An hour after the shift-end klaxon, Aldar Point fell silent. The dereliction and decay lent it the appearance of a post-apocalypse wasteland. There was no birdsong, no stray cats, no abandoned goats. The only foliage was the invasive grey-green Latchet weed, which bound itself around posts, pillars and poles, strangling vine-like. The sun hung low in the sky, darkening the dust cloud to an eerie amber smog. Silence prevailed.

Then, a thunderous boom. A deafening crash.

Reinforced concrete collapsed in on itself, steel rods jutting like splintered bones through flesh. The mass of rubble and crushed-flat machinery was sucked down into a black chasm, swallowing the wreckage before dust had chance to rise. The roar of toppling concrete was muffled the further down it sank, the sound trapped inside a grave a hundred metres deep.

The swallow hole opened in a second – devoured in less.

For a fraction of that moment, Cole screamed, his petrified eyes staring without comprehending. A lonely instant of utter terror – face white, hands reaching out, failing to grasp a handhold over death's own abyss.

Then nothing. No one.

In the space of two unbuildings and in the place of a precious life lost, yawned a vast, black hole.

PART TWO

WITHOUT A MAP

CHAPTER TWENTY-ONE

The shift-start klaxon was accompanied by a wail of sirens. The Emergency Division had been called at first light after a security guard almost stumbled into the gaping swallow hole. He had tottered on its brink, staring at where the tannery and the disused factory used to be. He couldn't look down. The horror of the hole was too much to bear.

The Emergency Division had arrived before the bleary-eyed workers streamed from the tramway stop. They cordoned off the site, widening the hazard zone to include the adjacent buildings in case of further collapse. Workers at those buildings, plus the absent tannery, were sent home without pay. There were no security guards or night workers at the tannery. And, taking into account the old factory had been vacant for years, it was reported that, mercifully, there had been no loss of life.

"As if that'll make a difference," said Blix, arms crossed, pacing her office.

Wulfwin stood before her, impatient. "We'll tell them it does," he hissed. "Today, of all fucking days."

"We've time on that score. Messaging on the hole must be

dealt with immediately. It doesn't take long for fear to spread, for the hysteria to take hold. Pull back some of your men. I want units on the street. Order must be maintained."

"Governor, the event—"

"The event is tonight. Fifteen hours away. You have time to divert resources to manage this potential crisis. Insurrection can be avoided with the precaution of swift intervention. Lest you have forgotten, mass hysteria can be triggered by exposure to a shared stimulus. This second hole could have infected citizens with a latent virus. All it takes is a single person's over-reaction to wake it up. Rideout, Wulfwin. I'm sure you don't need reminding."

Wulfwin stared at her, frustration erupting. "With all due respect, Governor," he said, failing to keep his voice level, "it is the memory of Rideout that is at the forefront of my mind. The Music Makers are finally within our grasp. We hold the upper hand. I will not stand by and let us squander this opportunity by pre-empting panic over a sodding hole."

Blix faltered, momentarily unnerved by the strength of his reaction. She was well aware of his reputation, played it to her advantage even, but had always managed to keep him on side. Wary of his volatility, she sought to concede ground without losing face. "We seek the same end, Commander. So yes, we can spare the Deaf Squad. Keep them in Glos. But I want troopers on the streets. Muscle, to send a message."

"As you wish, Governor."

"Good. I shall visit the base this afternoon to assess readiness. We can review the citizen issue then." She hesitated, about to say something else, but changed her mind. Instead she said, "Dismissed," with considerably less authority than she had intended.

Wulfwin clipped his heels, turned on the spot and marched out.

Blix stared at the open door. A cadet, stationed on the other side, stepped forward to gently close it. The moment she heard the latch, Blix spun around and hurried to her desk. Hands trembling, she fumbled with the silver pillbox, dropping its contents to the floor. On hands and knees, she picked up three of the small white pills and swallowed them. She remained kneeling on the floor, eyes closed, willing forward the effect.

—

Dent Lore sat beside the driver in the cab of an Ops truck. Behind him, either side of the truck's canvas-covered rear, sat twenty Allears. They were facing each other in silence, faces operation-grim.

Dent stared through the passenger window, sensing the friction that gripped the city. He noticed how citizens peered sideways at their truck, trying to look without looking. Others scurried into open doorways, swallowed by the darkness within. The tension was palpable, mixing with the cloud to create an atmosphere too heavy to bear. Throughout the entire journey, Dent only witnessed one moment of seeing. A small child had stood and stared, pointing as they passed, too young to feel afraid.

The truck veered left, joining a concrete track that led to a sports field in Glos. The state-owned facility had been commandeered by Special Forces, and an all-unit base was in the throes of being erected. The truck pulled up and the Allears disembarked to join colleagues already on site. Dent left his unit and marched towards the Operations Control tent that dominated the centre of the field.

At the awning's threshold, he hesitated. Ever since he had received orders to mobilise, he'd felt burdened by a spectral dread that haunted his consciousness. It struck him as akin to muffled background noise picked up by a field radio or ghosting on a monitor when the signal carried interference. It both came from him and not. He took a moment, trying to shake the feeling before facing the confrontation he knew was about to come.

Wulfwin denied him the opportunity. "Lore," he called from inside the tent. "I see you. Get your arse in here."

Dent exhaled slowly, pushed his shoulders back and stepped into the shade of the tent. He marched over to Wulfwin, who stood before a bank of radios and their trembling operatives.

"Just having a pep talk," said Wulfwin. "Want to make sure they fully understand the consequence of fucking this up." He glared at the operatives, who stared at their screens, faces either flushed red or bloodless pale. He turned back to Dent. "Come with me."

He led Dent over to a makeshift cubicle, formed of six-foot high partition screens on all sides and a small opening in one corner. Inside the cubicle was a desk and two chairs. They sat down opposite each other. "Your turn," said Wulfwin.

Dent looked squarely at Wulfwin. The routine felt familiar – a display of feathers he had yet to be intimidated by. He knew his responsibility, felt passionately the desire to fulfil it with success to spare. He even suspected success meant as much to him as it did to Wulfwin, albeit for different reasons. Maintaining eye contact, he waited calmly for the inevitable.

"This has come sooner than expected. Your fresh blood ain't ready. Disappointing how your previous failure still hangs around like a bad smell. Tell me there's good news regarding your last batch of graduates."

"They all passed the final assessment. Fully qualified and eager to enter the field, sir."

"That's a relief. For you, I mean. For me, I know what's riding on this. And you really don't want to be fucking this up again because of a lack of resources."

"I am confident the Allears will deliver all that is required of them."

"You'd better be right. 'Cos I'm telling you now, Lore, with the intel we have aside, the Deaf Squad still rely on the Allears. That kills me every time, but that's the way it is."

"We won't let the Authority down, sir."

"Yes, of course. Your textbook loyalty. Stuck record. Makes it sound… I don't know… Like you're spouting the bullshit you think I want to hear. Is that it, Lore? Are you taking the piss?"

"No, sir." Dent willed his conviction to generate passion. Instead, the ghosting flickered again. He forced it back, stared harder at Wulfwin and said in slow, deliberate words, "Success means everything. The Allears will not fail."

Wulfwin sat back, hands clasped behind his head, smiling. "You intrigue me, Lore. I don't know why. Blix appears to doubt you, questions your loyalty. But I've backed you up. Stuck my neck out. Do you know why?"

"Because of my performance?"

"Ha! I like that. But no. It's because I see a little of me in you. Despite your infuriating lack of passion, your slab-of-meat expression, I can see something else, something beneath all that. Something we might have in common."

Dent glared at him, tense now, trembling inside. His breath quickened as he held back the fury that had risen so suddenly from his gut. He struggled to swallow, forcing down the vile pill Wulfwin had just fed him. In all his years of abuse, he felt this was, by far, the most offensive thing Wulfwin had ever said to him.

Utterly oblivious, Wulfwin stood up and gestured for Dent to do likewise. "Come on. Enough. We have a raid to prepare for. This time we're gonna win, Lore. We're gonna get those damn Music Makers. The curtain's about to come down on those fuckers and they don't even know it."

—

All day, the Glos base was a frenetic field of activity. Military vehicles arrived in constant convoy. By mid-afternoon, all Deaf Squad units were on site, dressed in full combat gear and readied for action. The Allears had dispersed, strategically spread across the north-west corner of the city. Whisper dishes were manned by teams of three; all other units were scattergun spread, achieving maximum coverage. Special Forces cadets had erected a temporary detention centre on the playing field: ten cubicles made of steel fence panels, each one capable of holding fifty detainees. Beside it, a generator the size of an Ops truck electrified the perimeter panels.

Governor Blix sat on the back seat of her state vehicle. She had instructed her driver to take the direct route to Glos, avoiding the swarming masses that she imagined now filled the city centre. Parked up outside the Operations Control tent, she prolonged the moment with its precious relief of air-conditioning and tinted glass.

When it felt too conspicuous to delay any longer, Blix opened the passenger door and stepped out. She smoothed down her sharp grey suit and lightly touched her immaculate silver bun. Lips tight and eyes set in a determined stare, she walked towards the tent.

Wulfwin emerged from the shadows of the tent's interior. He had seen the vehicle arrive and had been waiting for her. "Governor Blix," he said, with a lacklustre salute.

"Chief of Command. The latest," she barked, slipping back into role.

"Deaf Squad are ready. Soon, they'll move closer to the expected zone, minimising response time. Commander Lore and his Allears are in position and active. We've several hours until the event is due to start. However, if there is any precursory sound that could lead us to the exact location, we will gain a valuable head start. Other Special Forces units are patrolling the area, looking for potential Users heading to the event. Our intention is to arrest them on sight, bring them back here for questioning. We only need to persuade one of them."

"Meanwhile, the decryption efforts."

"Still working to decipher coordinates. Intelligence Division will continue until the moment has passed. If they break it in time, Comms will radio all units immediately."

"Good. That leaves the matter of your sleeper. His source can negate the need to break the code."

"Chase is under direct orders to bring her in. He maintains that he doesn't know where she works or lives but expects her to approach him today in order to take him to the event. He's under surveillance. Only…"

"Tell me."

"Currently, we don't have eyes on him."

Blix glared, her breath quickening.

Wulfwin noted and ignored her reaction. "Last sighting was three hours ago by a street sweeper in Tempur. A WatcherCam was locked on, but there was a break in connection. Irritating, but nothing more. There are enough eyes on the ground to pick him up. Besides, once his source makes contact, he will Code S the details of where she's taking him."

"Your confidence in his loyalty surprises me."

"My confidence lies in our procedures. I checked his records. He had his implant refreshed last month. His system has enough Chromatofen in it to guarantee conformity. Besides, when I last spoke to him, I elaborated on the consequence of failure. The graphic detail was more for my amusement; he did not look entertained. He is under no illusion about what will happen to him should he fall short of expectation. And besides, his consistent cooperation means I am not unduly concerned. I imagine his initial reluctance to reveal his source was motivated by some foolish fancy for the woman. I know for a fact that his hatred of the Scene is deep-rooted. It will override any superficial desire when the time comes."

"Reassuring to hear. And you had better be right. Something tells me this event is our last chance. The mention of 'contest', whatever that may be, is significant. It has the ring of 'now or never'. And I will not countenance 'never'."

"With the information already at our disposal, we are well placed to succeed. I have every intention of doing exactly that."

"See that you do." She glanced around the tent, her cold eyes surveying the hundred or so uniformed officers and troopers carrying out orders. There was an urgency to their movements, a sharp focus in their expressions. The sense of purpose was palpable. Blix nodded slowly, then said, "I am returning to the Complex to take up position in the Comms Control Centre. Any development, make sure I am the first to know."

Wulfwin watched as Blix turned and walked out of the tent, her torso rigid. He took a moment to relax his strained composure, his face twitching. Then he marched over to the nearest radio operator. "Get me Commander Lore. Now."

—

A warm breeze skimmed the Nanso Trail, relieving the burden of sultry heat that had made for a gruelling climb. Dent Lore knelt on the ground, straining to detect the unheard. Sweat ran down his bald head. His beard prickled.

He had spent the last two hours darting between whisper dishes, issuing orders to blind, blank faces. Even after all these years, he could not get used to reading the expressions of the adjusted.

The sighted and the more agile of the adjusted Allears were alongside him on the Heights, listening. He had trained and re-educated all of them, knew them by name instead of number. He knew what they'd be feeling, what they'd be thinking. The programme of Chromatofen and indoctrination made that reliably predictable. That was why they were so effective. It was how they would, one day, win.

Will it be today? he thought, struggling to imagine the prospect. A goal, so long sought, had become incomprehensible as a reality. Mission accomplished was synonymous with purpose served. He couldn't imagine a 'what next?' because the concept held no meaning.

More tangible for Dent was the 'what now?' A familiar dread. Taken in isolation, his role as an Allear was a peaceable intervention. Actioned in concert with the Deaf Squad, it was the precursor to brutality. This shift in the nature of the part he played jarred in his psyche – a circumstantial contradiction that, he felt, placed him at the mercy of context. As always, he repressed the jabs to his conscience and focused on that which he could control: his responsibility, his duty and his loyalty to the Authority.

His radio crackled to life.

"*Alpha-Charlie-One. This is Delta-Charlie-One. Do you read? Over,*" came Wulfwin's voice, charged with static.

"Delta-Charlie-One. Copy that. Over."

"*No confirmation on location. Take up position 'bravo five'. Repeat, position 'bravo five'. Over.*"

"Wilco. Over."

"*Deaf Squad will mobilise at twenty-hundred hours. Rendezvous at twenty-thirty, south gate, Nanso Trail. Over.*"

"Wilco. Over."

"*And Alpha-Charlie-One. Don't fuck this up. Over and out.*"

The radio fell silent. An Allear to Dent's left turned away, as if to pretend he hadn't heard.

The orders brought Dent's mind back to the mission at hand. "Allears, listen up," he shouted. The fifty-strong unit gathered around him. "The moment is approaching. But detection is possible at any point. Be ready. Orders are in. It's B-five formation. You know the drill. First row, take up positions 120 metres from this point. Second row, thirty metres back from them. And so on. Hold formation and maintain separation. Keep your ears to the ground. The sound will come. Only we can hear it. I don't need to tell you what that means. Any questions?"

"No, sir," came an earnest chorus.

"Good," he said, then saluted. "Into position."

CHAPTER TWENTY-TWO

Chase hid in a dilapidated goat shed on the verge of Darlem Fields. The air was rancid, a noxious blend of stale straw, rotting vegetable matter and goats' piss. His two bleating companions stared at him through button-hole eyes. Exhausted, Chase lay curled up on straw. His intention had been to sleep for an hour or so, but the stench and the heat denied him the rest he craved.

He had been on the move since he left the Telltale Circus the previous evening. With a surveillance order on him, the tramway was out of the question. He knew that if he was going to make the Contest without being followed, he would have to get there on foot and by the most discreet route possible. After several lengthy detours, including a loop through the agricultural district of Wickerwild, his confidence that he was off radar had begun to grow.

There was still a great distance to travel. In order to reach the Nanso Heights, he had to head west, beyond the city's limits. He could not travel north, in the straight line that would lead him directly to his destination. Between him and the Contest was Cinder Hill – residential district of the A elite. Before that, Glos – temporary home to every Allear and Deaf Squad trooper in Wydeye.

Hiding behind closed eyes, Chase rehearsed his impossible plan for the hundredth time. He had no idea if it would work. In the absence of a viable alternative, he had decided to reject doubt and risk all in the attempt. This was because everything had changed. It was no longer about his trade with the A for a price paid years ago. It was no longer about his mission to unravel the Scene. It wasn't even about Wella anymore. By striving for all of that, he had placed Ursel in danger. Ursel, who had stirred something in him, something nebulous he had yet to name. An unconscious reaction that left an aftertaste of self-realisation – the acid burn of guilt and shame.

He touched the scar above his left shoulder and suffered the pain of discovery.

His plan was desperate. It would not make amends. If he was lucky, it might limit the damage caused by what he had already done.

–

As Ursel rode the railmotor on her circuitous route to the Contest, she gave no thought to consequence. Instead, she relished the prospect of what was to come. She hungered for the communion, the relief of being surrounded by people who thought and felt the same. It was the only time and place where she could be true to herself.

For followers of the Scene, life was a lie. Overground was a deception, both in terms of the Authority's narrative and the fact that followers had to appear to align themselves with it. Denial became a detested means of survival. Yet their commitment would not waiver, no matter the risk. They knew the truth; no amount of danger could undermine that knowledge. They also knew the reward. Despite the cost, what they gained by attending an event transcended everything.

Underground, followers relished the freedom.

Underground was honesty.

Only there could Ursel be herself: Hydrie Eursella Lindel, Chief follower and music lover.

—

The sand-clogged gloaming lent the Heights an eerie shroud.

Chase crouched behind a jutting rock, his chest heaving. Ahead, shadows shuffled in silent line. *Which are they?* he thought. Deciding in favour of followers over the A, he crept forward and merged with the line. The people around him turned in alarm. Chase nodded briefly and crafted a smile, wondering too late if there was some secret sign. The man closest to him returned the smile and placed his hand on Chase's shoulder. The pilgrims looked ahead, climbing the final stretch of overground.

As dusk gave way to a murky darkness, the vertiginous horizon loomed black above them. Ahead, followers gradually disappeared — a point of extinction edging ever closer until it reached Chase. He, too, slipped between folds of stone, into the mountain and then down, underground.

The stream of followers splayed and contracted according to the width of passageways. Chase pressed forward, weaving past men and women, young and old, repeatedly whispering his one-word question. "Ursel?" He was met with silent replies: a head shake, or shoulder shrug, or a mouthed 'sorry'. Eventually, a young woman nodded and pointed ahead. Chase felt his stomach tumble and his heart quicken. He hurried forward, offering silent apologies to those he passed.

"Ursel," he said in barely a whisper. He reached out and touched her shoulder.

Ursel turned her head. Recognising Chase, she smiled openly, eyes bright in the darkness. "You made it," she whispered as he fell in step beside her. "Clean tail?"

"I would've turned back if I had any doubt. I promise."

They walked the rest of the way in silence, matching the caution of everyone around them. As they dropped deeper into karstic subterrain, periodic gas lamps illuminated their way. The undulating passage delicately danced with the lights' faint flicker, shadows bobbing as the followers descended. At intervals, caves opened up before them: fishbowls of space in which some followers lingered, waiting for friends back down the line.

It was in one of these that Chase pulled Ursel to one side. He noticed her make-up, kohl heavy yet subtle; her tunic, short and black with the Chief emblem he recognised from before; her buckled boots, dusty from the long hike. "We need a plan," he whispered, his tone urgent. "Once we're in there, we might get split up. Or the music might, you know, distract." He tried to curb the adrenalin and remain focused. "I need you to take me to Wella. Not go off and find her first. Take me with you."

"Okay. Then what?"

"Then I think we should leave."

"What?"

"Escape. Before the A strike."

"They're not going to find us, Chase."

"You must've seen them today."

"Parading for effect. Besides, it's no different to last time. Only, this time we'll be deeper. With half a mile of solid rock above us, there's no way they'll hear the music. And even if they did, they won't know the way in."

"Still, it's a risk. We should find Wella and leave."

"Look, I told you when and where. We came alone. You're here for Wella. I'm here for the Contest. For Chief. I'm not leaving until the show's over. Besides, the risk is an unavoidable consequence of a choice already made. It's a price I'm willing to pay."

"But the A—"

"Least of all because of the A. I will not let them deny me my freedom."

"They will destroy it if they catch you."

"Let them try." She stared hard into his eyes, daring him to push her further.

Flustered and frustrated, Chase stared back. He saw his options narrow, his so-called 'plan' unmasked for what it was: a self-centred illusion of how to get his own way. *Why am I even here?* he thought, watching the gaps in his narrative render his whole conceit unstable. *I used Ursel to get me here and I still expected her to leave with me?* He had felt a connection, had dared to consider it might be mutual. Then he thought of Wella, their relationship coolly benign at best. *There's no way I'll persuade either of them... What was I thinking?*

Seeing, but misreading, his hesitation, Ursel softened. "Look. Tonight is special. And not just because of the Contest. Cole sacrificed everything to invite us here." She faltered and looked down. Then, taking a deep breath, she raised her head, determination lighting her eyes. "You've made it this far. That's half the danger gone, right there. The other half is getting home. It makes no odds if you face it once you've spoken to Wella or at the end of the show. You may as well make the most of the time in between and discover something important. Maybe even learn something, too." She took his hand and led him back to the line. "Come on, or we'll end up at the back."

—

Deep in the bowels of Lyun Mountain, the towering peak of Nanso Heights, the stages were set. A central cavern offered the choice of three passageways, each one leading to a vast cave, dimly lit by gas lamps and their reflection off sweat-drenched bodies. The air was warm and damp, hazy above the heads of the gathering crowd. At one end of each cave was a performance platform, on which the players' gear was set up. Eager eyes scanned the darkness behind the platforms, searching for signs of movement that could signal the Troubadours' arrival.

The atmosphere was charged with anticipation. Everyone knew this was an extraordinary event. Despite not knowing the intricacies of the Troubadours' peculiar politics, they grasped enough to appreciate the gravity of the occasion. The scale of the stakes. The prize at the end.

Before them, cloaked in shadow, waited the Troubadours and their players, instruments in hand, clad in their characteristic attire. Chief and her players wore patches of grey, leather-strapped and sleek, with androgynous faces and silvered hair. Pale Dexter and his players wore leather trousers and vest shirts, their bare arms a canvas for complex tattoos. Bend Sinister and his players wore black.

Bend Sinister bowed his head and closed his eyes, focusing his mind on the buzz beyond the shadow's cover. All day he had been preoccupied with thoughts of Saltire, Bluemantle and the coming Contest. He had long since moved beyond fear and the threat of capture. The risks were a given; no amount of dwelling on the fact could influence their scale. Stoic resignation had released him from that concern. What remained was still in the balance. The future.

He knew his opportunity to shape what that future may hold hinged entirely on his performance during the next few hours. He harnessed the thought, channelling energy from its roots in fear and anticipation. Then he relished the hunger, craved the feast that he would soon make manifest. Fired up and alive from the inside out, he held up his head and opened his eyes. He was ready to play.

Chase and Ursel entered Chief's cave and stood amid the crowd, arrested by the palpable atmosphere commanding the space. "I will be in here," said Ursel. "We'll find Wella now. After that, do as you like. But this is where I'll be staying." She led them back up the artery through which they had arrived. "The Troubadours are about to come on. Which means Wella will be out in the crowd, down there," she said, pointing at the third passageway. They hurried down it, entering the cave just as Bend Sinister took to the stage.

The gas lamps went out, the amplifiers crackled and the crowd roared. Bend Sinister grasped the microphone and said in a calm, deep voice, "We play to live and to remember what it means to live. Come, join us. Together we can raise hope above the limits of a dream."

From the first strike of the guitar and the thunderous rumble of bass, the crowd were captivated. People surged towards the stage, arms raised, faces beaming. The energy radiating from the stage penetrated their flesh and ignited their souls, rousing a passion and fervour that rivalled the players'. The music was powerful and charged with intent – a potent mirroring of the exchange taking place.

Chase stared at the stage, utterly entranced.

Ursel glimpsed him and smiled, unsurprised. She watched his face, which had become animated and bewitched; she saw the muscles relax and reform into an expression of joy. She withdrew from his side, leaving him oblivious as to her departure, and hurried off in search of Wella. She knew time would fly; she had to find Wella so that she could return to Chief and her own escape through rapture.

—

Overground, in pockets of reluctant association, the diametric mood hung heavy. Family members lit candles for the Deep, pleading for the safe return of loved ones. Friends of suspected followers peered through shuttered apertures, dreading signs of action that might spell detection.

Naylor stood on guard, seventy-eight floors up, scanning the sprawling city, watching for what he knew would eventually come.

Evan lay curled on a bed in a friend's cramped quarters. He thought about Bend Sinister, imagined what it might be like, right then, in that moment, underground. He wouldn't let himself think of anything else, only Bend Sinister's show. That was the closest he could get to thinking about Cole without breaking down.

CHAPTER TWENTY-THREE

"*Alpha-Charlie-One. This is Trooper Three-Seven. Positive detection. Repeat. Positive detection. Over.*"

Dent's heart skipped. He stood up, scanning the darkness. "Trooper Three-Seven. This is Alpha-Charlie-One. Copy that. I can't see your beacon. What's your grid position? Over."

"*Position eight-four. Beacon flashing. Over.*"

Dent looked to his right and spotted the blinking light. "I see you. Hold your position. I'm coming now. Over and out." With his path lit by helmet lamp and hand torch, Dent ran towards the beacon, dodging rock and boulder. He flicked the channel on his radio and called out, "Delta-Charlie-One, this is Alpha-Charlie-One. Positive detection in upper-right quadrant. I'm moving in to verify. Over."

An instant response fired back. "*Alpha-Charlie-One. This is Delta-Charlie-One. Copy. On our way. Out.*"

Dent reached the Allear. "Hold the beacon as high as you can," he said. "Deaf Squad are coming." Then he knelt down, closed his eyes and concentrated on the layers of sound and silence. He took his time, slowly delving deeper to discover distant traces.

"For crow's sake," he hissed, and dropped his head. He didn't need to strain to hear the thud of combat boots, far in the distance, growing louder as the Deaf Squad approached.

They eventually reached the location, Wulfwin leading the charge. "Lore. Tell me your boy ain't imagining things," he said, his voice taut with anticipation.

"I was just attempting to confirm." Dent had remained on the ground, head down, in the pose of interrupted business.

Wulfwin stood back and turned to his men. "Silence. I don't want to hear you fucking breathe."

Dent closed his eyes once more and resumed the task. The technique of stripping back layer after layer, discarding lost echoes and organic murmurs, was painstaking, yet reliable. There, deep in the heart of the superficial silence, was the quarry. He stood up and faced Wulfwin. "Detection confirmed."

For a fraction of a second, Wulfwin's face shone with anticipated glory. It was immediately masked by concrete composure and fierce control. He barked a barrage of orders. "Trooper Fifty-Eight. Radio Comms. Report 'confirmed detection' and initiation of procedures for source invasion and recovery." He turned to someone else. "Trooper Nineteen. Radio Ops HQ. Surveillance. I want every WatcherCam they've got covering this cursed mountain." Then to a third, "Trooper Twelve. Get your unit together. Rig the lights and fire up the generator. I want this place lit up like it's fucking high noon." Then to other men, "Troopers Twenty, Twenty-Five and Thirty-Seven. You know the drill. You're our fish net. Spread your units out. Go as wide as you can. It's down to you to catch any bastards that try to escape. I'll send other units to cover the north face, but this side is likely to be their main route down and, possibly, their only route home."

Wulfwin turned to the remainder: eighty or so men, clad in combat gear, heavily armed with coshes, chains, electroshock prods and tranquiliser guns. Clamped to their helmets were their ear defenders, poised ready to protect. "Men. Listen up. You know what to do. And you know what it means to get this done right. The Governor has said this could be now or never. For you, there is no fucking option. This is it, boys. Time to destroy the Scene and the bastard User scum. Most of all, time to put an end to the Music Makers, once and for all. Dead or alive is the order. Do I make myself clear?"

"Yes, sir!" came a terror-hungry roar.

"When I give the signal, ear defenders on. They don't come off until the job's done. Keep your in-helmet radio on open frequency. We follow the Allears until they pass the baton, then we take over. You know what to do from that point on, so don't cock up. Failure is a finger up to me and, let's face it, you don't want to be the one giving me the bird." He hesitated, allowing the consequence to be fully imagined. "Radios on. Helmets on. To attention," he barked, watching the men follow his orders with practised precision.

He turned to Dent and dropped his voice. "It's true what I said. The Governor believes it. Are your blind gimps up to the job?"

Unfazed, Dent nodded. "Yes, sir."

"Then lead on. Find me the source so we can get those fuckers."

—

Blix had heard the confirmation transmission the moment it came in. From that point on, the Comms Control Centre in the Authority Complex became a blur of movement and white noise. Concentrating on the strain of composure, Blix pictured the scene, superimposing what she imagined would be happening on the Heights like a cinematic palimpsest. The simultaneity was disorientating, blending realities of here and there into a single image. She closed her eyes and grabbed hold of a desk edge, resisting her body's inclination to shut down and pass out.

In the darkness, fresh calls of "Incoming!" drew her back. With effort, she pulled herself together and returned to her surroundings. She strode over to the officers seated at the bank of raised desks. "The latest," she said.

The officer nearest to her stood up and saluted. "Communication from the Chief of Command, Governor. Allears have located the source. They're handing over. Deaf Squad ready to move in."

—

"You're taking the piss, right?" Wulfwin looked at Dent Lore, incredulous. He had removed his helmet and ear defenders, which he held up as if redundant.

"No, sir. I'm absolutely certain."

"From under the fucking mountain?"

"I've had Allears monitoring the source from different positions. We're detecting distinct variation in reverberation time, as well as patterns of high and low frequency, with a predominance of low-frequency sound."

"Cut the crap, Lore."

"I believe the sound is coming from a network of caves directly below us."

"Great. And how, precisely, are we supposed to get to it?"

"We're tracing the higher frequency sound, the sound that's escaping. Where it comes out will give you your way in." Dent watched Wulfwin attempt to process the implications. "This could work in our favour," he added.

"And how the fuck do you figure that?"

"With limited ways in, there will be limited ways out. If we can locate all exit points, your men can have them covered. The Music Makers will be trapped inside. The Scene is a sitting target."

Wulfwin's eyes widened. His sneer stretched to a smile. "Good work, Lore. How long?"

"We've already found two openings. It's possible you can gain entry straight away. We'll continue to listen for others. With regards the first two, I'm handing over. We can't get any closer."

"Understood. My men will take it from here. I'll leave enough men above ground to stand guard. If you find any more exits, inform Trooper Twelve immediately. He'll ensure they're covered." Wulfwin put his helmet back on. Before placing his ear defenders into position, he said, "I knew I was right about you."

—

The music swelled around Chase, a tangible force connecting him to its source. An umbilical cord, feeding and sustaining, lifegiving. He was aware of the crowd surrounding him as they shared the wave he was riding. They had congressed as many and now engaged as one. They stood, swayed or danced, in exaltation.

Before them, Bend Sinister played on. Their instruments had become prostheses, making them whole once more. As Bend Sinister sang, surveying the crowd, all thoughts of the Contest, of Saltire and Bluemantle, dispersed into the heady air. He inhaled the scent of contact, drank its sweet nectar and felt revived.

Ursel approached Chase, a woman at her side. The woman, slightly taller than Ursel and a year or so older, looked serene. Her fair hair was short and gelled back, her eyes darkened by liner. A small tattoo lay like a promise on her left cheekbone.

—

It hadn't taken Ursel long to find Wella.

When Ursel had approached her, Wella had greeted her with a warm embrace and a wide, open smile. It was impossible to speak and be heard where they were, so they had slipped out to the antechamber that connected the three venues. There, with an uncanny drop in volume, they were able to talk.

"I've explained you're safer here, but he wanted to see for himself," Ursel had said.

"He's never been bothered about me before. Why now?"

"I think you need to ask him that. But he *is* bothered. Enough to come here. Twice. He thinks he can persuade you to return overground. I've tried to discourage him, but he's determined."

"That sounds about right," Wella said, sighing.

"Will you at least hear him out? If I'm reading it right, there's something changing in him. That," she said, gesturing towards the passageway that led to Bend Sinister's cave, "will have an impact. I know it. If you explain, I think he'll understand. Then he can respect your decision, feel like he's done his 'big brother' bit and move on."

"I'd be surprised if it were that easy."

"But will you? Just listen to what he has to say. That's it. No discussion."

"Okay. But I'm doing it for you, not him. You're a kind person. You've gone and taken him under your wing, made his cause your own. No doubt you'll feel like you've failed him if he doesn't get to say his piece."

Ursel shrugged, eyes down.

Wella smiled. "It's not a criticism. You're doing a good thing. Just a shame it's not for someone who deserves it." She put her hand on Ursel's shoulder. "I'll go and speak to Chase; you return to Chief. All this time you're fighting Chase's corner, you're missing their show. We can't have that. This is a Contest. Headcount is the deciding factor."

—

The Deaf Squad poured through the passageways, following the breadcrumb trail of gas lamps down into the bowels of the mountain. Sixty troopers, combat-ready, thirsting for a fight. Had Dent been listening, he would have heard their roars reverberate through karstic arteries as the mountain moaned from within.

Instead, Dent was tumbling down one of those arteries. He was drawn to the sound, a siren song luring him to a promised haven. Yet he was not powerless to resist; he knew he still had time to overcome its potency and pull back. But he did not. There was something in the sound, something fundamental in its core, that felt like reunion. He had to know what it was, this compelling force bidding him come. As he stepped through the gap and into the warm cave, beholding the man and the music, he found the answer.

Moments later, the first wave of troopers crashed into the antechamber, deaf to the screams of followers caught moving between the caves. The troopers witnessed the terror that their ears could not apprehend. With nowhere else to run, followers fled down the three dead ends, leading the troopers straight to their prey. Orders were shouted over in-helmet radios, units split. Troopers piled into the three caves, their jolting headlamps casting chaotic beams of light.

Bend Sinister, Pale Dexter and Chief were still playing, so

sudden was the raid. Their followers were still staring stageward, oblivious to the Scene's invasion. Time slowed in the moment when reality dawned. A freeze-frame of realisation while the gossamer layer between then and now was peeled away. Then instant recognition. And terror.

Bedlam flooded the caves. People screamed, eyes frantic. Some tried to resist or fight back, only to be beaten with coshes, slashed with chains and debilitated with agonising electroshocks. Others held up their hands in gestures of surrender, which were studiously ignored. Denied their sparing, they used their arms to protect their heads from repeated blows.

Troopers barged through the crowd, pushing people to the floor, trampling over their bodies. Some followers cowered against the cave walls, trapped and weeping. Others vented their fear, shouting inanely, refusing to accept.

Numbers dwindled. Followers were leaking through cracks hidden by the darkness. More barked orders. Troopers searched the caves' perimeter. They moved with urgency, desperate to stem the flow. Narrow crevices were found and blocked. The depleted audiences were shepherded into the centre of the caves. Gas lamps were raised, bleaching the scene.

Wulfwin stood in the middle cave, his helmet off, ear defenders shed. He climbed on top of the abandoned stage and looked around him, his face contorted. "Where are they?" he roared. He darted towards the rear of the stage, eyes scrutinising the seemingly impenetrable rock. He returned to the front of the stage. "Where are the Music Makers? People don't just disappear. For fuck's sake, find them."

Deep in the darkness of a limestone fracture, Wella led Chase away. Ahead and behind them were a dozen or so others who had fled Bend Sinister's cave moments after the

Deaf Squad had stormed. They edged forwards in silence, dreading the sound of pursuit.

The passage was narrow and perilous, requiring them to scale smooth rocks above deep chasms. One man fell. He bit on his arm to stop himself from screaming. His leg had snapped on impact, bone splintering and jutting, red on white, through flesh. Two people stayed with him, insisting they couldn't leave him behind. They exchanged names in stilted introduction. The rest filed past, promising to get help. Torn, Wella hesitated. Chase stared at her, imploring her through terrified eyes. They moved on.

In the centre of Chief's cave, surrounded by the captured and guarded by the Authority, stood Ursel, impenitent, yet utterly afraid.

CHAPTER TWENTY-FOUR

Dawn. As first light diluted the darkness, the forest stirred. Chase lay awake, listening to its life signs: tentative birdsong, the chatter of squirrels, the plaintive cry of a circling buzzard. He looked up at the perforated canopy, weak light revealing where the forest ended and the sky began. It had been pitch-black when they had arrived, breathless from their escape through the Heights. Wella had insisted on making camp in Wickerwild forest, avoiding the city while the Authority went on the rampage. She had said she knew of a place. Chase hadn't the will to argue.

He had lain awake all night, his tortured mind in a fist fight. Shame grew like a tumour, swelling with the gradual realisation of who he had become, how he had betrayed his own, what he had done to Cole. Then there was last night. The indescribable impact of Bend Sinister's performance, finding Wella, the terrifying raid. Ursel's arrest.

He knew she'd been caught. Friends of Wella's, the last to slip out of Chief's cave, had seen it happen. Ursel had been trapped in the crowd, couldn't reach the passage in time. Ursel, whom he had meant to save. Ursel, whom the Authority knew to be an active member of the Scene, a prize capture, a potential source of information. Chase bolted upright and retched to his side.

The noise woke Wella. "You alright?" she said, propping herself up on one arm and rubbing her eyes.

"Sorry to wake you."

"That's alright. We should get on the move anyway."

Chase didn't respond. He sat with his knees up, his head bowed.

"You want to talk about it?"

He shook his head.

Wella watched her brother, noticed the tremble in his shoulders and how his ribcage stopped moving as he held his breath. She got up and walked away, far enough to keep an eye without intruding.

Wretched, Chase wept.

After a while, Wella returned. "We need to move on," she said. "I suggest we head further south for a while to give Wickerwild Mine a wide berth. Then east, parallel with Aldar Point. The woods are dense there. We should have plenty of cover. Any objections?"

"I'm sorry…"

"What for?"

"I'm supposed to be looking after you."

"Says who? I don't need looking after."

Chase looked up at her, bewildered. He barely recognised his younger sister. "No, you're right. You don't."

"Glad we've got that straight. You, on the other hand…" She helped Chase up onto unsteady legs. "We should get going."

They walked in silence for several hours, Wella leading the way. By the time she stopped and declared, "We can rest for a while," Chase was physically and emotionally exhausted.

Taking cover beneath the wing of a low branch, they sat on their heels. "Here," said Wella, holding out her canteen. Chase accepted it without meeting her eyes. "I say we wait until dusk before we head back into the city. I reckon that's three or four hours away. That gives us time to go wide and avoid cutting through Aldar Point. If we can find a way to cross the Spire, we could sneak back in through the east edge of Creaser."

"I can't go back."

"The A'll be done raiding by then. They would've had all day. And they would've started in Creaser. We should be fine, if we're careful."

"No. I mean it. I can't go back."

"What are you talking about?"

"The A are watching me."

Wella studied Chase, brows raised. "Why? What've you done?"

"Nothing."

"Yeah, right."

"I don't know. They've got something on me. I didn't fancy stopping to ask."

Wella sat back, rigid. "And you still came to the Contest? Even though they had eyes on you?"

"I had to speak to you."

"Yeah. So Ursel said."

"I was careful."

"You… It was you. You led them to us—"

"No! I lost them. I swear. I wouldn't have carried on otherwise." He stared at Wella, eyes wide. "You've got to believe me. I wouldn't have done that. I was there to save you."

"I don't need saving."

"Ursel kept telling me that. But after Brann—"

"What? What has this got to do with Brann?"

"I had to do something. What if you were in trouble? I couldn't stand by. You're my sister—"

"That's sod all to do with it and you know it. Where have you been the last five years? Why didn't you help me then, when I could've used a bit of brotherly support?"

"I didn't know—"

"No. Of course you didn't. How could you? That's my point." Wella sighed. "You've not been around. That's your deal. So don't expect you can step in and play the hero when it suits you."

Silence. Wella picked at brittle leaves. Chase boxed inside himself.

"I'm sorry," he said eventually, voice taut and trembling. "No excuses. I should've kept in touch."

"In the meantime, you've got yourself in trouble. What's the score with the A?"

"I told you, I don't know."

"Bullshit."

"Look, it's complicated, okay?" he said, his teeth gritted. "Suffice to say I can't go back into Wydeye. Not for a while, at least."

"And the alternative is? You can't stay out here. And there's nowhere else to go. Unless you steal an Authority truck or stow away on a goods train, you're stuck. There's a reason for that and you know it. Don't go pretending you've got options." She glared at Chase, trying to read his hunched shoulders and fidgeting fingers. "What's the deal with Ursel?" She watched him flinch and turn away.

"I found a copy of *Bluemantle* in your quarters with her name on. She said she'd help me find you. She took me underground."

"She must've trusted you." This time she saw a pained wince contort his face. "You like her, don't you?"

Chase dropped his head. "There's something about her. I don't know. She made me open my eyes. I started to see things differently." He held his hands to his face. "I can't bear to think—"

"Another reason why we've got to go back. If you care about Ursel, you can't hide out here while they've got her. You know the score. You know what they'll do to her."

"But what can I do? There's no way—"

"So what? You just give up? You don't even fucking try?" Wella stood up. "Shame you didn't get to know the Scene a bit better. It could've taught you a thing or two about loyalty." She strapped her canteen to her belt and started walking.

"Wait! Where are you going?"

"Creaser. Coming?"

—

The raids on the city had been swift, the violence indiscriminate. Quarters were ransacked, taverns battered by havoc. Although some arrests were made, the modus operandi of the Authority's blanket attack prioritised message and mayhem. Besides, the Deaf Squad had succeeded in capturing just shy of two hundred followers in the Nanso caves. Along with those still in custody since the last raid, the detention centres couldn't cope with many more.

Two hundred followers caught in the act. The Scene finally discovered. The nest destroyed. Yet, the mood in Blix's office was bleak. She stood before Wulfwin, eyes wild. "Without the Music Makers, this means nothing. We've achieved nothing. The mission has failed. And I will not tolerate failure."

Wulfwin glared at her, fighting back his own outrage. He had spent hours tearing through the network of tunnels and caves, roaring as he beat the unyielding stone at each dead end. The Music Makers had been there; he saw one of them on stage, playing, the moment he had entered the cave. He knew they couldn't just disappear. Yet, somehow, that was exactly what they had done. His chest burnt, a hothouse for fury. Composure was a vulnerable mask that he struggled to preserve.

"They are down there," continued Blix, pacing the room in stilted steps. "If we can't find them, we force them out. Gas them. Or flood the caves. I don't care how it's done. Dead or alive. I want bodies. I want proof."

"I will assess all options and report back with a plan."

"You have one hour."

"It will take—"

"One hour."

Wulfwin held her eye contact in wordless challenge. He feigned salute and was about to leave, when Blix said, "Wait. Commander Lore. Perhaps he could have done more."

"As I have detailed in my report, his Allears made a timely detection. Lore confirmed the sound and located the source. He ascertained that it came from underground. It was him who found the way in." He stepped forward, scrutinising her face. "What is it? What bothers you about Lore?"

"He is weak. That makes him vulnerable, which makes me lack trust."

"I vouch for the man."

"Loyalty is a weakness too."

"It is not a question of loyalty," he hissed. "I have witnessed his performance. His actions speak for themselves. If anyone could've done more, it's the sodding sleeper. He's still off radar."

"Your confidence in him was misplaced."

Wulfwin winced. "As I've made clear in my report, precautions were followed. Medication checked and up to date. For all we know, he got caught up in the fall-out. Probably lying unconscious somewhere, beaten up by us or them. Either way, we'll track him down and haul him in."

"I demand that you do."

He stared at Blix, fighting the urge to speak his mind. Instead, he said, "If I have one hour to achieve the impossible, I must make a start." With exhausted effort he added, "By your leave, Governor."

Blix moved over to her desk and grasped the back of her chair. "Dismissed," she said, without looking at him. Wulfwin nodded slightly, turned and left the room. She slid down into her chair, her hands splayed on Wulfwin's report that lay open on the desk. She stared ahead, scratching the back of her hands. Eventually, she picked up a small, black device that sat, blinking, beside the report. She held it to the side of her face, flicked a switch and said, "Get me Allear Commander Dent Lore."

—

In his cramped quarters in the Authority Complex, Dent stood before a mirror. He stared at his reflection, into the eyes of a man exhumed.

He had fled the cave in a daze, intoxicated by revelation. The discovery was partial, glimpsed through a diaphanous veil of comprehension. Yet the hint of truth was so compelling, so absolutely known, it irreversibly altered his perception of reality. He could only hope that the veil would fall and the full scale of truth would be revealed. In the meantime, all he had was instinct. When the Deaf Squad had stormed the cave in which he stood, he had known he mustn't be seen there, that he had to escape. He had to pretend he hadn't witnessed Bend Sinister.

How do I know his name? he thought, staring into the eyes of his reflection. *And yet I do. More still. I know the man.* He trembled now, just as he had on the side of Lyun Mountain, emerging from the crevice into the warm night air, eyes scanning the dark sky for the dot of red light that would spell WatcherCam. He had hurried silently beneath the cover of darkness, switching on his headlamp when he heard voices in the distance. He had rejoined his unit moments before Deaf Squad troopers emerged with the first batch of handbound captured.

He studied his reflection, a face that was not his own. He raised his hand and touched his left cheek, covered by the dark hair of his beard. His fingers lingered, stalling. His heart raced, anticipating the incontrovertible, knowing the verdict before it was called. Swallowing hard, he leant in towards the mirror and slowly, with trembling fingers, parted the hair.

There. A small tattoo. A diagonal line.

Beeping, louder than it should have sounded, made him start in alarm. He looked down at the pager strapped to his belt and felt his blood drain. Recognising the number, he knew it could mean only one thing. He dialled in, dreading the confirmation that inevitably came.

By the time he crossed the Complex and arrived outside the office of Governor Blix, he had mustered some small degree of self-control. *Forget what you know now,* he told himself repeatedly. *Think only of what you thought you knew.* Pausing to take a deep breath, Dent pushed back his shoulders, lifted his chin and knocked on the door.

"Enter," came Blix's voice from within.

Dent obeyed, closing the door behind him. He stepped forward into the centre of the sparse office and stood to attention. Blix was standing before the tall window, her face bleached by the wan light outside. She turned slowly to face him. "I am curious, Allear Commander Lore. The raid last night. Your assessment in the context of mission objective."

Dent stared ahead, his body rigid. He had the urge to swallow, but his mouth felt dry. "Governor. We successfully detected the music and located its source. The raid led to both a substantial number of arrests and the discovery of the nest. I believe the latter is an important objective successfully accomplished."

"Explain."

"With the nest exposed, it is effectively destroyed. This will disrupt the Scene. They will have to find somewhere else to operate. That will be difficult to achieve in the context of your expanded Special Forces and associated deterrents."

"You've yet to make reference to the single, most fundamental failure in your duty to obey orders."

"Apprehension of the Music Makers."

"Indeed. Flows from the tongue as if you take your orders seriously. And yet your performance contradicts."

"Governor—"

"The Scene is context, superfluous. Our detention centres are already overflowing with Users. The only objective that truly mattered was the capture or killing of the Music Makers. We believe there are several. And yet the raid delivered me none. My assessment would be thus: comprehensive failure."

"From the perspective of the primary objective, Governor, I agree."

"How accommodating of you. But just to be clear," she said, stepping up close and forcing eye contact, "there is no hierarchy, no primary over secondary. There is and there has always been only one. One order. One objective. One measure of success. And, once again, you have not delivered."

Dent knew better than to respond to the judgement. He stared ahead and waited.

Blix circled him, her eyes trained on his face. "Interesting. Wulfwin describes you as lacking passion. Yet, I detect a distinct agitation."

"With due respect to the Chief of Command, I suspect the passions that Wulfwin and I feel are of a different order. I doubt he would recognise mine, just as I am unable to identify with his." He blinked, choosing his words with care. "I am moved by the knowledge that I have disappointed you. The privilege of service to you and the Authority is all I've ever known and all that matters to me. To know that I have failed you pains me."

"Such loyalty. I wonder where you place your family in the light of this apparent devotion to the cause."

"Without the benefit of experience I can claim my own, family is an abstract concept to me. As you know, I was adopted at a young age by the Authority. This is my home and my life; I've known nothing else. If you will accept family to be the community to which I feel bound by loyalty, then it is the Authority, under your sovereignty. As such, I place my family above all else."

Blix stepped back, as if to gain a fuller perspective of the man stood before her. Her own agitation had begun to bubble below the surface, slowly building, like the relentless itch that tormented her. She hesitated, debating how hard to push. Eventually, she said, "Just as Wulfwin described. Textbook." She moved to her desk, closer to the silver pillbox in its top drawer. With trembling fingers poised on the handle, she stood erect, eyes delving into Dent's. "Regurgitation is one thing. Let's see how it holds up when put to the test. Dismissed."

CHAPTER TWENTY-FIVE

It was dusk by the time Chase and Wella passed the outlying dwellings and re-entered the city proper. They crept through the southern corner of the Wallace Estates, pausing briefly to leave a message in Naylor's mailbox, then sought obscurity in Rader's concrete maze. Time was against them. With curfew fast approaching, they were forced to abandon stealth and run the remaining blocks.

"It's this one," said Wella, stopping outside one of several hundred identical tenement buildings. "Follow me."

Chase, with weary resignation, did as instructed.

They hurried up the concrete stairwell. With half their faces obscured by dust masks, Wella was confident they looked as anonymous as the few citizens they passed. Chase, on the other hand, still turned his head away when they saw anyone. Rader was rampant with Meezel addicts; he was in no doubt there would be eyes all over, eager to trade a sighting for a wrap.

Breathless, they reached the fifth floor. The corridor was deserted. A piercing wail blared from all directions as the curfew siren cried.

"Down here," whispered Wella, crouching low to duck pillbox apertures that opened onto the corridor. She stopped outside an unmarked door and knocked three times. Then once. Then twice more. The door opened the inch of security chain. "Wella Newell," she whispered through the crack. "The minstrels sing to me." The door yawned and they were drawn into darkness.

A small form cloaked in shadow led them down a dark corridor that dog-legged abruptly. They passed through a door into a narrow passage, then through a smaller second door into a box room. The low glow of an oil lamp illuminated the space. Beside it stood their guide: an elderly woman, long silver hair hanging limp over her stooped spine. She didn't say a word. Instead, she smiled warmly at Wella and cast a suspicious glare at Chase.

As soon as she left, closing the door silently behind her, Chase grabbed Wella's arm and whispered, "Are you sure about this? Did you see the way she just looked at me?"

"Trust me, you're safer here than anywhere in Wydeye. I've known Quince for years. She's a champion of the Scene. Her den is the most secure hide that we have overground. As long as you stay quiet and don't leave this room, no one will know you're here."

Chase grunted and sat on a low bunk, squinting at their surroundings. The room was cramped and aperture-less. Above him was another bunk. In the centre of the room, two rustic chairs and a small wooden table, on which stood the oil lamp. Against the opposite wall, a standpipe and bucket. To the right of that, in the corner, another bucket covered over with a piece of cloth. The walls were bare concrete block, the floor and ceiling, cast concrete slabs.

"At least it's cool and dust-free," said Wella, watching her brother's expression.

Chase shrugged.

"Okay. That's enough," she said, straining to keep her voice low.

"What?"

"Sit." She pointed at one of the chairs.

Stunned, Chase complied.

She sat down opposite him, the lamp flickering in the space between them. "I help you escape from the raid. I show you the way through the woods to avoid crossing the city. I use up a not-insubstantial lifeline and bring you here. You have shelter, running water and the luxury of two square meals a day. You are safe. And yet you sit there, turning your nose up and shrugging like an arrogant fucking arse. It's your turn to give, big brother. So, tell me. What's the score?"

"What? What do you mean?"

"What do I mean? Are you fucking serious? The A, Chase. What've they got on you?"

"I told you—"

"You told me bullshit."

"I swear, Wella."

"Don't go down that route. If this arrangement is going to work, if our relationship, for all that it is, is going to last, then you have to tell me the truth. I saw your face out there. In the stairwell. You were terrified. The A aren't watching you for some minor misdemeanour. They've got you so on edge, you can barely hold it together. An oppressive, autocratic state it may be, but it doesn't tend to instil that level of terror among the innocent. Even followers aren't that afraid. So, what is it? What's the real story?"

Chase faltered. He couldn't face the truth himself, let alone admit it to someone else. Gagged by guilt, he sought to deny. "Listen, I honestly don't know."

"You're lying. For crow's sake, Chase, I'm giving you the chance to explain. To come clean, whatever this is about. And believe me when I say this, you won't get the opportunity again. When the truth does come out, whatever it is you're hiding, it's going to go down a whole lot worse if you lie about it now. Because I'm convinced. You're hiding something. Not about the A. About you."

Chase rubbed his temples, staring at grain lines in the table, following their flow as they came together and pulled apart. He wanted to tell her, to expose and expel his guilt, rather than leave it gnawing at his conscience, devouring him from the inside out. Yet he couldn't bring himself to say it; he couldn't put into words the betrayal he was gradually coming to comprehend.

Wella watched, witnessing the battle. She stepped up the pressure. "What about Ursel?"

Chase jolted, eyes wide. "Ursel? What do you mean?"

"I presume you care enough for her that you don't intend to stand by while she is tortured to within an inch of her life for information that, I absolutely believe, she will never give up?"

"Oh no… Ursel… But what is there…?"

"How to save her? I've no idea. But as far as the A are concerned, she's just another 'User', so she stands a chance. Not like…" She faltered, then shook her head, forcing back her grief.

The Troubadours had shared word of Cole's reported capture, which had left the underground community devastated. They were under no illusion as to what would become of him in the hands of the Authority. To Wella, he had been both *Bluemantle* and a good friend. The news had hit hard.

She looked up at Chase, pulling herself together. "There's hope for Ursel," she said. "You insisted on saving me, who you've cared little about over the years; me, who didn't need or want to be saved. So, I'm assuming, given whatever fondness you have for her, that you'll at least want to try."

"Of course. I'll do anything."

"Then you have to tell me. Don't you see? I have to know what we're up against."

Chase's face crumpled. He held trembling hands to his eyes.

Wella softened her voice. She reached out and placed her hand on his shoulder. "You can't do this alone. And I want to help. But I can't do that unless you tell me the truth. It won't work otherwise."

Dropping his hands to the table, Chase took a deep breath and fixed his bloodshot eyes on the lamp's glowing mantle. "It started fifteen years ago," he said. "Brann had been in custody for five years. He couldn't cope. You remember what a gentle kid he was back then? So kind and easy-going. He wasn't tough enough to handle the detention centre. As the years passed, he was steadily deteriorating. You know this; you saw him. When his parole was refused for the fifth year running, he went downhill. He couldn't survive in there much longer. That's when I decided. I'd stood by for too long, watching him suffer. I had to do something to get him out. So, I went to the Exchange.

"I didn't have a plan, had nothing to trade. But everything has a price. So, I asked what they'd want for Brann's release. I despised the A for arresting Brann, loathed them for the way they were treating him. Yet, I knew the only way I could save him was to do what they wanted. I agreed to their price and we struck a deal. I would join their eyes and ears on the ground, feeding back any information on the Scene, in exchange for Brann's release."

Wella raised her eyebrows, but she didn't respond. Watching Chase intently, she waited for him to continue.

"I should've known," he said. "When I thought it was all sorted, they upped the price. Turned out it wasn't to be just the once. They were obsessed. They kept going on about 'Music Makers', how they had to be caught at any cost. They also knew about me, about my attitude towards the A. Turns out, they used my hostility to their advantage.

"Remember that time I went away for a while? You still lived at home, I think. Well, the A took me in. I didn't have a choice. They put me on a programme – 're-education', they called it. Brainwashing, more like. They held a mirror up to my hostility so that it bounced right off and reflected elsewhere. Towards the Scene. Towards Users." He shook his head. "I don't know how they did it. But it worked. I came to blame the Scene for what had happened to Brann. If the Scene didn't exist, the A wouldn't have to come down so hard on those they suspect are part of it. I resented Users. Blamed them. If I could report back information that would lead to their arrest, I was happy to do so. I figured they deserved it. I was an informer for the bastard A and I still felt justified.

"Then it just went on. Somehow, I'd absorbed their rhetoric and thought it was my own. My resentment grew. I felt no shame. Brann was out and alive; they couldn't hurt him anymore, yet I carried on. The A's mission became my own. The Scene had to go. If it did, there would be no more innocent people arrested and made to go through what Brann did. No more Deaf Squad. No more midnight raids. All I had to do was have an annual medical and psychological assessment, and message my contact whenever I picked up intel I thought they might want to hear. Whatever they did on the medical, I didn't want to know." He reached up and felt the scar on his shoulder. "Each time, they'd replace an implant. I didn't ask questions; I didn't care. The trade would never be paid off, but I was okay with that. They'd already got me on side. And then you disappeared.

"When I found copies of *Bluemantle* in your quarters, I guessed you were somehow involved with the Scene. I couldn't believe it – couldn't understand why you'd even want anything to do with the Scene. It seemed impossible. Then I met Ursel. When I found out she was part of it too, I knew the A would want to know. I was angry with her. But, at the same time, I needed her to take me to you, so I could persuade you to come home. I couldn't just leave you, knowing what the A would do to you if you were caught. And there was every chance they would catch you, because, despite the danger, I still had to tell the A what I knew. Not about Ursel; she was my way in. But about the event. Chief's show. I told them it was going to happen."

Chase sensed Wella move in her seat, could feel her eyes bore into him. He didn't dare look up to meet her eyes; he couldn't face the judgement he knew he would find there. Swallowing hard, he pushed on. "I went to the Chief event with Ursel. She refused to tell me exactly when and where it was to be held, thank crow, so I couldn't tell the A. I just told them which day it would happen. Then I saw Chief, heard their music, and everything started to unravel." He felt the scab, the deep scar of betrayal. "After, when Ursel and I had escaped, I cut out whatever it was they had put in my shoulder.

"Things became confused; I didn't understand. I saw something in Ursel: a strength and conviction I admired. I still resented Users, blamed the Scene, but I felt differently towards her. Also, I couldn't get Chief out of my head. The euphoria I felt at the event was short-lived, but it left an impression I couldn't ignore. I felt conflicted without knowing why. That's why the A started watching me. They were pushing me to give up Ursel, but I wouldn't. Not because I needed her, but because I was protecting her. They knew I was hiding something and they got suspicious. Now they'll know for sure. And they won't give up, I know it. They'll keep on until they find me. But I didn't realise that before. Even last week, I still thought I could have it both ways. The doubt had started, but it wasn't strong enough. It couldn't undo fifteen years of influence. It wasn't enough to stop me. Stop me from…" Chase buried his head in his hands, his body hunching over, cowering from the horror.

Wella waited, giving space through silence. Eventually, she pressed. "The Contest. Ursel told you where and when. You told the Authority."

"No! I swear on my life. She told me everything: the time, the coordinates. She trusted me. And I couldn't betray that trust. Also, I'd begun to realise. All the confusion, all the conflict; things began to separate. Parts of it started to make sense. You've no reason to believe me, I know. But I promise you, I didn't tell the A about the Contest."

"Then what? What can be as bad as…" Then she faltered, her voice breaking to a stifled cry.

Chase forced out the words. "I led them to Cole. I figured, if I stopped *Bluemantle*, the Scene would struggle to survive. The change in me came too late. I thought… I still thought it had to be done. I… I'm so, so sorry." He finally raised his wretched face and met her eyes.

Tears welled and rolled down her cheeks. Her tightened lips trembled.

"Wella…" he said, daring to reach out a hand.

"Don't touch me." She slowly rose, gripping the back of her chair for support. She looked around, wide-eyed, as if comprehension was an ornament she might find in the room. "Cole," she murmured. Then she turned to look at Chase, her face flushed and contorted. "You…? Oh, crow. Cole? I can't believe… How could you?"

Chase dropped his head. He felt his skin burning, his pulse racing.

Wella stared at him, her eyes black wells of disgust. "You have no idea," she said. "No idea at all. Who he was, what he did for us. The sacrifice." She slumped down on the bunk. "The person he was. A good man. Generous, kind, honest. All of that… And all that he stood for, what he achieved, you destroyed. All because of your fucking arrogance and spineless self-righteousness."

She glared at her brother, who cowered, head down. Then she closed her eyes and let silence say the rest.

Chase did not move.

Eventually, she got up from the bunk, took a deep breath and said, "I'm going out."

Chase looked up in horror. "But it's not safe. The A… The curfew—"

"The A are watching you, not me. And I don't care about the curfew. I'm used to hiding."

"Please—"

"Stay here. Do not leave this room. They will catch you if you do." She moved towards the door. "I need some time." Then she slipped through, closing the door silently behind her.

Alone, Chase became the sole judge of his actions. His scrutiny was brutal and thorough. He despised himself. Thoughts about the implant resurfaced now and then, but he suppressed these diversions. He would no longer entertain excuses. He had betrayed Cole, put innocent lives at risk, caused untold suffering. And now the A had Ursel.

He couldn't think beyond that horrifying fact. He felt appalled by his actions; hated the person he had become. He wanted to suffer, to face and endure the punishment for every consequence he had caused. Yet, the moment he thought of Ursel, the pain was too much to bear.

He sat on the hard floor, leaning against the concrete wall. The table eclipsed the light from the lamp, leaving him in a welcome half-light. Wallowing in the pitiful penumbra, Chase waited for Wella, both willing and dreading her return.

CHAPTER TWENTY-SIX

The three Troubadours stood in silence. A solemn triumvirate.

Their retreat had been swift. The precautions they had taken had paid dividend. They had evaded capture, as had every one of their players.

However, despite their best efforts to protect their followers, they knew a number had been trapped, unable to flee. They had heard their screams reverberate through the mountain's arteries. Heard the shouts of their captors as they stormed the caves and marched them away. The Troubadours mourned, fearing the fate of their lifeblood.

Pale Dexter chose his moment to change the subject. "We must consult the adjudicators," he said, his voice tentative.

Bend Sinister spun around and glared at him. "What? You dare raise that issue now? After what's happened?"

"We don't want to make it all for nothing."

"Nothing? Don't you see? It was all for *everything*."

"Now, let us maintain perspective…"

Bend Sinister stepped forward, bearing his greater size down upon Pale Dexter.

Chief slipped between them, forcing them apart. "Stop," she said. "Division will get us nowhere."

Pale Dexter crossed his arms. "Bend Sinister is adopting the moral high ground because he was opposed to the Contest from the start."

"And for good reason," said Bend Sinister. "But mistake me not, I take no pleasure in being proven right."

"Ha!"

"I mean it. My point is, consulting the adjudicators is not only inappropriate, it's entirely irrelevant. We have been forced down into the furthest reaches of this forsaken warren, potentially trapped and, thereby, doomed. There is the capture and likely demise of Bluemantle. It is possible we have lost a significant proportion of our followers, on whom our lives depend. Our underground haven, the one place it was possible to perform with a degree of safety, has been breached. In the face of this devastation, what relevance is the role of leader?"

Lacking a comeback, Pale Dexter huffed, expressing objection through a scornful glare.

"I was in favour of the Contest, as you know," said Chief. "Now, however, I agree with you, Bend Sinister. The question of leadership is redundant. The Scene is all but destroyed. If we are to survive, we need a plan. We have each performed and connected; we are satiated. But it is only a matter of time before we will need to perform again."

"There is a more immediate issue," said Bend Sinister. "For many years we have succeeded in evading capture, thanks to our karst kingdom. Now, our fortress has been discovered. It is only through our ingenuity that we escaped last night. But our hunters will be back – of that I am certain. And they will not leave until they have flushed us out."

The three Troubadours looked to each other, a common recognition forming between them.

The notion of departure had been raised before, but only ever as a flight of fancy. They had never regarded it a viable option because they had each believed it inconceivable. Now, with the luxury of choice removed, the idea took form, became solid, turned into necessity. Their minds rallied in new and different directions, connected by a single thread that drew them to the same conclusion.

It was Pale Dexter who spoke first. "Would we leave together?"

"That would be my preference," said Bend Sinister. "Our differences aside, we have shared our lives for two hundred years. You are my family. Our Scene is my home. Those fundamentals are noncontingent upon place. However, it is for each of you to decide. You are free to make your own way in the world, just as we did in the centuries before we found Wydeye and each other."

Chief and Pale Dexter remained silent, gently handling the option, feeling its weight, the shape of its contours.

Chief turned to Bend Sinister and said, "I am with you."

Bend Sinister bowed gracefully towards Chief. They both turned to Pale Dexter.

Pale Dexter nodded gravely. "As am I."

They stepped forward and placed their hands on each other's shoulders in spontaneous ceremony, forming a union. They held the moment, each struggling to conceive what had, for so long, felt beyond hope. Elsewhere.

Eventually, they broke away.

"With that decision made," said Bend Sinister, "I suggest we formulate a plan for our departure."

"Let us summon our players," said Pale Dexter. "Between us all, we can explore our options and agree upon the detail."

Bend Sinister smiled. "A good idea. Let us call them forth." He hesitated, then added, "However, before we do, there is something I must share with you."

"Please do," said Pale Dexter, intrigued.

Chief stood beside him, her cobalt eyes bright in the half-light.

"Last night, in the moment before the Authority's arrival, I saw a man in my cave. He emerged from one of our escape runs, dressed in military uniform. I thought then that we had been raided, but I was wrong. He stood there, watching me, listening. The instant I saw his face, I knew." He paused, looking at his expectant comrades. "It was our lost drummer."

"It can't have been," said Chief.

"You must have been mistaken. A trick of the light," offered Pale Dexter.

"I swear on the lives of every one of my players, I was not deceived. I know with all certainty that it was he. Twenty-six years it has been since he was taken from us. Whilst I held out hope for many years, I have long since feared him gone. My players and I have never stopped grieving his passing. And now, in such strange circumstances and in such alarming attire, he has returned."

"Did he know you saw him?" asked Chief.

"I believe so. But the moment was so very brief. An instant later, the Authority came crashing into the cave. There was no time to call out to him, to take him with us."

"Do your players know?" asked Pale Dexter.

"Not yet. I felt obliged to inform you both first. I appreciate the apparent risk. I need to know that you trust my certainty before I tell them. But tell them I must. He is their brother, after all. Do I have your blessing?"

Chief pulled at one of her silver dreads, absorbing the revelation.

Pale Dexter stepped in to fill her hesitation. "No matter the circumstance, if he were one of my players, I would know it. There would be no doubt." He bowed his head. "You have my blessing."

Chief studied Pale Dexter's face and slowly nodded. "Yes, you are right. As would I. I have absolute faith that I would." She turned to Bend Sinister. "Forgive my hesitation. I, too, grant you my blessing. This is wonderful news."

Bend Sinister's face lit up in a rare expression of joy. "Yes, it is wonderful indeed." Then the light dimmed. "Although, I don't know where that leaves us. Without knowing where he is and with no means to contact him, there is little I can do."

"He knows where you are," said Pale Dexter. "He will come back to find you."

"Yes. He will. You are right. I just hope he does so soon. With our decision to leave now firmly made, and the threat of the Authority returning to hunt us down, time is against us. I will not ask you to wait for him and put the lives of your own players at risk." His eyes turned dark, his voice strained. "After all this time, he returns to me. Yet he remains out of reach. Twenty-six years gone. And all he has left is a matter of days, or even hours, to make it home."

CHAPTER TWENTY-SEVEN

Dent Lore ran the Nanso Trail, as he had done every day for as long as he could remember. Reaching the track's summit, a limestone plateau at the foot of the Nanso Heights, he stopped to catch his breath. Ordinarily he would marvel at the view; Wydeye appeared so peaceful and welcoming from this very distant, distorted perspective. This time, however, his eyes were trained on the ground beneath his feet, his thoughts lost in what lay hidden below.

Had a part of me known? he thought, wondering if there had been another lure that had drawn him, daily, to the Heights. *Can I feel it now?*

He sat on a rock and closed his eyes, a warm breeze touching the cheek that bore the mark of old. Bewildered, he felt dislocated, his true self trapped in the body of a doppelganger. Unanswered questions tormented him, triggering ever more in their wake. All he knew for certain was that he had known the man and the music. Bend Sinister. Not mere association, or some past acquaintance. This was something much stronger: a bond reawakened the moment he saw him. *This is who I really am,* he thought, *not the person I've become.*

Aspects of his life began to make sense for the first time. He had no memories from his childhood. The fact of his adoption by the Authority was something told to him, rather than an experience he recalled. The Authority and the Allears was all he knew. He had put it down to absorption in the role. It had taken over his life; it *was* his life. And he had accepted that, just as he had accepted and championed the Authority's manifesto. *Do I believe in it? Is it really what I want too?* Even as he asked himself the question, he thought, *Yes. The Music Makers are a threat to the Authority. They are dangerous. They must be captured at all cost.* Yet the thoughts came ready-made; precast and constructed like so much of Wallace's concrete legacy. *I know this. But do I believe it?*

He searched deep inside his buried self, fighting to ignore the man on the outside. In the depths of his gut, his instinct had been a gagged voice, but at times he had heard its muffled cries. Those instances of opposition, of downright disgust, he had had to suppress and deny. They would have been regarded as weakness, disloyalty. The Authority's brutality was justified as a means to an end. A questioning of those means would have been deemed a lack of commitment to achieving that end. Not quite treason, but close enough.

Dent had questioned the means, repeatedly. But only ever to himself. His loyalty was ingrained. He was impeccably trained. At times he had almost felt ashamed of the doubts. It was as if, even by thinking them, he was already failing Governor Blix and the Authority.

His mind turned to his meeting with the Governor the previous day. He had been on edge from the outset. Then came her strange behaviour towards him, denigrating his performance, probing without questioning. *It's as if she suspects something*, he thought. *But how can she? I don't even know myself.* Serving her will had always been his personal mission, more than mere duty. Her goal was his, her motives his own. With the commitment to achieving a mutually desired end, he had felt genuine respect for the woman.

He had regarded her as strong, determined, ambitious. Now he felt wary of her, intimidated, threatened. You don't cross the A; that wasn't hearsay or reactionary rumour to an inflated reputation. It was fact. And Dent knew the consequences. Whilst he was loyal through conviction, he knew of many troopers whose obedience was motivated by fear. For the first time in his memory, he knew how they felt.

What can I do? he thought. *I don't even know... I don't understand... But how can I carry on?*

As if putting him to the test, his pager beeped. Recognising the number, his heart sank. Helpless as to an alternative course, he forced the questions back and grasped hold of the attitude that was second nature. Disguised beneath familiar skin, Dent ran back down the trail, not stopping until he reached the towering gates of the Authority Complex and the nearest telephone.

The number had been Wulfwin's office. When Dent dialled in, a junior officer relayed the message. He was to report to Detention Centre C immediately.

Dusty and sweat-streaked from his run, Dent reluctantly abandoned his plan to shower and headed straight for C-Block, the highest security penitentiary on the Complex.

Dent had very little to do with detention and nothing to do with interrogation. The order to meet Wulfwin inside C-Block rattled his already agitated nerves. He approached the building with a foreboding that its bleak exterior encouraged. A vast, concrete structure, jutting at angry angles, its looming façade was pierced by narrow apertures like multiple stab wounds.

"You look a wreck," said Wulfwin, emerging from the main

entrance as Dent approached. "And I made the order twenty minutes ago. Where the fuck have you been?"

"I was running the trail."

"That's why you stink like a goat's groin. No matter. Smells a damn sight worse in there," he said, nodding to the block behind him.

"With your permission, I'd like to shower. If there's time."

"There isn't." Wulfwin spun around. "Follow me. I'll fill you in on the way." He marched into the building with Dent on his trench coat-tail.

They passed through a reception foyer and down a narrow passageway, dismal grey. Fluorescent tubes hung from the ceiling at intervals, emitting a faint buzz – amplified white noise to Dent's sensitive ears. He struggled to hear Wulfwin's explanation.

"New orders from the top. Governor wants you to diversify your talents. You're to assist with questioning."

"But I don't…" Dent stopped in his tracks, stunned. He had to jog to catch up. "I spoke with the Governor yesterday. She didn't mention anything."

"Well, whatever you did talk about, it appears you've pissed her off. She wants you hands on. Playing nasty. Hence 'C', rather than the poke and tickle in the other blocks."

"I didn't say anything. She asked me about family."

"Ain't my problem, trooper," he said, holding up a hand as he continued marching down the hall. "I'm just following orders. But I reckon this is going to be *your* problem. Don't think I don't know. I just can't work out what it's about – if it's because you're squeamish or you're just too fuckin' soft. Same difference. I tell you, if you were in my squad, I'd have beaten it out of you by now. Sorted your spineless aversion to the tooth-and-nail approach to law and order. Ain't I right, Lore?

You're a fucking weak sister."

"I'm an Allear. And I'm good at my job. Violence is not a prerequisite."

"Whatever you say, Lore. It's still written all over your yellow-bellied face. That's why I know you're not going to enjoy what's about to happen. And why you'll try to worm your way out of following this particular order, like you did with recruitment. I happen to agree with your rationale behind the Test reforms. The Governor, however, seems to have detected the whiff of bullshit. These are her orders, not mine. She wants to see you get your hands dirty."

They turned left into a stairwell and climbed two flights in silence. They emerged in a corridor identical to the one they had just walked down. "First, training," Wulfwin continued, still walking ahead, his back to Dent. "And today is a dive in at the deep end. Observe the master."

Dent heard Wulfwin's smile as he said this, a saccharin tone of self-amusement coating his voice. His heart sank with lead-weight dread. For the first time since his revelation in the cave, he felt utterly trapped, imprisoned inside the person he had become. Now desperate to break free, he knew he would have to bide his time, play along so as not to arouse suspicion. If he displayed any form of resistance, Wulfwin wouldn't hesitate long enough to blink before hauling him up for insubordination. Common knowledge of the associated punishment contributed to the staggeringly high level of discipline in the ranks.

They branched right and stopped at the mouth of a wide corridor, brightly lit with steel doors running down its length on either side. A security guard at the corridor's entrance snapped to attention.

"Here's the deal," Wulfwin said, ignoring the guard. "In cell thirty-two we have ourselves a little gem. User. Apprehended at the Scene. Source of one of our sleepers. She's connected to the

Music Makers. We don't yet know how close, but close enough to make her a special case. And, we assume, close enough to make her a tough fucker to break. Hence, she's mine." He leant forward, his eyes twitching. "Watch and learn, Allear."

Wulfwin turned and led Dent to one of the steel doors, followed by the security guard. The guard wielded a cluster of keys and inserted one into the brick-like lock. There was a low, metallic clunk as multiple bolts slid from their mortices. Wulfwin pushed open the door and entered. Dent followed. As the guard closed the door behind them, the sound of the lock's engagement reverberated, trapped by impenetrable walls.

The cell was four metres square. The walls and floor were rendered and painted in washable grey emulsion, although the option to clean was unused. Against the far wall was a steel rack, six feet by four, heavy-duty straps hanging limp like broken arms. Paraphernalia lay scattered on a table on the left. On the right, a bucket and standpipe. On the floor in the centre, wearing a brown, sleeveless tunic, slumped a slight figure, hair wet from water, sweat or blood, Dent couldn't tell.

At first, he averted his eyes, but he knew the gesture was empty. He was there, in the cell, on the side of the Authority. He made himself look. Any lingering loyalty needed to be exorcised by witnessing atrocity. He knew this was Blix's test. He also knew he'd be applying utterly different criteria by which to judge success. So, he stared at the crumpled figure, his face rigid, screaming from the inside.

"She's unconscious," said Wulfwin, circling the prisoner. "We'll leave her for the moment, let her body recover just enough to survive another round. In the meantime, lesson number one. Take note. Interrogation is a game, the prisoner your opponent. The game itself is ironically subtle: a delicate dance between strategy and puzzle-solving. Essentially, your opponent has something that you want, much like territory in Ribatchi. To win, you have to take that territory. To lose, your opponent must deny you the pleasure.

"In this game, you are obviously playing for information. You need to select and apply the most effective strategy in order to win the information your opponent is holding from you. And, like any game, there are penalties. Push too hard in the wrong direction and your opponent dies, taking the information with them. Death is their greatest defence. Your supreme offence is to make a move that forces your opponent to surrender the information before that happens.

"In short, you need to locate their weak spot. Their own particular breaking point. That could be some form of personal injury to them, perhaps. A threat to parent or partner. The untimely death of their child, even. Who the fuck knows. It's your job to find out. That's the point of the game. Got it?"

Dent nodded, too sickened to speak and pull it off.

"Thus far, our opponent here has proved adept at the game. She doesn't want to share. We've even made it easy for her. Narrowed it down. One question is all she needs to answer. One simple fucking question. But she's holding her ground. My colleagues have applied some pressure, as you can see. Their powers of persuasion haven't won us any territory, unfortunately. So now it's my turn. Time to find her weakness. And this, Lore, is your training." He stepped up to Dent, their faces close. "Watch. Don't react. Don't say anything. Witness. Let it happen. Learn."

An agonising groan came from Ursel's slumped form.

"Ah, she wakes!" Wulfwin walked over to the cell door and banged twice with his fist. Four troopers entered, dressed in black fatigues, faces expressionless. Two stood either side of Ursel; the other two moved to either side of Dent.

Dent looked at them both, then at Wulfwin, alarmed.

"Don't look so fucking freaked," said Wulfwin. "I know you're yellow. They're there to make sure you keep watching." He sneered and turned back to the troopers beside Ursel. "Strap her to the rack. Tight. Restrain her head."

Once stretched out on the steel frame, the extent of Ursel's injuries became apparent. Her face was bruised and swollen. Congealed blood stuck to cuts on her cheeks and her arm. The skin where her right arm should have been was burnt, the flesh beetle-black and blistering. Her bare legs were whip-slashed. Battered and bloodied, it was only her eyes that retained any sign of life. They darted around the room, assessing, counting, weighing up. Finally, they landed on the man before her and darkened, obsidian-hard.

"Welcome back," said Wulfwin, with twisted conviviality. "Round one went to you. I'll hand it to you, you're tougher than you look. Now we enter round two. Same rules. I ask you a question; you answer it. Let's see how we get on, shall we?" He cocked his head, playing to his audience. Then he removed his trench coat, laying it carefully on the table beside him. His bared arms made for a bold statement of strength. Rubbing his hands together, he approached Ursel. "Let's practise. I say: where are the Music Makers? And you say?" He held a cupped hand to his ear in a mock-listening pose.

Ursel glared at him, unflinching. Her face was white. Her clenched teeth and trembling upper lip hinted at the agony her eyes denied.

"And still she plays tough. So, User, let us be clear. Round two is different. My colleagues have provided the warm-up. Now, we get down to business. You've proved that you can withstand a little general pressure. This time, I'm going to hit you where it hurts. By way of example, let's start with this," he said, pointing to the question mark tattoo on her arm. "Good at asking questions, but not so great at answering them, is that it? A little ink joke? Well, it ain't fucking funny."

He walked over to the table and picked up a scalpel and a wad of lint. He returned to Ursel and, without hesitation, made an incision on her upper arm, level with the top of the tattoo. Holding the knife steady, he said, "I ask, you answer. Where are the Music Makers hiding?"

Ursel stared ahead, then closed her eyes.

"You asked for it, bitch." He drew the scalpel down, cutting a long, straight line through her skin. Blood oozed, extending the line down her arm before dripping to the floor. In slow, deliberate movements, he cut a square around the tattoo. Then he said, "Where are the fucking Music Makers, User scum?"

Silence.

He held the lint against her seeping flesh and in one, swift movement, he tore the square of skin from her arm.

Ursel screamed.

Dent retched and attempted to turn away. His trooper guard held him by the shoulders, forcing him to face forwards. Dizzy and white, he made his eyes glaze over, fighting back the urge to vomit.

"Sort it out, for fuck's sake," hissed Wulfwin to the troopers beside the rack, while he went over to wash his bloody hands under the standpipe tap. One of the troopers held the lint to Ursel's bleeding wound, while the other fetched a bandage from the table and wound it around her arm, covering the crimsoned wad.

Ursel's eyes remained tightly shut, tears leaking uncontrollably from beneath swollen lids. She breathed quickly, flinching with each rise of her diaphragm as bruised ribs pushed against broken skin.

Wulfwin glanced at Dent, then spat at the floor. His

demeanour had changed – the jovial showman replaced by a dark ruthlessness and violent fury without bounds.

He stared at Ursel, fists clenched, slowly nodding. "Okay, here's the score," he said. "That was my pre-amble. I hope it set an appropriate tone for what's to follow. If it has, I'm going to be kind and give you the benefit of a heads-up. If you know what's coming, you might prefer to deny me my amusement. Save us all some time and save yourself considerable loss. With that in mind, let us talk long view. Apart from your life, what have you only got one of? What part of you can you least afford to lose?" He grabbed her arm around the makeshift bandage, causing Ursel to cry out. "That is my end game. Do yourself a fucking favour and avoid the unnecessary pain in reaching that conclusion, because it will take some time to get there. Understood?" He glared once more at Ursel, trying to hold her blinking, rolling eyes. "Let's try again. Where are the motherfuckers hiding?"

Dent trembled, willing her to speak. His trooper guard maintained a firm, two-handed grip on his arms. He looked about him, frantically searching for a means of intervention.

Ursel said nothing.

"Okay, play it your way," said Wulfwin. "For my next move, I claim something I assume is of significant value to a User. You flout the law of the Authority so that you can indulge in your addiction. How would you feel if you were unable to hear your precious music ever again?"

Ursel stared at Wulfwin, her eyes suddenly wide and steady.

"Well now, I seem to have your attention at last. Let's make the most of the moment, shall we? Last chance. Where are the Music Makers?"

Ursel held her stare. Then she closed her eyes tight, bracing herself. Her swollen lips remained defiantly sealed.

Dent yelled, "No!"

Wulfwin spun around. "Shut up, Lore. Whose fucking side are you on?" He looked back at Ursel and spat in her face. "User Scum deserves it."

He strode over to the table and took a moment to select his means. Grabbing a pencil, he returned to Ursel's side. Her contorted face was wet with tears. Her eyes and mouth were firmly shut.

"Your loss," Wulfwin hissed, as he held the pencil to her left ear, placing its sharpened point inside the canal. With the heal of his other hand, he slammed against the end of the pencil, forcing it far enough to pierce the drum.

This time, Ursel's scream was acute and unending.

With her head firmly braced, she was unable to move as Wulfwin crossed to her right side and held the pencil tip inside her other ear. He did not hesitate; there was no second chance.

At the moment of impact, the screaming stopped and Ursel hung limp. "For fuck's sake. Find a pulse, quick," he said to the troopers. "Keep her alive. She's not getting out of it that easy. She's not going to win. I will not let the bitch beat me."

He stormed past Dent and kicked the door twice. On the threshold, he turned around and said, "This is what we're up against, Lore. This is why the Users deserve every fucking thing they get."

CHAPTER TWENTY-EIGHT

"I didn't think you were going to come back," said Chase. He was sat on the floor in the hide, knees up, numb. He had no idea if it was night or day. The measureless time since Wella had left had opened up into a single, gaping chasm, deep and lamentably dark. A hole for soul-searching.

"Neither did I," said Wella, sitting on the lower bunk, her back straight.

"But you're here. Why?"

"If you care for Ursel, you'll want to help her. If you've anything more than the slightest trace of regret for what you've done, you won't stand back and let her die for nothing."

"Of course I want to help her. I'll do anything; anything to make up for what I've…" He shook his head, his face drawn.

"That's why I'm back. I have to find a way to save her. And to salvage the Scene. Strikes me I might need your help to do that."

"Anything."

She moved to sit at the table, her taut features unsoftened by the lamp's amber glow. "Get up off the floor and sit here," she said, nodding to the chair opposite her. "Let's start with what I've missed while I've been away. Talk to me. Tell me what's been happening. Tell me everything you know."

Chase hauled himself off the floor and sat opposite Wella. He laid his hands on the table and studied them as he spoke, addressing cracked knuckles in favour of more judgemental company. "First, there was the swallow hole," he began. He rattled off the developments of the last three and a half weeks, barely pausing for breath, as if a running start was the only way he could bear to admit his part in their escalation. "The A raided Cole's quarters. Ursel's convinced they took him; he'd left a note or something, saying he'd be there. Although the A didn't know who Cole was, they knew all about *Bluemantle*. Ursel said there's no way he'll break. She's certain the A will know that, so they won't even try to keep him alive. She said that, without *Bluemantle*, the Scene won't survive. She said she couldn't stand by and let that happen. She's made up her mind. She's determined to take on *Bluemantle*."

"What?" Wella's eyes grew wide.

"She said that she knows where Cole's workshop is and where the drops are. She knows who taught Cole encryption. She believes that, if she can keep *Bluemantle* alive, the Scene stands a chance of surviving."

"That's it. We have to get her out of there. She won't tell them shit, I know it. If, by some miracle, Cole's still alive, they'll have him in Itherside Hold. There's no way of getting him out. But, as far as the A are concerned, Ursel's just one among hundreds they arrested. She won't mean anything to them."

Horror drained the blood from Chase's face; sweat beaded on his brow.

Distracted by her glimpse of hope, Wella didn't notice. "I've no idea how," she said, "but if we could get her out, we'd not only be saving her. We'd be saving everything."

Chase's panic drew a curtain across the truth. "Whatever influence the A had over me," he said, breathless, "whatever they did to control me, that's gone. I still don't give a damn about the Scene. I won't fight for *Bluemantle*. But I will do anything, *anything*, to save Ursel."

Wella stared at Chase, attempting to read his expression in mute inquisition.

"Look," he said. "I know you've no reason to trust me. I'm surprised you're even speaking to me."

"If I felt there was a choice—"

"But I swear I'm done with the A. I want to make amends. I can't undo what I've done, but I can do the right thing from now on. And that means helping Ursel." He held up his hands to his temples, his eyes searching hopelessly. "But how? We can't exactly storm the Complex, break in to get her out."

"Of course we can't. We need help. That's why I'm going back."

"Underground? No. That's crazy."

"It's necessary."

"Why? What can they do? They're hiding under a mountain, for crow's sake."

"Don't underestimate them."

"Then I'm going with you."

"You're kidding me, right?"

"I'm serious. I have to help Ursel. I don't care about the risk."

"I don't give a shit about the risk to you. I'm thinking about the Troubadours. You're an informer to the fucking A. And they're watching you. You think I'm going to take you underground and have you lead them directly to their so-called Music Makers? You're out of your mind."

"I've told you. I'm finished with the A." He held out his hands, palms up. "How can I make you believe me?"

"I'll tell you how—"

"Please. Anything."

"If you seriously want to put things right, you've got to face up to what you've done wrong. You've got to be honest about it. Admit the truth and face the flak."

Chase swallowed hard, tasting the rancid bile of denial. "I've told you everything."

"Not me. Brann."

"What…? No—"

"Admitting the truth is only meaningful if it matters who you're admitting it to."

"He'll hate me."

"With good reason."

"I can't tell him… I did it for him in the first place. He couldn't cope. It was the only way to get him out."

"Don't make excuses. You know full well that won't hold with him. He would never have wanted you to be a grass on his account. It doesn't matter why you did it. And you know that. That's why you don't want to tell him."

"Please—"

"I'm not doing this out of spite. What do you think it took me to come back here? After what you've done? I can't forgive you, but I need to know I can trust you going forward. I decided that the only way is for you to admit what you've done to someone who really matters. In the absence of Ursel, the only other person is Brann."

Chase gripped the table, his eyes wide.

Wella rose and climbed up to the raised bunk. She lay down on her back, closed her eyes and sighed. "I'm glad you think it's such a big ask. Gives me confidence. I'll give you a few hours to think about it. Let me know when you've made your decision." She turned her head and looked at Chase, broken, on the chair. "And just so you know, if you refuse to tell Brann, we're through. You can stay here for a few days, let the dust settle. But I will leave. And, this time, I won't come back."

—

When Wella led Brann out of the hide, Chase was left alone to endure the sting of self-loathing. He sat at the table, head in hands. It had been the most painful ten minutes of his life.

Wella returned and sat on the lower bunk in silence.

"He hates me," said Chase, gut-sick.

"Yes, for now. But he'll get over it."

"I doubt it."

"Quit feeling sorry for yourself. He's disappointed in you. Feels betrayed. But now's your chance to make amends. So, drag yourself out of that hole of self-pity and pull yourself together."

"I did it for him—"

"Enough, Chase. That might have been your reason to begin with. That doesn't account for the subsequent fifteen years." She stood up, arms folded. "You fucked up. Admit it. And now put it behind you. Atonement can be found in what you do from here on in."

"That's why you've got to let me go with you. I did what you asked. You said."

"I know. But Chase, they've got Watchers on you. Eyes on the ground. Whilst you may not betray the Troubadours yourself, leading the A directly to them is just as bad."

"I'll shave my head. Or wear a wig. I'll go in disguise. We could go through the woods again, back the way we came. Skirt the city altogether."

"It'll take us all day to get there."

"Please. How can I help if I'm trapped in here?"

Wella rubbed her forehead, her eyes glazed in the process of option-weighing. "You can help, in time. Just not with this."

"But you said—"

"Trust doesn't come overnight. And my loyalty is to the Troubadours. There are rules in place to protect them. I'm not about to break those rules just because you decide to stamp your feet and insist on proving a point. Stop for a second and think about what it is you're asking. To them, Cole *was* *Bluemantle*. And *Bluemantle* is crucial to their survival. So no, Chase. Not this time." He was about to interrupt, but she held up her hand. "I acknowledge what you've just done in telling Brann, how hard it was. And I know why you did it. So, I'm telling you, I'm on board. We work together. We'll find a way to help Ursel. You'll have to play a part in that. But going underground? No. This is where it works both ways, big brother. I'm asking *you* to trust *me*."

—

Dusk was yielding to darkness by the time Wella reached the Nanso Heights. The temperature had dropped slightly, but the air remained sultry and dust-clogged.

Her journey through the city had been a trial. It was forty-eight hours since the Contest and the Authority's intimidating presence on Wydeye's streets remained pervasive. Taking a circuitous route, Wella had managed to avoid attention until she met a Deaf Squad roadblock on the approach to Westgate Arch. A chance encounter and offer of a ride with a carter she knew saved her. He was bald and burly, with a small tattoo, peeping through stubble, on his left cheek. When they were ordered to halt, the carter did the talking, presenting bona-fide papers for his cargo of scrap metal. Wella, donning the low-brimmed hat the carter had lent her, stared ahead, feigning nonchalance.

When they had safely passed through and were out of sight, the carter pulled up. Wella jumped to the ground, reaching up to shake his hand. "Thank you."

"Be safe," he said, smiling. With a brief nod of his head and brush of his cheek, he called to his goats to trot on.

Once outside the city's limits, Wella had hiked the remaining distance off-road and unseen. Constantly glancing over her shoulder, she had scaled the lower Heights, grateful for the failing light. Eventually, she reached a barely perceptible fissure in the flank of Lyun Mountain. She slipped through the crack and disappeared.

Underground had become her home long before her permanent move there nearly a month ago. She passed through the limestone arteries with warm familiarity, heart-bound haemoglobin. She relished the soundtrack of dripping water and the percussive echo of her footfall.

The sounds distracted her from thoughts of Chase, which had laid claim to her mind since his admission. His confession to Brann had served its purpose, bringing partial relief. Yet, she still felt disgust at his betrayal. Trust would be a long time in coming – forgiveness possibly never.

The descent into the depths of the mountain was long; yet, as she neared the sanctuary of Bend Sinister's camp, her spirits revived. Her loyalty had always been to Bend Sinister since her first visit to the Scene. When she'd moved underground, she had become one of only a handful of followers who had made the commitment to work for them as part of their retinue. She knew she would never be able to enjoy the same protection as the players themselves. However, the high risk was her lowest consideration. Her allegiance had become a calling; her life in the Scene far more fulfilling than the one she had endured overground.

The confidence that had propelled her through the city waivered once she reached her destination. This was not the way of things. You didn't just knock and ask to speak to a Troubadour. There were protocols. Conventions to observe. *Will he agree to see me?* she now thought. *Without prior request and appointment?* As she faltered before his bunker, the deepest, most fortified of his camps, she began to doubt herself. Then she remembered why she was there and forged confidence out of necessity.

She picked up a rock that lay at the foot of a narrow opening and struck the limestone wall four times. Silence, then soft sounds approached: cautious steps on stone, breathing from beyond the aperture's shadow.

"It's Wella," she whispered.

"Wella!" A face appeared, then a body, stepping out from the crack to embrace her. A young man, head shaved, wearing khaki shorts and sandals.

Wella returned the embrace, her anxiety abating. "Estrin. It's good to see you."

Like Wella, Estrin had forsaken life overground to work for the Scene. "It's good to see you too," he said. "I've been so worried for you. For everyone. We feared the worst. But look," he said, holding her by the shoulders, overcome with emotion, "you're here."

"I've come to request an audience with Bend Sinister. I know that's a tall order, out of the blue like this. Do you think he'll see me? Only, I have news he must hear. It's important, about *Bluemantle*." She stared at Estrin, alarmed. "What? What is it?"

"They've left. All of them."

"What? That can't be true."

"In the early hours of this morning. The Troubadours and players called us together for a meeting. They told us their decision, explained why they had no choice but to leave."

"I can't believe it—"

"I know. I couldn't at first. They invited us all to go with them, the whole retinue."

"Why didn't you go?"

"For this very reason. Someone had to stay behind, to explain to any followers who appeared. I doubted any would, not after the Contest. But I had to make sure they knew the truth. I hated to think of people assuming the Troubadours had run away, tail down." His face brightened momentarily. "And then you appear. I did the right thing. Now that I've told you, you can spread the word. Make sure followers know. They had to go. The Scene couldn't survive."

"But this is what I've come to tell Bend Sinister."

"What?"

"That it *can* survive. There's someone who'll take on *Bluemantle*. Ursel. A friend of mine."

"Really? She could do that?"

"She was close to Cole. She knows the whole operation."

Estrin shook his head slowly. "Incredible as that is, I don't know if it would be enough. The Troubadours explained it all. They have to play. And now the A knows where they hide. It was either leave or be hunted down, gradually fading away while delaying the inevitable. They had to leave in order to live."

"And how will their followers live? We need the Scene as much as they need us. How will *we* survive?"

"They're sensitive to that. That's part of the reason they've never left before. They know they can't be followed."

"So, what's changed?"

"They lost the choice to stay."

"I can't believe they've gone. I don't know what I'll do…"

"But this is why I stayed. To let people like you know. When the Troubadours find somewhere to settle, they'll send word. We can spread the message. You can join them. Others too. It needn't be over."

"You said yourself, most can't follow. And I can't leave. Not now." She leant against the cold stone wall, eyes closed. "This can't be happening."

Estrin held out his hand and touched Wella's cheek, tracing a finger over the tiny line of ink. Most wouldn't know it was there. He touched his own badge of allegiance. "Bend Sinister lives. That's the most important thing. As long as he does, we can too. Trust in hope. We'll find a way."

–

Wella sat at the small wooden table, her head in her hands. Had the hide boasted apertures, the diluted light of dawn would reveal shapes in a retreating darkness. As it was, the gas lamp glowed on – a timeless beacon in a never-ending night.

Chase sat opposite her, his face transformed.

She hadn't noticed the change. Her body was exhausted from the long journey back to the hide, her mind and spirit weakened by her mission's failure. "I didn't expect they'd just give up," she said.

"But they haven't, have they? From what you said, it sounds like they're doing the opposite."

"They're saving themselves, but they're giving up on the Scene."

"Did you honestly think they could do something about Ursel?"

"Yes." She faltered. "At least... I don't know."

"The A would trade every single follower they've got banged up for a Music Maker."

Wella glared at him.

"Sorry," he said, "a Troubadour. You know that. The A's obsessed. How could the Troubadours intervene? What could they even do? And now that the A have found their hiding place, they won't stop. They'll be on the scent, hunting day and night. I'm afraid I agree with your friend. What choice did the Troubadours have?"

"It's alright for you. You wanted an end to the Scene. You said so. Now you've got your wish." It was only then that she noticed a glint in his eyes, a relaxing of the muscles that had contorted his expression since his admission. "That's it, isn't it? It's written all over your face. Your Music Makers have fucked off. Mission accomplished."

"That's not true."

"Of course it is."

"That's what I thought before, yes. But while you were gone, it all fell into place. The things that Ursel said to me. How I felt after seeing Chief. The effect Bend Sinister had on me. I don't know… I've been sat here for hours on end, going over and over everything. Then it dawned on me. I understand now. I get what Ursel was saying." He countered Wella's sceptical stare with an enlightened smile. "Ursel said that *Bluemantle* is a map, an invitation for citizens to seek and discover the truth for themselves. She likened it to the Telltale Circus, how it's a means to an end. Revealing the way so that the audience can engage and learn on their own terms. I didn't get it before—"

"I don't get it now."

"Don't you see? She believes the answer is in enabling citizens to ask the question, challenge a broadcast, decide for themselves. She said that a question only becomes a problem if it's not addressed. That's what the Authority relies on to maintain dependency. All their broadcasts, their reassuring clichés. They tell us what to think. Who to believe. Who to blame. They deny alternatives. Erase elsewhere. With no apparent way through, people forget to ask the question. Ursel said that, as long as we keep asking 'why', we'll discover the truth eventually. Others can too. If they're shown alternative paths, people will realise they're free to decide for themselves."

"Can I stop you there?"

"I know, it's okay. I didn't understand it at first—" he said, swept away by the rush of revelation.

"No, Chase. You're talking to the converted. I challenged the A's narrative. I went to a show because I wanted to make up my own mind. Sure, I was curious. I'd dabbled in drugs a few years back. I was up for giving music a go."

"So, you get it, then? You know what I'm saying."

"No! Where's this leading? I want to salvage the Scene and, crow help me, save Ursel. But banging on about the sense she talked isn't going to save her."

Chase slid a piece of paper, covered in pencil scrawl, towards her.

She eyed it from a distance. "What's this?"

"A story."

"I don't believe this. I've just risked my neck going back underground while you've sat here writing a sodding story?"

"Ursel said the theatre aims to help their audience discover universal truths within a story. So, I've written one about the truth she taught me."

"Oh, this is priceless—"

"Hear me out." He stared at Wella, the glint in his eyes sharpening with crystalline intent. "The theatre families will be devastated by Ursel's arrest. Take this to them, explain that I've written it as a tribute to her. Suggest they turn it into a play that they perform in the Circus, to raise awareness of her case and raise funds to campaign for her release. They'll want to do something and, hopefully, this will appeal. There's a guy on security; he's helped me before. Explain you're my sister and you're there about Ursel. He'll get you in and introduce you. I would go myself, but I can't risk leaving here."

"I still don't—"

"Listen. If the audience pay attention, they'll pick something up. An unease. An earworm of doubt. If it works, the story will hold up a few mirrors. Force them to look afresh at what's going on around them. Actually listen to the broadcasts, rather than dismiss the white noise. Actively look at the murals and posters and recognise the face of their neighbour in the red-eyed rats."

"This is all very noble, Chase. But you can't change people's attitudes overnight."

"We don't. They change their own. That's the point."

"And this helps Ursel how?"

"Because, in the absence of *Bluemantle*, we need to find other means of showing the way. The story is a signpost. But it's only the start. A precursor."

"To what?"

"My plan to save her."

CHAPTER TWENTY-NINE

With every step up the rocky ascent, Dent Lore struggled to erase the images, feign deafness to the screams that resonated in his head, not reel at the stench of blood, shit and vomit that clung to his clothes. His senses were haunted by determined souvenirs of the last twenty-four hours.

He had escaped having to torture anyone himself, but it was only a matter of time. If he went back.

What he couldn't work out was why. *Does she know about me?* he thought. *Is this a punishment? Or a warning?* All he knew for certain was that Governor Blix had personally insisted that his training in interrogation be protracted and thorough, forcing him to observe the most brutal and inhumane of techniques. Men and women, young and old, children. Even now, he dry-retched at the memories. Foul bile burnt his throat. He climbed.

If he went back... He kept the option open with a token question mark, yet he'd decided the moment Wulfwin rammed the pencil into that woman's ears. He knew he would forever hear her screams. He would remember, always, the defiance in her face, right up until the moment the first eardrum was ruptured, when everything about her was agony.

He doubted she was still alive. He believed she'd be better off dead.

Whatever her motives, Blix's intervention had merely expedited the decision that he knew he'd make regardless. He had to find Bend Sinister.

Dent crept up the Heights. He avoided the main trail, knowing it would be teeming with troopers. He also knew Special Forces would be on the south and east sides of Lyun Mountain, guarding the known entrances to the caves, searching for others. Scaling the less accessible north face, Dent finally found the narrow crevice that had led him to the cave the night of the raid. He knew Bend Sinister wouldn't be there. He just hoped some buried instinct would lead him the rest of the way.

Deep inside the mountain, he found himself in a small stone chamber that gave the impression of a lobby to a far greater space beyond. He faced a wall of rock with a deep gouge in its surface. He stood at the opening and listened. There, hidden by a false silence, he detected breathing. He held his own breath to eliminate the possibility. The faintest of sounds remained, irregular and afraid. "Who's there?" he whispered.

No response.

"Please. I mean no harm. I'm looking for someone." The breathing resumed, this time with staccato indecision. "Bend Sinister."

Hesitation, then a face emerged from the shadows of the gouge. "Who are you?" the young man said, eyes wide and uncertain.

"A friend. Of the Scene."

"What's your name?"

Good question, thought Dent. "Grey," he said, seizing the first word that came to him. "Please, I've come to see Bend Sinister. Can you take me to him?"

"If you're part of the Scene, then you know it doesn't work like that."

"I know," he said, guessing too late the faux pas. "But this is important." Then an idea struck him without knowing its origin. "I can prove I'm to be trusted." He stepped forward and turned his left cheek to the man, parting the hairs where the ink lay hidden.

"Why didn't you say?" said the young man, stepping into the chamber and smiling warmly. He held out his hand. "I'm Estrin. Welcome, Grey."

Dent shook his hand, bewildered by the agency of instinct. "Pleased to meet you. So, Estrin, can you help me?"

"I'm afraid I've bad news. Bend Sinister and his players have left. As have Pale Dexter and Chief. Their retinues, too. All gone."

"Gone? No…"

"Yesterday, early. Their departure was a forced hand. Hopefully it will prove a fortuitous one in the future, once they're established elsewhere."

"I… I have to see him."

"I'm sorry, friend. It's been well over twenty-four hours since they left."

"Where? Where have they gone?"

"I don't know. They'll send word once they've found somewhere to settle. Could be some time, though. It took them forever to find Wydeye, so they say. We've got to sit tight and wait. It's the only way."

"No…" Dent shook his head, unbelieving, wishing he'd acted on impulse the moment he felt it. "I must find him. Which way did they go?"

"I've no idea. It'd be impossible to track them down. They'll make sure of that. And besides, once they cleared the Heights, they could've headed in any direction. All I can show you is the escape passage they used. Beyond that, your guess is as good as mine."

"I'm learning to trust mine. Please, show me the way."

Estrin hesitated only briefly before yielding to Dent's determined expression. "I still think you're best to wait with the rest of us. But, if you insist…" He handed Dent a dynamo torch and kept hold of a second, pumping the handle. "Follow me." He turned and led the way through the narrow opening.

After several metres of squeezing through tight bookends of rock, they entered a cavernous space, cathedral-high. Dent trailed behind in awe, distracted by the enormity of the cave that dwarfed them both.

Ever descending, they moved through dark passageways and smaller caves, past traces of domesticity hinting at the home it had so recently been: carved goblets, blind gas lamps, books, a pair of leather sandals. Estrin picked up a paperback and stuffed it in his shorts.

Eventually, they reached a wall of apparently solid rock. "They left through here," said Estrin.

Dent looked from Estrin, to the wall and back, his eyes asking the question where words failed.

Estrin grinned. "I know," he said. "Good, isn't it?" He ran his hands over the stone, his fingertips gently reading surface texture as if it were a Braille love letter. His hands gripped two imperceptible holds. Then he locked his arms straight and stood, legs braced, pushing his bodyweight into the wall.

Dent observed, mystified at first, then dumbfounded as the stone began to shift. Inch by grinding inch, a lozenge of limestone receded, leaving a coffin mould gradually sinking into the wall. Then the stone gave, revealing a slice of black, through which Estrin disappeared. Dent followed.

On the other side, their torches illuminated a passageway of a different character. Low and angular, this was a tunnel, chiselled into the mountain's rock-flesh. Estrin crouched down, his head level with the tunnel's mouth. "They've spent years making these escape shafts. Just in case. And thank crow they did. It's how they dodged the A at the Contest. And with Special Forces guarding the visible entrances, these last resorts were their only way out. They used this one yesterday morning."

Dent stared into the handcut hollow and the blackness beyond their torches' reach. He anticipated the slow, difficult crawl ahead. "Thank you for your help," he said, turning back to Estrin. "What will you do?"

"I'll wait. Where you found me. In case others come."

"But the A... I saw them up there. They're getting ready to come in. If not today, then surely tomorrow. I... I've heard rumours. They're planning to flush the caves. Toxic gas. Apparently."

"Doesn't surprise me."

"So, you can't stay. You've got to get out."

"No."

"What do you mean? They'll kill you."

"I offered to stay, so that's what I'll do. Even if it was one person, it would have been worth it. As it turns out, you're the second. More may come. Wella, the one before you, she'll spread the word. The Scene will live on, elsewhere."

"Surely that means you've done your job?"

"I'm the rear guard. A self-appointed pursuivant, defending the door. I will not desert my post." He pulled out a pencil from his shorts' pocket and opened the paperback he had stuffed into his waistband. He ripped out the first page and wrote on it. Then he folded the scrap of paper and handed it to Dent. "If you find Bend Sinister, or any of the Troubadours, please give them this. It's important." Then he smiled with pride and placed his hand on Dent's shoulder. "You should go, brother. I don't know how you'll ever find them, but I admire your determination to try. This tunnel is over two miles long. Take it slow. Oxygen levels will be low. I'm afraid I need the torch back, so you'll be crawling blind. But you can't get lost; there's only one way forward."

Dent returned the torch and shook Estrin's hand. "I've not witnessed bravery for so long, I can't remember. You are doing a remarkable thing."

"Go," he said. "I hope to crow you find them."

Dent nodded, then turned to face the tunnel. On hands and knees, head low, redundant eyes closed, he began the long, black crawl out of Lyun Mountain.

—

Blix stared at the bank of monitors, her heart racing, fighting the urge to itch. "Look at them," she said to Wulfwin. "Like flies around a corpse."

They were stood in the main surveillance room in the Comms Control Centre: a tech-manifestation of the vision captured by the Authority's compound eyes. Fifty monitors displayed as many different scenes around the city – a greyscale montage of real-time action, exposing unsuspecting citizens with their illusion of freedom.

Blix's stare shifted between four of the screens. They revealed groups of people, loitering. "An agitated swarm," she said. "Poised. Your assessment, Commander."

Wulfwin stood two steps behind her, watching the screens with weary disinterest. "A feeble attempt at making a stand," he said, stifling a yawn. "They're obsessed with the swallow holes. Apparently, the state isn't doing enough to protect its citizens. Whatever that means. But they're not even saying anything. They're just hanging around on street corners, looking gormless."

"They are restless. Look at their eyes. Most are probably high."

Wulfwin smirked at the hypocrisy. He studied Blix's wrought-iron posture and sculpted steel bun, searching for cracks in composure. "Whilst they appear to have the potential for mischief, I assure you their pathetic gesture is harmless. We've Special Forces on the ground, plenty of muscle to set the tone. A few carefully crafted messages will ease their minds."

"Perhaps. But we must be on guard." She stared at the biopsy's shadowy forms. "They gather, multiply. Bacteria, feeding off each other, bloating and spreading. A contagion." She pulled her gaze from the screen to scrutinise Wulfwin. "The man behind *Bluemantle* is still at large. Whilst Intelligence succeeded in decoding part of the last edition, they failed to crack it entirely. His skills in cryptography outsmarted our entire unit."

"He uses a different key each time, but we've found connections. The team are still on the case. I hear they are close to establishing a pattern."

"Comprehensively missing the boat. Meanwhile, he walks free." She turned back to the monitors. "He's an insurgent. It wouldn't surprise me if he's agitating these packs of rats – a vector, spreading paranoia about the holes."

"We have his papers, a full description and control of his quarters. Surveillance have marked him a priority target. We'll find him. Besides, he can't be that smart. He'd stashed a copy of every single edition of *Bluemantle* under his bed. Vanity may be his own undoing."

"While you find hope in his failings, the fact he's still out there is yet another failure on the part of your men."

Wulfwin gritted his teeth. "Is that all, Governor? I have matters to attend."

"No." She glanced around her at the various Comms officers, all studiously occupied. "Follow me."

She walked out of the room and down a long corridor, into an empty office at its far end. She turned and perched, arms crossed, on the edge of a desk that stood in the centre of the space.

Wulfwin entered the office, closing the door behind him. He slumped on a chair opposite the desk.

"You've been working on her for two days," said Blix. "She must have nothing left. If she's still alive, that is."

"Touch and go."

"You're under orders, Commander. I want her kept alive. Everyone has a breaking point."

"And I would have argued the same, before I had the challenge of finding hers."

"Don't tell me she's winning."

"She's playing tough, but I will not be beaten." He stood up, his mood altered by an aggravated nerve. "So yes, I have every intention of keeping her alive, regardless of my orders to do so. I've left her to recover, wherever that is physically possible. Tomorrow, we're down to the ultimate test. I'm confident, she will break."

"Make sure she does. The search of the caves concludes tomorrow. The following day we gas them. We need the location of the Music Makers from her to avoid casualties. I'd rather breathing prisoners over poisoned corpses. The end will ultimately be the same, but the former makes for a far more impressive trophy to parade."

"I will do my very best."

"And I want Commander Lore to watch. In the context of interrogation, you at your inimitable best is something I want him to see."

"If he can pull himself together by then."

"Explain."

"He didn't show for duty this morning. Signed himself off sick. Lily-livered wuss. Kept chucking up."

"You've gone to see him."

"No, of course I haven't. He's authorised to sign off. And I don't give a shit about what state he's in. The man needs to toughen up. That ain't going to happen if I start checking up on his bloody wellbeing."

"I don't trust him."

"Which is the distinct impression I get, Governor. What is it? What aren't you telling me?"

She shot him a glance. "Nothing, Commander. And watch your language. You've a mouth like a cesspit amongst the troopers, but keep it clean in front of me."

Wulfwin glared, his nostrils flared. "Of course, Governor. I apologise." He stared ahead, through Blix, to an imagined point in space.

"And I don't accept your reading of the citizens' behaviour. I recognise the signs. You have to learn lessons from failures like Rideout. Early detection is a preventative measure. Then it's a matter of swift intervention. Containment. Stop the disease from spreading. And, from what I just witnessed on those monitors, the symptoms are there. Do something about it."

"As you wish, Governor. Do you have specific orders?"

"I have specific demands. Total control. Your suggestions."

Wulfwin hesitated, weighing the options. He was tired of managing her paranoia. Frustrated, he decided to abandon the attempt entirely and, instead, indulge her need.

"Chromatofen," he said, deadpan. "We dope the city. Ensure unwitting compliance."

Blix was captured. "Continue."

"The water supply. We use Project Alpha. The excavation shaft cuts through the water source that feeds the spring in Spire Wells. We halt production at the purification plants, so that the spring is the only source of drinking water. As a gesture of the Authority's goodwill, while the plants are closed for unspecified repairs, we increase production of bottled spring water and distribute it gratis. After two or three days' worth of consumption, the citizens of Wydeye will have enough Chromatofen in their system to be eating out of our hands."

"This is genius." She could barely contain her delight. The prospect of such control, however deviously achieved, was giddying. She grasped the plan with greedy hands. "Do it. Implement immediately."

"The protocols?"

"Bypass."

"As you wish. Taking into account the time it will take for sufficient contaminated water to reach the spring, plus production time for bottling, I'd say we are looking at a week to ten days."

"I want it distributed on the streets in four." She held up a hand to stave objection. "And Wulfwin, this is strictly between us. Keep quantities of the drug as low as you dare, while still achieving the desired effect. The citizens will be none the wiser. And many of our colleagues are already medicated to varying degrees." She glared at Wulfwin. "This goes no further. That's an order."

CHAPTER THIRTY

In the pale light of dawn, the Troubadours stood on the brow of a steep hill, each gazing out in a different cardinal direction. They had long since walked free of the cataract cloud that still blinded the city. With the benefit of clear air and an elevated vantage point, they surveyed expansive horizons.

Below them, hidden beneath a wooded dell's dense canopy, lay their temporary camp. Players and their retinue slept, recovering from the exhaustion of a hundred-mile hike. Beside them, four horses held their noses to the ground, feasting on the lush grass that flourished under the trees' shade. Four small carts stood beside them, heavily laden with the players' instruments and stage gear. Dangling from the sides like ballast were cloth sacks containing the troupe's scant possessions.

The Troubadours stood, assessing terrain.

"I say west," said Pale Dexter.

"And I say east," said Chief.

"If only we had a map," said Bend Sinister, shaking his head. "Or better still, the memories of our long journeys that led us to Wydeye. We each arrived from a different direction;

we have a collective experience of the terrain in all but one. Alas, two centuries is a long time to remember the features of our passage." He turned and gazed down into the dell. "Our troupe are already weary."

"We had to push on," said Pale Dexter. "The Heights were crawling with troopers. Any one of them could have caught sight of our escape and followed close on our heels. At least our people sleep with some degree of confidence that the A are not on our tail."

"Agreed," said Chief. "It was arduous, but necessary. However, with the tonic of food and rest, they will wake restored. I say we rouse them now and resume our journey."

"Now?" said Bend Sinister. "Surely we afford them longer? Our players can keep pace, but we have a retinue of followers to consider, some of an age we'll never know. We must take their different needs into account, else we shall find ourselves with an exhausted troupe, too weary to make the distance."

"They know the danger," said Pale Dexter. "They made the choice. Whilst they may lack our endurance, I have faith that they will discover reserves of energy from which to draw."

"I hear your concern, Bend Sinister," said Chief. "However, I fear it's a case of needs must. We should continue on our way."

A noise from behind startled them and they each spun around. A player appeared, scrambling up the hill, breathless. "What is it?" said Bend Sinister. "What's wrong?"

"Someone approaches. A man. Running."

Without a sound, the Troubadours fell to a crouch and followed the player down the hill, into the cover of the dell. They were met by wide-eyed stares of the entire troupe. Breaths were held. Ears trained on fragile silence.

Into the camp stumbled a man, who collapsed at the feet of Bend Sinister.

"Water, quick," said Bend Sinister, turning to his players.

His bassist rummaged behind them and returned with a canteen. He slowly approached the stranger, who lay sprawled on the ground, face down.

Bend Sinister stepped forward and took the canteen from his wary bassist. He knelt beside the man, gently rolling him over onto his back and lifting his head. The man's lips were cracked dry, his chest heaving. He choked as the water trickled into his parched mouth.

A follower stepped forward. "I can attend to him," he said, his tone a blend of reverence and fear.

"No," said Bend Sinister, cradling the man's head, coaxing him to swallow. "No. I must."

Pale Dexter stared in horror. "Have you forgotten yourself? What is this?"

Chief stood beside him, her mouth agape.

"I know this man," said Bend Sinister. "As do you."

"I hardly think so…" said Pale Dexter.

The stranger looked up into Bend Sinister's face, his eyes bloodshot and near-blind. Tears welled. He tried to move his swollen lips, croaking a whisper, barely audible.

Bend Sinister leant forward, bringing his ear to the man's face. He heard the words and shook his head. "Enough," he whispered gently. "Speak no more. You must drink. Let's get you well."

"Bend Sinister?" said Chief. "Are you going to share what only you appear to know?"

Bend Sinister looked up, his eyes welling. "After… After all this time… He's finally returned. My drummer."

Chief and Pale Dexter stared at the broken man. There was a sharp intake of breath among the players as they shuffled forward, peering at the stranger in desperate hope, searching for confirmation that this was, indeed, their long-lost brother.

All Dent Lore could do was breathe. He had run over a hundred miles. Twelve hours, without food, water or rest, fuelled only by the desperation to be reunited with his chieftain. Exhausted and dehydrated, he clung on to consciousness by relief's weak grasp. His chest burnt no more; the agony that had tortured his body slipped away. There was no space to feel. All he could think was, *I've found him.*

It was some time before Dent was able to speak. Two followers had propped him up against a tree. He sat, legs out, arms limp. Bend Sinister and his players knelt beside him. Pale Dexter and Chief stood apart, separated by scepticism's wary distance.

"I didn't know I was lost," said Dent in a quiet, hoarse voice. "I don't know who I am. All I know is that I know you." He looked up at Bend Sinister, then slowly, at the wide eyes of the players. "All of you."

"When I saw you at the Contest, you were in military uniform," said Bend Sinister.

"I am… was, an Allear."

Players gasped.

Pale Dexter said, "Perfect," and crossed his arms, teeth clenched.

"Hear him out," said Bend Sinister, sensing the antagonistic glares of his counterparts. He nodded to his drummer. "Go on."

"My name is Dent Lore and I work for the Authority. At least, that was the life I believed to be mine. Then I saw you at the Contest and I knew, in an instant, none of that was real. Everything disintegrated. Left in its wake was a single realisation. I should be here, with you. Like I once was."

"You don't remember?" said Bend Sinister.

Dent shook his head.

"You are a player. Our drummer. Twenty-six years ago, the Authority raided an event. You turned back to help a follower who'd fallen in the rush to escape. It didn't give you enough time to save yourself. They caught you, tranquilised you and dragged you away. We didn't know what happened to you. We've contacts overground, but nobody could find any information. The Authority had you but said nothing. As the years passed, we came to fear the worst."

Dent stared, seasick with dichotomous reactions to words he both disbelieved and knew to be true. "I remember nothing of before. Only ever the Allears."

"Bend Sinister. A word in private," said Pale Dexter, retreating into the shadows, Chief by his side.

Bend Sinister placed a hand on Dent's shoulder and smiled. "Look after him," he said to his players. "Food. And more water. I shan't be long." He slowly rose and left the awestruck scene.

He approached Pale Dexter and Chief on the camp's fringe, meeting their glares with an expression of calm resolve. "I know what you're thinking."

"No. I don't think you do," hissed Pale Dexter. "We've risked everything. We have forsaken our life underground to seek sanctuary elsewhere – our only chance to survive. And now we have an Allear in our midst and you welcome him with open arms. You feed him from your own fingertips as if reviving a dying brother."

"He is my drummer."

"He *was* your drummer."

"And so he remains. Whatever they did to him, however they were able to control him, it does not negate who he is inside. I can see that. As could you if you resisted the urge to let swift judgement cloud the perspective of calm reasoning."

"Says he who knelt before a single question was asked. This could be a trap. Whatever control they've had over him, perhaps it remains still. They could have sent him to lure us into the hands of his paymasters."

"Pale Dexter has a point," said Chief. "As an Allear he has, for many years, sought to hunt us down and destroy us. Why the sudden change of heart? How can we possibly trust him?"

"Ask the question if you must," said Bend Sinister. "I have no need. I know. My drummer has returned. He has my trust, without doubt or hesitation. I offer no explanation because the fact is not contingent upon one."

"But the risk to our troupe—"

"Risk requires doubt. I have none."

"We doubt. We recognise the risk."

"In which case, I urge you both to trust *me*. Although it may not appear so, I do not make this call lightly. I accept my reaction was swift, but not all knowledge takes time to dawn. You both know me well. I urge you to let that influence the conclusions you draw."

"I've drawn mine," said Pale Dexter, his voice serrated. "If you bring him in, then I and my players will depart. We'll pack up now and head west. I will not endanger my players, nor risk my own life, because you want to believe you've regained a life already lost." He turned to Chief. "You and yours are welcome to follow."

Chief glanced between her comrades, her eyes wide in desperate appeal. "No. We should remain together. We gain strength in our number. Can't we resolve this?"

"There is no resolution to be found," said Pale Dexter.

"You are mistaken," said Bend Sinister. "This can be resolved and we'd do well to try. I'm mindful that we should be on the move as soon as possible. But please, spare a little time. Listen to what he has to say."

"Even if we did agree to stay together, he will slow us down. He's barely conscious, let alone able to walk. We have another hundred miles to travel today."

"I will carry him on my back if it comes to that," said Bend Sinister. "Please, I entreat you. A short while longer. Then do as your will dictates."

Chief looked to Pale Dexter, who folded his arms, eyes defiant. Without a word, they followed Bend Sinister back to the heart of the camp, loitering on the periphery – satellite testifiers.

Bend Sinister knelt once more, but further away from Dent than before, widening the sphere that connected them.

Dent looked at him, then at Pale Dexter and Chief, his face pained. "I know you doubt me. You've just cause to. The things I have done, the cruelty I've been party to, even if not wielded by my own hand. Such atrocities. You have every reason to cast me out."

"I'm more interested in hearing a reason why we shouldn't," said Chief, her eyes dimmed to a dull, dark blue.

"I don't know what to say, how to prove it to you."

Chief stepped forward. "How did you find us? We left no trail."

"I went back to Lyun Mountain – the only place I could think to start. There, I met one of your followers. Estrin. I showed him the mark on my cheek. He took me for a follower. He showed me the escape shaft. From there…" He trailed off, searching for words to explain what he could barely comprehend himself.

"Yes? From there?" Pale Dexter prompted, impatient.

"From there, I ran. Ran as fast as I could, wherever my instinct led me. I felt this pull, a profound magnetism, drawing me onward. Something inside me responded. Somehow, I knew which way to go."

Pale Dexter raised his eyebrows in exaggerated gesture. "You ran, non-stop, for a hundred miles? In that time? Is that even possible?"

"I appreciate how it sounds. But that's what happened."

Pale Dexter shook his head. "It's all a little farfetched to my mind. I say you've got some Authority truck parked beyond the rise." He looked up at the pin-hole gaps in the canopy above. "There are probably Watchers overhead, recording your little performance. What will it earn you? A medal? Promotion? Bring in the 'Music Makers', dead or alive. We know there's a price on our heads. Estrin knows that too. He shouldn't have shown you the shaft."

"He saw the tattoo. He believed me." Dent shifted to one side, reaching a hand inside his shorts pocket. He pulled out a piece of paper, roughly folded. "I forgot. He asked me to give you this."

The three Troubadours looked to each other. It was Chief who stepped forward to take the note. She slowly unfolded the paperback's torn page and read Estrin's scribbled message. Her eyes widened as she reread the words. Bend Sinister and Pale Dexter rushed to her side to inspect the cause of her alarm.

"This is remarkable news," said Bend Sinister, still staring at the note. "I had feared there was no other able to take on the role."

"I know of Ursel," said Chief. "She was a friend of Bluemantle's. And she is one of mine." Her eyes brightened. "This changes everything, does it not?"

"How?" said Pale Dexter. "Whilst I agree that this is wholly unexpected, our hand has been forced. We've left. The Scene is no more. Regrettable as it is, what good could *Bluemantle* do now?" He turned towards Dent, face flushed. "Assuming its former creator and champion has perished, that is. The A took him, didn't they? Raided his quarters. Is he alive? Or have you tired of his silence and brought his torture to a merciful end?"

"I… I don't know. I'm not aware of any raid. But that doesn't mean anything. I sat on the Council of Command, but its governance is a charade. Between the two of them, Wulfwin and Blix do what they like. Also, I wasn't involved in detention or interrogation, so I don't know who they're holding. Apart from…"

"Yes?" pressed Pale Dexter.

"A woman. Two days ago. I was forced to watch…" He faltered, sickened by the memory. "But the man behind *Bluemantle?* He'd be high value. If they did have him, he'd most likely be in Itherside Hold. If he's still alive, that is, which I doubt. Not if you think he wouldn't break."

The three Troubadours bowed their heads, their grief renewed by the implication.

Chief broke the mournful silence. "Then this brave offer of Ursel's proves a timely lifeline. Yes, we have left Wydeye. But that decision was born of little choice, was it not? With *Bluemantle* restored, we'd have options. We could still communicate with our followers, spread word of a show."

"And where would we perform that show?" said Pale Dexter. "Underground is lost to us. The Authority will have scoured those caves. Our home, our sanctuary, is destroyed. And there is nowhere overground that can evade their detection." He turned to Dent, face taut. "That's right, isn't it, Allear? You've got overground sewn up so well you can hear a goat dream."

Dent hung his head, eyes down, and nodded.

"Then we take it with us," said Chief. "The Scene is the people, not the place. If we had *Bluemantle*, we could reach new audiences. Build a new following. Connect."

"We don't need *Bluemantle* to do that elsewhere. If we ever found a new audience, we would have no cause to rely on coded messages, created by an emissary risking all in the act. But there's the rub. You know this. We've always known it."

"What?" asked Dent. "Why can't we just go elsewhere?"

"*We?*" echoed Pale Dexter.

Bend Sinister intervened, speaking softly to Dent. "You don't remember. Before we each came upon Wydeye, we were travelling minstrels in search of an audience." He explained how the four Troubadours and their players had come to find Wydeye after untold years of searching. "Nowhere else did people connect with our music. And it's this connection on which our survival depends. That's why, over time, we feared the worst for you. We clung on to blind hope for so long, until the impossibility forced us to replace hope with grief." He looked at Dent, blinking. "You haven't performed in over two decades. Without that to sustain you, it's a miracle you're alive."

Dent shook his head, unable to account for his survival.

A silence fell on the camp. The players sat dazed, overwhelmed by the unexpected return of one of their own. The retinue of followers hung back, uncertain of their place in such unfamiliar territory. Dent closed his eyes, grappling with the pieces of two different puzzles.

By that time, dawn had dissolved into a new day. The dell provided dappled shade — welcome shelter from the sun's full force. Insects buzzed, filling the silence with light-winged industry. The horses snorted, pulling at their tethers, swatting flies with their tails.

The Troubadours looked to each other, then rose and withdrew to the edge of the camp, out of earshot. Still, they kept their voices low, with an urgency sharpening their register. "We're wasting time," said Pale Dexter. "We should have been on the move at first light."

"But this news has changed things, surely?" said Bend Sinister. "We would be wise to pause and reassess."

"What's there to reassess? We've nowhere safe to play. While that remains the case, we've no option but to leave."

"We still don't know if we'll find anywhere else to settle. If it was just us, we would find reserves to keep searching. But our retinue? They have made great sacrifices by coming with us. We have a responsibility to consider their welfare."

Chief spoke up. "The same stalemate. Don't you see? This is why Ursel's offer could open doors. Create alternatives, in place of this hopeless situation."

"I admire your determination," said Bend Sinister. "But even if *Bluemantle* could play a part in some way, the fact remains that the person who has offered to take it on, at immense personal risk, is currently incarcerated. Without Ursel, we are left with nothing more than the blind hope that has led us thus far."

"I agree," said Pale Dexter. "That's why we need to send your drummer back to get her."

Bend Sinister flushed in alarm. "What?" he said. "A merciless proposition. Absolutely out of the question."

"He's spent the last quarter century working for the Authority. Assuming they still think he's on side, he will hardly draw attention if he's seen in the vicinity of her cell. She was arrested for attending the Contest, along with so many others; they've no cause to regard her as of notable value. I'm sure he has the wherewithal to devise a scheme to extract her. That's if he's to be trusted, of course. The man has a great deal to prove. This presents a fitting opportunity to test his newly recovered loyalty, wouldn't you agree?"

"No," said Bend Sinister, struggling to keep his voice down. "It's insane. He can't just walk out with her. The risks. It's impossible. They'll kill him if he's caught. Besides, you've seen the state he's in. He can barely walk. It'd take him a week to crawl back to Wydeye."

"We'll give him one of our horses."

Bend Sinister turned to Chief, desperate. "Second me,

Chief, please. He's proposing a suicide mission – for Ursel, as well as for my drummer."

Chief hesitated, tugging at a silver dreadlock. "I'm thinking of Ursel," she began. "If there is any way of saving her, bearing in mind what she may be able to achieve for us all, then…"

"Chief, I implore you. We don't even know if she's still alive. If we send my drummer in, we're sure to lose them both."

"I don't deny the risk. But think what it could mean if he succeeds. The potential for *Bluemantle*. The potential for us all."

Pale Dexter grasped the sway of favour. "With a point to prove and an opportunity to save the day, I propose we put the plan to your man. With conviction, mind. We must stand united before our troupe. Since Saltire and the absence of a leader, that's what we agreed. Bend Sinister, you always champion the merits of democracy. I say we put it to a vote, between the three of us. Do we send the drummer back?"

CHAPTER THIRTY-ONE

It was the first day in over a fortnight that the dust cloud choking Wydeye had begun to clear. Citizens were able to see beyond arms' reach, could risk breathing without the protection of a mask.

Naylor had relished the relief during the short walk from his apartment in the Wallace Estates to the Rader Tenements. Now, sat inside the hot, airless hide, the relief felt like a mirage that had tricked his senses.

Despite her resistance, Chase had managed to persuade Wella to bring Naylor to the hide. "I have to speak to him," he had insisted. "And you know I can't leave here."

"I can explain the plan to him."

"I need you to explain it to Tinashe. And to your friends, work colleagues, fellow followers. Anyone you can trust."

"So why not add Naylor to the list?"

"Because he's my closest friend, a man for whom I have deep respect. And when the time comes for me to tell him the truth, I want it to be in the context of the actions I've taken since to put things right."

They had argued about Chase coming clean with Naylor

and Tinashe. "It's not another test," Wella had said. "It's about honesty. And besides, I don't want to be complicit in your deceit."

"Look. If I tell Naylor now, he won't be on board. I know him. It'll take him weeks to process. I'm not saying I blame him. He has every right to hate me for what I've done. And I'm prepared for that. But right now, we need him on side. That makes it sound like I'm using him. I'm not. At least, I don't mean to. I just know he'd want to help Ursel. And he'd want to make a difference to how things are, with the A and all that. But if I tell him now, he won't be able to get past it."

So, Wella had reluctantly agreed, on the condition the confession came after. "Apart from Ursel," she had added. "Crow help us, if she survives and we see her again, you have to tell her. Up front. No stalling. Promise?"

The prospect of telling Ursel made Chase feel sick. The mere thought of her at all, the horror she would be going through, was unbearable. He believed she was still alive. He knew she'd never talk and the Authority would take care to spare her life because she was too valuable. The consequence of the stalemate was unthinkable. He wrapped up the thought of her and carefully tucked it away. "I promise," he'd replied, both dreading the moment and praying it would, one day, come.

When Wella had brought Naylor to the hide, she left them alone, heading back out to recruit Tinashe.

Naylor sat opposite Chase at the small wooden table, looking around the dim, cramped room. "I don't get it," he said. "What have they got on you?"

"I don't know. I just know they've eyes on me. Maybe someone's grassed about me going underground." His stomach turned at the irony.

"So, how long are you going to stay here? What about your job?"

"That depends. You see, I've come up with a plan. To help Ursel, but also to go further than that. To change things, for everyone. That's why I asked Wella to bring you here. We need your help."

"I'll do anything I can to help Ursel. She's a kind person. I can't bear to think…" He trailed off, shaking his head.

"I know."

"And if the wider angle is to do with the A, well then, you know my feelings on that score. But how? You don't mess with the A. That's why we are where we are."

"But that's exactly what got me thinking." He sat forward, hands splayed on the table. "I thought to myself, they must have a weakness. A chink in their armour. Something to aim for. And I've worked it out."

"Tell me."

"The A are obsessed with increasing productivity to maximise income from exported goods. To help achieve that, you need a healthy, hard-working, line-towing workforce. So, the state introduces perks to grease the wheels. Free public transport, free education, free healthcare.

"Meanwhile, citizens have come to believe they depend on the perks. They need their free tramway pass because they wouldn't be able to afford their own vehicle, even if they were allowed one. Their health isn't great, what with the dust from the quarry, the fumes in the furnaces, the climate's strain on work-weakened lungs. How would they cope elsewhere, without free health? Where else could they live that had modest, capped rents for all, leaving a few spare ketrels to blow on booze or Meezel on their one day off in seven?

"We know all this. But what I hadn't appreciated before is the consequence for the state. The bungs amount to a costly sweetener. And it's not like we're talking subsidies either. The

A must be reliant on a hefty net income to fund such generous welfare.

"Now, whilst the A boasts about so-called zero unemployment, they've created a problem for themselves. You know as well as I do the pressures the last few raids have created. The more innocent people they throw in the detention centres, the more jobs left vacant. Employers have to keep the positions open. Even if they were allowed to fill them, they can't because everyone's already got a job – excluding Wethers, but the A's made damn sure they're not fit to work. And that puts huge pressure on the rest of the workforce, having to extend their hours, for no extra pay, to cover absence.

"Workers are struggling under the strain of distributed hours. Employers are pissed off at losing key staff through indefinite absence. Meanwhile, that precious productivity target that the A promote as a personal goal we should each be striving to achieve, is balancing on a knife edge. Reduce the workforce and, I believe, the balance could swing. If output drops, the A's income begins to fall, then the bills don't get paid. And therein lies their weakness. Whilst the A have made the citizens of Wydeye believe that they're dependent on the state, the state is equally dependent on them."

Naylor sat back, nodding slowly. "I've never considered it in that way, but you're right. It leaves them vulnerable. They need us. But that's all promising in theory. What do you propose we do?"

"We strike from the inside. Target key dependencies that will have greatest impact. I'm thinking the tramways, the only means for most to get to work; the quarry, as the source of raw materials; the furnaces and processing plants, to slow the manufacture of goods for export. We infiltrate, persuade likeminded people around to a certain way of thinking, then encourage them to down tools.

"Wella's speaking to Tinashe now. Tinashe is in a state over Weldon, but she'll want to be involved, I'm sure. Hopefully she'll know people to target in the tramways. I know you've got solid people in processing. Wella's got the furnaces covered. I know some good guys in the quarry who'll jump on the ride, no hesitation. I'm not saying it's going to be easy. But, if we can encourage people to see that a gradual walkout could turn the tables, shift the balance of power, then we're in with a chance."

"How do we do that? You're talking about upending a whole mindset that the A have spent decades carefully crafting."

"The way I see it, there are two distinct camps who have a particular gripe against the system. The first are the workers struggling under distributed hours. The second are the friends and families behind the faces on the Wall of the Missing. They don't make a stand because they fear the cost. Dissention is met with punishment; the very perks they rely on are withdrawn. And Wethers are proof of the consequence, emasculated to the point of destitution. But if citizens feel, with sufficient numbers behind them, that there's a chance to make a change, then I think they'll take the risk. We point out that, by downing tools together, we throw a floodlamp on the state's dependency on people picking them up again. Then we find ourselves with a bargaining tool. Something to trade. That's when we suggest the exchange."

"Ursel?"

"Ursel. And the release of every innocent man, woman and child held without charge or hope of a trial. My feeling is that the A's need for citizens to return to work will outweigh their preference for keeping their examples behind bars."

"How can you know that? They won't just release people, surely?"

"If that's the only exchange on offer, I think they will. A fair trade for keeping the economy alive. And besides, they don't give a damn about the citizens they've got banged up. They're just an example. And the example's already been made."

"But the chance to interrogate. The A are desperate for intel on the Scene."

Chase looked down, his passion for the plan eclipsed. "They must know by now."

"Know what?"

"Followers don't talk."

—

Ursel lay on the mattress, foetal and shivering.

It was not cold in her cell. The cramped space was sultry, the air dense with a putrid stench. It was also dark. The single bulb, a tiny torso hanging from the ceiling, was operated by a switch on the other side of the door. Not that she minded. She lived in darkness now, her eyelids too swollen to open. A desolately silent darkness.

She believed she spent long periods unconscious, although she had no sense of time. These episodes suited her. She could feel, think, remember nothing. Warm oblivion. Her only comfort. This was why she was unafraid of dying, which she believed would be the conclusion to this ordeal. She imagined death to feel much like these welcomed moments of tranquil unbeing.

Death would save her. It would be her escape.

But death didn't come.

Each time she neared the brink, she slid back. She would be left in her cell, on her blood-stained, urine-soaked mattress, to recover. Her spirit was prepared to yield, yet her body possessed a stronger will to survive. She felt herself slipping further and further back. Away from the edge. Away from the end.

Then sleep would take over.

Sleep was the worst. More painful than the torture. For in sleep, she retained the memory of sounds. In her nightmares, she was no longer deaf. Instead, she was tormented by her own deafening screams.

It was not cold in her cell. The shivering was from infection. Her wounds had not been treated. The raw flesh on her arm where her skin had been ripped off was swollen and weeping puss — tears of bacterial contamination. And the pain. It felt as if the man was still ripping her skin from her arm — a seamless, continuous action.

During one of her periods of 'rest', she discovered the woeful inadequacy of language in her new inescapable life. There were no words to describe the pain.

Only the screams in her dreams came close.

CHAPTER THIRTY-TWO

Despite the late hour, the Authority Complex was alive with activity. Black-clad troopers trotted between buildings, Ops trucks in convoy crossed the parade ground, silhouettes moved in and out of distant yellow windows. Movement choreographed by purpose and urgency.

Floodlights bleached the night scene, denying the cover of darkness. Dent Lore pressed his back against the towering concrete wall of the Comms Control Centre, hidden by a narrow strip of shadow. He fought to control his breathing, having run from the northern limits of Hole, through Welspek Breach, to reach Gedges Hill and the sprawling Complex. He had left the Troubadours' horse in a disused barn on the outskirts of Hole. His precaution would mean a long walk back to the barn, heavily burdened, should he make it that far.

He didn't have a plan. Throughout the journey from the Troubadours' camp, he had attempted to conceive of one, despite fearing the impossibility of the task. He was all too familiar with Complex security. Yet, despite his efforts, his mind would not focus. He could not get past the crushing disappointment of discovering his true self, only to be sent back to the appalling other world of cruelty and control.

Bend Sinister had not wanted him to go; he knew that. He could see it in his eyes. But the other two had. *Is it a test?* he had thought on the long ride back. *A punishment?* He could understand why this woman he was tasked to save was important to them. But to risk the lives of them both in a mission doomed to fail?

And now he was back. All trace of his manufactured loyalty was gone. In its place, an overwhelming revulsion at the regime that had been the architect and puppeteer of his convictions for a quarter century. He dredged up the mantras: *I am loyal to Governor Blix… I serve her will and the rule of the Authority… The objective of the Allears and the will of the Authority is all that matters…* Slogans of counterfeit allegiance. Attitudes ingrained with unwavering permanence like skin ink. He touched his own tattoo. *How could I have forgotten who I am?*

A noise behind him brought his attention crashing back to the present. The questions would have to wait. However impossible the task appeared, he had no choice but to make the attempt. To have any chance of succeeding, he knew he had to start by returning to his private quarters and changing back into issue fatigues to avoid drawing attention. He leant forward, his head breaching the shadow line, and assessed his path. Two hundred floodlit metres. All he could think to do was to run for it.

Then he realised, *I do this every day.*

Taking a deep breath, he stepped out of the shadow and started running along the concrete track to his block. An Ops truck drove up behind him, swerving wide as it passed. Two troopers left a building to his left and marched back the way he had come. Dent relaxed his shoulders. *Don't hide. They don't know.* As he jogged the final yards to his block, he almost felt like smiling.

Just as he reached out and grasped the door handle, a voice boomed out behind him. "Lore. What the fuck?"

Dent froze. His heart raced.

Wulfwin strode up and stood behind him. "Feeling better, I take it?"

Dent slowly turned around to face him.

"Shit me. You are proper ill. What in crow's name are you doing out running?"

"I… I needed to get out. Thought a run would do me good."

"Looks like it's near enough killed you."

"I… I do feel rough."

"Well, do me a favour and go back to bed. I need you fit for tomorrow."

"Tomorrow?"

"Ursel, the User Scum. It's her last chance. If she doesn't spill, the arm's coming off. Blix wants you there to observe."

Dent's mind raced, making the appalling connection between the woman he was there to save and the broken figure he'd witnessed be so brutally tortured. Choking on the memory, he fought to slip back into role. "My class-two recruits have got a field test first thing. Where we've fast-tracked them, I have to keep on top of assessments."

"I know. But she's insisting." Wulfwin rubbed hand over fist, eyes glaring. "Between you and me, the bitch has fucking lost it. Paranoid wreck. And high as the Heights."

"The Music Makers?"

"That's part of it. But she's freaking out about the citizens. Convinced they're going to revolt. Because of the holes. Like they've got the wherewithal. It's doing my head in."

"The citizens won't do anything. Those who aren't loyal are controlled by fear."

"Exactly." Wulfwin eyed Dent and sighed. "You see it like I do, Lore. I know it. You're there on the ground, among them. They're too friggin' scared to even look at us, let alone cause trouble. But she's up in her tower, staring at monitors, imagining all sorts of crazy shit." He stepped forward and lowered his voice. "She's even ordered the doping of the water supply. Can you believe it?"

"What? How?"

"Dump a tonne of Chromatofen down the Alpha site. Drug the whole city. Turn them into drooling pawns. That's how fucking insecure she is."

Dent swallowed, struggling to hide his horror.

"Anyway," said Wulfwin, "that's between you and me. Understood?"

"Of course."

Wulfwin straightened and stepped back. "Now, go rest. We start the final round of the game at zero-six-hundred hours. It's to be done in C-Block infirmary – contain the mess. You're to attend, whether you're fit to or not. And, right now, you look like shit." He sneered, about-turned and marched off.

Dent stared at Wulfwin's receding form. His hands, then his arms, then his entire body trembled. A wave of nausea almost floored him. He fought back the urge to retch and turned, struggling to open the door. He ran blindly down dim corridors, up stairs and past alarmed troopers. Finally, he reached the door to his quarters, fumbled with the keypad, relying on muscle memory to gain entry. Once inside, he bolted the door, ran into his bathroom and threw up in the basin.

Confident the need to vomit had passed, he stumbled out of the bathroom and collapsed on his bed. He hadn't slept in over twenty-four hours. The urge to give in to sleep was overwhelming. Feeling himself drift off within seconds, he sat up and forced his eyes open. He needed a plan. It was approaching midnight. Six hours to get Ursel out and away from Wydeye.

Warmth cradled him. Darkness enveloped him. Stillness embraced him…

—

Dent bolted upright, eyes wide, disoriented.

Reality was a landslide, hurtling towards him – rocks of realisation, smashing into his head. Amid the onslaught came a glimpse of the clock above his bed. It was ten past five. He had slept through his best chance of getting Ursel out.

Panicking, Dent's mind darted this way and that, grasping and discarding ideas as to what to do. Then a thought struck him. He held on to it, convinced it was the only way. Within five minutes, he was marching out of his quarters, dressed in standard-issue fatigues, heading straight for C-Block.

Troopers and Authority medical staff were crawling the building. As Dent strode through the corridors, they saluted him as he passed. No one questioned him.

He bypassed the door to Ursel's cell and walked straight to the infirmary, which was behind a pair of swing doors at the far end of the corridor. The room was vacant. He checked a door on the left-hand-side and, to his trembling relief, found it unlocked. Silently opening the door, he peered through the crack – another corridor, empty. Then he closed the door, grabbed a steel gurney and wheeled it through the double doors to Ursel's cell.

The guard at her door stood to attention.

"I've come to collect," said Dent, his voice flat.

"Sir?"

"Commander Wulfwin's orders. He is coming to interrogate the prisoner in forty-five minutes. I'm to take her to the infirmary and set up the apparatus."

"I knew she was going through, but I was told zero-six-hundred, sir."

"That's when Commander Wulfwin starts. I'm ordered to prepare."

The guard hesitated, until his doubt was assuaged by practical logic and the orders of a superior officer. "Yes, sir," he said and unlocked the door.

Dent wasted no time. He picked up the broken frame of his charge and gently placed her on the gurney. He looked over his shoulder to check the guard was out of earshot. Then, forgetting, he whispered to her, telling her not to fear, that he was on her side, he was getting her out, begging her not to scream.

Her body was limp and lifeless. Yet she was breathing, her chest rattling. With deadweight limbs, she offered no resistance. She barely even looked at him, aside from a brief glance through one swollen, bruise-blue socket. Strapping her down was a gesture for appearance's sake.

As he pushed her out of the cell, he nodded at the guard, who offered a parting salute. Then he wheeled her down the corridor and into the infirmary, in full view of passing troopers and staff. As soon as he was behind the swing doors and out of sight, he unbuckled the straps and wrapped a blanket around her. He knew she was conscious inside her lifeless body. He kept whispering to her, offering gentle assurances, attempting to calm himself by calming her.

From a cupboard, he took out a large piece of folded black plastic and laid it on the floor. A zip ran down the middle, from top to tail. "I'm sorry," he whispered. "I'm going to have to put you in here." Then he gently laid her in the body bag, leaving a gap in the zip, head end, so that she could breathe. "It won't be for long."

He placed the body bag on the gurney and pushed it towards the door on the left. Opening the door, he hesitated before the empty hallway.

This was the part of his last-minute plan that most hinged on desperation and hope. He knew the hallway led to a small morgue, where the deceased were stored until transported to the state's main facility in Itherside. However, he had no idea if the morgue would be attended by staff, or if the exit, where the bodies were collected for transfer, would be locked. Having made it this far, he had no choice other than to find out for himself.

A mixed result. The room was empty, but the exit was triple-locked.

Trapped, Dent's mind turned immediately to defence. He bolted the door through which he had come and set a cabinet below the handle. Then he unzipped the body bag and lifted Ursel out, laying her on a blanket, which he wrapped around her battered form. Still she did not move.

Time was running out. He knew Wulfwin would arrive early, eager to play his final hand. Dent looked around, desperation and determination producing a powerful cocktail of adrenalin and ingenuity. His eyes glanced from the refrigerated units against one wall, to a loaded gurney pushed against another. The body was of a young man in a prisoner's tunic. His flesh was a patchwork of grey, blue and black. His eyes were open, maintaining their terror in death.

In the centre of the room was an autopsy slab, crusted in dark brown blood. Beneath that, the floor was tiled, with a gully leading away to the right. Dent traced its course, as it deepened and widened before reaching the base of the outer wall – a drain, dropping down to an iron grilled cavity, which led to outside. A cavity just wide enough for a body to squeeze through.

The grille was badly rusted and gave way with little force. The clatter of iron on stone as he kicked it out could have easily raised alarm, save for an Ops truck that happened to trundle past at the same moment.

The feeling of good fortune was short-lived. When Dent lay on the floor to peer through the opening, his heart sank. On the other side of the wall was the parade ground. Every morning at half-past five, over a hundred cadets assembled for dawn drills. Within a matter of minutes, the entire square would be full of young troopers-in-training, formation marching and saluting the Governor's tower.

There wasn't a second to lose. He had intended to pick his moment, wait for a convoy for cover, perhaps, or the brief interval between patrolling guards. Such caution was denied him. If he waited until the drills were over, Wulfwin would already be in the building and Ursel's absence would be discovered.

He picked her up and lay her on the floor, next to the opening. Without even looking to check if the coast was clear, Dent squeezed his own body through, feeling his ribs straining within the too-small gap. Once clear, he crouched low and pulled Ursel through, still wrapped in the blanket. He picked her up and gently placed her over his shoulder, murmuring to her, telling her not to be afraid. Checking that the blanket covered her completely, he began walking, head down, away from the square.

He stopped dead in his tracks.

A hundred metres ahead, Wulfwin emerged from a building, flanked by several Deaf Squad troopers. Headed for C-Block's main entrance, they marched directly towards him.

Dent froze, staring at Wulfwin, his heart pounding. If he hadn't already been spotted, he figured he had a matter of seconds before he would be.

He spun around and hurried back the way he had come, in the direction of the cadet barracks. Just as he reached the far end of C-Block and the edge of the parade ground, wailing sirens filled the air: the call to dawn drills. Scores of cadets, in combat shorts and vests, poured out from the barracks and into the square – a swarm of young men and women, eyes fixed ahead, filling the space around him. He ducked his head and pushed against the current, grateful for the myopic obedience of Authority youth.

As the final cadets spilt through the doors, Dent crossed the road and slipped through a gap between barracks. He feared for Ursel, suspecting she had fallen unconscious, but he daren't stop. He still had to clear several hundred metres of Complex ground before he would gain cover in Welspek Breach.

Luck, or chance, continued to back his corner. Everyone he passed was heading somewhere in a hurry. If anyone did notice him, no one paid attention. He was an Authority trooper, just like them, dressed in fatigues, just like them. Only, he had a blanket thrown over his shoulder. And, beneath that…

Dent reached Welspek Breach and crawled through the gap in the chain-link fence that he had made on his way in. Only when he was far enough into the farmland that dominated the Hundred of Hole, out of range of the Complex's security cameras, did he stop to check on Ursel.

He laid her down on the unploughed edge of a corn field. She was unconscious but, mercifully, alive. He could not bear to look at the wounds on her arm and legs, the deep cuts and swelling to her face, the blood that had run from both of her ears, now dried and black-red.

Instead, he focused on tasks intended to comfort. He ripped off his shirt, bundled it up and placed it beneath her head. He took a canteen of water from his belt and let drops fall onto her cracked lips and trickle into her mouth. Her tangled hair clung to her head. He pushed it off her forehead with gentle strokes.

"You're safe now," he said, lullaby-tender. "They can't hurt you anymore." He kept stroking her forehead, repeating the words. Tears welled in his eyes and fell onto her face, rolling down her cheeks as if they were her own.

In this frail young woman, her tortured, broken body, Dent beheld the wounds of every innocent victim of the Authority's brutality. All the times he had turned a blind eye to stay true to the cause, resisted the instinct to intervene for the sake of loyalty, they played back before him now. He had saved Ursel, but he knew there were countless more he could have saved. Her wounds, her pain, came to represent all the suffering he had witnessed but walked on by.

The Authority had taken and made a monster of him.

He held his hands to his face and wept.

CHAPTER THIRTY-THREE

"What do you mean, 'she's gone'?" roared Blix.

The routine rhythm of morning drills had transformed into a cacophonous state of emergency. A clash of klaxon and siren, the rumble of combat boots on concrete, dogs barking in floodlit outposts, orders screamed.

Inside Blix's private quarters, the alarm intensified.

"Gone. Taken," said Wulfwin, his face contorted and crimson.

"How could that even happen? Why wasn't she guarded?"

"She was. I've not spoken to the guard yet. I came straight here."

"This can't be true…" Face white, her bloodshot eyes bulged. "How could you let this happen?"

"There's something else."

"What do you mean? What else could there possibly be?"

"Lore. He was seen in the building. He's gone too."

"No!" she screamed, and sank to her knees, fiercely scratching her hands.

Wulfwin grabbed her by the arms and pulled her upright. "I knew it. There's something about Lore. You know something. Tell me." He tightened his grip and shook her. "Tell me."

"I don't…" Blix stared at Wulfwin, her fury turning to fear.

"Don't lie to me. Tell me what you know."

"Let go. You're hurting me."

"Then I suggest you talk." Still holding her by one arm, he grabbed her by the neck with his other hand and squeezed.

"Let me go and I'll explain," she cried, choking. She struggled but failed to break free. Wulfwin tightened his grip. She stood, trembling, almost hanging from his fist clamped around her neck. "Dent Lore was… He was one of them. He was a Music Maker."

Wulfwin froze, staring at Blix. "You… You fucking bitch." He let go of her and struck her hard across the face. She fell to the ground and remained there, cowering on all fours, blood weeping from a cut below her right eye. He stood over her, fists clenched. "You're lying to me. Tell me you're fucking lying to me."

"It's the truth. It was Wallace's idea. No one was to know. I swore an oath. When I took office. That I wouldn't tell anyone." She dared to look up at Wulfwin, one arm over her head in futile defence.

"Lore is a Music Maker?"

"*Was*. But it's not how it sounds—"

"Not how it sounds? Are you for fucking real?" He reached down and grabbed her hair, hauling her up by her tight grey bun. She screamed as he yanked and twisted. The bun unravelled, loose hair hanging down her back like silver blood. "I should kill you for this."

"Please. Hear me out. I can explain."

"Explain? You know this, yet you've never told me? Now you want to explain?"

"I couldn't tell you before. And for good reason. The plan would never have worked if you knew."

"I don't believe I'm fucking hearing this…" He yanked her hair again. Blix cried out, arms flailing, trying to bat him off.

Grunting at her attempt, he let go of her hair and punched her hard in the abdomen.

Blix doubled over, then collapsed on the floor. She lay curled up, knees to chest, coughing. Through wide, terrified eyes, she stared at Wulfwin.

"Lying piece of shit," he said, spitting on the floor, just missing her head.

He backed off, turned and moved to the other side of the room. His breathing was heavy. Uneven. He clenched and unclenched his fists as he paced between desk and door. Back and forth, back and forth.

Blix did not take her eyes off him.

Eventually, Wulfwin stopped. He stood at a distance, arms crossed, facing Blix. "You reckon you can explain?" he said. "Talk, bitch."

Blix hesitated, assessing. Moving slowly, she stood up and leant against the wall behind her. She went to neaten her immaculate bun. What she found appeared to distress her more than the blossoming bruises on her face and stomach. Pride fought to restore itself, numbing pain, straightening posture. "There… There was a raid," she said, her voice hoarse and trembling. "A Music Maker was arrested."

"I know."

"Wallace insisted on handling the interrogation alone. It had been fourteen years since Rideout. He was beyond hungry; he wanted to relish in private what he had craved for so long. There were no witnesses, no reports, nothing on file. But the rumours were rife. Wallace was brutal, the interrogation relentless. Yet, his prisoner wouldn't break." She paused, reading his reaction.

"Go on."

Blix spoke with cold precision, intent on telling the whole story, now that the truth was finally out. "For three years, he tortured him. The entire time, Wallace wouldn't let me in. I pressed senior staff in the infirmary. They admitted to being called several times with orders to resuscitate. The only occasion I did see the prisoner was about two years after he was captured. He was in intensive care. Covered in wounds, old and new. He'd been starved for I don't know how long.

"Then, after three years, it all went quiet. I never saw the prisoner again and no one I challenged had either. I had high security clearance, but there was nothing on him. Meanwhile, Wallace went silent. He stone-walled my every attempt to find out what had happened. Again, rumours spread. Unchallenged, they became common knowledge. The prisoner had died and Wallace was covering it up.

"No one could prove anything, even if they wanted to. And Wallace knew there was no way he'd be investigated for causing the death of a Music Maker. Instead, his silence encouraged a blind-eye attitude. People chose to forget.

"Three years later, Wallace fell ill. When it was clear he wouldn't pull through, I put myself forward as his successor. On the day of my inauguration as Governor, he told me what had really happened to his prize prisoner.

"The Music Maker hadn't died, although he came very close by the end. Desperate to make him crack, Wallace had experimented with his toys. He devised a contraption to combine electroshock and sonic fatigue. Only, he thought the sonic element wasn't working. He increased the volume, assuming that was the problem. The prisoner started moaning. Although Wallace could still hear nothing himself, he turned it up higher; the prisoner cried out. He upped the volume to its highest setting; the prisoner screamed. It turned out the sonic device was emitting sound at a frequency higher than the range of normal human hearing. Yet, the prisoner could hear it.

"The Allears was still a small-scale operation. Most recruits were adjusted, with only a handful having the required level of aural sensitivity to avoid surgery. Now, here was someone whose hearing was so sensitive, the others were as good as deaf. That's when Wallace had the idea. Create the ultimate irony. Defeat the Music Makers by developing a weapon out of one of their own."

Wulfwin stood and stared, wide-eyed. His rage and this revelation were too much to process.

Blix, desperate to defend her actions, continued. "Wallace told me how he took the prisoner and hid him in a secret wing of the detention centre, what's now the morgue in C-Block. There, he held the prisoner, heavily sedated and insensible from constant Chromatofen ingestion. He fed him up, treated his wounds, slowly restoring his health. He also worked on the prisoner's appearance. He shaved his head and let his facial hair grow into a full beard. The prisoner's wounds healed, altering the contours of his face.

"Once convinced that his captive was unrecognisable, he created false ID papers under the name Dent Lore and handed him over to a trusted colleague, an expert in psychopharmacology. Wallace gave him orders to put Lore through a programme of intensive indoctrination and re-education, with a view to enlisting him into the Allears. He did not say who Dent Lore was, other than that he was an orphan of the state, family unknown. The colleague took him on and began the process of modification.

"Wallace told me this in confidence when I became Governor because he wanted me to push Lore to the limit. This way, Lore could be instrumental in the capture of the Music Makers – the same people he'd endured three years' horrendous torture in order to protect. Wallace relished the irony and was desperate that his scheme be realised, even if he wouldn't be alive to see it.

"When he told me the plan and I met Lore for the first time, I could see why. It was clear to me that Lore was a weapon: use him to his full potential and we could destroy the Music Makers. And that potential seemed boundless. His re-education had worked a dream. He had no recollection of his past. He absorbed and regurgitated state ideology with conviction. His determination to achieve the mission of the Allears and the will of the Authority was unwavering. And the irony was the icing on the cake. I monitored his progress closely, looking for signs of lapse, but there were none. Quite the opposite. After two years of re-education and psycho-manipulation, then nine years as a serving Allear, I promoted him to Unit Superior."

Wulfwin hissed through gritted teeth, "And I was appointed Chief of Command ten years ago. You and I have worked closely together in that time. You should have told me."

"I couldn't. Don't you see?"

"No. Of course I fucking don't."

"We both hate the Music Makers – for different reasons, but with an intensity matched. For you, it comes down to win or lose. As long as they walk free, they're winning. And that's your red rag. I understand and respect that.

"But we handle our hate in very different ways. You wear yours like a man on fire. Even if I was permitted to tell you, I knew you wouldn't have been able to work alongside Lore, knowing who he really was. You wouldn't have put aside your hatred in order to accept the plan."

"That's because your plan is bullshit. Create the ultimate irony? Use him as a weapon? He's a fucking Music Maker. He doesn't deserve to be anything but dead."

"But his hearing—"

"I don't give a fuck about his hearing. This is about you and Wallace and your damned obsession with control. Wallace was bad enough. But you've taken it to another level. You're obsessed to the point that it's turned you into a paranoid junkie."

She opened her mouth, about to speak.

"Shut it," he said. "You've said your piece. Now hear mine."

He approached her slowly, probing her sphere of personal space. "You've lost it, Blix. You're so doped up on Meezel, you can't walk straight, let alone think straight. You're so fixated on controlling the city, that you don't even realise you've lost control of yourself. I don't give a shit about your lame excuses. You should have told me about Lore. I'm his Commanding Officer, for fuck's sake. I backed him up. I..." Wulfwin faltered, remembering the last conversation he'd had with him, not seven hours ago. "You stupid, Meezel bitch. You should have told me," he roared. "That's it. You're finished."

"What...?"

"As your serving Chief of Command, I hereby advise you that I am triggering Article Twenty-One and, in consort with the Chief of Staff, I assume control of the Authority."

"On what grounds?"

"On the grounds that you are a drug addict, you have been complicit in fraudulent activity against the state and you have withheld vital information from your Chief of Command. Enough, or shall I continue? What would your Chief of Staff say to your little plan to contaminate the spring and dope the entire city?"

"That was your idea!"

"That's what you say. However, I've demonstrated that you're no longer to be trusted." He sneered and held up his hands. "I was merely following orders."

"That's a lie—"

"You should've told me. Instead, you've made a fool out of me. You'll pay dearly for that." He pulled a radio from his belt. "Trooper Five-Eight. This is Delta-Charlie-One. Do you read? Over."

"What are you doing?" cried Blix.

He ignored her. His radio crackled back.

"*Delta-Charlie-One. This is Trooper Five-Eight. Copy that. Over.*"

"Get your unit together and report to me immediately at apartment A, floor two-eight, residential block one. Over."

"*Apartment A, floor two-eight. That's—*"

"Governor Blix's private quarters. Yes. Get your men up here immediately. Do you read? Over."

"*Copy that, Delta-Charlie-One, sir. Over and out.*"

Blix stood, pale and floundering. "What… What are you doing?"

"I'm taking control."

"No—"

"I must speak with the Chief of Staff to initiate proceedings. Meanwhile, you are confined to quarters. That's an order. I suggest you don't resist. My men are armed."

"Commander—"

He eyed the silver pillbox on the desk behind her. "Indulge, why don't you? Knock yourself out." Then he turned and walked out of the room, locking the door behind him.

—

The Chief of Command wasted no time.

Within three hours, Wulfwin was stood in the centre of the parade ground, megaphone to mouth, barking orders. The seat of power was still warm. He relished the transition.

Passive on his leather coat-tails hung the Chief of Staff. Protocol for Article Twenty-One demanded that power be devolved to both the serving Chief of Staff and Chief of

Command until the incumbent Governor be investigated for the charges brought against them. All decisions must be jointly made. All interventions mutually ratified.

Wulfwin held the megaphone. The Chief of Staff hovered – a silent, visible nod to the rulebook.

All around them, the bustle of orders in action. Squads of troopers marched towards transit vehicles, kitted for detail. Officers darted between buildings, laden with crates or shouting orders into radios. A convoy of crawling trucks snaked along the road, north of the parade ground, towards the Complex's west exit. Their cargo was one hundred iron cylinders painted hazard-yellow. The troopers marching alongside the convoy carried gas masks and goggles.

"Trooper Forty-Eight," called Wulfwin through the megaphone. "Halt and report immediately."

In the distance, the Unit Superior leading the detachment turned around to those behind him. The squad halted and stood to attention. The trucks ceased their cautious crawl, stopping nose to tail. The Superior ran across the parade ground towards Wulfwin, arriving with a breathless salute. "Sir!"

"Trooper Forty-Eight. You lead only three units of men. You have 120 square miles of subterranean caves to treat. Starting tomorrow, you have two days to do it in. Tell me. How the fuck does that work?"

"Sir, the orders were for staged release. Health and safety."

"Well, the orders have changed. Leave your second IC to lead that rabble. While they march with the elephant line, I want you to assemble seven more units."

"Sir, there aren't enough gas masks."

"Then they'll have to hold their breath. Dismissed."

The Superior hesitated briefly, then snapped a salute and ran back to his squad.

In his place appeared another Superior, his face cement-grey and sweating. "Trooper Sixty, sir," he said, offering a trembling salute. "I received your message."

"Oh, good. And do you know why I ordered you to report to me?"

"The sleeper, sir. I... I assume you want an update."

"You assume correct. Meanwhile, bearing in mind the importance of your task, I had *assumed* I wouldn't have to fucking ask."

"Sir, I... I was waiting for something more... more concrete to report."

"I take it from that you haven't found our missing person?"

"No, sir."

"Trooper Sixty, it's been five days. I don't have a reputation for patience, so why are you testing it?"

"Sir, I—"

"You've got forty-eight hours. If you don't deliver in that time, consider the test a catastrophic failure. Now, get out of my sight and find the damned sleeper."

The trooper saluted, then turned and stumbled forward, fear compromising his balance.

Wulfwin surveyed the battle ground, selecting his next target. His gaze landed on the bleak façade of the Comms Control Centre. Switching from loudhailer to radio, he said, "Charlie-Bravo-One, this is Delta-Charlie-One. Do you read? Over."

The crackle of static, then a flustered, "*Delta-Charlie-One. This is Charlie-Bravo-One. Copy. Over.*"

"Change of plan. Proceed with the mandatory broadcasts immediately. Set the levels high. I want to hear those radios from up here. You read?"

"*Copy that, Delta-Charlie-One.*" A rattle in the background. "*Live on air. Over.*"

"Good. Keep it going all day. Monitor the figures closely. Alert me as soon as drop-off exceeds five per cent. Over and out."

Across the city, radios switched themselves on. Citizen's thoughts and conversations were swallowed by the blaring monologue, broadcast at a non-adjustable volume. Muddled minds were forced to focus on the day's message: *"Citizens of Wydeye, access to Nanso Heights is strictly prohibited. This is for security reasons. Do not be alarmed. Instead, stay focused on your work. Those production targets won't reach themselves. Workers of Wydeye, the Authority's priority is the prosperity of our great city and the welfare of all who call it home. The dust cloud has lifted, exposing once more the ferocious sun. To keep you healthy and hydrated, the Authority is gifting bottles of water, fresh from our very own Spire Spring. Watch out for bottle distribution stations on a street near you. Coming soon, so don't miss out. Beat the heat with free fresh water. You can't say fairer than that. Citizens of Wydeye…"*

Wulfwin heard the script in his head, written and recorded just an hour ago. He had inspected the monitoring procedures. Tweaks had been made, communication loops tightened. It was already impossible to turn off public radios. Now, if the owner of *any* radio, public or private, sought to tamper with their set, a break in reception would be detected and drop-off recorded.

Wulfwin rubbed his chin. *That leaves the water*, he thought.

Despite declaring, in his litany of allegations to the Chief of Staff, that Governor Blix had intended to secretly drug the entire population of the city, 'a despicable plan that served as proof of her lack of rational judgement and her consuming paranoia', Wulfwin had every intention of implementing his own idea. He did not share Blix's fear that the citizens might become out of control. He simply thought a doped, compliant populace made for an easier life. Then he'd be able to focus on the Music Makers, without the headache of a city to run.

When it had dawned on him that he had told Lore about the plan, he was livid. He would never suffer fools, yet he'd been the fool, he thought, trusting that spineless yes-man. At first, he'd assumed he would have to ditch the scheme entirely. It then occurred to him that, wherever Lore was hiding, wherever he'd taken Ursel, he wouldn't be back to blow the whistle. To return would be insane, he thought.

He hadn't decided what to do about the Lore situation. He found the deceit utterly abhorrent. Action had to be taken, yet he hadn't the headspace to properly consider his options. All he knew was that Lore wouldn't dare show his face, which bought precious time. To account for his absence, Wulfwin put word out that Lore's continued illness was contagious. He was to be quarantined in his quarters – no contact permitted under any circumstance.

Wulfwin's fury at the thought of Lore was trumped only by his feelings towards Blix. She had heard him vouch for Lore, had let him forge a trust built on a deception so vile and self-serving. *She treated me like a fucking idiot and made me into a fool,* he thought. *Well, that's her mistake. Right there. I won't ever let her forget. No one makes a fool out of me.*

This rage had ignited a determination to right the wrong. To set the record straight. *I ain't no fucking fool. And I'll prove it.*

There would be no interference from Governor Blix; he had made sure of that. He had elaborated on the accusations that he had put before the Chief of Staff. Their severity warranted a declaration of temporary martial law until a full investigation into the charges could be carried out. Wulfwin had insisted that this process be postponed until the more urgent matter of the Music Makers was resolved.

Meanwhile, Blix had been placed under arrest. She was detained in her private quarters, with an armed guard to ensure she remain there.

Wulfwin had free reign.

First step: doping the city. Once the Music Makers were destroyed, the dose would gradually be reduced, weaning the citizens off the drug over time so that they remained oblivious. Wulfwin thought his plan was simple; the challenge was how to implement it without raising suspicion. Significant quantities of the drug would be required, ideally in liquid form. It would need to be transported up to the Project Alpha site, in the northern range of the Nanso Heights, unhelpfully close to the operation to gas the caves.

Yet his mind was set; it would be done.

Wulfwin turned to the Chief of Staff and handed him the loudhailer. "Take this," he said. "Stay here and try to look like you're in charge. Aside from that, don't do or say a fucking thing."

The Chief of Staff held the device like a dead man's hand. "Where are you going?"

"None of your business."

CHAPTER THIRTY-FOUR

Ursel had decided to die.

She had chosen an end for herself. Without this, she knew the torture could continue forever. They kept leaving her to rest so that her body could recover sufficient strength to survive another round. She knew they'd keep it up, falsely believing that, eventually, they'd do something that would make her break. She saw an arrogance in their assumption and detested them all the more for it.

Before the man had come into her cell, she'd already decided. *The next time, I die.* It wasn't a case of giving up; it was simply drawing a line. With the decision made, she felt empowered and unafraid. A wilful intervention, rather than helpless submission. So, when the man appeared, in body and spirit, she let go.

It wasn't the usual man, the one with the coat. But he was still A and she'd seen him before. That time, he had watched, staring through her, effacing her with his cold, glazed eyes.

This time, he was different. His expression was wrought with urgency. His lips kept moving, as if mouthing hallowed incantation. She couldn't hear a word. But she knew he kept on and on, even when she had decided to close her eyes for the last time. She felt the faint touch of his breath as his words brushed over her skin, a buried vibration in his chest, which she could feel when he carried her over his shoulder and when he held her tight against him on the horse.

He was speaking to her, but she cared not what he said. She let her limbs hang limp in an attitude of closure. Her thoughts ceased as her awareness of her surroundings dimmed and died. Her mind became immersed in introversion. The shutters fell, outward consciousness extinguished.

Death would come.

At times, she thought it had. There were moments on the horse, if the jolting roused her into consciousness, when she believed death had already taken her. The end was protracted, yet painless, oscillating in and out of oblivion. With each hazy surfacing, she believed her body had already passed; it was only her spirit holding on. Stubborn to the last.

And still the warm touch of silent words brushed her broken flesh.

—

"Will she pull through?" whispered Chief. She stood before a makeshift tent in the Troubadours' temporary camp. Night had fallen.

The woman with whom she spoke had been a doctor in her life overground. "Yes. She has regained consciousness and is now sleeping. Her wounds are severe and the infection advanced, but not life-threatening." Her eyes darkened. "By the way, you don't need to whisper. She can't hear you. Those sick bastards have made sure of that." She described the trauma to Ursel's ears and speculated on the likely cause.

Chief paled. "That's... That's monstrous. How can they get away with it?"

"You have been underground for many years. In that time, the A have embellished autocracy with the power of impunity. They've been getting away with this kind of brutality for decades. No one will stand up to them." She sighed, shaking her head. "No one even tries."

"I hadn't realised they had stooped to such depravity. And against their own people? It's different for us Troubadours; we've known they've been after our blood since that tragic festival. But such barbarity against a citizen, whose only crime is participating in an innocent, harmless pleasure?" She raised her chin, face flushed. "No one even tries to stand up to them, you say?"

The woman shook her head.

Chief turned and strode into the heart of the camp, to a clearing lit by small fires and filled with silent, waiting stares. She stopped in the centre, her arms crossed, cobalt eyes gleaming with fury.

Bend Sinister and Pale Dexter rose and approached. "What is it? Will she not survive?" said Bend Sinister.

"Ursel will live." A murmur of relieved sighs rippled through the troupe. One of the followers, a young man with a mohawk, held his hands to his face, his body shaking. "There's more," said Chief, cutting short their relief. She described the most profound of Ursel's injuries. "To force her to speak, they destroyed what they thought she valued the most. Now she will never hear music. Never feel the joy that gave her strength to live."

"Their cruelty is truly abhorrent," said Bend Sinister, his face drawn.

"A despicable act of violence," said Pale Dexter. "Unthinkable."

"You articulate what is obvious, my friends. As did I. But we must not trail off with expressions of disgust, leaving our statements empty of deed."

"What do you mean?" said Pale Dexter.

"Our reaction should not end there. That's tantamount to complicity."

"Chief," said Bend Sinister, "we have not the strength nor number to take on the might of the Authority."

"So, what? We don't even try?" She looked from her counterparts to their silent retinue and addressed them. "Loyal followers. You have found a way. You have broken free from the influence of that oppressive sovereign power. Surely others can do the same? Please, explain for us. What holds their tongue? What binds them to their lot?"

The followers looked nervous, unaccustomed to such an invitation. It was the mohawk man who tentatively rose and stepped forward. "The A bends your ear. Gnaws at you so you see it differently." He hesitated.

"Go on," said Chief.

"They paint a picture, giving you enough to think it's the real deal. Free health, free education, free tramways pass. Rent's low, food's cheap, booze even cheaper." Passion gave him confidence. He spoke with bitter contempt. "The rate they dish out Meezel at the Exchange means the benefits of towing the line and grassing on those that don't is an attractive trade. It's no wonder half the city's addicted; Meezel's become a state-sponsored currency. You see, the A make life seem easy if you stay on the right side of the line. Meanwhile, they send a clear message to the switched-on minority who don't. Ask any poor, beggared Wether. That's what happens when you don't play ball. What they did to Ursel is unforgiveable—" His voice broke. He took a moment to pull himself together. "Sorry. She's a good friend."

"Take your time," said Chief.

"What they've done to her is horrific. But she ain't no way near the only one. The centres are brimming with cases like hers. That's why the Wall only ever gets longer."

"The Wall?" said Bend Sinister.

"The citizens' one and only gesture at making a stand. They post pictures of the people that go missing. Or those that are arrested and never released. The A put a stop to visiting rights years ago. If you're locked up, you're damned lucky if you ever get out again. There's no such thing as a fair trial 'cos there ain't no trial to begin with."

"So what value is the Wall?"

"It's a record. A way of letting the A know we're keeping tabs and we ain't forgotten. There used to be petitions, too, for parole, or compassionate release. But that died a death a few years back."

"Why?"

"Those pushing the petitions were seen as dissidents. They'd discover their rent cap had been lifted without warning and they were suddenly in the red. Or they'd have their tramway pass invalidated, so they couldn't get to work. Then they'd lose their job, right before they lost their dingy quarters for unpaid rent. That's when someone bends their ear, suggests a way out. Snippet of intel here, spread the word there. Before they know it, they're a regular at the Exchange, passing the Wall to trade in the interests of the A, walking right past the spot where they'd posted their petition. The handful strong enough to resist lose everything; they end up like a wretched gelded goat 'cos of what the A takes away.

"Once you're sucked in, you're part of the machine. More and more's feeding the machine. That's what binds them. That and the fact most have become dependent on the state. The freebies make it attractive to stay; the restrictions make it pretty much impossible to leave. While they grow to rely on the bungs, they ignore the fact they're not allowed to own their own vehicle, or telephone, or travel permit. That's why they don't make a stand. And it's why they never leave. That and fear. Dependency makes for a good reason to stick around."

"And if it's not Meezel they're doped up on, it's likely to be Chromatofen," said Dent Lore, stepping into the clearing, his eyes bloodshot and bleary. When he'd returned to the camp a few hours earlier, he'd made sure Ursel was taken care of before collapsing himself. He'd made the one hundred-mile journey three times in the last three days, with little rest. Once they knew he was asleep rather than unconscious, Bend Sinister's players had picked him up and carried him to their portion of the camp.

"Drummer," said Bend Sinister. "How are you feeling?"

"Better. Thank you." He bowed before Bend Sinister, then to Pale Dexter and Chief. "I awoke to hear this young man's account. I have further news of my own, learnt during my mission to save Ursel."

"What news?"

Dent addressed the Troubadours and the crowd of wary faces. "The Governor has ordered for Chromatofen to be released into Wydeye's fresh water supply. They plan to drug every citizen in the city."

A sharp intake of breath. Murmurs among the troupe. Even the followers, who were familiar with the true nature of the Authority's interventions, stared, mouths agape.

The Troubadours looked to each other in gravest alarm.

Pale Dexter turned to Dent. "What is this Chromatofen?" he said. "Will it cause harm?"

"It is a psychoactive depressant. It manipulates attitude and behaviour to achieve compliance. New recruits are treated with prolonged high doses to assist in their adjustment and re-education. They become malleable, believing, trusting. Obedience is easily won, until the effects of brainwashing make the drug an unnecessary intervention. They also dope civilians who operate on their behalf: members of the surveillance operation, field administrative staff, informers. They have an implant, slowly releasing the drug over time. Ensures continued cooperation."

"I've heard of the drug," ventured the mohawk man. "If this is true, the city is lost. The followers left behind, they'll succumb. They won't even know to resist. They'll see no reason to challenge. The A will control a city of docile puppets."

"There's more," said Dent. "Tomorrow, they plan to gas the caves beneath Lyun Mountain, along with other caves that they've located throughout the Heights. They think you're still down there. They tortured Ursel to find out where so that they can take you alive. Without her, they're down to last resorts: flush you out and kill you with toxic gas."

"Estrin…" said one of the players.

"I warned him," said Dent. "When I came looking for you. But he wouldn't leave his post."

"We left him in the belief he would be safe where he hid," said Bend Sinister, his expression grave. "We took precautions. There's no way he can be found. But poisonous gas…" He shook his head.

His keyboardist stepped forward, hesitant.

"Yes? Please, speak," said Bend Sinister.

"We have to save him," she said. "We can't know his fate and yet do nothing."

Bend Sinister nodded. "I agree. We must send word, fast. We must also alert him to the Authority's plan to spike the spring water. He could return to the city, warn the remaining followers at the very least. Even without *Bluemantle*, there must be ways he can reach them."

"Yes," said the mohawk man. "It's dangerous, but there are places where we gather. We can't talk openly, but we can pass messages."

"Follower, what is your name?"

"Nial, sir," he said, bowing before Bend Sinister, still rattled by the experience of addressing a Troubadour.

"Nial. Would you do this for us? Would you go back to Estrin, tonight? Tell him to leave his hide before they gas the caves and bid him return to the city to warn our followers? With fortune's favour, he can raise the alarm before too many fall under the influence of this drug." He looked squarely at the young man. "We place no pressure upon you. This is a request, which you are free to decline."

"I will be proud to serve you and the Scene," replied Nial, head high, heart racing.

Bend Sinister turned to Pale Dexter and Chief. "I apologise, I am ahead of myself. We have not discussed this."

Pale Dexter nodded slowly. "No, we have not. But your proposal is sound. And, if this brave man is prepared to act as messenger, then I believe it is a plan we are wise to follow. I know I have been pushing for us to move on, to achieve greater distance between us and our pursuers. However, this here," he gestured to the clearing and the shadows beyond, "will afford us safe cover in the short term. Even if our followers are unable to leave Wydeye to join us on our journey, I believe it is our duty to know that they are safe before we move on."

Bend Sinister raised his eyebrows. He stepped forward and placed his hand on Pale Dexter's shoulder. "I admire your loyalty to those loyal to you." He turned to Chief. "Are you in agreement?"

"Without hesitation," she said.

"It is decided then. Nial, our players will provide you with a horse and supplies for the journey. You have far to travel; you will need to leave as soon as possible if you are to make it in time. Do you remember the way back to the shaft?"

Nial opened his mouth as if to respond, then hesitated.

"I can draw you a map," said Dent. "I would offer to go myself, but—"

"But I wouldn't allow it," interrupted Bend Sinister. "You must rest. You've done enough already. We need you well."

Dent dropped his head, lacking the strength to protest. Then a thought occurred to him. "There was something else. I meant to tell you on my return. I don't know if it has any bearing at all, but I feel compelled to share it with you."

"What is it?"

"On the journey back, Ursel was slipping in and out of consciousness. Whenever she came around, she never spoke other than repeating one word. A name. 'Wella.'"

Bend Sinister's other players and several of their followers looked to each other. His guitarist stepped forward. "Wella was one of ours. She recently made the move underground to join our retinue."

"I know Wella, too," said Nial. "She's a close friend of Ursel's."

"There was something in the way she said the name," said Dent. "Urgent. Insistent."

"However abstract, we can't afford to misjudge the relevance," said Bend Sinister. "Nial. When you pass the message about the water to Estrin, also tell him this: Ursel is alive and safe in our care. Once he has carried out his task in the city, tell him we bid him come join us here. With Wella."

CHAPTER THIRTY-FIVE

Drayloc Market baked beneath the midday sun. Citizens realised the clearing of the dust cloud came at a scorching cost. Wella and Naylor took shelter in a slither of shade, ignoring the calls of beckoning barkers.

"We can't talk here," said Wella. She tipped her head in the direction of The Raven.

Although busy, the tavern held a subdued hum that made conversation possible. Wella commandeered two stools in a far corner, while Naylor battled at the bar. He returned with two Kitsons and a bowl of spiced barley breads.

"So, you've had a couple of days to think about it," said Wella. "Are you on board?"

"Of course. I told Chase I was."

"I just wanted to check. He's fired up about the whole idea. His passion is persuasive, but you might have had second thoughts once away from his influence."

"Not at all. I'm not convinced it'll work, mind. The theory is all well and good, but convincing people to take the risk? To stand up against the A, knowing the consequence? It's a massive ask." He paused, shaking his head. Then he sat up straight, shoulders back, and smiled. "That said, I know a lot of pissed-off people who haven't lost their fighting spirit. They're saying the A have gone too far this time. They're done with playing ball. I'd like to think we can drum up some level of support. I've already warmed up a crowd who've said they'll do it. But enough to make a difference? That's the part I'm not so sure about."

"I agree. But I also think it's worth a try. My hope is in momentum. It takes effort to counter the friction at first, to get the cart wheels in motion. But once they start to move, they keep on rolling, gaining pace. I'm banking on those wheels."

"I don't get what the play brings to the plan."

"He's done that for Ursel. Like a tribute to her. He knows it's possible she might not... You know." She blinked, staring ahead. "He means it to be *her* story, if you like. What he's learnt from her. So that it doesn't go to waste. He's realised how important it is."

"He read it to me. I get the moral of the tale, the whole 'judge for yourself' lesson, but that's hardly going to change anything, is it? The Circus seats, what, a couple of hundred, maybe? There's a *few hundred thousand* people crammed into this miserable city."

"It's enough for him that her story's told. Even if one person stops to think, he'd feel it was worth it. Another candle lit for Ursel."

A brief silence fell, accompanied by dark thoughts. Naylor forced them back, denying them airtime. "What did Tinashe say?" he said.

"She's on board. She's doing it for Weldon, in case... Well, anyway, she said the tramway company is full of operators and drivers who've had enough, like they've been wanting a nudge like this for years. She said it's as if they could never contemplate making a stand on their own, while the potential for joint forces felt too much to hope for."

"When are they going to start?"

"Tomorrow. A dozen or so have committed to walking out, or not turning up for their shift. Then she reckons plenty more will follow suit."

Naylor shifted.

Wella watched him closely. "What about your end?" she said. "You support the plan. When are you going to act?"

He filled his chest with the deep breath of decision-making. Then he exhaled slowly, let his shoulders relax and nodded, almost smiling. "Tomorrow."

He was about to elaborate when a young man entered the tavern, his eyes gleaming, his expression intense. He attempted to blend in, hanging back in the shadows, yet Wella felt his presence, glancing up as soon as he entered. Her body stiffened. She held her breath, immediately looking away at nothing.

"What?" asked Naylor. "Who is it?"

"Quiet. Don't look around." She stared at Naylor, anchoring her eyes on his. She lifted up her glass, then placed it back on the table without taking a sip.

The man weaved through the crowded room in a circuitous route. Naylor noticed two other people had a similar reaction to Wella's: freezing, as if caught in the act, waiting for some inevitable repercussion. As the man passed one, then the other, their bodies slowly sagged and downcast eyes attempted to follow his path.

When the man passed their own table, Wella's body did not sag. The man hesitated for a fraction of a second, barely long enough to tuck his left hand behind his back, two fingers pointing down. Wella caught the signal and immediately shifted her eyes back onto Naylor's face, staring but not seeing, her mind carried far away.

The man weaved through a few more tables then shrugged, turned around and left the tavern, apparently failing to find whomever he was looking for.

"Hey, hey," said Naylor, "remember to breathe. Do you know that guy?"

"Shush, not here." She picked up her glass again, a slight tremble in her hands, and took large gulps of her Kitson. "Drink up. We need to leave. But not yet. Soon."

"What? But we've only just got here." He stared at her, waiting for a response. Nothing was forthcoming. Instead, he polished off the barley breads and reluctantly rushed his beer.

After a few minutes and a surreptitious glance around the room, Wella stood up and said in an overly bright tone, "Come on, let's get going. I want to check out the stalls."

Resigned to whatever was happening, or was about to happen, Naylor downed the dregs of his drink and followed her out of the tavern, back into the bustling market. "I thought we were done here?"

"We are. I've got to go somewhere."

"Where? Who was he?"

"I can't say. Just meet me back here in half an hour."

Before he had chance to protest, Wella had disappeared.

Forty minutes later, she returned to join a sullen Naylor under the shade of a tea bar awning. Her face twitched as if it couldn't decide on an expression.

"Follow me," she said, turning to merge with the shuffling crowd. "Keep walking. I'll explain everything."

A carter came between them, leading his goats to a water trough. Naylor cursed, hurrying back to Wella's side.

"He's from underground," she said. "His name's Estrin. He came to find me, to give me a message." She glanced at Naylor, wide-eyed. "Ursel. She's alive. Someone got her out.

The Troubadours are looking after her. And they've... They've summoned me. Estrin is going to take me to them."

Naylor stared at Wella, bumping shoulders with passing citizens. He stumbled, struggling to process the news and still keep up.

"Listen," she said. "I need you to tell Chase. Go back to the hide, straight away. But you must be careful. Make sure no one's following you. Quince, the hide keeper, will recognise you, but you still need to give the code. Say to her, 'The minstrels sing to me.' Have you got that? Say it, now."

"The minstrels sing to me."

"Good. Don't forget, else she won't let you in. I mean it. Tell Chase I had no time to explain. Estrin is waiting for me. He said we have to leave within the hour. Tell Chase I'm sorry. He will want to know about Ursel, but I don't know anything more. Only that she's alive and safe. But she's been asking for me. The Troubadours think it could be important. I've got to go."

"How... How long will you be gone for?"

"I don't know. Estrin said the journey's long. But don't worry. I'll tell them about our plan. That I need to be back here. To make it happen." She stopped walking and grabbed his arm. "Naylor, this doesn't change anything. You said tomorrow. Tinashe is walking out with her lot in the morning. The followers I've spoken to are on standby. They'll act as soon as they're given the signal."

"But who'll give the signal? You don't know when you'll be back. We need the numbers—"

"There was another follower with Estrin – name's Nial. He's going to stay here and spread the word among followers about our plan – that it's happening and that we need them on board. And he's got to tell them something else too. Something you need to know and share with everyone you can. Clo, Chase, Quince. People at work. Anyone who'll listen."

"What? What is it?"

"Don't drink the water. The bottled stuff they're going to dish out for free. It's drugged. The A have drugged it."

"But—"

"That's all I know. Tell as many people as you can." She glared at him, tightening her grip on his arm. "You have to warn them. Before it's too late."

CHAPTER THIRTY-SIX

A dust-free dawn had paved the way for a still, hot day. Shimmering heat haze agitated the horizon. Outside the Wall of the Missing, citizens gathered.

Numbers were low at first. However, as the morning passed and word spread, more appeared in tentative ones and twos. The atmosphere was calm, with an edge of apprehension that kept voices low. The air hummed with a shared exhilaration, borne of knowing the stakes but taking the leap regardless.

Tinashe moved through the gathering crowd, placing her hand on the shoulders of those she knew, smiling warmly at strangers-turned-comrades. She approached Naylor, who leant against the Wall, staring up at the looming Exchange. "Wella was right," she said, tipping her head to a man and woman approaching the group. "Momentum."

"They've shifted the cameras. I've counted four all pointing this way. And over there," he indicated far left with his eyes, "a Watcher. Lights on."

"Hardly surprising, though."

"I know. Just makes me nervous."

"Well, try not to show it. Let them see that we don't care." She lifted her head in full view of the eyes above and smiled.

A military truck pulled up and a Special Forces unit piled out. Troopers took up positions around the area, circling the Exchange, the precinct at its feet and the long arm of the Wall jutting from its left.

"Oh, shit…" said Naylor.

"Don't panic. We're not doing anything wrong. They're just sussing us out. As long as we don't react." She glanced around at their growing number. "I'm going to mingle. I spy a few rattled faces. We've got to make sure they don't lose their nerve."

Tinashe slipped away, moving among the crowd. She caught fragments of conversation as she passed – a pendulum swing between faith and fear.

"…could be arrested for this. I've a kid to…"

"…can't touch us. I'd like to see them try. I tell you…"

"…is a mistake. I knew it. I should've…"

"…our chance. Make a stand. How long have…"

She paused before a satellite group, conspicuous in their silence. She exchanged nods in greeting, sensing a tangible union among them. She hazarded a guess. "Followers?"

A young man stepped forward, his hair casting a sun-dial shadow. "There are many more of us. They are coming. First, they have an urgent task. You've heard about the water?"

"I have."

"They're due to start distribution first thing tomorrow. We have to warn as many people as we can. As soon as our friends have spread the word, they will join us."

"How many?"

"There were several hundred of us, but many are locked up. Free, I'd say we're about 150 strong."

"Where do you all work?"

"All over the city. All sectors. We can reach many workers." He held out a slim, firm hand. "I'm Nial."

"Tinashe. Tramways," she said, shaking his hand. "Listen. We've some waverers here. Can you and your friends help me ease a few minds?"

"Of course."

They dispersed and moved among the crowd. Heads bent forward, quiet words spoken. All the while, new citizens appeared, merging with the gathered, which had spilt from the Wall to fill half of the precinct. Tension flowed in diminishing waves, its force gradually absorbed by those joining the crowd.

Two carters appeared, their goats hauling cargos of fruit, baked breads and steel barrels filled with chilled nettle tea. Trading was forbidden in front of public buildings, a fact which drew the swift attention of the sentinel troopers. The nearest two marched over to the carters, relieved to be given a reason to intervene. The carters held up their hands, faces open. "But we are not trading," one of them said. "See?" He held out a bava fruit to one of the troopers, broke off a chunk of baked bread and handed it to the other. "We are giving."

The troopers stared in confusion and backed away, reluctantly rejecting the refreshments. They reported back to the unit's apparent lead, who rattled something into his radio.

The two carters paid no heed. They gestured invitation towards the gathered citizens, who welcomed the unexpected charity.

On the radio's receiving end, a message was taken and relayed several times. Meanwhile, monitors in the Comms Control Centre were scrutinised for the slightest breach of law. Legislation on public protest was unambiguous. It would take very little to warrant swift, excessive intervention.

Had Governor Blix been at liberty to watch the bank of screens, to witness the growing throng from multiple high-angle shots and hovering bird's-eye views, she would have found the necessary justification. As it was, she remained in her quarters, detained by lock and guard, oblivious of the developments.

"They're not doing anything," barked Wulfwin into his radio.

He was up at the Project Alpha site, flanked by his Deaf Squad. It had taken them all morning to ship the falsely labelled barrels up the Heights to the excavation shaft. His men were poised, ready to pour the contents down the shaft, onto the subterranean stream below. "Protests are illegal. Marches are illegal. Demonstrations are illegal. It ain't illegal to hang around drinking gratis fucking tea."

"But, sir…" crackled the reply.

"Radio when there's a riot. I'm busy. Over and out." He cut the radio and turned around to his men. "Okay. Start pouring it in."

—

Chase sat alone in the hide. The lamp had gone out. He had not bothered to relight it, finding that the darkness leant his guilt small relief in obscurity.

Naylor had visited him late the previous night, had told him about Ursel and about Wella's summons to the Troubadours. "I've no idea how they got Ursel out," Naylor had said. "Not that it matters. She's alive and she's safe. That's all we need to know."

Chase had sat on the lower bunk, his face lost to shadow. He couldn't speak, could barely breathe.

Naylor had tried to read his reaction, debating whether to remain silent and give the news time to sink in or fill the void with bright-side reassurance. He opted for the latter. "Wella will be careful; she won't go taking risks now that there's a plan. And she knows we need her here. I don't know how far away they're hiding, but my guess is she'll be back before long. And she'll have more news about Ursel, how she's doing."

Chase nodded, silent.

"Listen, if you're pissed that she didn't come to tell you herself—"

"No, it's not that."

"Then what? I thought you'd be pleased."

"I am. Of course I am. It's just…" He sighed. "It's my fault."

"No, it's not. Ursel wasn't there just to help you find Wella. She would have gone to the Contest regardless."

"I know. But still. With the raid and everything. Wella and me escaping. It should have been me they caught, not Ursel."

In that moment, part of him had wanted to tell Naylor everything. The truth was like a deep, thick splinter, festering in his flesh. Pulling it out would hurt, but the relief after would be worth it. Yet he maintained it wasn't the time. The relief would be short-lived, and he needed to keep Naylor on side.

They had talked for a while – empty phrases skirting a topic too tender to touch. Then Naylor had left, saying, "It's late. And tomorrow's a big day. We start the walkout early, when the first shifts clock in. I've a dozen committed. They're fired up for it. I guess I'm a little wary. I've Clo, you see…" He had trailed off with a sigh, placed his hand on Chase's shoulder, then left.

Now it was noon. The walkout was happening.

Chase tried to picture the scene outside the Wall of the Missing. Yet the image was unstable, flickering with conflicting possibilities. He had no idea how many would take the risk when the moment came. He had felt so confident about the plan, but now doubted the pivot point on which success was hinged. It was a tall order. To expect people to walk out of their job, knowing the penalty for protest. To make a stand before such an arsenal of control.

He knew he would do it; but then, he had nothing to lose.

His thoughts were twisting and turning in zig-zag guesswork, when he heard voices outside the door to the hide. He froze, holding his breath.

The door opened and Quince's face appeared through the foot-wide gap. "Your friend is back," she said, letting Naylor slip through, before gently closing the door behind him.

"I've come to report on progress," said Naylor. "Can't stay long."

Chase jumped up and relit the lamp, fumbling with the matches. "How's it going? Have many turned out? What about the A? Will they crush it, do you think?"

Naylor held up his hands. "One at a time, okay?" He sat down opposite Chase and took a moment to catch his breath. "Alright. We've had a positive start. Word has started to spread. Once people saw that their mates were actually going through with it, they found the balls to follow suit. I reckon we must be approaching a hundred now. And the people from the scene, the 'followers', they're a huge help. I don't know how, but they've mobilised contacts all over the city. They've given us a way in to the factories in Aldar Point, into the Education Centres and Wickerwild Mine. Pretty much every sector. Even the Messam, although I doubt we'll get many from business, apart from maybe those with family locked up."

"A hundred… One to every three thousand workers. That won't come close to causing a problem."

"Give it time, Chase. It's only the start."

"And the A?"

"They're on our case alright. Cameras and Watchers recording our every move. Special Forces all over the place. We've made it clear to everyone: no banners, no chanting or raised voices, no posturing. But it's a terrifyingly fine line. And it'd only take one citizen to cross it. Then it's game over for all of us. We just have to hope to crow that everyone holds their nerve, no matter what."

—

Wulfwin stood on Lyun Mountain, gas mask in one hand, barking into the radio he held in the other. "They're freaked out about the holes, that's all. Order Comms to refresh the message, remind them we're on the case. Meanwhile, they'll soon realise they're out of pocket. The rate they waste money on Meezel and beer, they can't afford to bunk off for long. Report in if they actually do something. Over and out."

Radio communication from various Unit Superiors was proving relentless. With Governor Blix stripped of her authority and the Chief of Staff effectively gagged by intimidation, all decisions had to come through Wulfwin. Had he not been so distracted by the operation on the Heights, he would have relished the position of power. As it was, he had no time for trivialities.

"*Delta-Charlie-One, this is Trooper Two-Nine. Do you read? Over.*"

"Fuck this," he muttered, and switched off his radio.

He strapped on his gas mask and entered the mouth of the cave. Forgetting his goggles, his eyes began to sting. "Trooper!" he called to a passing man, pointing at his head. "Give me those." He snatched the man's goggles and put them on, his eyes already weeping.

All around him, Special Forces were streaming in and out of the cave. Many of those leaving were without protection, bar a sleeve to their eyes and a hand over their mouth. They stumbled out into the daylight, choking and near-blind.

Wulfwin shoved past them, cursing at the obstruction. "Where's the Duty Superior?" he called. "Who the fuck's in charge?"

After several minutes, two Unit Superiors appeared, their bloodshot eyes squinting behind the inadequate protective gear. "Sir!" they said in unison.

"Tell me you've flushed the fucking rats."

"Sir?" said one.

"The Music Makers. Where are they?"

"We've not found them yet, sir. It's vast. Caves everywhere."

"I don't give a shit. It's taking too long."

"Sir, we're working as fast as we can. We must be in the final section now. It's deep. Takes over an hour to climb down there. It's been a mission to get the gas canisters down safely."

"Safely? We're trying to kill the fuckers."

"Risk of explosion, sir. It'll cause collapse. The men—"

Wulfwin waved a hand. "Whatever. This last section. You think they're in there?"

"I don't know, sir. Unlikely. Oxygen levels are low. We're not seeing signs of habitation, like in other areas. But if they're down there somewhere, then this is the last place they can be."

"*If* they're down there? You'd better hope to fucking crow they are, 'cos it was your units that were guarding the exits when we stormed the place. If they're not there, it's because *you* let them escape." He prodded them both in the chest. One stumbled backwards with the force. "Go back and find those bastards. I want them carried outside in the next hour, breathing their fucking last."

—

Back in the Comms Control Centre, eyes still stinging,

Wulfwin screamed at Surveillance. "Why the fuck haven't you got me an answer?"

"Sir," stuttered the Unit Superior, "there's a lot of material to trawl through. We had the mountain well covered. There were fourteen Watchers in the Heights that night. There's over a hundred hours of footage."

"How many people have you got on the case?"

"Well… The whole unit, sir."

"Twelve men? You're taking the piss, right?"

"Sir, I—"

"Shut it. There's your answer, right there."

"Yes, sir."

"As many men as you've got machines. I want that footage scanned and a report in my ear in the next two hours. Do I make myself clear?"

"Sir."

"It is looking increasingly likely that the Music Makers escaped. If you did your job properly, one of those cameras will give us a direction. And if they don't? Well. Time for an unscheduled performance review. And I don't do constructive criticism. So, you'd best hope you find something."

"Yes, sir."

"Where's the other waste of space that runs this division? The one looking for our missing sleeper."

"Unit Superior Tumen, sir?"

"I don't know his name."

"Trooper Sixty."

"That's him. Tell him to report to me here. Immediately. Then start searching for that needle. Clock's ticking."

"Yes, sir."

"And?" He glared at the man, who faltered and froze. "Go! Go now, you piece of shit."

The Unit Superior scurried away, leaving Wulfwin to pace

the room. Radio operators fumbled with dials and switches, fingers trembling. Several of the messages that came in were for him. He had left his radio turned off, already tired of the relentless attention that came with being in charge.

A different Unit Superior came trotting up to Wulfwin, breathless. "Trooper Sixty, sir," he said, raising his hand in unsteady salute.

"Tell me it's because you've been saving up the good news."

"Sir?" His arm fell, limp.

"The reason you've yet to report on the whereabouts of our AWOL sleeper."

"Sir, we are doing all we can to trace him."

"If that were the case, Trooper Sixty, my missing sleeper would be here, at my feet, kissing my arse, apologising for getting lost. So, cut the crap."

"Sir, all WatcherCams are programmed to detect his ID. Static cameras, likewise. Our eyes on the ground have been on the lookout since he first went off radar."

"Remind me. That was how long ago?"

"Seven days, sir."

"Seven days… A week off radar and you've got the nerve to tell me you're doing all you can? Were you born a bullshitter, or did you learn it from your cock-sucking mother?"

The man flushed, eyes bulging. "I… I won't have—"

"You *won't* what?" roared Wulfwin, striking him hard across the face. The man stumbled backwards and fell, his left hand cupping a broken nose. Wulfwin kicked him in the abdomen, forcing him to crunch up in pain and foetal defence. "Tell me. Go on." He stamped down hard on the side of his ribs. "Exactly what the fuck *won't* you do?"

"I'm sorry, sir. I didn't mean—"

"You're off the detail, Trooper Sixty. And you're stripped

of Superior rank. When you've pulled your blubbing arse together, report to Sanitation. You like talking crap so much, you can start cleaning it up."

A Special Forces Unit Superior appeared at the door and froze, regretting his moment to arrive.

"What?" barked Wulfwin. He stepped over the huddled body of the demoted trooper. "What now?"

"Sir, I've just come from the Exchange. I tried to radio you—"

"You and every other damned Superior. So? You've found me. Spit it out."

"Sir, the crowd is growing. I estimate three hundred. Increasing by the hour."

"Are they blocking the Exchange?"

"No, sir. They've left a path for citizens to enter. Although…"

"What?"

"Well, hardly anyone is."

"For fuck's sake. We need the intel. There's still chance someone could've seen the Makers leave. Are you sure they're not barring the way? Intimidating people as they approach?"

"I'm certain, sir."

"So, what? They're just hanging around, obsessing about the bloody holes? Sipping tea and losing a day's pay? They're probably itching Meezels, too high to care."

"What would you like me to do, sir?"

"Get your men to start provoking. Stir some trouble. All we need's a little reaction. Meanwhile, liaise with Employment. Tell them to find out who's skipped class and threaten termination of contract. See how the loafers like that."

"Anything else, sir?"

"Yes. Stop wasting my time. I've got more important shit to deal with. I've given over enough resources for you to contain the situation. Just make the fuckers flinch. You've already got orders to go in heavy-handed the moment they do. So, go do your job and stop with the jittering. You sound like bloody Blix."

The man saluted and left.

His own mention of Blix riled him even more. He turned to take it out on the trooper on the floor, but the man had crawled away, betrayed by a trail of blood from his broken nose. Cursing under his breath, Wulfwin surveyed the room. Heads were ducked behind radio sets. The officers at the raised desks had their eyes down, studying pieces of paper. Those whose job it was to run the messages back and forth had appeared to disappear. Wulfwin snorted, kicked over a chair and left the room.

He marched over to the parade ground and glanced up at the tower that contained Blix's private quarters. He imagined her prostrate on the lounger, eyes rolling in doped oblivion. He had ensured she had constant access to Meezel, only not the discrete pill form she favoured. He had ordered a batch of wraps from the Exchange's supply. A trusted colleague in Pharmaceuticals had laced them with a compound developed for psychoactive torture. It combined a sedative with a powerful hallucinogen, rendering the subject powerless to wake from their visions – or, more often, their nightmares.

Wulfwin stared at the tower, hoping Blix was engulfed in an endless, terrifying trip, full of swarming masses, rising up to deliver her dreaded rebellion.

CHAPTER THIRTY-SEVEN

It was an emotional reunion in the Troubadour's temporary camp. Wella had been warned about Ursel's injuries, but nothing could prepare her for what she saw.

Ursel was laying propped up on a makeshift bunk near the centre of the camp. Bandages and dressings evidenced the quantity of wounds to her body. Her face was uncovered, however. Bruised swellings created their own expression. She still couldn't open her left eye. The dried blood had been cleaned from inside her punctured ears.

Beside the bunk stood the three Troubadours, their players a step behind. Among them, Bend Sinister's drummer, who had shaved off his beard, adopted the black attire of his fellow players and shed the moniker ascribed by the Authority. Behind the players stood their retinue: the followers that Wella had joined when she made the Scene her home just four weeks ago. Among them, Estrin, weary from the long journey through the night to locate the camp.

When Wella first saw Ursel, she fell to her knees and wept.

"Save your sympathy," said Ursel, her tone flat. "I am free. There are many who are suffering great cruelty as we speak. We must focus on them."

Wella began to say something, forgetting. Ursel raised a weak arm, gesturing to a pad and pencil at the foot of the bunk.

Her hands trembling, Wella picked them up. She held the pencil poised over the paper but failed to find the words.

"It's okay," said Ursel. "There's nothing you can say."

"Wella," said Bend Sinister. "We thank you for coming. We appreciate it was at no small risk to your safety."

Wella stood up, her pulse quickening. She had followed Bend Sinister for two years – had given up her life overground to work in their retinue. This was the first time he had spoken to her directly. "I had no hesitation," she said. "Ursel is a good friend. And I would do anything to help the Scene."

"We are grateful for your loyalty. I must warn you, however, your loyalty is about to be put to the test." He paused, watching Wella's expression. "Ursel has a plan to salvage the Scene and free those who might choose to follow it. It also seeks to liberate those still suffering at the hands of the Authority. This plan hinges upon your involvement to a significant extent. It also puts you at great personal risk. For this reason, know that while we value your loyalty, we do not expect you to accept without careful consideration of the consequences."

Wella stared at him, wide-eyed.

Pale Dexter addressed her. "We have been forced into a bleak dilemma. The proposed intervention carves the only desirable resolution. Whilst we acknowledge the danger it will place you in, we believe it may be our only chance."

"Hush, say no more," said Chief, glaring at Pale Dexter. "Look at her. She's as likely to decline before she's even heard the idea." She smiled kindly at Wella. "Do not be alarmed. I give you my assurance that you have the choice. A choice free of pressure and expectation. Come, sit on the bunk beside Ursel and let her explain. It is painful for her to speak and her voice cannot carry. I suggest you save your questions until the end. You can write them down, then Ursel or one of us will address them for you." She gestured towards the bunk. "Please."

Wella drew her eyes from the Troubadours to Ursel, who had been watching the exchange. Wella sat down beside her, held her hand and nodded for her to begin.

"The Authority have controlled the narrative for too long," said Ursel, her expression resolute. "It's time for change. But to achieve that, the citizens of Wydeye must hear the real story. They need to know that the *Tale of the Travelling Minstrels* has a new ending. In it, the minstrels leave the city because they are free to do so. Just as the Telltale Circus will become a touring theatre once more. The Wydeye that the minstrels and the theatre settled in and made their home has changed beyond recognition. Even the folklore of Wydeye Deep speaks of a city long since lost, destroyed by those sworn in to deliver protection and prosperity.

"Those in power have become consumed by their desires, controlled by their need to control. Instead of protecting the citizens of Wydeye, they tell them what to think. Now they poison the water to manipulate how they behave.

"Citizens must recognise they are no more dependent on the Authority than they are on the protection of the Deep. One is fantasy, the other fairy tale. They are free to leave, free to follow, free to choose.

"Estrin has informed us of your plan. It filled me with great hope to hear it. Those with open eyes and sufficient courage will seize the opportunity. You will have many who will come forward, empowered by union, hungry for the opportunity to make the stand together that they're afraid to make alone.

"However, Wydeye is a large city, its population bloated. To touch, you need to reach. To be heard, you need a voice. Cole knew this. He created a means to reach those ready to venture from the A's single track. He grew the audience by giving people a map, inviting citizens to follow a different path – to engage with the Scene, in order to make up their own mind about it. He had faith that, if they did, they'd become part of it. Who wouldn't?

"And now, here we are, in a very similar situation. Only, the stakes for engagement are significantly higher. Yet the reward warrants the risk. It's not simply choosing a different path. It's about choosing freedom by following it. And the tragedy is, most people don't realise that the choice has been there all along.

"So again, we need a voice. A map to reveal the way and express the invitation. Dear Cole…" Ursel faltered, then sighed, her eyes downcast. "I asked other prisoners, even guards. He wasn't there. They must have him in the Hold. They tortured me for four days and I know they were close to drawing a line. Cole was taken ten days ago. There's no way…" She swallowed hard and cleared her throat.

Eventually she looked up at Wella and said, "We may harbour hope in our hearts, but in terms of our actions moving forward, we must assume he's gone from us. Yet, the invitation he created lives on. In *Bluemantle*."

Wella wanted to withdraw her hand, sensing what was coming next, but Ursel held on tight, determined to get to the end. "Wella, we need you to resurrect *Bluemantle*. One edition. To tell the real story. No coded messages, no coordinates buried beneath text, lost to all without the means to decipher them. This time it needs to provide the map and make it plain as day there's a choice: to follow the path and don't look back.

"I can tell you where Cole's workshop is. Where the drops are. We'll get a message to followers. They'll pick up the bundles and distribute them by hand, giving them to citizens who've never even heard of *Bluemantle*. If you print a hundred thousand, we could have them handed out in a day. That's a third of the population. If only a quarter of them join the path, that's twenty-five thousand people who've opened their eyes for the first time in decades. It's also twenty-five thousand joining your walkout. That should make a dent in productivity. Then the A will have to listen.

"Believe me, I appreciate the huge risk. We all knew the dangers that Cole faced. And yet, I'm asking you to face the same. For this one edition. Then, if it works, we won't need it anymore. Presented with the truth about the A, I believe citizens will navigate their own way. Challenge the narrative, break the illusion of their dependency, take back control of their freedom."

She let go of Wella's hand and held out the paper and pencil to her. "So, what do you say? Will you do it?"

—

In the warren of Rader, the creeping light of sunrise could not penetrate the hide's concrete walls. Chase stood beside the table, his face lost in shadow. "I can't believe they asked you to do this."

Wella stood opposite him, weary from the arduous journey, yet wired by the prospect of her mission. "They say there's no other way."

"There must be."

"I don't think so. And were it not for the danger, it'd be the perfect solution. It'll boost the walkout in a way that the A can't possibly ignore, and in a fraction of the time. It'll get the message out to citizens in a way *they* can't ignore, direct and unambiguous. It could change everything, Chase. I see that. You must be able to as well."

"Were it not for the danger, then yes. But you can't extract that. You can't will it away." He reached out and held her arms. "The message won't be coded. When a copy falls into the hands of the A, which it will, it'll be over, for everyone. Every raid, every attack, even Rideout – nothing will compare to what they'll do. We're talking innocent people, kids. The A won't care. They'll come down on the whole city and they won't stop until everyone in possession of a copy is locked up or dead." He slumped down on one of the chairs.

Wella sat down opposite him, silent. She'd had the same thoughts when she first heard the plan. She'd battled with them on her journey back to the city.

Chase studied her face, looked deep into her eyes. "You know all this. Yet you're going to do it anyway."

She took a deep breath, then relaxed her shoulders. "Yes."

Chase closed his eyes and held his head in his hands.

Earlier, when Wella had eventually returned from her summons to the Troubadours, she had told him about Ursel and the brutality inflicted upon her. He'd felt the urge to retch. The thought of Ursel's suffering sickened and appalled him; he felt responsible and helpless, weak in every regard. Then Wella had added, "But you know, after all they did to her, she's still not broken. If anything, she's more determined. Stronger."

Those words came back to him now. He forced himself to picture Ursel as Wella had seen her: battered but not broken. Bruised but not defeated. He looked up at his sister. "I will help you," he said.

Wella stared at him, mouth open.

"I'll need to disguise myself somehow," he added, quick to block any objection. "Just to get me to the workshop. Then I'll help you put *Bluemantle* together. A hundred thousand copies is a lot. I can help with the printing, folding, packing them up. Even with the drops, if we think the disguise is good enough."

"Chase—"

"Please. I've been holed up here, unable to do a damn thing. Alright, the walkout was my idea, but it's action we need. I've so much to atone for. The story was for Ursel. This is for the Scene, for all the wrongs I've done to bring it down."

"Look, I've already decided I'll do it. I can manage on my own. You don't need to get involved. You're in enough trouble with the A as it is."

"I want to help. And whilst I know you can handle it without me, we can get it done faster together. Once the bottles of water start appearing, we've probably only a couple of days before people have enough of the drug in their system to take effect."

Wella studied Chase's expression, then slowly nodded. "Alright. Quince has a stash of wigs and clothes for disguise. You're not the first to have had to leave the hide before it's safe. The workshop is in Old Wydeye Town. We'll take the Elevated to Standings Cross and walk from there. Get yourself ready. We leave in ten."

—

Chase and Wella rode the railmotor in the silence of prey.

Sweat poured down the side of Chase's face. Beneath the wig, his head throbbed from the heat and itched unbearably. He couldn't see through the prescription glasses. The padded shirt clung to his body, raising his core temperature in the already sweltering heat.

Wella had adopted a more modest disguise – a precaution in case Surveillance tracked friends and relatives as a route to their target. She stared through the trailer windows, her eyes fixed on snatches of street between the arches of the Elevated.

The railmotor pulled into Standings Cross. They got off and descended to street level, following the underpass until it terminated at the crumbling limestone walls of Old Wydeye Town. Once lost in the maze of narrow streets, they felt able to speak for the first time since leaving the hide.

"Did you see them?" said Wella.

"I can't see a damn thing in these."

"Trucks. They're delivering the water. It won't be long before they start handing it out."

They weaved through cobbled streets between low limestone buildings, ducking to avoid sagging awnings and suspended wares. Chase held on to Wella's arm as she led the way.

"I know I can't see where we're going, but haven't we just walked in a circle?" he said after a while.

"Correct."

"Don't tell me you're lost—"

"Relax. Evasion tactic."

Eventually they reached their destination. Wella held them back on the opposite side of the street.

"What is it?" said Chase.

"One of the unknowns in the plan. The workshop is guarded by an old man. Some say he's Cole's father. Ursel told me the code so he'll let us pass. But that's assuming he's still there. Cole's quarters were raided eleven days ago. It's possible the old man destroyed the workshop as a precaution. But hope leaves a light on. Ursel isn't sure but believes the old guy would've waited."

"What if he hasn't? What if he's wrecked the whole operation?"

"Game over."

"Why didn't you tell me this before?"

"What difference would it have made?"

Chase sighed and shook his head.

They approached the ramshackle house, its shutters closed. Wella knocked on the door three times, paused, then knocked twice more. They held their breaths, straining to hear sounds in the foreboding silence. Eventually the door creaked open by a finger's width. Wella leant forward and whispered through the crack. "The crow flies low over Glade Park."

Nothing.

Chase squinted at Wella, who shrugged, palms up. Then the door slowly gave way and a frail hand ushered them in.

The room was dark. Splinters of light bled through cracks in the shutters, forming a faint constellation where they touched the dusty floor. The old man stood in the centre of the room, leaning on his crooked cane. His face was gaunt, his expression grave. "Eleven days gone," he said.

Chase recalled the last time he'd seen Cole. Recalled his own sickening betrayal. He heard the grief in the old man's voice and could not bear to look him in the eye.

"We have a plan," said Wella. "One that could lead to the release of prisoners. Crow willing, we'll reach Cole in time."

The old man shook his head slowly. "He's gone. They didn't take him. But he's gone."

"Then we'll find him. Or he'll come back. Once the dust has settled. He'll return."

"No. He's gone to the Deep. He won't be coming back." He looked at her with eyes that knew. "I'm afraid I can't help you. I'm sorry. You've endured a wasted journey."

Wella met the old man's gaze, trying to make sense of his words. Failing, she fell back on the urgency that had propelled her to his home. "You *can* help us. We've come to finish what he started. We have the Troubadours' consent. Please. If you are right, then let this be his legacy."

The old man studied the stars at his feet.

Chase fidgeted, sick to the stomach and desperate to leave.

Wella stood her ground, willing the guardian to agree.

Eventually, the old man raised his cane and pointed it towards the wooden cupboard at the far end of the room. "That way," he said.

Once inside the basement, Chase tore off his wig and rubbed his sweat-soaked hair, scratching his scalp with relief. Wella pulled from her tunic a piece of paper, covered in handwritten script.

"What's that?" asked Chase.

"The text. Ursel wrote it. We need to set it out in the fanzine format. Make the content clear. Then we start printing. Our target is to drop the bundles before dawn, then get a message to Naylor and Tinashe. They're going to explain to the followers their role in the plan."

They set to work in silence, typing up the blocks of text, cutting and gluing them onto the concertinaed master.

"It doesn't fill it up," said Chase, once they'd finished. "There are two sides left on the last fold. What do we do? Just leave it blank?"

Wella thought for a moment, then smiled. "This is a big city," she said. "Not everyone goes to the Circus."

Chase frowned, then the furrows cleared. "Really?"

"Why not? The story's message is consistent."

"Did you tell her about it?"

"I thought you could do that yourself. Or take her to see it when she comes home."

They both fell silent at the prospect. There was too far to go before it could feel achievable; too much could go wrong. For their own reasons, they pushed the thought away and focused on finalising the master. The print job would take several hours. Time was tight. That pressure alone made it possible to ignore all that couldn't yet be faced.

—

A hundred miles away, the three Troubadours sat in silence. They perched on the rise above the camp, keeping watch while their minds dwelt on the freedoms enjoyed in centuries past. Below them, their people slept.

Two in the camp who could not sleep were Ursel and the drummer who had been Dent Lore.

Ursel lay on her bunk, eyes closed. In her mind she cherished the memory of sound – of voices and of music. She played and replayed them in her head, her aural treasures, fearful of forgetting what she would never hear again.

The drummer lay on a blanket among his fellow players. He kept his eyes open, too afraid to close them lest he fall asleep and wake up in that other world where he was the hunter, not the hunted. He had returned to a dream from a nightmare. Neither one felt real.

Over the city of Wydeye, the celestial constellations disappeared in the fading night. Chase slipped through the deserted streets of Darlem Fields, his final drop delivered. His body ached with exhaustion, yet it paled beside a far greater suffering. This, he had made into a bundle all of its own, wrapped in a guilty conscience, which he carried in his chest. He bore it like a burden deserved and headed east across the city, back to the hide in Rader.

Wella was still in the Hundred of Wickerwood. She had made her final drop an hour before and now lay huddled in the shelter of a friend's backyard. Her eyes were closed, her body resting, but sleep would not come. Her mind knew to wait, alert, for the hour the curfew would lift. Then she could move through the city without the need for stealth, journey north, to Spire Wells and the steps of the Exchange. There she could discharge the last of her duties. Her part in the plan would be played.

At this early hour, the Wall of the Missing stood alone. The faces in the photos looked out towards the empty precinct, their 'remember me' expressions boring holes into the concrete. Soon, the citizens on the walkout would return, adopting their mask of passive presence and hoping that more would join.

In contrast to the awakening city, the Authority Complex never slept. The yellow windows of the Comms Control Centre never blinked. The parade ground never stood silent, jackboot free. And in Deaf Squad HQ, in the private quarters of the Chief of Command, the bedsheets were never wrapped around naked skin.

Wulfwin stood in his trench coat, staring at his desk. Behind him, pinned to the wall, were charts and tables: rotas, resources, contingencies, logistics. On the desk before him lay a map, the only one of its kind. All other maps detailed Wydeye: its Hundreds and districts, its roads and tramways, the ribbon of The Spire, starting from a needle point at the spring in Spire Wells. All other maps ended at the city's outer limits. Beyond that, the margin was narrow, the cartographic representation abstract.

This map was different. It revealed Wydeye as a patch of grey in the centre of a far wider, colourful context. It showed the mountain range to the north-west, the forest to the south, the plains to the east. Then it charted what lay beyond even those: the terrain and its contours, settlements and cities, roads and railways. It was not a map of Wydeye, but of what lay beyond.

It was also a battlefield.

And Wulfwin was preparing an army to go on the attack.

They're out there, he thought. *And I'm going to find them.*

CHAPTER THIRTY-EIGHT

"Overspill," said Tinashe. She was stood on the steps of the Exchange with Wella, who had struggled to find her in the crowd. "Naylor's leading the way. We're establishing a second gathering in Glade Park." She smiled. "Fitting, don't you think?"

"Nice work. And plenty of space. Once *Bluemantle* gets out, we're going to need it." She stood on her toes, scanning the crowd. "Where's Nial?"

"Over there." Tinashe pointed out a mohawk near a line of parked carters. Two had become six, distributing free food and uncontaminated water to the grateful gathered. Wella weaved through the crowd and joined him.

"Wella," said Nial. "It's good to see you again. All done?"

"Done. Are they ready?"

"More than."

He turned and signalled to a follower a few yards away who, in turn, signalled to others. Within a matter of seconds, a large gap appeared in the crowd where over a hundred followers had stood moments before. They disappeared, heading off in pairs to their allocated drop. From there, they would distribute the bundles, targeting places of work, cafés and taverns, public spaces and people's homes. The plan was tight. Nial had divided the Hundreds and districts into subdistricts; no part of the city would be duplicated or missed.

"They know to act fast," he said. "And not just because of the water. When the A, or anyone willing to trade, sees a copy, Special Forces will come down heavy. It's inevitable. But before that happens, we need to get *Bluemantle* into the hands of as many citizens as we can. Only then will we have the volume we need for the walkout to work."

"Do you think it will?"

"I have to believe it will, else what's the point? Which is why you did what you did last night. Right?"

Wella smiled briefly, subconsciously touching the mark on her face.

A man walked past, making his way to the Wall of the Missing. Wella caught her breath and held her hand to her chest.

"What is it?" said Nial.

"I've got to go. There's someone I need to speak to."

She darted off in the direction of the man, who was now scanning the photos through welling eyes. She caught up and stood behind him. "Excuse me. It's Evan, isn't it?"

The man turned around and gazed at her through red-raw eyes.

"My name's Wella," she said. "I knew Cole. From underground. He often spoke of you. Carried your picture."

He glanced over his shoulder, indicating the Wall. "His picture's here, somewhere. But so many have been added, even in the short time since…" He wiped his eyes with the heels of his hands. "Sorry. It doesn't get any easier."

"I saw his father. He doesn't think the A have him."

"I know. I beg the Deep that were true, but false hope is a fleeting friend."

"But, if they have him, isn't there *real* hope? If we win and force the A to release people, maybe—"

"Hope's all well and good if you think there's a crow's chance. But I don't. They will have tortured him, despite knowing he would never talk. It's been twelve days. I have to… I have to believe it's over, that he's finally at peace." He swallowed hard. "That's why I'm here. Why I've walked out. We've got to put a stop to it. To what they do to people. We've sat back for too long. Acceptance makes us complicit."

She looked at Evan, at the passion flushing his face and pulsing in his jaw. "I'm going to ask you a favour. You can say no, but I hope you don't."

"If it helps with this," he gestured towards the Wall, "then I'll do anything."

"Please speak to people. Anyone here who will listen. Tell them about Cole and what he did. What he created and what he risked his life for. Tell them about *Bluemantle* and why it was important. Not just to Cole and the Scene. But what it meant about making a choice. The freedom to choose. Tell them what it cost Cole to create that freedom for others. Tell them that he knew what the cost would be. And that he did it anyway."

—

Across the city, citizens began their commute to work. Delays on the tramways caused queues at the stops. Ordinarily reliable, the network was struggling to cope with an increasing number of absent drivers and signal operators. Commuters were unaccustomed to the disruption. They stood in line, anxiously clock-watching as their window to punch in approached.

Authority personnel manning the spring water distribution stations spotted the opportunity. Free bottles were handed out to those waiting in line. The morning was already warm; queuing commuters drank the water, grateful for the refreshment.

Followers also targeted the captive audience. Once the bottle distributors had moved on, followers worked down the lines, thrusting copies of *Bluemantle* into empty hands, murmuring, "Read this," and, "Spread the word." Citizens looked startled. Many dropped the pamphlet as if handed something contaminated. Most appraised the piece of folded paper with idle curiosity. Another tramway pulled in, then pulled out. The line shuffled forward. They had nothing better to do. So they read.

Murmurs rippled along the waiting lines, and in the cafés and tea bars where workers paused for breakfast. Citizens looked around them, wide-eyed, fearful they were in possession of some anti-Authority propaganda. Others looked at their free bottle of spring water, uncapped the lid and sniffed the contents. Above and around them loomed didactic murals: illustrated reminders of enemies of the state. Radios reinforced the narrative. "*Laziness feeds off idle hands, restricting productivity. Resist! Keep fit and healthy and achieve your work goals. Citizens of Wydeye, watch out for the rats. The nest is near. Protect your family – keep your eyes open and tell us what you see. The Exchange is waiting for you, twenty-four seven. You know it makes sense.*"

A jarring of voices. Conflicting messages.

Unease began to spread.

—

Up in the Authority Complex, the Council of Command sat in session. As acting leaders, the Chief of Command and Chief of Staff had called the emergency meeting. Eleven Commanders sat around a large, oval board table in the Authority's Operations HQ. The seat of the twelfth Commander was vacant, as was the seat at the head of the table. Either side of this sat Wulfwin and the Chief of Staff, both deputising as Chair. The Chief of Staff did not speak a word.

"To implement the plan with any meaningful chance of success," said Wulfwin, "we need adequate resources. It is my intention to mobilise the Allears, Deaf Squad and one hundred Special Forces troopers, as well as five transporter trucks, eight Ops trucks and the full fleet of field bikes."

The Commanders looked to each other, heads shaking, establishing mutual resistance and a shared reluctance to be the one to disagree.

With evident unease, Special Forces Commander Fentlow mustered the courage to speak up. His tall frame and broad shoulders diminished beneath the pressure. "But that would leave less than two hundred troopers to cover the entire city. I've still got men on the Heights, remember. What about the situation outside the Exchange? If anything, we need more resources to contain it."

"There's nothing to contain. They've been playing ring-a-roses around the site for three days and still nothing's happened. And nothing's going to happen. The scum wouldn't dare." *Plus, there's the water*, he thought, suppressing a self-satisfied sneer.

"But the numbers are growing. There's another group gathered in Glade Park."

"Banners? Loud-hailers? Badges with 'Fuck off, A' on their shirts?"

"No, but…" Fentlow looked around the table in search of support. None was forthcoming.

"You're a victim of influence," said Wulfwin. "The Governor's paranoia has rubbed off." He stood up, leaning on the table with stilt-arms. "The citizens fear us. Nearly forty years and we've not had so much as a hand in the air and a polite, 'S'cuse me, but…' What makes you think they're going to kick off now?"

"Then why are they gathering?"

"The holes. They assume we can control nature. Most are probably high; you can't employ reason. Once they see the dent in their pay packet, they'll be clambering for overtime."

"Let's hope so. We've had calls from Employment. Problems have started."

Wulfwin sighed. "We're preparing to mobilise troops on a vital mission and you bring up Employment?"

"They've raised concerns, sir."

"Don't they always?"

"But serious this time. I've seen their outline assessment. Productivity is down."

"Bullshit. It's only been three days."

"We've made the margins tight. Risk register is triggered if it's down zero point two. If the current trend continues, we'll hit that in a couple of hours."

"Relax the margin then." Wulfwin raised his hands, palms up. "What's the point of this Council if we can't exert a little power? Flex the rules? I suggest we revise it to zero point four. That should take the pressure off other Divisions too. If not, we'll have Trade kicking off before the day's out. Meanwhile, we can focus on more important matters. Yes?"

Fentlow raised a finger, about to say something.

Wulfwin cut in. "Good. The plan is agreed. We mobilise at sixteen-hundred hours. There's much to prepare. I declare this session closed."

—

Whether it was curiosity or conviction that drove them to the park, Naylor couldn't tell.

Throughout the morning, more citizens arrived. Some found friends or family already gathered; others loitered on the periphery, one hand still on the fence. Then, in time, groups formed, merging with others. Conversations were kept low, yet their intensity grew. Doubts dwindled as reason gave cause. "…And now they've drugged the water. What's left to say?"

This was the emerging backstop. First, in *Bluemantle*, spelt out in black and white; now, voiced among the gathered. The arguments were compelling. Confidence grew. "We just need more to join the walkout," citizens said. "Then they'll listen. They'll *have* to listen."

—

The disguise had worked when coupled with the cover of darkness. Chase dared not risk it in full daylight. Instead, he was forced to hole up in the hide, desperate to know how the plan was unfolding.

Eventually, Wella dropped in to update him. "*Bluemantle's* working," she said, her lips breaking into a cautious smile. "It can't all be the walkout. There's too many coming."

"What's the mood?"

"They know the rules. They appear subdued. But you move among the gathered and it's a different story. You should hear what they're saying."

"Like what?"

"Like we can win this. Together. Stand our ground. How we've suffered for too long and we're not going to take it anymore. How this is our chance to change things."

"But they're realistic, right? They know what the point is?"

"Yeah. *Bluemantle* made that clear. But still. It's momentum. There's a faith building. A belief that, if we can achieve this one thing, it's a first step in a journey towards change."

"I wish I could see it." He sighed. "I wish Ursel could see it."

"In time, brother. In time."

—

Ursel could imagine it. That was enough for her.

She lay on her bunk in the Troubadours' temporary camp. The midday sun penetrated the dell's canopy, casting heat spots on her wounds. The swelling had eased in the night. She could now open both eyes.

The drummer who had been Dent Lore approached, hesitant. She gestured for him to come closer. "It's okay," she said, holding out the pencil and paper.

The drummer knelt beside her bunk, his eyes dark and downcast. His hand trembled as he began to write. Without meeting her eyes, he handed her the note. "*I was there,*" it said. "*They made me watch.*"

"I know. I remember."

He scribbled again, faster this time. "*I should've done something. Stopped them.*"

"You had guards either side of you. You couldn't have taken on all five of them."

"*I wasn't myself. I was still mostly… him. But that's no excuse. Even if I was fully him, I shouldn't have stood by and let it happen.*"

"There was nothing you could have done. If you had kicked off, they would have taken you out. It wouldn't have changed what they did to me. You must know that." She reached out and touched his arm. "Since then, you've risked your life to save mine. I would be dead if it wasn't for you. I've everything to thank you for."

The drummer shook his head, his expression pained. Then he wrote, *"Do you think it'll work?"*

"Yes. I do."

"Why?"

"Because people are ready. Not everyone, but enough. Enough have been touched by tragedy. All they needed was an invitation. *Bluemantle* will give them that."

"I'm afraid to believe it."

Meanwhile, on the other side of the camp, the Troubadours sat close. It had been a long night, hoping for fortune's favour one moment, fearing fate's tribulation the next.

"We must have faith that *Bluemantle* will succeed," said Chief.

"What about whether the citizens will listen?" said Pale Dexter. "Their track record affords little ground for hope."

"This is different," said Bend Sinister.

"How so?"

"You heard Ursel. It's not been spelt out before. And they can't ignore this. Whichever side they take, they will listen. How can they not?"

Chief sighed. "We must be mindful not to underestimate the Authority's hold over them. They rule with a merciless whip, striking terror and intimidation. However well they listen, the citizens' fear may determine their actions."

"For some, yes," said Bend Sinister. "For others, I think not. Which is why we must be ready."

Pale Dexter and Chief looked at him, their silence questioning.

Bend Sinister obliged. "We made the decision to leave because we believed we had no choice. If the situation in

Wydeye changes, it may be that we have options. I'm not saying there will be such a radical change as would permit us to return and perform without threat of capture. That hope is beyond even my bright-side perspective."

"Then what are you saying?" said Pale Dexter.

"If *Bluemantle* succeeds, citizens may choose to leave. If they leave, some may follow. We need to be ready for them. They will look to us, the Scene's troika. We must be prepared to lead."

CHAPTER THIRTY-NINE

The crowd at Glade Park was growing. Troopers circled the area, glaring at those gathered in an effort to intimidate. The posturing was wasted. For the first time in decades, the citizens were unmoved.

Naylor observed them. "They're getting cocky. I can feel it."

"They're enjoying themselves," said Wella. "Quit worrying." She had headed to Glade Park after visiting Chase at the hide in Rader. It had taken a while to find Naylor in the crowd, which was over a thousand strong.

"All it takes is one person, one over-enthusiastic kid to cross the line. Look at the troopers. They're poised to pounce at the first excuse."

"Relax. Everyone knows the stakes. And those stakes have just been raised a notch."

"Why? What's happened?"

"There are rumours about the furnaces. Hundreds have walked out from there. Word is, the management have raised it with the A. Production has plummeted. They're worried they're going to face penalties."

"Then that could be it. The A will just force us to go back."

"They can't do that. They can't make us work."

"They'll find a way. Probably start arresting people, scare others into going back."

She gazed at the crowd around them. "Something tells me it's going to take more than that to scare this lot."

—

While Wella and Naylor beheld the growing gathered, troopers and trucks were amassing around the Authority Complex, filling the parade ground and surrounding roads.

Wulfwin stood before an Ops truck, the contraband map spread across its bonnet. Two Special Forces Superiors stared in wonder.

"Let's be clear," said Wulfwin, "you haven't seen this, alright?"

The two Superiors nodded, wide-eyed.

"Troopers on Nanso Heights have found a trail. Horse hooves, leading away from Lyun Mountain, heading northeast. Here," he said, pointing to a location on the map. "Note how the area is remote. A few tracks, but no infrastructure to speak of."

The Superiors stared at the map, attempting to absorb the layout of a landscape they'd never seen before and encouraged, since childhood, never to imagine.

"We'll spread out," said Wulfwin. "I'll take this line. You fan out, following routes here and here."

"Sir!" called a trooper, running towards them. "Chief of Command, sir," she said, snapping to attention. "Permission to speak."

"Denied," said Wulfwin, pouring over the map, not looking up.

"Sir. Urgent news."

He stood up and glared at the young woman. "I refuse you permission, and yet you speak anyway. How the fuck does that work?"

"Sir," she said, holding out a piece of paper.

"This had better be good." Wulfwin snatched the paper and scanned the contents. "For fuck's sake…" He screwed it up, grabbed the map, which he rolled and stuffed inside his trench coat, and marched across the parade ground to Operations HQ.

The two Superiors were left standing beside the truck, still stunned by a map that was never supposed to exist.

Within moments of receiving the news, Wulfwin stormed into the boardroom where a number of the Commanders from the Council had reconvened. "I don't believe this," roared Wulfwin. "Tell me it's a wind-up. Come on, make my day. Will someone please tell me this is someone's idea of a fucking joke?"

Special Forces Commander Fentlow stepped forward, now the reluctant designated speaker. "It was handed in to the Exchange half an hour ago. We don't know how long it's been out or who's behind it. But we do know one thing. This one's different."

He handed Wulfwin a crumpled copy of *Bluemantle*.

—

"This is what we've been waiting for," said Wulfwin, his voice brittle. "This is our reason to act."

The Commanders from the Council stood before him in the boardroom, their bodies rigid, braced for the full force of reaction.

"What do you propose?" ventured Commander Fentlow.

"Get your men down on the streets. Order to stop and search. Arrest anyone caught with a copy. Start outside the Exchange and in Glade Park. This must be why they're there. Game's over."

"What about the plan? Half my men are on the parade ground, ready to mobilise."

"Special Forces need to remain in the city and deal with this shit. I'll have to make do with the Deaf Squad and Allears. I'll also need a couple of Superiors." He forced out the words as if pulling a barbed thorn. "Lore's still laid up; I'll need help herding his gimps." He paced the room, mumbling as if talking to himself. "This... This fucking bullshit will delay everything. There's still stuff to prepare. We'll have to leave later. Which means we won't get far before sundown. And now with a fraction of the men. And all the while, the Music Makers are getting away." He trailed off, his fists clenched, strangling the pamphlet.

The Commanders waited in silence.

Wulfwin spun around, snapping his attention back to the room and his anxious audience. "Coordinate with the Police Commissioner," he barked. "I want every officer and cadet, every spare trooper, out there, on the ground. Then I want every fucking copy destroyed and every citizen carrying one to suffer beyond fair consequence. The slightest resistance or reaction, then full assault. City-wide. Understood?"

—

Troopers swept through the streets, a starved swarm on the hunt.

Citizens fled, seeking shelter in their homes, down passageways, behind bins. Railmotors were halted between stations, while troopers climbed aboard and searched terrified passengers. In the taverns and street cafés, chairs were upturned, glasses smashed, stools hurled against shuttered apertures. In Drayloc Market, crowds ran through the gangways, tripping over guy ropes, crashing into stalls. And everywhere, like pennants peppering the ground, *Bluemantle*.

The units dispatched to the Exchange and Glade Park generated a different reaction. Citizens stood unfazed, arms out, offering themselves to be searched. Not a single copy of the fanzine was found. No one was arrested.

The scant arrests elsewhere were small fry, nowhere near the level anticipated by the Authority.

Four Commanders remained on standby in the boardroom, poised to convene the depleted Council should the need arise. The four, including Commander Fentlow, stood before the trooper who had come to report the latest.

"It's been three hours," said one of the Commanders. "And only a handful of arrests. Maybe we jumped the gun? Maybe there were only a few copies in circulation?"

"I've heard the streets are littered with them," said another.

"Someone must have warned them we were coming," said the third.

"Warned the entire city?" said Fentlow. "No. The warning was given way before we even knew about it." The three Commanders looked at him, bemused. "Didn't you read it?"

"What's the point? It's just shit-stirring. All that stuff about the water. As if? I don't know why Wulfwin made such a big deal."

"Then look again." He held out the copy of *Bluemantle* and pointed to a text box at the bottom of the last page.

Printed in bold, upper case, were the words, "DROP IMMEDIATELY. DON'T GIVE THEM REASON. READ AND REMEMBER. SPREAD THE WORD. FOLLOW THE PATH."

—

By dusk, the walkout had peaked for the day. Citizens would soon drift towards their homes, harbouring feelings of both pride and relief. Wella, Tinashe, Naylor and Nial stood on the steps of the Exchange, reading the mood of those gathered.

"What do you think'll happen tomorrow?" said Naylor.

"Because it's Sunday?" said Wella. "I think they'll still come."

"But for a lot of them it's about work. The strain of distributed hours. Sunday's their day off. They'll want to be with their families."

"It might've started out that way. But they've been here for a while, some of them three days, listening to people talk. They'll see their own beef in the context of a far bigger picture." She tipped her head towards the Wall. "And a far more compelling one. I honestly think those who join the walkout because of work end up staying because of the missing. And now the A have added fuel to the fire. Drugging the water, storming the city, assaulting people. They ain't doing themselves any favours."

"Do you think we'll see more tomorrow, then?" said Nial.

"I wouldn't be surprised. Momentum is building. The cart was picking up speed. The A have just gone and shoved a friggin' motor on the back."

—

The new day proved Wella right.

Sunday morning. The walkout had near enough doubled in size. Whole families gathered, sitting on blankets in Glade Park. Enterprising café owners moved through the crowds, wicker baskets on their backs laden with baked breads and bava fruit. Carters spread themselves around the perimeter, between staring sentries, selling chilled teas and spritzers.

The trading restrictions didn't apply at the park. Besides, they could no longer afford to donate – the number of people had grown too great to fairly cater for all.

Not since Rideout had so many citizens amassed in Glade, nor anywhere else in the city.

This fact would not have been lost on Governor Blix, had she access to the monitors, or even the wherewithal to focus on their grainy images. Had she glimpsed the scene, the lingering throng, thousands strong, she would have perceived the manifestation of her greatest fear. Then she would have seized her justification and used it to purge the disease. Eradicate the swarm.

Instead, she lay on the lounger in her private quarters, barely conscious. The laced Meezel had taken firm hold, trapping her in a cycle of personal nightmares.

The significance of scale might have occurred to Wulfwin, had he the attention to afford it. However, the hunt for the Music Makers left no room for trivial observations.

He had convened his depleted army late the previous afternoon. As they were preparing to leave, two breathless Superiors had come running towards him. One had a black eye and a bandage taped over a broken nose.

"Reporting for duty, sir," they said in unison, snapping to attention.

"What the actual fuck?" said Wulfwin. The Superiors stared ahead, eyes wide. "Trooper Sixty. I thought I'd arranged things so that your head would be down the crapper for the foreseeable. Explain why that's not so."

"Sir, Commander Fentlow said my rank is temporarily reinstated. Under review."

"You are kidding me."

"He said extenuating circumstances, sir. Not enough men."

"Fucking bastard." Wulfwin turned away and looked at the sky's fading light, then growled through gritted teeth. He turned back to Trooper Sixty. "Your rank is not reinstated. But I need bodies. Useless as yours is." He shoved him by the shoulders. The trooper stumbled backwards. "Get in line and don't do anything that reminds me you're alive."

They had set off soon after, heading west, up Cinder Hill, towards the Nanso Heights. Within an hour of searching, they had located the hoof tracks leading away from Lyun Mountain and followed them for as long as there was light enough to see. They had eventually set up camp approximately twenty-five miles north-east of the Heights.

At the first glimpse of sunrise, they packed up and were on the move once more. The terrain steadily deteriorated. Wulfwin reluctantly ordered that they abandon all vehicles except for the fleet of field bikes, excessively modified with powerful engines and forgiving suspension.

One of the troopers carried a long-range radio. However, as they marched further into the lands of the map that shouldn't exist, the signal weakened, then was lost entirely.

Wulfwin didn't care. It just meant no more interruptions. The Council could deal with the city, he decided, especially now the water would be exerting its influence. It was no longer his problem. He was finally free to focus on the prize. He could feel the end approaching, smell the prospect of victory in the air.

Yet progress was slow. Sighted Allears had to lead their adjusted colleagues, strung together by lengths of rope which they clung to like a lifeline. The hoof tracks were faint or, in some places where the ground had no give, had disappeared entirely. Troopers fanned out, scanning the ground, until someone found where the tracks resumed. These interruptions slowed them down, as did the challenging terrain. They stumbled up steep hills and down sheer escarpments, through swathes of dense porcupine scrub, over rock-fall barricades, all in sweltering heat.

Wulfwin became impatient at the pace. He halted his army and barked orders, changing the strategy to one of advance party and rear guard. He commandeered the fifteen field bikes and called forth his best Deaf Squad troopers. The rest, he ordered to continue as before, following the trail of horse hooves as far and as long as their provisions lasted.

"We'll go on ahead," he said, jumping onto one of the bikes. "We won't be able to see the tracks, but we'll leave our own. We'll spread out. They must have made camps along the way. Left crap behind. We'll find signs, then come back to redirect you. With the bikes, we have the best chance of catching them up."

Not one among his men dared to challenge.

The selected troopers mounted the bikes and, with vague orders as to direction, Wulfwin revved his engine and sped away. The other bikes followed, fanning out, creating a new dust cloud that choked those left behind.

—

The three Troubadours stood before Ursel's bunk. Ursel was sat on the edge of the bunk, recovered from the infection caused by her untreated wounds but still too weak to stand for any length of time. Beside her sat a young woman, pencil and paper in hand – Ursel's ears. The drummer who had been Dent Lore stood to one side, proud to be called to attend the meeting but self-conscious before the Troubadours. Eyes down, he waited to be addressed.

"Ursel. Drummer," said Bend Sinister. "We seek your counsel. We have debated through the night, yet we remain without consensus. In strictest confidence and with sincere respect, we invite your thoughts on the matter at hand."

Ursel's scribe wrote fast. Ursel looked from the words on the page to the drummer, who shared her expression of cautious anticipation.

"The question," said Pale Dexter, "is whether we should break camp and resume our escape and our search for a new place to settle, or remain here, in a location known to two of our troupe back in Wydeye – our only link to the followers we leave behind. We find ourselves favouring different options, yet the time has come to decide. Your informed perspectives will, we hope, enhance the context of reason."

"Ursel," said Chief, "you possess an understanding of the citizens of Wydeye, both followers and not. Drummer, in the guise of your other self, you possess a valuable knowledge of the Authority and its intent. These unique insights can inform our deliberations and help us reach a decision. If you would be so kind?"

Ursel scanned the page, then looked up. "Of course."

"An honour," said the drummer, nodding for Ursel's benefit.

Chief turned first to Ursel. "Our question to you relates to your plan. You were born into a travelling theatre that has remained resident for nigh on eighty years. You are loyal to the Scene, which existed as a subterranean secret, trapped by a city it both relied on and was hunted by. You live among people who never leave, despite the oppression, fear and suffering that has become the fabric of Wydeye. Yet, your plan is based on the premise that citizens will awaken somehow and suddenly feel free to move on. Why?"

Ursel read the words and blinked. She thought of the tattoo that had once been a badge of conviction upon her arm. Slowly rising from the bunk, she stood to deliver her reply. "When a dark cloud lifts and you see things clearly for what they are, the revelation is a catalyst to an irreversible process. The discovery of something you can't unlearn. The realisation of truth that you can't unknow.

"The citizens of Wydeye have been sleeping. The A have kept them asleep with their laced lullabies. I believe that, if we wake some, they will wake others who will, in turn, wake more still. By waking, they will perceive things differently, including their own freedom. By that, I mean freedom to think for themselves. Freedom to ask questions. Freedom to no longer accept. That's in everyone's grasp and it has been all along. They've just forgotten they have the option." Her point delivered, Ursel sat back down, her legs unsteady.

The three Troubadours looked to each other in silent conference.

Then Bend Sinister turned to his drummer. "You are yourself once more. Think back to the person they made you, what you knew from that perspective. We were once welcomed by Wydeye, made legends in their tales, championed for our music. Then everything changed. For decades, they have hunted us, fuelled by a motive that evades us. We mean no harm, yet they demonise us. They persecute those who follow us. They appear relentless in their drive to destroy us. Why?"

The drummer took a deep breath, forcing himself back into the mind and memories of Dent Lore. He felt nauseous in that dark, distant place. "The Authority is ruled and the city controlled by the will of two people: Governor Blix and Wulfwin, her Chief of Command. Their motives appear aligned, but they are not. Wulfwin is intent on destroying you, the 'Music Makers', whom he despises without due cause or justification, other than the fact you have evaded capture thus far. It is a battle of win or lose, and he will not tolerate losing. Governor Blix is intent on destroying you because you threaten her grasp of absolute control — a delusion she obsessively strives to maintain. Neither will cease in the attempt. Blix, because while you exist, you remain, in her eyes, a potentially destabilising influence on the vulnerable masses. And Wulfwin, because he is evil incarnate; he is determined to win and will stop at nothing to do so."

Once again, the Troubadours stood in silence, absorbing the assessment, formulating their own.

It was Pale Dexter who brought the assembly to a close. "We thank you for your consideration and insight. We must now withdraw and deliberate further, aided by the light you have shed."

All three bowed graciously, stepped back and slipped away between the trees of the dell. Out of range of eye and ear, they reconvened.

"Illuminating, indeed," said Chief.

"A most fruitful consultation," said Pale Dexter.

Bend Sinister said nothing. His eyes darted this way and that; his breathing quickened. His counterparts watched with curiosity, distracted by his sudden agitation.

"Tell us," said Chief. "What are you thinking?"

Bend Sinister looked them square in the eye. "They've demonised us for decades. That's not who we are. It's not what we do. But, if it works, it could be how we defend ourselves."

"What are you suggesting?" said Pale Dexter.

"Something our pursuers would never expect."

CHAPTER FORTY

"Get the Chief of Command on the radio. Immediately!" snapped Commander Fentlow.

It was early morning. The Comms Control Centre was in chaos, radio operators unable to cope with the volume of traffic. Messages were being delivered by hand, their senders having given up on the clogged frequencies and jammed telephone lines.

Disruption was widespread. Half the tramway network was closed, the other half congestion-clogged. Queues of commuters lined the streets around the tramway stops, begrudging their forced dependence on the service. These were the citizens who had heard but had not listened, too loyal or too afraid. All around them walked those who *had* listened. Wide-eyed, awake, they moved calmly through the streets, filling the underpass, trapping authority vehicles attempting to ferry troopers to their posts.

The walkout was working.

Tens of thousands had joined the movement, crippling the infrastructure to the extent that many who wanted to work found themselves unable to do so.

The industrial engine of Coxen Lyme had stalled. The furnaces were non-operational, their huge smoke stacks breathing clean air. The neighbouring processing plants lacked the manpower and materials to perform their function. Power had been cut to Aldar Point and Ulden Cross, leaving a wasteland of lifeless factories and industrial units. There were no trains running to the limestone quarry, forcing production to grind to a halt. The freight depot waited, empty.

"What's taking so long?" said Fentlow, fuming. "I want Wulfwin on the radio, now."

"Sir," stammered an operator, "we've been trying for several hours. We can't reach him. Nor any of his men."

"Damn it," roared the Commander, staring at the monitors. "We're in meltdown and our de facto leader goes off grid."

He knew the situation was escalating.

Chase knew it too. In his hide, shut away from the world, he sensed the moment was at hand. And he knew he couldn't miss it.

Ignoring the risk, he put on the wig and costume that Quince had lent him to make the drop. In the dim lamplight, the disguise was passable. In the bright glare of day, he knew it would be a different matter. Yet he no longer cared.

He scribbled a note for Wella and Naylor – a precaution in case one of them dropped by to update him. "I'm walking out," was all it said.

With the tramways down, he had to travel on foot from Rader, through a ghost town Brolan, to the district of Glade. The pseudo-rush hour had passed, leaving the streets eerily quiet, apart from long queues of anxious commuters still trailing from each tramway stop. Here and there, aperture shutters on apartment blocks were left closed, flaunting an air of neglect. On street corners stood abandoned water distribution stations, unopened crates piled head high.

Trodden into dust lay disowned copies of *Bluemantle*. All around, an air of desertion. A sign that could be foreboding or auspicious, Chase thought. He hoped to crow it was the latter.

When he crossed the Spire and made his way down the Bayley Road, his hope was realised. Whilst in the hide, he had spent countless hours imagining the scenes. His mind's eye impression had failed to come close to the reality of this altered overground.

He stood before Glade Park, its boundaries erased, drowned by a sea of citizens. Gone were the seated groups of family and friends in nervous union. Instead, everyone stood, statuesque. They maintained their attitude of passivity, yet they were acutely alert, attuned to the change. They knew the tide had turned; something was going to happen.

Chase realised he had little hope of finding Wella, or Naylor, or Tinashe. That didn't bother him. He was there, witnessing the spectacle, blown away by the scale. It was impossible to know; he could only guess. *Twenty thousand?* he thought. *Maybe more?*

Around the crowd, sentinel troopers had been forced to expand their circumference considerably, now stretched to the point of precariously thin. They maintained their posturing, hands on weapons, strained eyes fixed on the crowd. They had long since abandoned their attempts to provoke. Utterly overwhelmed, every trooper recognised their means of control had become woefully inadequate.

Meanwhile, up in the Operations HQ, Commander Fentlow continued to bark pointless orders. Several Council members hovered on the periphery, unwilling to speak up lest it result in taking on responsibility. Behind them hung the Chief of Staff. Whilst he was the only person present with any legitimate authority, he studiously obeyed Wulfwin's parting orders to do nothing.

"Sir. Excuse me, sir," said a young officer, addressing Fentlow.

"Yes? What is it?"

"Employment, Transport, Trade and Industry, sir. They demand an emergency meeting with the head of the Council. Representatives from each Division are already here, sir. They're very insistent. What shall I tell them?"

"Why are you asking me? This is for the Chief of Staff. He has the Chair." He spun around. "Where is he? He was here just now."

"Sir, it was the Chief of Staff who instructed me to speak to you. He said he's had to withdraw temporarily. He says you are to take his place. Until the Chief of Command returns."

"This is ridiculous—"

"Sir, the representatives are waiting. What should I say to them?"

—

One hundred miles away, unaware of the escalating crisis, Wulfwin was closing in. He had stopped to sleep only briefly before resuming the chase, determined to catch up with his prey. No food or water had passed his lips for over twenty-four hours. Light-headed, he attributed the dizziness to adrenalin. He knew he was on the right path. He could feel it – hear it, almost. Wydeye was gone from his mind. His sight was fixed firmly on the prize. Revving the engine, he lifted the front wheel and laughed.

A mile ahead, perched on a rise, a follower spotted his dust trail. She ran down to the dell, raising the alarm.

Wulfwin gripped the handlebars, his hands numb from the constant vibration. He glanced at the petrol gauge – half-full. More than enough, he felt sure. He regretted his lack of provisions, however. Water would be good. Even if he was as close as he hoped, water would still go down well. It reminded him of the contaminated bottles back home and a twisted smile cracked his face. *That'll keep them quiet*, he thought.

In his haste, he'd not only forgotten provisions; he also lacked a helmet and ear defenders. Wrapped in encroaching delirium, he failed to notice the fact.

Feeling a jolt in his chest, he broke hard and skidded to a standstill. He listened to the engine, detecting something different in its sound. Then he realised it wasn't the bike at all. There was another sound – beneath it, beyond it. He turned the key and the engine fell silent.

He could hear it.

Up ahead, half a mile, maybe. The sound that had caused the jolt in his chest. A sound that pulled at him now, luring him forward, influencing his limbs to dismount and walk forwards.

Music.

The melody reached out to him, touched him, enticed him. Had he the wherewithal to resist, he wouldn't have wanted to. He stumbled forward, almost running, desperate. He had no thirst for water now; the music was all he craved. Already he felt it reviving his body. It washed over him, penetrated his skin, coursed through his veins, caused his heart to race.

He climbed the rise. As he reached the summit, the volume swelled. The music was coming from beneath the trees below him, the sound reverberating around the hollow. He crouched down, arms wrapped around himself, drinking the music, revelling in the revival.

Then he wanted more. He had to get closer.

He slipped down the bank and into the dell. Beneath the trees' canopy, he caught his first glimpse of the source. Five figures, dressed in black. His mind was numb, unable to process thought beyond what his senses made apparent. Five figures, making music. That was all. And that was enough.

He stood close by, eyes closed, in rapture.

—

Commander Fentlow sat at the board table in the Council Chamber. Opposite him sat senior representatives from Employment, Transport, Trade and Industry.

"Productivity is down by over two per cent," said the man from Trade.

"That's nothing," said the woman from Industry. "If we can't get the furnaces and processing plants operational in the next few hours, it's going to be far higher."

"We haven't the manpower," said Employment. "We're receiving reports of approaching fifteen per cent clock-in failure. We can't run the machines without sufficient staff. Health and Safety."

"Half of those who haven't clocked in are stranded, waiting for a damned railmotor," said Transport. "The tramways are screwed. Nothing can move. We're missing too many drivers and signal operators. Half the rolling stock is in the wrong place. Where we do have drivers, the routes are blocked."

"We're reaching crisis point," said Industry. "If the Authority doesn't intervene as a matter of urgency, production could grind to a halt entirely. One day's output lost will have a disastrous knock-on effect for the week's targets."

"She's right," said Trade. "Even if everything returned to normal tomorrow, which looks highly unlikely, it'll be impossible to make up the shortfall. That'll make the month-end targets unachievable. Which then has serious implications for Revenue."

"Talking of whom, they're on their way," said Employment.

"The Authority must intervene," reiterated Industry, slamming her fist down on the table. "What do you propose to do?"

"I…" began Fentlow, then broke off. The representatives glared at him, red-faced. "I will convene an emergency session," he said, wondering if he could actually do that, without the conferred authority. "We shall discuss the crisis and report back."

"When?" demanded Industry.

"It'll take some time to gather the members."

"When?"

"One o'clock. Return here at one."

The representatives looked at each other and nodded, apparently appeased. They rose and left the Chamber.

Fentlow remained in his chair. The practicality of what he had just committed to do, plus the fact he had no idea how to do it, left him blood-drained and winded.

—

Bend Sinister played without pause. They had no power, so the set was fully acoustic. This did not diminish the impact on their audience. Wulfwin was suspended in reverie.

Chief and Pale Dexter approached him from either side and stood close, their faces leaning in, almost touching his. They were cautious, wary lest the influence falter. They also had no idea if the next part of their plan would work.

Chief spoke first. "How many more are coming?" Her voice was flat, hypnotic.

Wulfwin's expression remained unchanged, as if he was unaware of both the company and the question. Yet the words somehow penetrated his subconscious. Without thought or self-control, he responded. "Others far away. I am alone."

"What are your orders?" said Pale Dexter, half whispering into his ear.

"No orders. I'm in charge now. I do what I want."

Chief and Pale Dexter exchanged puzzled glances. Bend Sinister played on, captivating their audience. Their drummer fought to focus, desperate to avoid meeting the eyes of their captive.

Chief nodded to Pale Dexter, who said, "What news of the Governor?"

"Blix is out of the picture. She won't get in the way no more."

"And Dent Lore?"

"Fucking bastard," said Wulfwin, his voice dropping to a low growl.

Both Pale Dexter and Chief stiffened, fearing they had disrupted the enchantment.

Yet Wulfwin kept his eyes fixed on the band, his breathing steady. "He's one of them."

"Who else knows the truth about him?" said Chief.

"No one. She said it was a secret. Should've told me. The fucking bitch."

"No one knows? Only you?"

"Only me. And I'm gonna kill him."

CHAPTER FORTY-ONE

This time it was the drummer's idea that he return to the city. The man who had been Dent Lore was once again clad in Forces-issue fatigues, courtesy of the insensible Chief of Command. He sat astride Wulfwin's field bike, pushing the engine to its limit, racing towards Wydeye. As he swerved left and right, between boulder and brush, he fought to resurrect that other consciousness. *For the last time,* he swore to himself. *Then Dent is dead.*

Bend Sinister hadn't wanted him to go, had insisted the risks outweighed the reward. Even when his drummer had pushed the plan, arguing that it was necessary to help Ursel's scheme succeed, Bend Sinister had resisted.

"They don't know the truth about me," the drummer had said. "Worst-case scenario is they just don't listen. But while they don't know who I am, it's got to be worth a try. And anyway, I'm confident they will listen."

He had stood before the three Troubadours on the edge of the camp. A short distance away, several of Chief's players maintained the continuous lullaby before a recumbent Wulfwin, locking him in blissful catatonia. They had moved away from the camp to avoid over exposure of the Troubadours' retinue who, they feared, could be equally mesmerised by the uninterrupted performance. The players had also taken the precaution of binding Wulfwin's arms and legs, although it was proving unnecessary. He lay on the ground, his head propped up against a tree, stupefied.

"What makes you so sure?" Pale Dexter had said.

"Because without Blix and Wulfwin telling them what to do, they're incapable of making a decision. The Authority may appear to exert great power and control, but it rests entirely in the hands of those two individuals, now absent. The remaining chain of command is an empty gesture. Left to their own devices, the Council will be floundering, unable to act without instruction."

"That still doesn't account for why they'll listen to you," said Chief. "Whilst I applaud your courage, I fail to see how your return can make a difference."

"If Ursel's plan is working and the walkout is gaining traction, then the Council will be forced to act. If productivity is compromised, they'll recognise they have no choice. It's the benchmark for stability. Maintained output powers the machine; a dip could stall it completely. Yet despite this, no one will have the courage to make a decision, not while there are ten other people in the room who could do the honours. They've forgotten how. Cue Allear Commander Dent Lore."

The argument had swayed Pale Dexter and Chief. When it was put to a vote, Bend Sinister's objections were overruled. His drummer offered solemn assurances of caution before withdrawing to pack supplies and prepare for the trip.

For his plan to work, the drummer had to dress as an Authority trooper once more – a prospect that left him sick with abhorrence. A couple of followers had stripped the oblivious Wulfwin of his fatigues, replacing them with a loose grey tunic. It was then that they discovered the map stuffed inside a pocket – the incompatible chart of lands unknown.

Before leaving, the drummer had sat beside Ursel. He wrote on the notepad, *"If I don't return, I beg that the truth perish with me. I would rather die a thousand times than have a follower discover who I had become. I cannot bring shame to the name of Bend Sinister. I have no right to ask anything of you, yet I ask you this. Please, let this part of the story remain untold."*

She read the words, shaking her head. "You carry these burdens of guilt and shame unnecessarily. You are not the same person. You are not to blame."

"I wish that were true," he wrote. *"But in going back, I hope to make some small amends. So please, can you do this for me?"*

"I give you my word."

Finally, he had taken leave of Bend Sinister, saying, "I am sorry that I do this against your wishes. But please know, it is for you that I go. For all of us here. And for all those still persecuted in Wydeye for choosing to follow. I have faith I will succeed. Please, forgive me. And trust I shall return."

Bend Sinister held him firmly by the shoulders and squared his own. "You go with my blessing. Be safe. And mind you do come back."

As he sped through the wilds, the map in his pack, he forced himself to think only of the Authority and the detestable dogma of Governor Blix. He dredged the depths of his consciousness and found the remains of their creation.

Skin crawling under skin, he became Dent Lore once more.

—

Amid the cover of the crowd, Chase grew in confidence. WatcherCams buzzed overhead; troopers stared from the periphery. He ignored them, keeping his head down, blending with the movement around him, his eyes straining through the prescription glasses. He listened intently, catching snippets of hushed conversation.

"…says the tramways are fucked. No drivers…"

"…first time since Rideout. Never thought I'd see the day…"

"…like something's gonna happen. You can feel it…"

"…that's why they're not doing anything. It's like they know…"

The gathering citizens had grown in confidence too, buoyed by the scale, the comradery and the heady buzz of defiance.

As he left Glade Park and headed north-west, through the Pentagon, the atmosphere changed. Citizens still on the fence, or crouching behind it, loitered around Five Wents like nervous dogs. They flinched at passing troopers, anticipating the start of the end through a lens of terror. Those who had witnessed Rideout felt their scars tear open – old wounds turned fresh and bleeding.

It was already noon. The sun was at its peak, reducing shade to washed-out slithers of relief. Chase walked up First Went, which would normally be busy by that hour, its stalls and cafés drawing the early lunch trade. Yet, the street was all but deserted. Cafés stood blind, their shutters bolted closed. Kerbside traders were scattered islands amid deserted pitches, regular stall holders having shifted to cater for the gathered in Glade. The few businesses that were open for trade were doing little. A group of children ran across the road. They laughed, carefree, making the most of the unexpected closure of their Education Centre. Above them, the Elevated stood silent, redundant.

Ahead, the Exchange loomed large, transformed by the human context. The precinct had long since disappeared, as had the steps leading up to it and the road beyond. The

Wall of the Missing had become a parenthesis amid the silent throng, although the spectacle spoke for itself.

Chase stood before the building, overwhelmed. Then a hand grasped his arm and he froze.

"What are you doing out here?" hissed Wella.

Relief replaced the panic. He smiled at his sister. "I couldn't stay there, knowing what was happening. I had to see it."

"And what if *they* see *you?*"

"Relax, they won't. Not with the wig." He tipped his head to the crowd around them. "And not with all this going on. The cameras are trained on the masses. That's the threat."

"Still, it's a risk. You were safe in the hide."

"I couldn't miss this. You've got to admit, it feels incredible. Being part of something so huge. Doing something that might actually make a difference."

Wella sighed, relenting with a softening smile. "Yeah. It's special alright." Her expression darkened slightly. "Only…"

"What?"

"I didn't expect it to happen so quickly. It's escalated. Significantly. Just today. And the tension…"

"I know. I can feel it."

"It can't be contained. Either the A will crack or the mood here will reach a tipping point. One way or another, something's going to happen. This, here? It's too volatile."

"So, what do we do? We can't get this far only to fail because someone can't take the heat and it all kicks off."

"I say we've achieved a critical mass. Partly volume, but also the impact it's having. The walkout's causing chaos. The A will be paying attention. They'll want it to end."

"You think so? Already?"

"We're there. It's time."

—

Around the board table in the Council Chamber sat nine red-faced Commanders. Between them, four empty seats. They had been in session for nearly two hours. In that time, they had repeated the obvious and skirted the issue. Tension was building; the clock was ticking.

Commander Fentlow had found himself chairing the meeting, despite declining the unanimous call for him to do so. "Commanders, please. If I can bring the discussion back to the most pressing matter. Again. Representatives from a number of key Divisions will be at our door, expecting an answer, in less than half an hour."

"Then we send them away," said one Commander. "We cannot rush a decision of this magnitude."

"I suspect that will not go down well. They were insistent this morning and the situation has worsened since then."

"Who is in charge here, them or us?" pipped up another, immediately sinking back into his chair.

"Hierarchy is not in question," said Fentlow. "Hence their appeal this morning. They were right to raise the alarm. The fall in production has far-reaching consequences. We must intervene before it drops further. Whilst the timescale for a decision from the Council is challenging, it is, nevertheless, necessary. So, I ask again, do we have any further suggestions around the table?"

Commanders drew lines on their notepads, or stared at a spot mid-table, or stifled a cough lest the noise be misconstrued.

Fentlow sighed, glancing up at a clock on the wall. "Okay. Okay. Let us return to what we have so far. The obvious option is to order military intervention. Special Forces and the state police move in and arrest all those who refuse to return to work."

"The detention centres are full," said one Commander on Fentlow's left. "There must be in excess of twenty thousand out there. We haven't the space or resources to detain them."

"Objection noted. Anyone else?"

"Chief of Command insisted we must not intervene unless they do something," said a Commander to his right. "So long as they don't act, they're not in breach of the law. That's what Chief of Command said."

"I don't dispute that," said Fentlow. "However, I put it to you that Governor Blix would view the assembly of so many citizens as doing *something*. Congregating en masse like that. There's no way she'd allow it."

Heads nodded around the table. Murmurs rumbled like a collapsing hole.

"Perhaps…" ventured a Commander at the far end. "Perhaps, in the absence of the Chiefs of Staff and Command, we should consult her?"

"Commander," said Fentlow, "I trust you are fully cognisant of the conditions of Article Twenty-One?"

"Of course."

"Then you are aware that Governor Blix is under arrest, pending full investigation, and her rank suspended."

"Yes."

"So why, in crow's name, do you propose we ignore this critical provision in our governance arrangements by seeking her advice?"

"She's ruled this city decisively and successfully for twenty years. Whilst I'm not disputing the charges brought against her, whatever they may be, I'm just saying she hasn't been investigated yet. It might all be a mistake. And she might know what to do."

Another murmur, this time more cautious. The notion appealed. They had trusted their Governor. She would know, they felt. She would be able to decide.

Fentlow sensed the sway of favour. "Colleagues, I must remind you of the seriousness of this proposal."

"But without the Chiefs of Staff and Command," said the same Commander, gaining confidence, "who's to say we have the authority to decide anything anyway? It's not been brought into question before. We have no mandate. Is not our only recourse to defer to the leader who still, technically, holds the office, albeit subject to investigation?"

Fentlow stared at the faces around the table. Above all others, this was one decision he was not prepared to make. "Colleagues, please. Division representatives will be here any moment—"

There was a noise at the door.

Fentlow looked up, startled, unprepared to handle the confrontation. A man entered. Fentlow stared, confused, then smiled in recognition. "Commander Lore, I almost didn't recognise you without the beard. We were informed you were unwell and confined to quarters."

"Commander Fentlow. Colleagues," said Dent, saluting briefly and taking his seat. He fought to catch his breath and feign composure. "I was unwell, yes. But I am on the mend. I am aware of the gravity of the situation and felt I should make every effort to attend this emergency session. I can only apologise for my late arrival."

"Apology unnecessary. And we are pleased to hear your health has improved."

"I appreciate time is of the essence, but perhaps you could appraise me of the discussion thus far and I'll add my contribution."

"Certainly." Fentlow felt like a lifeline had appeared from nowhere. He grabbed it with desperate hands. Revitalised by relief and hope, he outlined the situation and the proposals discussed. He concluded by saying, "We welcome your thoughts, Commander Lore," drumming his fingers on the table.

"I must admit, I am astonished by the suggestion to consult the detained Governor, bypassing the restrictions imposed by Article Twenty-One. That would constitute a criminal act. I, for one, would not be party to that. Indeed, I am surprised that any member of this Council would." He looked around the room. All eyes were averted. "Secondly, I believe the proposal for military intervention in the absence of any criminal behaviour would be a contentious move, let alone an unwarranted one. Granted, we apply a heavy hand when the situation demands it. Justification negates the need for caution. However, I hardly think the fact that citizens have collectively decided to peacefully gather, displaying no sign of protest whatsoever, warrants forceful arrest and incarceration. And that is regardless of whether or not we have capacity in our centres to detain them, which we do not."

"Yes, yes," said Fentlow. "A point well made."

"Meanwhile, it strikes me your deliberations have overlooked something that is rather obvious."

Everyone looked to Dent.

Fentlow's brows raised in hope. "What might that be?"

"The citizens are not demonstrating. There is no sign of protest. Yet they must be there for a reason. Twenty thousand people standing in the same place, at the same time, is beyond the realms of coincidence. Has anyone actually spoken to them? Asked them why they are doing this?"

"I, er... I hardly think that appropriate."

"Why? They have decided to forgo several days' pay. Whatever their reason for doing so, it must be important enough for them to make such a sacrifice. To my mind, their actions suggest they want something. And, in order for us to get them back into work, it would be helpful to know what that something is. Would it not?"

"But we can't go striking deals without the Chief of Command."

"Where's the Chief of Staff?"

"Ahh…"

Dent knew full well that the Chief of Staff would have withdrawn without Wulfwin's coat-tails to hang on to. He took a moment to calm his nerve. He felt it was going well. He didn't want to blow it by appearing over-confident. He tried to emulate his former demeanour and held back.

After a pause, during which everyone around the table appeared to be waiting for him to continue, he said, "We have a chain of command, the limits of which have been exposed. Both Chiefs are absent and yet a decision must be made. There is no precedent to follow, and I know of no protocol. Meanwhile, the suggestion to speak to a representative citizen is merely fact-finding. It is not contiguous with any particular course of action. You asked me for my thoughts. It would appear to me to be the most sensible thing to do, given the circumstances."

Fentlow detected a chance to pass the baton. "I agree. A decision must be made and this is a sensible first step. You speak with conviction, Commander Lore. Have you sufficient certitude to stand behind your proposal? Are you, with the backing of this Council, prepared to give the order?"

"I have confidence in my reading of the situation. I also have confidence that the Chief of Command would share my view. We see things the same. Wulfwin has said as much in the past. So yes, with the support of the Council, I am prepared to give the order and accept full responsibility for the consequences."

A simultaneous release of breath came from around the table, with much smiling and relaxing of shoulders. The Commanders either side of Dent turned to him and shook his hand. Fentlow rose, beaming. "Colleagues, with your consent, I hand over to Commander Lore. Does any member object?" He looked around the table, returning the smiles. "Excellent. In which case…" He held out a hand, passing on the burden he could not wait to shed.

As he sat down, Dent Lore rose. "Colleagues. To my mind, asking the question of the citizens is a straightforward move that does not compromise our position in any way. We act discretely but swiftly. We contact the Senior Duty Officer in the Exchange, order them to make themselves visible in the entrance to the building. Citizens will interpret this for what it is. An invitation to parley. Once we hear what it is they want, then we will be in a far stronger position. We retain the upper hand. No ground will have been lost. With your agreement, I propose we action this immediately. A show of hands, please. All in favour?"

Within moments, orders were sent to Comms Control. A call was received by the Duty Officer, who made her way through the great hall of the Exchange and stood in its main entrance, dwarfed by the scale of all around her. She waited, nervous and exposed.

Dent took his seat once more and helped himself to a glass of water from a pitcher in the centre of the table. Remembering in time, he refrained from drinking any.

Meanwhile, the delegates from Employment, Transport, Trade and Industry arrived, joined by their disgruntled counterpart from Revenue. Fentlow made what he felt was a gracious gesture, offering to entertain them in an adjoining room and occupying them with refreshments, thus buying time.

Outside the Exchange, word spread. The citizens were ready; they had been ready for days. They could tell their moment was at hand, however it might play out. They had the A's attention – a most unfamiliar and precarious position to hold.

Within minutes of the Officer appearing, the unspoken invitation reached Chase and Wella.

"I told you," said Wella.

They looked at each other, acknowledging the turning point and the question of what next.

"You do it," said Chase. "I would. I want to. But what with them watching me…"

"Okay. But only if you're sure. This was all your idea."

"I'm sure. But be careful. It could be a trap. I don't trust those bastards."

"I've plenty of witnesses if they try anything dirty."

She took a deep breath, then made her way through the crowd. People parted, clearing a path. Those close by patted her back or touched her arm. Everyone who could see her attempted to communicate their encouragement in barely perceptible ways. They knew they couldn't react now, not when they had come this far, when they were so close.

Half an hour after giving the order, Dent was back in the Chair, all eyes upon him. In his hand was a message transcript. "Colleagues, we've received news. It appears I was right. They are there for a reason."

"What is it?" said Fentlow. "What do they want?"

"They've proposed an exchange. The citizens want to trade."

CHAPTER FORTY-TWO

The negotiations were protracted. The Commanders could not adjust to the altered authorship of influence. The situation made clear who held the upper hand, yet the majority of the Council were incapable of accepting the fact. The crisis was unprecedented. They felt their control waning. They dug in their heels and braced themselves.

Meanwhile, productivity plummeted. The knock-on effect of the walkout on infrastructure, supply chains, manufacturing and commerce escalated at a staggering rate. As the negotiations continued through the night and into a new day, the Divisions of Trade, Industry and Revenue were warning of a state of emergency. "The long view," they insisted. "Look at the long view." Targets missed could not be caught up. The forecast shortfall in gross domestic income could not be recovered. Significant cuts in spending would have to be made to fill the predicted deficit.

The pressure was mounting on the Council to accept the trade.

"They're not even criminals," said Employment, face flushed in frustration. The Council had agreed to hold a joint meeting with the Division representatives, who refused to leave the building until a decision was reached. "The prisoners they want freed haven't been convicted. Why not release them?"

"The detention centres are full to capacity," chipped in Revenue. "If there's one obvious way to claw back money, it's to clear them of citizens who needn't be there. Do you know how much the state spends a day running those centres?"

Throughout the negotiations, Dent had remained quiet, biding his time. He made contributions when necessary, but they were passive, non-committal. He felt he had succeeded in his masquerade; he was wary of jeopardising the whole plan by pushing the point through impatience. He remembered how things worked, the habitual deference of the Council. If Blix or Wulfwin were present, he knew the situation would be in stark contrast. They wouldn't have entertained the idea of listening to the citizens' demands, for a start. Their leadership style demanded dependency. In their absence, the lack of direction was unsurprising, the arduous debating of the issues inevitable. Dent held back, waiting for the invitation that he knew would come eventually.

By one o'clock, twenty-four hours after the trade had been proposed, six days after the walkout began, that invitation came. An hour into the joint meeting, Fentlow turned to Dent and said, "Commander Lore, this was all your idea. Yet you've remained characteristically quiet. I urge you to speak your mind. We must resolve this. What would you propose we do?"

—

Wella emerged from the Exchange, bleary eyes blinking in the bright sunshine.

The majority of the gathered had remained outside the building and in Glade Park throughout the night. Their representative spoke for them all: they would maintain their presence for as long as it took. Volunteer messengers were on standby to make the cross-town dash to the park the moment there was word.

It turned out the word was a gesture. With thousands of expectant faces upon her, there was only one way to spread the news. She held up her fist in triumph.

The crowd roared.

All attempts to contain emotion were abandoned. The gathered swelled, a tsunami of elation and relief.

Troopers circling the crowd aimed their guns, trigger fingers trembling. Unit Superiors barked into radios, demanding new orders between shouting, "Hold your fire!"

The gathered ignored them. Their victory held no place for intimidation. They had no room for fear. Instead, they looked to their representative and returned her salute. Then came the surge, flooding the great hall of the Exchange.

Around Glade Park, outnumbered troopers braced themselves, weapons raised. The twenty thousand-strong crowd took no heed. News of the deal reached a small group on the park's northern tip. Within seconds, word spread across the masses. Within minutes, the gathered began to drift in the direction of Five Wents.

Special Forces attempted to bar their way. Unit Superiors screamed into their radios. "We've lost control. Permission to fire."

In the main surveillance room in the Comms Control Centre, Dent and Fentlow studied the bank of monitors. Fentlow's face was white, his eyes twitching. "What do you think?" he said, holding up his radio. "Should we give it?"

"No," said Dent. "Wait. Watch. See how they move?"

"They've stormed a state building. We have staff in there. They're at risk."

"Look at them. And think about it. Why kick off now? They've got what they wanted. Why throw it away?"

"They're out of control. We must maintain order."

"*Look* at them."

The bank of monitors showed citizens sitting in the cups of whisper dishes, standing in front of propaganda posters, covering tannoy speakers with cloth sacks. Everywhere, whatever their gesture, citizens were looking up at the cameras they knew were trained on them. Their faces were serene, their eyes bright with defiance.

"These people have not lost control," said Dent.

"Well, we have, which is tantamount to the same thing."

"Open fire and you'll have a full-scale massacre on your hands. Do you want to be responsible for that?"

"But—"

He turned to Fentlow and held out his hand. "I'm happy to be held accountable for the decision."

Fentlow hesitated, glancing between Dent and the monitors. Then he handed over the radio. "The mistake is all yours."

Dent wasted no time. He switched the channel on the radio. "All Units. This is Alpha-Charlie-One. Permission to fire denied. Order your men to stand down. I repeat. Stand down."

Outside the Exchange, the troopers slowly lowered their guns, as stunned by the order as by the scene before them. Unit Superiors stared with gritted teeth, hungry for the denied reprisal.

Inside the Exchange, citizens filled the great hall. One by one, they opened the eighty doors around its perimeter. Climbing on each other's shoulders, they draped fabric, torn from their clothes, over the eighty numbered boards.

The Duty Officer hung back, dreading the rumble of combat boots and the brutal consequence that would surely follow.

At odds with her fear, the citizens were jubilant, yet calm. This was no riot, no violent retaliation. Not because their hard-won trade would be jeopardised, but because of what they'd achieved besides that.

They just wanted to see signs of the change they had already brought about.

—

The gathered gradually made their way up to Leven Hyder, forming a silent congregation outside the gates of the Authority Complex.

By dusk, the first detainees were released. Hundreds of men, women and children emerged from the detention centres and staggered through the gates. Many were weak, malnourished, bearing the wounds of interrogation. Yet all were smiling, scanning the mass of faces for loved ones.

The Authority had agreed to release all prisoners deemed low risk, awaiting charge or trial. This amounted to over three thousand citizens. They had also agreed to release them before five-thirty the following morning, when the first shift klaxons would sound. If all prisoners were not released, the gathered would not return to work.

The Authority honoured their commitment.

They also honoured the commitment to terminate surveillance of all citizens for whom they had no evidence on which to bring trial.

Chase could walk free.

Yet he remained with the masses, witnessing emotional reunions. He remembered how he'd felt when Brann was finally released after five long years — how his young brother had emerged a broken man, crushed by the state who claimed to provide and protect. He thought of all those he had betrayed, who had ended up in one of the centres because of information he had supplied. All the suffering he had caused through his self-righteous war against the Scene. The ever-persecuted Scene, which was not to blame for Brann's arrest in the first place. Then he thought of Ursel, until the shame grew too great to bear. Surrounded by elation and tearful liberation, Chase felt wretched.

Tinashe also stood among the crowd, watching the steady stream of detainees emerge. Her eyes scanned their faces, desperately searching, allowing hope to blossom into faith. For hours she persevered, asking the freed, "Do you know Weldon? Was he with you? Have you seen him?" When she eventually found someone who had briefly shared a cell with him, the limited information they had was enough to obliterate all hope. She didn't require confirmation; it could only have ended one way. Surrounded by the joy of reunion, Tinashe stood alone, her hands covering her face, confronting the horror of loss.

Wella remained among the crowd too. She had left Chase to rejoin her new family: the followers who had been incarcerated, or who had worked tirelessly for the last five days to fight for their comrades' release.

She stood beside Nial. Both had returned overground to fight for the Scene and for the sea change they believed was possible: a change in perspective that could help grow the Scene in ways that would never have been possible before. *That's Cole's legacy,* she thought. *Bluemantle woke them. And now citizens know. Now they can stay, or leave, or they can choose to follow.*

Wella had already decided what she would do. She confided in Nial as they stood amid the crowd. "I'm going to return," she said. "To work for the Scene, wherever they end up."

"A group of us are leaving tomorrow," said Nial. "There's a couple of hundred ready to go. We don't want to wait for the

Troubadours to find somewhere else. We want to search with them. Come with us?"

"I can't. Not yet."

"Why not? There's nothing for us here."

"There's one last thing I need to do. Then I'll join you."

—

Once the agreement had been signed and the first wave of detainees released, Dent Lore had prepared for his final withdrawal.

The majority of troopers were deployed throughout the city, with orders to suppress celebration through intimidation. "We have agreed to their terms," Fentlow had said, "but we will not lose face. Special Forces will be firmly in theirs, watching their every move. That's control. Wydeye will do well to remember that."

Fentlow's insistence meant that the Complex was relatively quiet. Dent had been able to refuel the motorbike and load his few possessions and basic supplies unnoticed. He had also signed himself off sick, citing a relapse, buying himself three days before his absence would be noticed.

Before leaving, he had addressed a package, marked 'Confidential and Urgent', which he took to the Comms Centre. He spotted a trusted messenger, to whom he gave the package, along with a visual description of the addressee and where she might be found.

By the time he arrived back at the Troubadours' camp, the drummer had shed his other self for the final time. He hoped Dent Lore's parting deed achieved some small measure of atonement for the cruelty and suffering caused by his actions as Allear Commander.

—

"You have done a remarkable thing, drummer," said Bend Sinister. "You have made me and our players proud. And you have acted with tremendous courage in the interests of our family, followers and the survival of the Scene. We are all indebted to you and are most relieved at your safe return. Welcome home."

The drummer who had been Dent Lore stood in the centre of the camp's humble court, surrounded by the three Troubadours, their players and retinue. Ursel stood next to Chief, leaning on a makeshift crutch, her scribe at her side.

"I have an admission of which I am ashamed," said Pale Dexter. "I mistrusted you. I was sceptical about your sudden return and cynical as to its motive and timing. It was I who suggested we put you to the test. For that, I most sincerely apologise. The risks you have taken for the benefit of us all cannot be overstated. I admire your courage, respect your loyalty and warmly welcome you home." He stepped forward and embraced the drummer.

"I, too, doubted you," said Chief. "For so long I had believed you gone. Grieved your passing as if you were one of my own. Despite our allegiances and personal interests, we are all as one in the Scene. Yet, when you returned, I knew who you were, but I did not trust you in the light of who you had become. I doubted the legitimacy of your claims. I supported the proposal to test your word and was prepared to cast you out if you refused. Forgive me. I should have had faith in the man we knew. And now, you have proved yourself beyond what we could have hoped or expected from you. The selflessness and courage you have shown has served to remind me of the true merit at the heart of the Scene. Community over sovereignty. Saltire knew this. It characterised her leadership. In my preoccupation with the Contest, I had lost sight of that balance."

She looked to Pale Dexter, who nodded, eyes cast down. She turned back to the drummer. "You have reminded me what it means to be part of the Scene. I owe you a great debt, not only for your actions to help save it, but for reasserting what it is we were striving to save. Please, forgive my doubt and accept my heartfelt gratitude." At this, Chief stepped forward and held out her hands. The drummer accepted them.

"I thank you all for your kind words," said the drummer. "But the apologies are not warranted. We must not erase the fact that for twenty-five years, albeit unwittingly, I have worked for the Authority and proactively hunted you down. I have trained countless cohorts of Allears, many of whom were children, taken from their families and grossly mutilated. My actions since returning have not been to prove my loyalty in return for trust but acts of expiation for those deeds that are so abhorrent to me. To my mind, I have been neither brave nor courageous, merely desperate to right those wrongs."

He turned to Ursel, speaking slowly so that her scribe could keep up. "To you, I owe the greatest apology, for reasons I have already shared with you. And yet, the more I listen to you, the greater that debt becomes. I have heard your views on the citizens' plight, your understanding of and sympathy for their situation, your unbending belief that, with a little help, they have the freedom to free themselves. In respect of your faith in them and, again, as a small gesture of reparation to you personally, I hope that I provided some of that help before I returned here."

Ursel scanned the notes, her eyes welling at the words. "You've already made amends. Whilst you do all this for others, grant me a special favour and do one thing for you?"

The drummer frowned, signing his question.

"Forgive yourself," she said.

—

Two days later, Ursel began the long journey home to Wydeye.

Before she left, Nial and over two hundred followers had already made it to the camp, having left the city for good. There was not enough room in the dell, so they pitched a makeshift bivouac on the other side of the rise.

They had reported the news that all troopers were returning to base, the search for the 'Music Makers' having been permanently called off. They also said that there were rumours surrounding the disappearance of the Chief of Command but that there was nothing to substantiate them, nor clues as to his whereabouts.

Meanwhile, Wulfwin remained intoxicated by the influence of music, which the players had performed, uninterrupted, for forty-eight hours. He lay strapped to a bunk, eyes glazed, humming the earworm melody that had been played incessantly to him.

The night Nial arrived at the camp, he had sat with Ursel on her bunk, pencil and paper in hand. *"You're returning?"* he wrote. *"I don't understand. Why?"*

"I had two homes, but I never had to choose between them before," said Ursel. "That's why I never made the move underground. Now that the Scene is leaving, I'm forced to make the choice. But it's okay. The Telltale Circus is important to me. I believe in what we do. I also believe that we will be moving on, too, before long. Become a travelling theatre once again. There's nothing to keep us in Wydeye anymore. I just need to help the founders see this, if they haven't already come to realise it for themselves."

The next morning, she bade her farewells, including an emotional break from Chief and her players. Her scribe offered to join her, but Ursel declined. She was touched by the young woman's gesture but unwilling to separate her from the life she had chosen.

Estrin proposed he escort Ursel back, suggesting that she was still too weak to travel alone. "That's kind of you," she replied. "But you don't need to do that. Stay with the troupe. You've done more than enough."

He took her pencil and notepad. "*My job isn't finished,*" he replied, smiling. "*I'm the rear guard, remember? The pursuivant defending the door. I know there's no door to defend anymore, but I still need to show people the way.*"

"What will you do?"

"*Remain in Wydeye until the Scene is established. Then I'll join them, bringing with me anyone left who wants to follow.*"

Ursel recognised the glint in his eye and knew she'd be a hypocrite to challenge him. She accepted his offer, finding herself grateful and unexpectedly relieved to have the company.

—

When Ursel left, the three Troubadours withdrew to the rise and stood in the glare of the midday sun. Below them, the quiet hum of excited anticipation reverberated through the dell. The news that they were no longer hunted fugitives had lifted a heavy burden from the shoulders of them all. Their own dark cloud had finally cleared, revealing a horizon of hope and the prospect of a new life, overground, elsewhere.

"If news had also come that the law against live music was revoked, would you consider returning?" said Chief. "If we could perform, at liberty, overground?"

Bend Sinister looked to the north. "Had you asked me that before we left underground, I would have said yes." He closed his eyes and breathed deeply, relishing the sun's warmth on his pale skin. "But now it's different."

"Even though we still don't know if we'll be able to connect elsewhere? We could journey for years and still fail in our search."

Bend Sinister did not respond. His eyes remained closed, his expression serene.

Chief turned to Pale Dexter. "What about you?" she said. "If the law had changed, would you remain?"

Pale Dexter also looked to the north, eyes wide. "No. I would not."

"Why?"

"When we agreed to leave, our hand was forced. Now that we are free of those caves, we face horizons on which there lies choice. I know we are still unable to remain and play at will. But neither would I want to, even if the law allowed."

"I agree," said Bend Sinister, slowly opening his eyes and turning to his comrades. "There is much to be said for fresh air and a fresh perspective. Listen to them." He gestured to the dell below. "The new arrivals have reinvigorated our troupe. They've replenished our supplies of optimism and faith. For they, too, felt trapped in caves of their own making. But they found their freedom and grasped it with both hands. They have inspired me to do the same."

"Well said, my friend," said Pale Dexter.

Chief looked to them in turn, marvelling at the distance they had already come. "The light suits you both."

"It's decided then? We leave tomorrow?" said Bend Sinister.

Chief and Pale Dexter bowed their assent.

"Which leaves us the question of direction."

"North," they both replied.

—

By noon the next day, the Troubadours and their troupe had packed up camp and gained over ten miles' distance.

In the centre of the abandoned dell, Wulfwin's wrists and ankles bled. The wire used to bind them cut into his flesh as he fought to break free. Flies gathered and settled. The rope around his chest was tight. The tree to which he was tied, unyielding.

The Troubadours had debated what was to be done with their captive, deciding that their only option was to leave him behind.

"We can't possibly take him with us," Pale Dexter had said. "If we stop playing, his senses will return. As will the danger to us all."

"But we can't leave him here to die," said Bend Sinister.

"Your drummer spoke of the troopers' cultivated loyalty towards this man," said Chief. "They will come looking for him. His bike tracks will lead them here."

Seeing no safe alternative, they had tied him to a tree, then gave him water and something to eat before they had left.

Bound as he was, Wulfwin could drink no more. Three hours after the troupe's departure, his throat was dust-dry. The mesmerising effect of the music was abating, enabling his wits to return. Fury dominated, numbing the pain as he wrenched his wrists, the wire cutting deeper.

Then he froze, held his breath. His senses still felt compromised, lacking his trust. Yet, there, in the distance, he felt sure he could hear it.

The growl of an engine.

As the sound drew nearer, Wulfwin's hope became certainty. It was an Authority Ops truck, he had no doubt. "Hey," he screamed. "Over here!" He knew it was pointless; they wouldn't hear him over the noise of the engine. Yet desperation made him persist. "In here, you bastards."

The growl was loud now, coming from just beyond the rise. It peaked, so close. Then it began to fade. "No!"

Wulfwin tugged his ankles, the wire cutting down to the bone. He guessed they were looking for him. If they missed him now, it was unlikely they'd return. He'd be left there. Left to die. "Come back!" he cried.

He suddenly fell silent. The engine's sound had changed in pitch. The truck was in reverse. His heart pounded as the motor cut out. "I'm in here!" he yelled, his voice breaking.

He heard the snap of brushwood and rustle of leaves as someone slipped into the dell, approaching him from behind. Wulfwin struggled, twisting his shoulders, but he was tied too tight. "Who is it? Face me. I can't fucking move."

The man lingered in Wulfwin's blind spot.

"I recognise the sound of the truck. You're a trooper. Show yourself."

The man remained out of sight.

"What the fuck, man? Untie me already. That's an order."

Silence.

"I know you're a trooper. I can smell your boot polish. You wouldn't have stopped and come looking for me if you weren't."

Nothing.

"What are you playing at? Face me, you fucker."

The man took a step backwards. Then another.

"Hey, what are you doing? You fucking bastard. Help me." He wrenched his wrists, the blood now coating his clenched fists. "You can't leave me here." A branch snapped, far behind him. "I'll kill you for this, you hear me? I'll get out of here and I'll track you down. I'll sniff you out, you piece of shit. Don't think I won't. You're gonna die for this."

The man scrambled back up the bank, desperate to get out of the dell and away. He'd come back to round up the last of the Deaf Squad troopers. They'd all been ordered back to base. The Allears were already there. He was the last one to return. *Which means no one will find him,* he thought. *No one will know.*

With that realisation, the panic subsided, replaced by a calm assurance. He looked down into the shadows of the dell, deaf to the threats of his screaming Chief of Command.

Shoulders back, face composed, Trooper Sixty returned to his truck and drove away.

—

Establishing the whereabouts of the Chief of Command became a priority in theory. Little was done in practice.

The cerebral whereabouts of Governor Blix was also unknown – this, despite the fact she was conscious and confined to quarters.

Gone was the immaculate bun and sharp grey suit. Blix spent her days huddled in a corner of her room. Tributaries of silver hair fell on her shoulders and over her face. The skin on her arms was red-raw. Bleeding scratches covered her legs.

Her wide eyes beheld harrowing hallucinations that tormented her day and night. Crouching in the corner, rocking on her heels, she whispered warnings to herself.

Too late came Fentlow's discovery of her supply of laced Meezel.

She was lost forever down a fathomless hole, in the company of her imagined horrors.

—

Ursel had expected to see Wella at Wydeye's Eastgate arch. Instead, it was Chase who met her. She saw him linger, eyes downcast, as she dismounted the horse and bade farewell to Estrin.

She approached Chase. They embraced briefly, Chase awkwardly, then they walked in silence, over the bridge that spanned Wydeye Deep, towards Standings Cross and the Telltale Circus. A Special Forces Ops truck drove past them. Ursel flinched and looked away.

Once they reached the other side, Chase stopped and held her arm. Reading his expression, Ursel handed him a notepad and pencil. *"There's something I need to tell you. It can't wait,"* he wrote.

Ursel studied his face, then nodded. She led him to a tea bar next door to the reopened tramway stop opposite the Circus.

They sat in the shade of the bar's awning, either side of a pallet-top table. Chase stared at his glass of iced green tea, trembling hands knotted in his lap. He had longed to see Ursel again, had feared that he never would. Now he couldn't bear to look at her. And it wasn't because of the scars that etched her face.

"Talk to me, Chase."

So he did. He wrote slowly at first, telling his story from the beginning. Then, once he overcame the hurdle of starting, he found he couldn't stop. Or, he was afraid of stopping, afraid of missing something out, failing to make a full confession. He scribbled frantically, his writing barely legible.

Ursel read his scrawl, not saying a word.

His confession complete, Chase dropped the pencil and sat on his hands. By slow degrees, he dared to look up. He still couldn't meet her eyes. Instead, he looked at her mouth, watching it move, reading her reaction in her lips alone.

Ursel did not speak. Not for some time. Her mouth tightened. Chase felt sick.

Eventually, she said, "I think you know what I'm going to say."

Chase sighed, his eyes dropping to the table. He picked up the pencil again and slowly wrote a single word in tall, capital letters. "WHY."

Ursel didn't respond. He knew she wouldn't. It was down to him to answer the question he had been asking himself since the Contest, when Ursel had been arrested and his house of cards collapsed.

"*At first, I thought it was because of Brann,*" he wrote, "*but that was an easy excuse. Then, I thought it was because I blamed the Scene and I wanted revenge. But that was just another get-out. I even let myself think it was because the A had a hold on me, that I was in too deep. Lame, but easy to believe.*" He paused.

Ursel read the words. Her mouth did not move.

His chest tight, his heart stone-heavy, he continued to write. "*They were all excuses. Truth is, I didn't do it because of anyone else. I felt like I'd gained something. A sense of power, I guess. Control. It got so as I needed it, like it set me apart, made me stronger. And that's the real reason. That's why. I did it for me.*"

Ursel bit her lip and slowly nodded. She took the pencil from him and said, "Look at me."

He hesitated, afraid, then dared to meet her eyes.

"I appreciate your honesty," she said. "I know that must've been hard. I'm afraid what I'm about to say might feel even harder."

He stared at her, uncomprehending.

"What you did – it upsets me, but it doesn't surprise me."

Chase almost choked from the blow.

"Hear me out," she said. "I knew from the start you had your own agenda. Your search for Wella wasn't for her benefit. You did little to hide your prejudice of the Scene. You failed to ask the right questions because you kept your mind firmly closed. You didn't even try because you assumed you already knew the answers. So, no, I'm not surprised.

"But that doesn't matter because that's not you anymore. I thought I saw something in you, hoped that your experience of the Scene would open your mind. And it did. It has. You've changed, Chase. I read the story you wrote. I know the walkout was your idea. You're putting right the wrongs of a different person. And that's okay, because he's not around to do it himself."

She reached out and touched his arm. "Let your honesty lay to rest your guilt. Be who you've become and make a better job of it." She handed back the pencil. "Now, enough wallowing. Where's Wella?"

He struggled to process her words and recover from her touch. He blinked, disorientated by the sudden switch, then wrote, *"I'm not sure. She said she had to do something. She's going over to Naylor's later. I'm staying with him for a while. Just in case."*

Ursel cocked an eyebrow and half-smiled.

"You know what she's up to?"

"Not as such. But I have an idea." She finished her tea and stood up. "I've got to go home. See my family and friends. Speak to the founders. But I'd like to drop by later, if that's alright? At Naylor's. To see what Wella has to say."

—

Chase sat at the table in Naylor's quarters, stealing glances at Ursel's silhouette. She was stood by the window, looking down on the sprawling city. Naylor lingered in the doorway, leaning against the jam, arms crossed.

"I've never known anywhere else," said Ursel, her back still turned. "Neither have the rest of my family. Only the oldest founder has travelled elsewhere, but she was a young child at the time and can't remember." She turned around and joined Chase at the table. "But that's about to change."

Chase and Naylor both raised their eyebrows, asking the same question.

Ursel smiled. "The founders have decided to live up to our purpose and become a travelling theatre once more."

Chase slumped, deflated.

Naylor read the situation and stepped in. "*That's exciting news. When will you leave?*" he wrote.

"In a month or so. It's been eighty years; there's no rush. And there's a lot to pack up and prepare. Performances will run for another couple of weeks, then we'll start to dismantle the big top. They decided to keep the new play running for a final fortnight; it's proving popular." She smiled at Chase, who missed the intended gesture.

There was a faint knock at the door. Naylor went to let Wella in. Chase stared at a point in the centre of the room, pained by the presence of Ursel now that he knew he was about to lose her again.

Wella entered, her face beaming. She walked over to Ursel and embraced her warmly. Then she stood back and looked around her. "Where's Clo?"

"In her room," said Naylor. "Why?"

"Ask her to join us. She needs to see this too."

While Naylor disappeared, Ursel leant towards Chase. "Will you scribe for me?"

Naylor returned, his arm draped over his daughter's shoulder. Chase sat rigid, pencil poised.

"I received a package," said Wella. "Since then, I've been in Cole's workshop, preparing this." She moved over to the table. Naylor and Clo gathered around. Wella pulled from her tunic a piece of paper, folded concertina-style. "A master template for an unexpected print run. We thought *Bluemantle* was over, but it turns out there's need for one final edition."

She opened up the folds to reveal text on one side. It was a letter, explaining about the Test and its true purpose. It detailed what the resits were actually for. It went on to account for the hundreds of children who had disappeared over the decades, revealing the truth about what had happened to them, who they had become – adults now, and altered. The letter closed with a lengthy apology, expressed by its author, Allear Commander Dent Lore, on behalf of the Authority of Wydeye. It also confirmed permission to publish the letter, along with a document it referred to as enclosed, to be distributed among the citizens of the city.

Wella turned the paper over, revealing a reproduction of something that should not exist. A map that was not of Wydeye.

N
W
E
S
Way Lode
Drey Lode
Pen-Axen
Govian
Pol
Lake Mistry
Wydeye
The Spire
Zentenda
Lake Rex
Mastfeld
Monan
Kasperan

ACKNOWLEDGEMENTS

I have received so much help, support and encouragement throughout this project, for which I am deeply grateful.

I am indebted to freelance editor Donna Hillyer for her excellent editorial skills on an early draft of the book. Her comments enabled me to extract the story from where it had become buried and to let *Bluemantle* breathe. It is a far better novel for it.

Thank you to my wonderful early readers: Mark Langston, John Turvey, Amanda Jane Franklin and David Franklin. Your honesty, insight, constructive feedback and plot-themed cakes were invaluable. You also gave me the confidence to know I was on the right path – welcome reassurance on a journey without a map.

Talking of maps, the two illustrations that bookend *Bluemantle* are the work of the super talented Shirley Bellingham. Shirley transformed my amateur scrawls into two beautiful maps – one of Wydeye and one of elsewhere. Thank you for helping to bring this world to life.

I am extremely grateful to graphic designer Jan Massie of Brilliant White Design for her help, expertise and fantastic creative talent. A warm thank you to Leanne Turvey for her unwavering love and understanding and for suggesting I build a garden in my mind in which to refuel. Also, my thanks to friend and fellow author Ray Dafter, for his ongoing encouragement and for calling me a writer.

Most of all, I thank my husband, Mark, whose belief in me and my ability to write a story worth reading is the reason this book exists.

Bluemantle is also in your hands thanks to The Book Guild, who found potential in its pages and thought it worthy of publication. With their professionalism and wealth of experience, they have been a pleasure to work with.

Finally, I would like to thank the amazing bands and artists who make me feel the way followers do when they watch the Troubadours perform live. In particular, a special thank you to Haken and Caligula's Horse, whose unforgettable gigs in London in 2017 provided the inspiration for this novel.